In one brutal instant, he lost ———
his freedom, his pri———————.
What does————————?

HIGH PRAISE FOR JAMES W. HALL
AND
RED SKY AT NIGHT

"ELECTRIFYING . . . you know the old saw: *Red Sky at Night,* reader's delight."

—People

"Mr. Hall has always been a top-drawer writer, but now he has fully realized his ability to frighten and baffle—prerequisites for a winning thriller."

—The Washington Times

"JAMES W. HALL'S WRITING RUNS AS CLEAN AND FAST AS THE GULF STREAM WATERS."

—The New York Times Book Review

"EXCITING . . . [An] exploration of pain and loss and how people live with both."

—The Miami Herald

"HALL IS ONE OF THE FINEST AND MOST LITERATE OF THRILLER WRITERS."

—San Francisco Chronicle

"Thorn has long been one of the most appealing and complex characters in crime fiction. Melding the magnetic pull of the archetypal hero on a quest with the flesh-and-blood humanity of a vulnerable man trapped between conflicting needs, Hall masterfully works both ends of the genre street, transforming the beach-bum sleuth into an everyman."

—Booklist

Please turn the page for more extraordinary acclaim. . . .

Books by James W. Hall

UNDER COVER OF DAYLIGHT
TROPICAL FREEZE
BONES OF CORAL
HARD AGROUND
MEAN HIGH TIDE
GONE WILD
BUZZ CUT
RED SKY AT NIGHT

JAMES W HALL

RED SKY AT NIGHT

A DELL BOOK

Published by
Dell Publishing
a division of
Bantam Doubleday Dell Publishing Group, Inc.
1540 Broadway
New York, New York 10036

This novel is a work of fiction. Names, characters, places, and incidents either are the product of the author's imagination or are used fictitiously. Any resemblance to actual persons, living or dead, events, or locales is entirely coincidental.

Copyright © 1997 by James W. Hall

ISBN: 0-440-22574-4

Reprinted by arrangement with Delacorte Press

Printed in the United States of America

Published simultaneously in Canada

July 1998

10 9 8 7 6 5 4 3 2 1

OPM

———————————

This book is dedicated to my uncle, Scott Hall, whose courage is powerful medicine for all of us.

My deepest thanks go to Dr. Charles A. MacNeill and Gale MacNeill. Great and inspiring friends who opened their lives and helped me find my way through difficult material. I couldn't have done this without you.

And to Patrice Flinn for her valuable technical assistance, and to Pam Brown of the DEA, who filled in several crucial blanks.

And as always, for Evelyn, who was there at every stage with intelligence, good humor, and love.

"What falls away is always. And is near."
—Theodore Roethke

CHAPTER

1

It was Monday around two on a painfully bright April afternoon. Overhead a flock of white ibis labored by like gorgeous aeronautical blunders. The sky was scrubbed clean of clouds, as it had been for weeks. No rain, no sign of it. What grass there was in Key Largo had yellowed and turned crisp as toast.

In the saltwater tank two of the dolphins were nosing against the scar on Thorn's arm—a glossy pockmark where several years ago a lump of lead had passed through the meat of his shoulder in a red-hot hurry. For the last few minutes the larger of the two dolphins had been bombarding the shiny, thickened flesh with her sonar. *Echolocation,* it was called.

"Does it tickle?" Monica asked. She was treading water beside him in the twenty-foot-square pool. So far none of the dolphins had homed in on her. Monica's short blond hair was bright in the midday sun, plastered against her head, revealing the shape of her perfect skull.

"More than a tickle," Thorn said. "Like my shoulder's a tuning fork."

"Bliss with flippers," said Roy Everly. "That's what some California idiot called them last week."

Roy sat on the edge of the dolphin tank, feet dangling in the water. He was the owner and caretaker of the dolphin center. He'd been a year behind Thorn at Coral Shores High back in medieval times. Roy had the distinction of being the first person on the island to own a computer. Built it himself; the thing filled half a room. He'd won a scholarship to Stanford in computer science, but had to turn it down because his mother was dying of cancer. That was twenty years ago and she was still dying.

These days Roy weighed well over three hundred pounds, most of it hanging over the waistband of the red thong he wore continually. He still cut his thick blond hair the same way he had his whole life—in a one-inch burr.

"Big debate these days," Roy said. "Are dolphins aliens from outer space come to enlighten us, or are they angels?"

Thorn smiled civilly.

"Bunch of California horseshit," Roy said. "Dimwits eating way too much granola and alfalfa sprouts."

The Down syndrome kids in the adjacent pool had quieted. No more screams of fright, rapturous shrieks. Now all Thorn could hear were soothing gurgles and low croons coming from over there, ten kids and their two teachers, bobbing amid the angels. And in the third tank the cancer patients and paraplegics were finished with their session and were being helped out onto the wood deck by a large black man in a white uniform.

"Now they go back to their van and do the blood tests. Doc Wilson draws a few cc's before they go in, then after the half hour in the tank he gets another sample. Looking for elevated levels of beta-endorphin, lipotropin, serum cortisol, and catecholamines. Brain chemicals, pain regulators. Trying to pin down exactly what's happening, why their intractable pain subsides. Why they suddenly start performing better on all the tests, mental and physical and psychological."

"Bean Wilson's working here?"

"Last year or two," Roy said. "Nice old man. Good doctor too. Helping out some VA clinic down in Key West. Saddest bunch of assholes I ever saw—twisted, mangled old vets. But they seem to get a kick out of the dolphins. They go home happy, anyway."

The two dolphins that had been analyzing Thorn's scar backed slowly away to the far end of the pool. They hovered there for a moment as if in serious deliberation.

"They're getting another angle on you. Sonar's so highly developed, they can spot a shark a half mile away, tell whether its stomach is empty or full. Doesn't work as well up close."

Suddenly the water surged in front of the two dolphins and they headed directly toward Thorn, twenty miles an hour in less than ten feet. His skiff with a one-fifty Evinrude couldn't accelerate that fast.

As they rushed forward, Thorn held his position, less from bravery than a lack of any other option. Then a foot from his face, the duo split apart like fighter jets passing in review, each dolphin whispering against one of Thorn's shoulders. A moment later they circled back and once again focused their pings on his gunshot wound.

"Wow," Monica said. "What the hell was that about?"

"They're trying to figure out his scar," said Roy. "Violence, guns, bullets. It upsets them; it's too weird. They don't understand it."

"Neither do I," said Thorn.

A small bottlenose had finally taken an interest in Monica and seemed to be nuzzling against the belly of her black bathing suit. Monica's smile relaxed and her head dropped back in the water. There was a rule against touching the animals. Everyone was instructed to let the dolphins determine all contact.

"Oh, my god, he's doing it," she whispered. "He's pinging me."

"I can't watch," Thorn said.

"Been verified with EEGs." Roy stood up, stretched lazily. "Half hour in the tank, brain waves are smoother, more regular. Left brain and right brain in much better harmony. Neurological functioning on a much higher level. Half hour swimming with them boosts the immune system, increases T-cell count. Even evidence it can shrink tumor mass. What I think is the sonar is causing cavitation inside the soft tissue of the body. *Cavitation,* as in cavities or bubbles, you know. Those echoes you feel are ripping apart your molecules, opening up spaces."

"Sounds painful," Thorn said. "But this feels good."

"You wouldn't feel molecular pain. A little buzz, that's all. It's like your molecules are being rolfed, loosened up, all the calcified masses broken apart. It's pain, but a pain you don't feel. A pain that stimulates endorphin release, which, *voilà*, creates the deep relaxation and increased T-cell production."

"You know a lot about them," Monica said.

"Of course, on the downside," said Roy, "as the

word spreads about the beneficial effects of swimming with them, every charlatan from Miami to Seattle is starting to trap dolphins, open healing centers. Angels for rent.''

Roy stood there staring gloomily at Thorn and Monica, as if they were the first wave of barbarians.

Monica groaned, eyes closed, off in a euphoric cloud.

Since January, Monica Sampson had been renting a downstairs apartment next to the dolphin center and she and Roy had become friends. For weeks she'd been badgering Thorn to come swim with the dolphins, but he'd resisted. Among other things, he didn't want anyone to get wind of his connection with the place.

When Kate Truman, Thorn's adoptive mother, died a few years earlier she'd left several million dollars' worth of income-producing property to Thorn. He immediately signed it all over to Millie Oblonsky, a cranky Russian matriarch who'd practiced law down in Islamorada for the last sixty years. Nearing ninety, Millie had been Kate's closest friend and had shared her fierce dedication to preserving the Keys in as natural a state as possible. Thorn never asked what charities or environmental groups were receiving the financial help. The money was no longer legally his and he wanted absolutely nothing to do with it. The scant income he got from selling his bonefish flies to local tackle shops and a handful of guides was sufficient to get him through. Anything more was a burden.

Ordinarily Millie kept him out of the loop. But last December, on her Christmas card, she'd scratched a quick message: *Chech out Kate's dolphins.* Included was a photograph of the Key Largo research center, three connecting tanks carved out of the limestone behind a conventional concrete block house that sat alongside a mangrove canal a half mile east of US 1. The eleven dolphins were penned inside the wire fences and were available as swimming partners seven days a week.

Thorn knew the place well. He'd passed by it hundreds of times over the years. Just another shabby roadside petting zoo, as far as he could tell. He'd pictured a bunch of fat, noisy Midwesterners trying to straddle the dolphins' backs, yee-ha. But he'd been wrong.

Last week when Monica finally coaxed him into going, Thorn found the place to be quiet and meditative, and even though penned in such small tanks, the dolphins seemed as amused by the humans as the other way around. Roy admitted tourists only when he didn't have sufficient sick or damaged folks to occupy the tanks.

Thorn had come back twice, though today was his first swim. It had been pleasure enough to stand with the usual gathering of onlookers and watch the sick and crippled slip into the dark pools with those powerful creatures and thirty minutes later to watch them climb out with the exhilarated expressions of the newly sanctified.

"Better than a hit of morphine," Roy said. "Dolphins discover what ails you and more often than not they set about making it right."

Thorn found himself agreeing. The two dolphins who'd been bombarding his glossy pockmark with their invisible rays seemed to be trying to ease the tension in his scar. A tension he hadn't even realized was there until now.

"Your time is up," Roy said. "I'd let you stay longer except I got a busload of schizophrenics coming in at five. I want to clear the place out before they arrive.

There's only ten of them, but what with all their multiple personalities, it gets a little crowded around here.''

Roy didn't smile, didn't seem to get his own joke. A lifetime of caring for his mother had sapped the humor from him. He might even have been beyond the help of dolphins.

As Thorn and Monica were toweling off, he noticed a tall, heavyset man standing at the back of the half dozen tourists gathered at the fences. He'd seen the same man on one of his other visits that week. The guy's paunch was so pronounced it looked like a German helmet beneath his shirt. He wore a red baseball hat with the brim tipped very low and a pair of gold-rimmed aviator sunglasses. But what snagged Thorn's attention was the way the man wasn't watching the dolphins or the swimmers. His gaze was fixed on Roy Everly as he went about his duties, opening and closing the gates between the pens to keep the dolphins circulating among the groups, turning the pumps on and off, tinkering with the aerator. As Monica ruffled the towel across her hair, Thorn watched the man insert his thumb into his mouth and work at something that was lodged between his front teeth. When he got it free, he examined it briefly, then flicked it over his shoulder into the grass.

All that night Thorn's scar tingled. Monica came over for dinner and they talked for hours on the upstairs porch, stars flooding the sky. They laughed and held hands and shared a bottle of excellent red wine she'd brought along. If there were any mosquitoes, neither of them noticed.

"Something's wrong with me," Thorn said. "I feel too good."

"It's like we're getting the afterglow without the sex."

"You feel that good?"

"Better," she said, smiling. "Like all my knots have been untied."

They watched a twinkling sailboat motor along the distant Intracoastal. In the woods nearby an owl shrieked. A pair of bats fluttered close overhead, skimming bugs from the breeze.

"I wonder," Thorn said. "The dolphins make us feel this way, but what do we do for them? What the hell do they get out of it?"

"Maybe they're altruistic. They get pleasure from giving it."

Thorn looked over at her. Her legs were propped up on the porch railing, sleek and burnished with moonlight. She sipped her wine and stared out into the boundless dark. With her free hand she reached across and trailed her fingertips over his arm as delicately as fog. Thorn took a long drag of the sweet night air. He couldn't remember the last time he'd felt so good, so relaxed.

And it worried him. It worried the hell out of him.

CHAPTER

2

The man suffering from phantom pain lay naked on top of the clean pink sheets. His name was Frank Hanes and he was a few years younger than the doctor, forty-two, forty-three. Another Vietnam vet, Frank had a small beer belly, a sunken chest, and his paralyzed legs had withered away to bones. His hair was gray and stringy and hung over his shoulder. He was a nice man, polite, never cursed once in the six months he'd been at the clinic. And he didn't whine about his pain like most of the others did. Just a wince now and then, a quiet moan.

Frank had fashioned bracelets out of tinfoil, which he wore around his ankles and his wrists. He told Pepper that he believed space aliens were beaming rays into his body and that was what caused his terrible pain. The tinfoil was supposed to bounce the rays back into outer space, protecting the vulnerable spots. So far it had not worked. Frank was convinced it was his own fault for not getting all the creases out of the tinfoil. He spent hours and hours in his room at the clinic trying to flatten away all the tiny wrinkles.

Over in the corner of the cabin, sitting primly with

his white Panama hat in his lap, was Tran van Hung, the money man. He was wearing shiny gold shorts and a gold shirt he'd bought on Duval Street. He studied everything the doctor did and made little Vietnamese noises in his throat. For the last month Tran van Hung had been living at the Marquesa Hotel, supervising the project, waiting for the experiments to finally pay off. At night Pepper's job was to sit with the man in strip joints and bars, try to explain what was going on around him, and make sure he didn't say or do anything that would get him hurt. The doctor had also let her know that she was to tend to any other desires Tran van Hung might have, however weird or disagreeable they might be.

Outside the starboard window of her ancient fifty-foot Hatteras she could see the roofs and widow's walks and dormers of Old Town a couple of miles away, and the bright flags lying limp behind one of the big hotels along Key West harbor. The water was as smooth and blue as the empty sky overhead.

They were anchored in a leeward cove off Christmas Tree Island. Not a human being in sight. On the distant flats a tern swooped low over the water, about to strike at a fish, but it changed its mind at the last second and fluttered back into the sky. Pepper looked back at the doctor, watched him fill his syringe from the vial and then hold the syringe up to the light to check its level. She could see the milky solution as he tapped the plastic cylinder with his fingernail to get the bubbles out.

While the doctor prepared his syringe, she continued to swab Frank's flabby belly with purple-tinted iodine. She coated the area again and again, because even the smallest speck of bacteria crossing the blood-brain barrier into the man's spinal canal could kill him quickly and spoil the whole experiment.

Frank Hanes was looking up at her. All of them did that, because they didn't want to watch the syringe. Old soldiers who'd gone running out of foxholes into Japanese machine-gun fire or who'd fought in the jungles of Vietnam or out on the endless deserts of Iraq, never knowing what waited beyond the next hump of sand, and here they were, afraid of syringes. So far, six soldiers had come aboard the cabin cruiser, different ages, different races, different wars, but all six had looked at Pepper the way Frank Hanes was looking at her. Doing it so he wouldn't have to watch the needle moving toward his belly.

The doctor was tall and handsome with blond hair and complicated blue eyes. He was a veteran too, and he had seen terrible things and had been injured over there many years ago, and a lot of those things still lived in the blue of his eyes. But Pepper loved his eyes anyway, and his tall thin frame, and she loved the way he talked, so slow and calm, so few words. And she loved the way he stood now, straight and strong and steady beside the bed, looking down at the naked man on the pink sheets.

The doctor told Frank that there'd be a small burn when the needle entered. Frank nodded, his eyes on Pepper. He had stubble on his cheeks and bloodshot eyes and his penis was shrunken to the size of a thimble and hid in his nest of gray pubic hair.

Pepper liked it when their dicks shriveled. These tough men who wouldn't look at the needle. She liked when they looked at her as this man was doing, studying her face, falling in love with her because she might be the last woman they ever saw. She even liked it when they died—the gray film that rose to cover their glossy eyeballs as they watched her.

She hoped Frank wouldn't die. She hoped it for the doctor's sake, for the sake of his experiment, which he wanted so badly to succeed. And she hoped it because it would mean Tran van Hung would go back to the other side of the world, leaving his pot of money behind. And then everything good, everything she had been hoping for, could start to happen.

But if Frank did die looking at her, she knew she would enjoy it. It pleased her being the last thing a man saw, the face he remembered for eternity. Pepper's face, floating out there in the dark empty stretches of afterlife.

The doctor bent over the old soldier and Pepper lifted the iodine swab and dropped it into the waste can. The doctor felt for the pump embedded in the man's belly. He ran his fingers around the edges of the device until he located the small port where the rubber membrane was. Pepper could see the outline of the pump through Frank's flesh—like he'd swallowed a yo-yo.

She watched the doctor lower the needle and press it to the man's flesh, guiding it carefully into the membrane, and then she turned back to the naked man. He was staring into her eyes, drinking her in, longing for her.

The doctor withdrew the needle, set it aside, and picked up the black transmitter wand from the bedside table. A wire ran from the wand to his portable computer, which sat on the deck beside the bed. The doctor held the black wand a few inches over the man's belly and pressed the start button. Once the pump began working, the drug took thirty seconds to snake through the catheters around to the spinal cord.

No one spoke. There was only the moan of the gray wind.

The old soldier took a deep breath and his face relaxed and the doctor asked him if the pain in his legs had decreased at all. The naked soldier smiled at Pepper and his eyes glowed with blissful light. The doctor put his hand on Frank Hanes's shoulder and shook him lightly and asked again if the pain had decreased. But the man didn't seem to notice him. The soldier blew the air from his lungs and inhaled again. Sucking in air and more air and more until Pepper thought his chest would crack open.

The doctor's face had grown tense and dark, and he asked again what the man was feeling. Would he please try to describe the sensations. The man emptied his lungs in one loud rush like he was blowing out marijuana smoke. Then he smiled up at the doctor.

"Nothing," the soldier said. "Nothing at all."

"No pain?"

"None," said the soldier. "Zero. Nothing. Everything's gone. I feel like I used to feel. Before everything."

And the doctor nodded. Pleased but cautious. The doctor reached out to feel the soldier's pulse, looking at his own wristwatch to count the seconds.

And Pepper watched as that fine mist began to cloud Frank's eyes, the man still smiling at her but starting to drift deeper inside himself like he was sinking below the surface of a tub of dirty water. His face rippled with little expressions coming and going, spasms in the facial muscles, nerves misfiring.

Then suddenly Frank sat up.

He grinned at Pepper.

"I'm fine," he said. "Jim-dandy. Ready to rock and roll."

He pivoted on the bed and slung his feet over the edge. The doctor took hold of his arms, gripped him hard, and Pepper grabbed him around the waist, but Frank was all muscle and gristle and sudden fury. He was stronger than any man Pepper had ever touched. Stronger than her father, stronger than her football-playing high school boyfriends. She'd had years of experience wrestling with boys, trying to push them away, or drag them into her arms, but they were all weaklings compared with potbellied Frank.

Frank got his feet on the floor, jerking from Pepper's grasp, shoving the doctor aside, and he started walking toward Tran van Hung.

There were no muscles left in his legs, his spinal cord was severed and he was paralyzed from the middle of his chest down, but somehow he kept his balance and swung his arms high like a German soldier and made two miraculous steps toward the little Vietnamese man dressed in gold, Frank crying out the high-pitched hoot of a rodeo cowboy when the gate's thrown open. That old soldier filled with a million volts of energy, like the space aliens had finally gotten their beams inside him and were zapping him full of powers no other earthling had.

He raised his hands like he meant to strangle Tran van Hung, and the little Oriental man ducked and cried out in gibberish, then all at once Frank halted, tottered for a second, and crumpled to the deck.

The doctor and Pepper lifted him and carried him back to the bed and lay him down. He'd started to sing some low quiet song, a funeral hymn it sounded like, moaning it deep in his throat.

They got him on the pink sheets and the doctor shook the old soldier's shoulder again. Frank stared at Pepper, his eyes disappearing inside the fog, as his hymn got quieter and quieter and finally ceased.

The doctor cursed. He felt for Frank's pulse and cursed again.

There was no CPR, no shock paddles. They had used those before and found that nothing could revive the old soldiers once they were gone.

"Well, at least it worked for a minute or two," Pepper said. "That's an improvement."

The doctor looked at her, his blue eyes blank. Pepper took a breath. Like a big, dangerous dog watching you, he might be about to lick your face or tear your throat out. She could never tell, when the doctor's eyes collapsed like that.

White birds sliced through the ice-blue sky and Frank Hanes lay dead on the pink sheets. After another few moments the doctor dragged in a breath and came back into his body from wherever he'd been, his eyes deepening and letting Pepper into them once more.

"So what happened, Doctor?" Tran van Hung said. "What's your excuse this time?"

The doctor was staring at Frank's dead body. The invisible fumes of that old soldier's soul rising from his corpse.

"It's okay," Pepper said. "This is better than before. We're making progress. That's what counts."

The doctor looked at her. Studying her face like he was just that second noticing her, and for the first time considering that Pepper might be someone he could reach out for and touch and kiss and lie with and love and marry and have a brood of children with. Looking at her with those tormented eyes full of sad electricity. Her blond doctor.

But he didn't say anything. He just kept running his eyes over her face, then over her white blouse and burgundy skirt. Looking and looking at her while the dead man lay naked and cold on the bed between them, and the doctor stared at her without a word on his lips, eyes depthless again like that big, dangerous dog.

"Well," Pepper said. Hurrying now to get some words into the air, anything to move his eyes off her face, her clothes, her body. "I think we should all be happy and quit fussing. We're getting closer."

Finally, the doctor broke off his staring, and looked down at the dead soldier on the pink sheets. The man carrying Pepper's face off into eternity.

"We need more material, Pepper," the doctor said. "You can go tonight."

"Tonight?"

"Something more important on your schedule?"

She took a quick look at the doctor's eyes.

"No," she said. "I'm available. Sure, of course."

"Good," the doctor said. "I'm so very pleased."

Pepper Tremaine hated working with Yankees. They were so goddamn pushy, for one thing. Near as she could tell, everybody in Miami was a Yankee, always in a big hurry, everybody nervous, doing you a favor to say hello.

First words out of the guy's mouth when he picked her up at the Islamorada 7-Eleven was that he didn't want to know her name.

"My name's Pepper. Pepper Tremaine."

"I just said I didn't want to know your fucking name. What're you, retarded?"

"Well, now you know it, you're out of luck. You can't go back and not know it at this point."

The guy looked at her for a few seconds, then went back to smacking on his gum, weaving through the light traffic. Red baseball cap scrunched down tight, a pair of dark glasses, aviator style. Driving with them at night, he looked like some old blind piano player.

Pepper was an inch under six feet. Her eyes were olive, but she could make them darker if she wanted, just by staring hard at someone. Tonight, for the assignment, she had on a pair of black leggings and a loose-fitting black blouse with flap pockets. She wore her auburn hair shoulder length, parted in the middle with a frosted strand running down each side of her face. Pepper had the same body as her daddy. Rawboned, with rangy, gristly arms and long legs. Like her daddy she was hard-muscled from years of deep-sea fishing. Only difference was she had breasts. Good ones, hard and high like grapefruits cut in half. And a good swell at her hips, shapely legs. She knew she was pretty because she'd been runner-up Homecoming Queen. And now, six years later, there were a dozen guys in Key West who'd marry her in a minute. But she had her sights set higher than local boys. Dumb conchs with the smell of fish guts on their hands. Pepper was headed a hell of a lot higher than that. All she needed was a little more womanly sophistication. Help with her makeup, her posture, maybe a hint or two about her wardrobe. None of it that hard to learn. All of it right there in the little how-to sections in the magazines she bought every week, *Vogue, Elle, Cosmo, Mademoiselle.* She'd had a deprived childhood, hadn't had a mother or older sister to help her master all the feminine tricks other girls picked up naturally. But that was coming. She was studying the magazines, getting advice from the cosmetics girl at Sears. She felt good. Within shooting distance of her goal. A doctor's wife.

Anyway, tonight this big guy in the baseball hat was Pepper Tremaine's partner. Acting like her boss, the way he talked, explained the job, what Pepper was supposed to do, taking her through it step-by-step. Real bully.

Within a half hour of being in the same car with the guy, Pepper was ready to pull out her #15 scalpel, press it to the guy's aorta, drain him down a few gallons, then kick his fat carcass out of the car, forget the whole assignment.

"I took care of this same job three times before already. I guess I know how it's done."

The big man looked over at her.

"You could've told me that at the beginning," he said, "saved me the fucking trouble explaining everything."

"I was being polite," Pepper said. "Letting you have your say."

The big man muttered something under his breath.

Pepper reached up and touched the scalpel through the cotton of her black blouse. The lead handle gave the knife the extra heft of a first-class tool. It was an expensive instrument, but like her daddy used to say, never scrimp when choosing tools. He was referring to rods and reels, of course, but it was just as true with scalpels. One quick swipe with that #15 and Pepper could forever change the way a man looked at the world.

It was two in the morning as they coasted over the

noisy grating of a bridge and the headlights lit up the sign for Key Largo. The moon was in the west, cocked on its side like a sickle about to harvest a field of flimsy clouds.

They passed the goofy-golf places, bait shops, gaudy liquor stores, Pepper looking out at the trashiness. Give her Key West any day. Say what you would about the T-shirt shops and the ten thousand bars on Duval Street, she'd rather be down there where there was some kind of pulse, than in the upper Keys where everybody was always half-crocked on embalming fluid.

Ten more minutes. The big guy turned off US 1 at a shopping center, driving past a bank, couple of gas stations. Everything closed up on that weeknight. Real quiet out there, nobody walking around, hardly a car on the highway. All the old-timers drooling into their pillows by now.

The big guy wheeled the rental through a dark neighborhood and parked on the shoulder of the road and turned off the engine.

"Down there," he said. "Couple hundred yards."

"You're not coming with me? Don't want to get your feet wet?"

"Yeah, I'm going with you, make sure you don't fuck up. I been scoping this place out for the last few days."

"Know how I got my name? Pepper?"

"I don't know and I don't give a rat's butthole."

" 'Cause of these."

She pulled a smoked *habanero* out of her pocket, one of the miniature chili peppers she carried everywhere. Came out with the scalpel at the same time. Holding both of them in her right hand, Pepper capped the chili, flicked the stem away and popped the rest in her mouth. Imported from the Yucatán, it was fifty times hotter than a jalapeño. Rated at three hundred thousand Scoville units, which was off the charts on most people's tearjerker scale.

"Jesus, where'd the doc dig you up, state mental ward?"

"Wanna try one?"

The big guy just kept staring at her through those dark glasses.

"Well, hell, at least feel how hot it is."

Before the guy could jerk his arm away, Pepper reached over and dabbed a speck of *habanero* juice on his forearm, and it took only half a second.

"Jesus Mother of Shit!"

He rubbed at his arm, cocking his head back and staring up at the rental car ceiling.

"You eat one of these," Pepper said, "you damn well better keep your hand off your dick for eight hours. Unless you're one of those Marquis de Sade types."

Pepper got out, took the gym bag from the backseat, and waited till the big guy managed to open the door and stand up. Invisible steam rising off his back. She followed the big fellow down the road. Nobody had anything to say. Pepper was usually quite the talker, but this guy wasn't bringing out the best in her.

At the high fence, Pepper set the gym bag down, unzipped it, and took out a pair of heavy bolt cutters. She snipped the lock, dropped it on the ground, squeaked the door open. There were no lights on inside the nearby house, just a couple of noisy window air-conditioners churning away. You could probably set off a small nuclear device out there and no one inside that house would hear it. No lights anywhere along the street. Music was coming from somewhere, but with all that water nearby, it could be miles away.

Pepper stepped inside the gates and the big guy followed her, still in the sunglasses and baseball cap. While the guy slipped over to the water valves, Pepper took a minute to look down at the dolphins circling in the dark, making their clicks and whistles as they slushed through the water. The big guy hissed at her to get a move on.

After they cranked open all three valves, the two of them went over to the edge of the canal and watched the water pour out of a big pipe. The splashing was noisy but the breeze carried off most of the sound.

The man rubbed at the spot on his forearm and watched the water splash into the canal. After a minute he stooped down, dug through the athletic bag, and came out with two handguns, both with silencers. He handed one to Pepper and held his down by his side, just standing there chewing his gum like he was waiting for her to lift the barrel, give him a reason to shoot.

Just then, from down the street, a car horn honked, one single blast. The big guy swung around and stared down there, and Pepper took that opportunity to jam her silencer into the guy's kidneys.

"My name's Pepper Tremaine. Now I'd like to hear you say it back to me. Put it in a sentence. Say something nice. 'Hello, Miss Pepper, how you doing this fine evening?' Something like that. Go on, say it. Use my name in a sentence."

"Pepper Tremaine," the big guy said, "you're one fucked-up individual."

Pepper chuckled politely, then waited a second or two, waggling the barrel against the guy's kidneys, letting him sweat.

"Do it again. Something not so insulting this time. Use my name."

"I think we should begin doing our job now, Miss Pepper. How's that?"

Pepper watched the water coming out of the drainage pipe. Down to a trickle now. Behind them the dolphins were making different noises. Squeaks, little whimpers, flopping around on the concrete floor, lost all their agility. Pepper angled the man over to the edge of the pit, where they could see the big gray dolphins shiny in the moonlight. Looked like a bunch of blind grub worms you'd find under a rock, all of them squirmed and bumped into each other. Gasping and snorting.

"Okay, that's better. You and me, we didn't have the same upbringings; our folks must've used different etiquette books. But that doesn't mean we can't still get along."

Pepper took the gun out of the big man's kidneys and stepped away.

"Through the tails now," Pepper said. "Be careful. We don't want them dying right away."

The guy turned and peered at Pepper for a minute or two like he was considering testing her reflexes, then he sighed real loud and raised his pistol out to the side, and aimed down at the dolphins and let go.

Professionally trained shooter like he was, it still took the big guy eight shots to hit five dolphins. Pepper went six for six. She guessed island girls were good at some damn things.

"Well, enough fun," she said. "We got work to do."

Pepper drew the heavy Deiner's knife from her gym bag and climbed down into the tanks to commence the surgery. She took one last good swallow of the cool night air and shook her head.

God help her, the shit she did for love.

CHAPTER

3

Thorn had decided they should celebrate Monica's dollar-an-hour raise at the newspaper by having lunch at Sundowners, and that's where they were when the news came on the overhead TV. It was the lead story on the Miami station. Eleven dolphins had been killed in Key Largo. Shot and butchered. All eleven had been decapitated and most had been disemboweled.

Thorn set his conch fritter down, stared at the screen. A young Hispanic woman stood beside the dolphin pool with her microphone and notepad and a queasy smile.

"I must warn you," she said. "The scene you are about to see is graphic."

As the camera panned over the carnage, Thorn felt the scar on his shoulder flare.

"Jesus," Monica said. "Christ Almighty."

Someone on the other side of the bar laughed.

Thorn cut his eyes to the man. A short guy with the bullish neck of a bodybuilding geek. His three friends were iron pumpers too, all of them wearing shorty T-shirts with the sleeves torn off. The guy caught Thorn's eye and held on, grinning.

When Thorn looked back at the screen, the reporter was interviewing Roy Everly.

"For the last several years, Mr. Roy Everly has been allowing various scientists to use these dolphins in their research studies."

Roy took a deep breath and peered into the lens. He wore a starched white shirt with a turquoise string tie that seemed to be strangling him. He looked as dazed as a man who'd just stepped out of the wilderness into the bright lights of television.

"So, Mr. Everly, could you tell us, please, what exactly is the significance of the loss of these animals, in scientific terms?"

She jabbed the microphone close to Roy's mouth. Across the room one of the barbell idiots said something funny and his friends foamed up with laughter.

"The significance of their loss? In scientific terms?"

"That's right, Mr. Everly. Were the scientists close to any important findings?"

Roy frowned.

"You're not asking the right question, lady. The question is, who the hell did this and why? What kind of world is it where this kind of shit could happen?"

The reporter pressed her earpiece deeper and smiled awkwardly.

"All right then, Mr. Everly, do you have any idea who would do such a thing?"

"A monster," Roy said. "A soulless, bloodless, god-awful monster."

The iron pumpers hooted and cheered and Thorn got down off his stool.

Monica rested a hand on his arm.

"Thorn."

The little man with the grotesque neck was grinning his way.

"What's the point, Thorn?"

"There isn't any," he said. "None at all."

He walked to the other side of the bar. By the time he arrived, the group of muscle freaks had drawn apart and were striking poses, arranging themselves in full display. Lats, biceps, quads, a regular anatomy class. The little man had a single emerald in his left earlobe, and he wore heavy gold rings crusted with jewels on most of his fingers. High-fashion brass knuckles.

"Something funny over here?" Thorn said.

"There is now," one of them said. Head shaved, walrus mustache. His ear was dotted with an identical green stone. Probably their club insignia. Steroids Anonymous.

They were drinking Coors Light. A fresh round just laid out on the bar in front of them. Thorn had never cared for that brand—like drinking carbonated snow.

As he stood there, he felt the bullet scar grow warm. The television was off to a commercial, dogs singing about their relief from fleas.

"Dead dolphins make you laugh? You stump dicks find that real funny?"

"Oh, help me, I'm wounded," the little guy said, pressing a palm to his heart. "The gentleman called us stump dicks. Insulted our masculinity."

"He's partaking of the stereotype," one of his buddies said. "Muscle men with inferior sexual apparatus."

"Go ahead, Dingo, show him what you got. Haul it out for him."

"Slap him upside the head with it, Dingo."

Thorn said, "What I'd like, Dingo, is to hear what's

so goddamn funny about dead dolphins. Or maybe you could tell us a knee-slapper about beating up old ladies or having sex with parakeets. Come on, I know you can do it, a guy like you, highly trained sense of humor. Go on, scoff at something for us, show us how it's done. Tough guy doesn't give a shit about anything but making his neck thicker. Tell us a goddamn joke, man, something hilarious about slaughtering dolphins. I want to hear that. We all do, don't we?''

Thorn glanced around the dining room. Several tables full of tourists, some local businesspeople. Nobody moving. All the fish sandwiches growing cold. The dazzling expanse of water was spread out behind them, fishing boats and Jet Skis zooming by, the world on vacation.

"That's who you are, isn't it, Dingo? Big guy who doesn't give a damn about anything. Everything's a fucking cartoon. So go on, tell us something funny, man, we're all ears.''

Dingo was giving Thorn the dead man's stare.

"I'm not gonna try to make you laugh, asshole. You aren't going to be laughing for a long time.'' Saying it very quietly. Same drama coach as all the other tough guys.

Dingo stepped away from the bar. Thorn shuffled back a half step. The martial arts class he'd taken last summer had been all about fending off blows, neutralizing your opponent without hurting him. Shunting his hardest shots off into harmless trajectories. It was a nonviolent defense meant to demonstrate to your opponent that he could not hurt you and you would not hurt him. Though the class ran against his instincts, Thorn had to admit it had twice saved his life, helped him put a couple of very bad men on the floor, desperate for breath. However, that was months ago and Thorn hadn't been keeping up his practice.

Rusty as he was, he managed to brush aside the first two chopping blows that Dingo threw, and slid away from a stiff karate kick and a leaping side kick. Dingo was a lot quicker and more limber than he appeared. Thorn's sidestepping only seemed to fire Dingo up, and he heard the guy's friends cheering and chairs scraping behind him and the voice of the bartender yelling for them to take it outside, and he felt the scar on his shoulder growing hot, the strange energy those dolphins had beamed into it.

He dodged another low kick and watched as Dingo feinted with his right hand and ducked his shoulder, looking for a chance to unload with a crushing left hook to the body. And all those hours Thorn had spent in the gym last summer choreographing counter-moves had taught him how to handle that particular blow when it came, to step inside the punch, swivel and hook the arm around his waist and use his opponent's weight and the momentum of the stroke to spin the attacker harmlessly away.

But instead, Thorn halted abruptly, held his ground, kept his guard up. He'd decided he didn't want to demonstrate anything to this guy. He didn't want to tire him out, convince him that fighting was useless. What he wanted was a lot less complicated, a lot less philosophical.

He watched Dingo slit his eyes, inch forward. Smiling coldly at Thorn's possum trick. As Thorn held his ground, the small man showed him again that feint with the right, the load-up with the left, Dingo the one-trick pony.

Dingo circled right, then came back quickly to his

left and let go with the punch. Thorn's blocking jab was a half-second late, and the blow glanced off his forearm and grazed Thorn in his right ribs. The lights in the room broke apart, turned to sparkling confetti as the breath blew out of his lungs. He heard cheers, Monica's shout. He saw the brilliant outline of Dingo's body as the man stepped back to admire his handiwork.

A block of cement had fallen on Thorn's ribs from ten feet up. Little guy like that, a foot shorter but probably ten pounds heavier than Thorn. Zero body fat. Clearly this wasn't the day to play rope-a-dope. One more cement block and Thorn was going to be orbiting the Milky Way.

Slumping forward, hands on his knees, Thorn managed to keep his head tipped up, watching the small man who didn't give a shit about dolphins, who found their massacre funny, watching this man inch forward and rear back, cocking his thick right arm, aiming for the soft bone above Thorn's left ear.

With a groan, Thorn swung his head to the side, sucked down a painful breath, and shot a right hand at Dingo's throat. Made contact with his Adam's apple. Not much weight behind the blow and not much behind the next one or the one after that. Just enough to turn his voice box to mush and send Dingo backpedaling toward his friends. That husk of muscle hadn't protected him. He clutched his throat like a man strangling on his own breath, a drool of blood appearing at the corner of his mouth.

In two strides, Thorn had him by the front of his T-shirt. He set his feet and spun and hurled the man toward the bar, at the last second steering Dingo's face into the brass railing. Dingo lifted his head, nose mashed a half inch to the right, eyes fogged, blood bubbling from his mouth as if he'd been feasting on fallen game.

"You happy now?" Monica was at his side as Thorn limped toward the door.

The other carnivores gaped at Thorn and didn't budge, apparently content with the current alignment of their noses. On the telephone the bartender was describing the event to the sheriff's dispatcher, making it sound like a bigger deal than it was.

Outside in the sunny parking lot, Thorn halted by Monica's ancient Chevrolet Impala. Its blue paint had faded almost to white.

"Jesus, Thorn. What the hell was that about?"

He didn't reply. It was about nothing. About everything.

Monica opened her door and got in behind the wheel. Thorn climbed in the passenger door. The vinyl seats were simmering. They seared the back of his thighs. The pain felt fine, just right.

"I saw a suspicious-looking guy at the dolphin tanks yesterday," he said.

"What?"

"Red cap, aviator sunglasses. Tall with a beer belly."

"That's suspicious? Red cap, sunglasses?"

"He wasn't looking at the dolphins or the people swimming, he was checking out Roy. Watching all the mechanical stuff very carefully, like maybe he was casing the place so he could come back later and tear it apart."

Monica studied him for a moment. A stinging light flittered in her eyes.

"I'll drive you down to the sheriff's office. You can

describe the guy to them." In her voice was the quiet burn of ice. "If that's what you want."

"All right," Thorn said. "For all the good it will do."

"Yeah, well, you did a lot of good back there now, didn't you? A barroom brawl. What the hell was that supposed to accomplish?"

"It was the way he was laughing."

"He was an asshole, Thorn. You could pound on him for a year, he'd still be an asshole. What's the point?"

"I had to do something."

"Start a fight, hit a guy in the throat. Wow, that makes the world a better place. Very mature, Thorn."

"I was supposed to walk out of there, go home, tie more flies. Catch some fish, brush it all off?"

"You wasted your time with that guy, Thorn. He's not the problem with the world."

"Maybe he is."

Monica looked off at a line of palms along the highway. She took a long breath and let it out. Cleared her throat and set her shoulders. She looked at him briefly, then back at the roadway palms.

"I had a friend in college," she said, then halted and shook her head.

"What?"

"Nothing," she said. "Never mind."

"You had a friend in college."

She looked back at him, grimacing as if she doubted it was worth the effort.

"Okay," she said. "All right. His name was Paul Nottoli. An art major friend. We were very close. Smart kid, very talented. Professors were in awe of him, art dealers coming up from New York, talking to him about doing a show. Paul wasn't blown away by any of it. It was like fine, okay. Happy, but not overwhelmed.''

Thorn watched the body builders troop out of Sundowners and get into a blue Ford van. Dingo looked over and did something with his eyes that was supposed to vaporize Thorn. It didn't work.

"Then, his senior year, right after Christmas break, Paul's parents and kid sister were killed in a home invasion back home in Virginia. All of them tied up and shot. The family was very close. Very close. When Paul came back to college, he could barely function. A month later he quit, just left, didn't tell anybody but me where he was going. He drove to San Francisco, joined a Buddhist temple. Zen meditation. He'd been playing around with Zen for years, but all of a sudden it was extremely important. He put aside everything, college, a great career, all so he could find some peace.''

She was gripping the steering wheel, staring straight ahead out the windshield, navigating the back roads of her memories. Thorn watched the blue van pull out of its space, back slowly in their direction.

"So Paul's in San Francisco, one day he's sitting, doing his meditation with maybe thirty, forty other people. He's been there a few months, working very hard, dedicating himself and making progress, feeling that particular day like he's flirting with a major breakthrough, when outside in the alley a woman screams.

"A second or two go by and it's clear what's happening. Her head is beating against the opaque windowpane. Everyone in the meditation hall could tell the woman is being raped. Paul and a couple of others jump up, but the Zen master orders them to sit back down. He tells them this had happened before, and it would happen again and again. This was the way the world was. Nothing they could do would change it. He tells them to listen to the woman's voice, to remind themselves why they were there. For them to use the horror of this woman's pain to spur on their own pursuit of salvation.''

Thorn looked over at Monica. She was gripping the wheel, giving it little nudges as if the car were hurtling out of control.

''The Zen master told them they had to choose. Did they want to wrestle endlessly with the problems of the world, or did they want to solve the most important problem? It was only ego that made them think they could deliver justice, that they could judge who was right, who was wrong. And anyway, if Paul or any of the others went out in the alley and tried to save that girl, how would they know where to stop? There's always someone screaming in the next alley and the one next to that. A mugging, another rape. Always sirens in the distance. Always another problem. Where does it end? When do you stop trying to save others and get back to the thing that matters most? The reason you're here in the first place. To save yourself. To find understanding.''

''And if that was you in the alley?''

''Sure, it's terrible,'' she said. ''The world is full of awful things, rapes, murders, slaughtered dolphins. But you can't take on every problem. Right every wrong, feed every hungry person, give a dollar to every beggar. It's just not possible.''

''So what'd he do, your friend?''

The blue van was parked right behind them now.

Ten feet away. Windows tinted so dark, the muscleheads could be aiming shotguns at them, it'd be impossible to see until the windows exploded.

"Paul went through the window."

"Hip, hip."

She looked over at him.

"The rapist slashed Paul across the face. Then the man slit the woman's throat and walked away. The woman died. Paul nearly did."

"Good God."

"He wasn't allowed back in the Zen center either. I haven't heard from him in years. I don't think anybody has."

Thorn heard the wheels of the van crunch across the gravel and he turned. As the van passed by, the sun caught the side glass at a different angle and Thorn could make out four butt cracks pressed hard against the windows. Four hairy moons rising in the west.

"It's not worth it, Thorn. That bodybuilder might've had a gun, or one of his buddies. You could've been killed in a barroom fight. For what? Some trivial bullshit?"

Monica shook her head. A sweat stain was darkening the center of her denim shirt. It was shaped like a heart. Not a pretty pink valentine, but that dark lump of muscle that drove her body.

"Okay, you're right" he said. "I was an asshole. I should've just walked away."

"Look, Thorn, I feel terrible about the dolphins too, but it isn't something worth losing your life over."

"Okay," he said. "You're right."

"Nothing's worth that. No war, no cause, nothing."

"Nothing?"

Monica looked at him for a long moment.

"Nothing I've ever encountered."

Thorn stared into the endless blue of her eyes. Finally she let go of a breath and looked away. She started the car, pulled out of the lot and onto US 1.

Thorn looked out his window as she brought that big car up to speed. He snuck his hand around to his bruised ribs. Growing more tender by the second. He slid a finger inside the arm of his dark green T-shirt and touched the bullet scar. It had stopped tingling. It was no longer warm. Just a scar again, thickened flesh.

In the second-floor laboratory at the Eaton Street clinic, the doctor gave Pepper Tremaine another chemistry lesson as they worked from midnight to dawn. He took her through each step of the process, saying aloud everything he was doing. Someday soon Pepper was going to take over this part while the doctor spent his time on marketing the drug.

First, he filled a small-gauge syringe with a saline solution and inserted the needle into the spinal column and forced the fluid through. Then he isolated the bone marrow cells, washed them and suspended them in an assay medium. After that he acidified the sample using hydrochloric acid and then passed the solution through a Sep-Pak column. He showed Pepper how to wash the column with trifluoroacetic acid and elute it with methanol. They dried the resulting solute with a nitrogen stream.

That residue was what they were after. A powder so fine it was nearly invisible.

From ten that evening till four the next morning the doctor took her through the whole process, step-by-step. Pepper kept up with him, stayed focused, because that's what he wanted from her, what he expected. At the end of it, they had enough powder for two more injections. Eleven dolphins, two more shots.

CHAPTER

4

Greta Masterson spent her last afternoon in the Eaton Street clinic watching television in the sitting room. It was Tuesday, but her body still felt relaxed from the Sunday swim with the dolphins up in Key Largo. The other disabled vets also seemed more calm than usual. Eight of them hanging out, waiting for their suppertime injections.

Only Randy Gale had fallen back into his normal funk. Randy sat in the corner of the room in one of the folding metal chairs and stared at the painting of Christ that hung on the wall. A dark oil of the Crucifixion, the one with four soldiers squatting below the cross on a blanket as they threw dice for the purple robe. Randy had no arms. He'd lost them over twenty years ago in a land mine explosion, but he still felt them there. He imagined that they were sticking straight out to his sides. Randy felt compelled to turn sideways to get through doors. He couldn't walk down the sidewalk in Key West without angling away from people. Christ on an invisible cross. His phantom arms cramping constantly from the strain of holding them upright.

But everyone else seemed to have stashed their pain for the afternoon, watching the soaps, then the talk shows. A couple of the older amputees drinking Budweisers, the cans hidden in small paper sacks. Ginny, one of the two Desert Storm spinal cord paraplegics, was doing wheelies in her chair beside the window that looked out on Eaton Street.

"Oprah should do a show on us," Ginny said.

"Too much of a downer," one of the Korea vets said. "Bunch of freaking losers with missing limbs, whatta we have to say to America?"

"I think we could be very inspirational," Joe David, the 'Nam double amputee, said.

"Yeah, right," said Ginny. "Cheer up, Mrs. Middle America. Your husband may be running around with young boys, but hey, things could be worse. Your amputated arms could feel like they were boiling in the deep-fat fryer every minute of the day."

"You should get Oprah's number, call her up. Suggest that for a topic."

Greta rolled her chair back a couple of feet, faced the group.

"I'm leaving tomorrow," she announced.

"Yeah? Giving up on the cure?" Ginny got her chair up on balance, footplates a few inches off the hardwood floor. She held it there with tiny movements of her push rim.

Randy looked over at Greta. He'd fallen in love with her during her six-week stay. She'd seen it developing early on and had done all she could to keep him from getting serious, but it happened anyway. Randy couldn't understand why she was leaving. For the last several days he was angry all the time, ready to cry.

"She's going back to Miami," Randy said. "Rent an apartment, sit in the dark all day."

"No, I'm not."

"You got any family, Greta?" one of the Desert Storm guys asked.

She said no, none. Alone in the world.

"Sit in a dark room and feel sorry for herself," Randy said.

Ginny was looking expectantly at Randy, seeing a little drama ready to erupt. They erupted frequently around the pain clinic. Somebody screaming the worst words ever said to another human being, filthy, outrageous obscenities. Ten minutes later everyone's watching TV again, the jokes rolling along.

Greta was going to miss that group.

Without another word she rolled out of the room, Randy studying the floor with a clenched mouth. No one told her good-bye. Have a good life, it was fun knowing you. None of the pleasantries of polite society. Greta didn't expect it, would've even been a little insulted if they'd made an exception in her case. That was the one rule in the Eaton Street pain clinic. No bullshit. A lot of happy faces, balloons and hugs and kisses, would've been major bullshit. Like everyone else in this room, Greta was in terrible pain. She'd arrived in pain, she was leaving in pain. There'd been no relief. A bunch of happy bullshit was out of the question.

She rolled back to her room, shut the door. Greta rolled her chair into a swatch of sunlight that was leaking through the untended banyan tree in the adjacent backyard. She was wearing gray jeans today, a white crewneck T, white tennis shoes. The leather purse in her lap was natural cowhide clumsily hand tooled by her daughter, Suzy—a summer camp project from two years before.

Greta rolled over to the cheap deal desk and pulled open the drawer. She curled her fingers over the guide bar in the back and pinched out the small photograph she'd smuggled along. A fairly dangerous risk, given her situation, but one she felt compelled to take. The snapshot had been taken by Greta's mother. It was a color photo of Suzy and Greta the previous summer at the beach on Key Biscayne. Greta squatting by her trim, blond daughter, holding her around the waist as a wave crashed over their backs. Both of them laughing wildly. Greta stared at her own legs from a year earlier. Muscular and tan. Nothing like the shriveled appendages she had these days. She looked at her daughter's easy laughter and her own. All of it changed now. Nothing easy anymore.

Greta let her mind wander through some of the other images she'd stored away. Suzy sitting primly at her school desk with her hand straight in the air. Suzy reading a book by the window, so focused and serious. Suzy holding the flower basket out in the sunny backyard at her grandmother's Coral Gables house while Granny clipped roses. Suzy rigidly asleep in the same narrow bed where Greta had spent her own childhood nights.

For these last six weeks Suzy had been staying with her grandmother. That was the hardest part of Greta's assignment. Just a weekly phone chat to see her through. Stealing down Eaton Street to a public phone at the Laundromat. Watching the door as she talked. Besides that phone conversation, Greta's only other comfort came from invoking Suzy's image every chance she could, hoping her daughter could feel the telepathic tingle of her love.

Greta had fallen. That was how it began. Last September, balanced atop a brick wall, four feet above her patio, she had been stretching up to prune one of her new orchids, *oncidium,* the dancing lady. Reaching out to snip off one of the cascades of blooms—an inch from her grasp, no more than that. On her tiptoes in the white Keds with the pebbled soles, on the bricks that were always damp and coated with the green slime of mildew from Miami's perpetual hothouse climate. Reaching up for a cluster of blooms, something she'd done a thousand times.

Only thirty-two years old, for godsakes. In the best physical shape of her life. Just out of DEA boot camp at Quantico, where for four months she'd jogged five miles a day, done countless push-ups, stretching, weight lifting, target practice. She was an excellent marksman, with better scores than all but one of the men in her class. She was no tomboy, had never even held a handgun before—no father around to show her how to shoot. But it turned out she was a natural. Never wavered as she squeezed, never flinched at the blast or winced at the recoil.

That was Greta Masterson's major skill. She didn't flinch. Didn't dodge, didn't try to sidestep or bullshit herself. A spade was a spade was a spade. A failed eight-year marriage ended in a weekend of battering. She nearly lost an eye, nearly lost Suzy. But she didn't cringe, didn't feel sorry for herself. Greta had the bastard hauled off to jail, stayed around till the trial was done, looked him in the eye when they took him away. Then she went home to Miami, to her mother's galling told-you-so's. She hadn't flinched at any of it. Did what she had to do, got on with it, never second-guessed, never winced as she pulled the shrapnel out of her gut, piece by piece.

How she decided on the DEA she couldn't say. One of Miami's growth industries. Maybe it was her ex-husband's love affair with amphetamines, maybe her mother's medicine cabinet always crammed with a bright array of mood adjusters. In any case, Greta Masterson was an exceptional shot and studied hard, and graduated second in her class at Quantico.

Everything was going so well. Good money for the first time in her life. Able to move out of her mother's suffocating house, rent a two-bedroom cottage on a South Miami avenue, a house where the patio was always in shade, the bricks growing green slime. Five orchids, six orchids, seven. Blooming. Everything blooming for Suzy and Greta. Daughter with blond ringlets, mother with dead aim.

Until slick pressed against slick, the blooms just an inch away and Greta lurched backward, dropped four feet through the air and cracked her spine against a ficus tree's gnarled root that thrust up from the earth like an iron fist. She lost contact with her legs, everything below her navel. Lying there on her back looking up at the perfect blue Miami sky. Her rented backyard, her rented clouds, her bricks. Feeling nothing where her legs had been.

Conus medullaris. Severe violation of the sacral cord and lumbar nerve roots within the neural canal. Dead from T-4 down. An emergency operation—steel rods implanted to steady her spine. Then a week into rehab, a wheelchair for life, the pain began—a fire raging in her numb legs. Violent cramps in muscles that were no

longer operable, pain that roared through the senseless flesh. Each toe burning separately. For a week she
woke every morning with her legs drawn into a brutally
tight fetal curl. Except they weren't truly drawn up.
Her legs were paralyzed, lying flat and dead on the
mattress. But they felt that way. Cramped and burning
with her knees locked hard against her chest.

It came and went when it pleased. No warning. A
phantom that poured scalding oil on her flesh and
made the dead nerves howl. Greta writhed in her bed.
It took her breath, burned for hours, then disappeared
as abruptly as it came. The medical staff tried all the
drugs, but none of them could touch the pain. They
looked at her, the doctors, her mother, her friends,
they stared at her legs and listened to her groans, and
she could see they didn't fully believe. As if it were
something in her head. Greta, the hypochondriac.
How could she possibly feel her legs? They were dead.

But no, they were not dead. They burned and
burned as though the flesh were turning to charred
cinder. There was a scale they used to measure pain,
zero to fifty. One of her young doctors had informed
her of it. Amputation of a digit was at the top, a 41,
childbirth a few slots lower, then phantom limb pain at
27. Twenty-seven. Not as intense as childbirth, which
Greta remembered vividly. Only difference was, this
pain was forever. There was nothing out there to stop
it. No drugs, nothing. Never going to be an end to the
fire, no healing, no soothing salves, no return to normalcy. And to make it worse, they told her it was a
problem in her brain, her neural map still showed two
legs down there, a lifetime of neurological habits, the
brain still sending electrical messages down the circuitry of nerves every split second to verify the legs'

existence and every split second those messengers came howling back with garbled screams, the white noise of pain. If she'd lost her legs from the slow death of frostbite or even gangrene, her brain would have had time to redraw its diagram and there would be no phantom pain. But with sudden traumas like her fall, or a gunshot wound or car accident, the brain held on to the old map—forever showing a continent that no longer existed. There was no way to instruct the brain to let go of its faulty script. There was nothing Greta could do at all, nothing but lie on her bed and feel her dead flesh boiling. A 27.

Then one rainy afternoon Brad Madison came to visit, no fanfare, just pushed open the hospital room door and walked in, smiling but serious. Special agent in charge. Ran the entire Miami office of the DEA, responsible for several hundred agents, all of Florida and the Bahamas, toughest drug beat on the planet. Greta knew who he was, of course, but never suspected Brad knew her.

He stood beside her bed for a few awkward minutes, condolences, all that, then offered her a new assignment. He'd found a spot for her in one of the MET operations. Mobile enforcement team. A service provided to local law enforcement agencies around the country—some sheriff in over his head calls, they go.

Greta listened, her gloom lifting slightly. The impossible weight of her despair. Brad Madison himself doing her a favor. Or maybe not. Looking at him, she wasn't sure, his anxious smile.

Here's how it would go, he said. You finish your rehab down in Key West. There's a doctor there, your injury fits his profile. He runs a clinic with ties to the VA system. He's doing some sophisticated pain treatment. Trouble is, he's been prescribing some big numbers—narcotics, opiates, in quantities that wouldn't make us flinch if he were a licensed pain clinic. But he's not. Like maybe he's using the VA system as a cover, big bureaucracy, get lost in the paper shuffle, working with dead-end guys everybody else has given up on. He specializes in amputees, paraplegics. Focused on the same kind of phantom limb pain you've got. Guy's a highly trained specialist, Harvard Medical, Johns Hopkins postdoc. With all that going for him, the man's decided to work with vets, taking government wages. Regular Father Teresa, this guy.

Or maybe not.

Greta would rent a room right in the clinic, go through his process, listen, keep her eyes open. They'd clean her up, a new identity. No living relatives, no child. She'd be Greta Masterson, Marine Corps lieutenant. Injured in a training exercise at Lejeune. A fall, nothing fancy. Keeping it as close to the truth as possible.

This doctor, he's not a quack—nothing like that, Brad Madison said. You'll be perfectly safe. Hell, he might even do you some good.

What it is, the VA internal police are convinced he's diverting Schedule Two drugs, writing way too many scripts, then recruiting some of these sad sacks to go sell the Percodan, Darvocet, pure morphine on the street, kickback his share. The money's there. If he takes his time, goes slow, he could get rich selling just a fraction of what he writes. Down in Key West, who would notice, a few more drugs floating around? But this is serious, and we need to check it out.

Who're you trying to kid? she said.

What?

I'm sorry, Greta said. But this is make-work. Trying to be nice, distract me. You don't send someone under-cover for that. You call in the Medicaid Fraud Unit, or you seize his records, refer him to the state medical board, or you use informants. That's not what Mobile Enforcement is for. Anyway, this is a Diversion Program issue. If the guy's diverting drugs for profit or self-medication, it's Echeverria's bailiwick.

Lecturing her boss, like he didn't know already.

Well, yes, he said. That's true normally. But this is a sensitive case, Greta. It requires some nonstandard arrangements. I couldn't just drop this on Echeverria's desk.

Sensitive? What's that mean? Nonstandard?

It means there are some toes we can't step on here. Sensitive toes.

What? Our doctor is some U.S. senator's son?

Something like that, he said. But trust me, it's serious business. If this guy is dirty, I don't care whose son he is, we're going to nail his ass to the wall. No fudging, no sweetheart deals. We're playing this straight. The last week or two I've been working on this, trying to come up with a plan, a way to run an undercover operation, then this happens to you, your fall, and I'm thinking, this is perfect . . . well, *perfect*'s not the right word, of course, but it's a good matchup. You know what I'm trying to say, Greta.

Pardon me, she said, but how come you're here? Special agent in charge. You're working street-level cases all of a sudden?

I have a personal interest.

What? This is your operation? You're running it by yourself, is that what you're telling me?

He considered that for a minute. Then, okay, yeah.

It'd be just you and me. Official, but not official. A gray area. Please, Greta. You'd be doing me a personal favor. That's how it is. You find out anything, it's between us. No reports, no paperwork. But if this guy is dirty, he doesn't get a pass. We jump on him with both feet. Ride him to the ground.

Not even thinking about it, weighing what it would mean to Suzy, not really caring if it was make-work or not, Greta said, sure, why not. Thread me on the hook, throw me in, see what bites. Sure, what the hell else've I got to do?

It was a short-term operation, six weeks max. She had a tiny room, a hot plate, had her run of the building all day. She could watch, sniff around. Talk to the other patients. Perfect vantage point. A couple of weeks into it, what she found was, she liked the doctor. A good guy, doing damn good things. Treating the vets with chronic, intractable pain dumped on his doorstep by VA hospitals all over the country. Guys who'd had all the operations, all the rehab and therapy and were still hurting like hell. No one knew what to do with them anymore. Some old warhorse guzzling a gallon of morphine a day, he's still screaming and complaining, so they ship him off to Key West, end of the road. Good-bye and good riddance. But the doc took them in. Worked his ass off for them. "Father Teresa" was right.

As the weeks passed, the doctor seemed to take a special interest in her condition, tried different approaches with her phantom pain. A few things dulled the burning for an hour or two. Epidural injections, the trigger point shots, deadening nerve junctures in her back.

To be perfectly honest, she'd have to admit, after six weeks of seeing him every day, she'd fallen a little. Early forties, lanky athletic body, handsome, very natural, with an easy smile, always joking around. Shaggy blond hair and dark blue eyes that every once in a while took all the accumulated pain that had settled in them and sailed off to some warm place and returned a moment or two later refreshed. But most important, this man absolutely believed in Greta's pain, the only one of all her friends and family whose sympathy never wavered.

Greta decided the only reason he was writing a lot of scripts for Schedule Two drugs was that he was up to his neck in intractable pain. That's how much narcotic it took to make a dent. Way more than the DEA guidelines. The man wasn't diverting. She was sure of it. She talked to his other patients, listened, snooped a little, file cabinets, even prowled in his computer late one night. The guy was clean. What he was prescribing was what he was injecting, nothing getting siphoned off for street sales.

The only thing wrong were the guidelines. Written by puritan assholes back in Washington who'd never been on a pain ward, heard the screaming, the nightmare agonies of excruciating suffering. So worried about addiction and diversion, they had no idea what it was like in the trenches. Six weeks in those trenches, Greta was a convert. Let the narcotics flow, dole out the opiates, whatever it took. Quit counting cc's. Why should anyone have to suffer, for godsakes?

Of course she knew why. That's the way the world worked. People in quiet offices with their pie charts and their religiously uptight constituencies, deciding policy for blood-and-gristle people whose pain was unimaginably brutal. Let them eat aspirin. Lots of aspirin, if that's what it took. Stiff upper lip. Bite the bullet. All that stoic bullshit.

But then Greta's tenure was finished. The six weeks up, she was turning back into a civilian, headed home to Suzy. Greta wondering if she should say something personal to the doc before she left, give him some sign how she felt. But deciding, no, she'd go home, have her conference with Brad Madison, give the doc a clean bill of health, write her report. Then she'd see how she was feeling a month later, and if the emotions were still there, she could always come back down, pop in the clinic one day, ask him out for supper. Greta, the modern woman.

At five-thirty, as Greta was finishing packing her bag, Pepper Tremaine, Dr. Wilson's head nurse, tapped on her closed door and said the doctor was ready for her. One last injection for the road. Greta rolled quickly over to the desk and slipped the snapshot into the drawer and closed it. When she swiveled around, Pepper was standing in the doorway, smiling at her innocently.

Greta followed her down the hallway to the treatment room, and Dr. Wilson was there, in rumpled khaki trousers and a blue work shirt. Looking more like a classy beachcomber than an anesthesiologist. He helped her out of her chair, up onto the examining table, his strong hands on her, giving her that tingle.

With Pepper standing beside the examining table Dr. Bean Wilson lay Greta on her stomach, drew up her blouse, proceeded with more trigger point injections, the usual stuff, Marcaine Hydrochloride, Depo-Medrol, tetracaine, she couldn't keep them straight. A prick of local anesthetic at four nerve sites in her lower back, then the deep injection, four inches down, using the flexible needle so he could turn it subcutaneously, fanning the drug to a larger area.

When he was finished, the handsome, kind, sweet, wonderful doctor turned her back over, smiled down at her, and said she was going to sleep now and when she woke up she would be in a different place.

"What different place?"

"I'm moving you," he said. "Pepper's boat. It's quite comfortable."

"The *Miss Begotten*," Pepper said. "My father named it. He was a rumrunner, among other things."

The doctor fastened one of the restraining straps across her torso, pinning her arms.

"Boat?" Greta smiling uncertainly. "What're you talking about? We're going on a cruise?"

"Something like that," Pepper said.

The doctor tightened the strap across her ankles.

"You want to be rid of your pain, Greta, don't you? The burning?"

"What's going on?"

"You'll be fine," he said. "You'll fall asleep in a minute or two and when you wake, I'll be there and we'll try some new things. Some better things."

"I'm leaving town tomorrow," she said. "Did you forget?"

"It's a simple procedure."

"What're you talking about? Are you drunk?"

Greta twisted against the restraints, but he had her by then. Four webbed bands holding her tight to the stretcher.

"There's just one important issue, Greta, the question I must ask every patient in your situation. A formality, really, but I have to ask.''

Pepper was smiling at Greta. The room getting hazy.

"Are you sure you can tolerate a foreign body inside your body?"

"What!"

"You know the routine, Greta. One-hour procedure, small incision in your belly, nestle the pump in a pocket on top of the muscle tissue, tunnel the tubing around your side and then guide it into your spine, one-day recovery, very little pain. Tomorrow you'll wake up, your stomach will be a little sore, but that's all.''

"Wait just a goddamn minute. You can't do this. Hey!"

He patted her on the shoulder and left. When the door shut, Greta Masterson cried out, then she bucked and twisted and fought the restraints, but they didn't give. Pepper stood beside the bed, still with that small smile.

As the anesthetic kicked in, Greta began to sweat and a rush of panic swept over her. She squirmed and wrenched an arm, managed to free it, but by then she'd lost all dexterity and could not loosen the other straps. Lathered in sweat, she flailed her free arm and began to babble. Picturing Brad Madison parked down the street waiting for her to come rolling down Eaton. Coming to pick Greta up, take her back to Suzy, to her old life, her new life. Coming tomorrow. Tomorrow afternoon to take her home.

Pepper stood over Greta and stared down at her, eyes empty. Then she refastened Greta's arm beneath the strap and walked away. And Greta began the long descent—a heavy sleep dragging her down into its breathless depths, its immense gravity.

''She was clawing and screaming. All I could make out was this. I was supposed to tell whoever answered the phone that she was in terrible trouble. To come right now and kick down the door.''

Dr. Bean Wilson sat at the desk and stared at the slip of paper Pepper had scribbled on. He touched the corner of the paper with his finger, straightening it, lining it up with the edges of his desk.

''Shit,'' he said. ''Shit, shit, shit.''

''You want me to call the number, find out who answers?''

''No.''

''I don't mind. It might be a good idea. She could have some family we didn't know about. A boyfriend or something. Somebody who'd come looking for her later and could cause a lot of trouble.''

''Goddamn it, I already know whose number it is.''

''You do? Who?''

The doctor crumpled the paper. Mashed it between his hands, rolling it into a tight little ball, which he dropped on the desk in front of him.

''His fucking name is Brad Madison.''

CHAPTER

5

Wednesday morning Thorn finished his morning coffee out on the wood dock. Blackwater Sound was as sleek and gray as dolphin flesh. A couple of miles out, two white fishing boats skimmed south abreast of one another. An easterly breeze carried their muffled exhausts, along with the scent of grated ginger and cheap beer gone stale, the morning smell of mangroves. Seaweed rode the swells along shore; a paper cup, a length of rope bobbing near the pilings of his dock. The blue was just seeping back into the sky for another long day of uninterrupted sun. The National Weather Service had been playing its unvarying message since the end of February. It was never going to rain again. Never, ever.

Thorn watched Rover stalk butterflies in the lantana. Pointing, taking one careful step after another, holding his profile low. Such poise, such focus. Another step, another, closing to within a yard, the magic distance for butterflies, then holding there, cocking his body like the tightest of bowstrings. Then, at some mysterious signal, he leaped toward the thicket, a beautiful strike. But somehow the clumsy insect with its speck of brain and foolhardy trajectories lurched away from him. Saved itself again from Rover's jaws.

When he'd finished his coffee he went back upstairs and for the next couple of hours he tied Crazy Marys. It was a bonefish fly he'd created a month ago after his friend Sugarman dropped off a grocery sack full of red hair he'd discovered behind the beauty shop next door to his office. Turned out it was Mary Fitzroy's hair, an old salt who'd been cultivating that mane for over eighty years. Most of that time she'd been an offshore fishing guide, taking the three-hundred-dollar-a-day crowd out after dolphin and sail and marlin. Years of sun hadn't dulled its deep cherry hue, but lately Mary had come to believe that the weight of her hair was robbing her brain of vitality. How else to explain her sudden lapses of memory, or an occasional inability to sight the subtle roughening in the ocean's surface caused by a passing school of dolphin. Mary told Lisa Ann at the Hairport to just whack it off, shave it down to the shiny scalp. The stuff was too much damn work to take care of anymore and it required more goddamn energy than she could spare to keep lugging it around.

For the last few weeks Thorn had been working his way through the hair, pinch by pinch, shaping flies with bright silver bead chain eyes, crimson Mylar over a Mustad 3407, fluorescent green Flashabou, and Mary's hair for the saddle hackles. Proud Mary was the name he'd given the flies, but as soon as the guides discovered the source of the hair, they started using the same nickname they'd always used for Mary Fitzroy. Crazy Mary. At first there were a group of them who refused to touch the flies after hearing they were made from Mary's hair. Some kind of sacrilege. But after word got around that the lures were catching fish, all the superstitions blew away.

By eleven that sunny morning, Thorn's fingers were dull and clumsy, and his back was tight from stooping over his custom vise. It was Wednesday, two days since the dolphin slaughter, and so far he'd kept his word to Monica. He'd left it alone, kept himself locked up inside the meditation hall. Though to be honest, his mind was not fully cooperating in the venture. He thought of little else.

While he had considerable work to do on the Chris-Craft to get her back in service, Thorn decided instead to make a run down the highway, take his backlog of five dozen Crazy Marys and offer them to a few of his tackle shop buddies. His cigar box was down to less than a hundred dollars, enough to get through the month, but without much cushion.

That's what he told himself as he ate a quick lunch—turkey sandwich and iced tea. And that's what he said aloud to Rover when he set down the dog's breakfast of leftover fried grunt fillets and white rice. Thorn was simply going out to sell flies, something he'd done a few thousand times before. Nothing to feel guilty about, nothing to explain to Monica later. Going out to sell some Crazy Marys. Simple as that.

Roy Everly was lying on a yellow chaise beside the empty dolphin pens when Thorn pulled his VW bug convertible into the driveway. The Keys Cruiser was over thirty years old and was starting to show some serious wear. For the last few years the convertible top had been stuck in the down position, and the upholstery had taken a hell of a beating from the rain and sun. Lately a few rust spots had eaten all the way through the floorboard near the accelerator pedal, so now Thorn could watch the asphalt highway speed by between his legs. A new thrill.

Thorn wore a pair of gray canvas shorts and a white polo shirt. He'd selected the pair of running shoes Monica had given him a month back when she was trying to convince him to join her in a shape-up campaign. The shoes had plastic bubbles in the soles so you could see the air you were walking on. They were red and silver and looked like they might glow in the dark. He'd put them on because he thought they might be just the ticket for a long day of selling flies.

Thorn went through the open gate, glancing at the mangled lock lying in the sand. Roy continued to stare out at the empty tanks as Thorn took a seat beside him in a webbed aluminum chair.

Roy was wearing his red thong and a Panama hat that looked like he'd rescued it from a week in the middle of a busy highway. Roy's flesh was as dark and oily as tobacco juice. His coppery eyes might have been sized right a couple hundred pounds ago, but now they were dwarfed by Roy's ten-gallon head, like two old pennies sinking into a bog. There was a three-day grizzle on his cheeks, silvery and thick. He had a rum lover's overripe nose and a couple of scars Thorn had never noticed before, one near his eye that curved just above his eyebrow and another at the corner of his mouth. They had the look of feminine slashes, some outraged flick of nail file or cuticle scissors, as if this boy whose mother would not die had once or twice leaned in too close to check her breathing.

"Hey, Roy."

The big man grumbled hello.

"Sorry about this. It's a shitty thing."

"Shitty as it gets," Roy said.

"What do you do now?"

Roy snorted.

"I sit here. Maybe they'll come back, slice me open."

"Who was it, Roy? You have any idea?"

Roy glanced over at Thorn, then past him toward the house. Thirty feet away his mother was sitting by an open window with her head bent forward as if she were knitting, but Thorn could see her left ear aimed in their direction. Roy turned back to the empty tanks.

"When'd you start jogging, Thorn?"

"I haven't," he said. "Monica gave me the shoes. I'd sure as hell hate to mess them up by running in them."

"Monica's a good lady. You should treat her right."

"I'm trying, Roy. Trying hard."

Roy Everly took a deep breath and polished the bulbous tip of his nose with his big right paw.

"How the fuck should I know who killed my dolphins? You think if I knew who did it, I'd be sitting here?"

Thorn leaned forward, elbows on his knees.

"No suspicions?"

"Whatta you doing, Thorn? You visited this place exactly three times your whole life. What the hell do you care who carved up my dolphins?"

"What do the police think?"

Roy touched his chin to his chest and watched a bead of sweat run down the dark hump of his belly. He cut his eyes to the window. His mother wasn't there any longer. Probably went to get her hearing aid.

"So, you're taking this up? You making this a project, are you?"

"No," Thorn said. "I'm just being neighborly."

"Monica send you over here?"

"I'm here on my own. In fact, I'd rather you not say anything to her about my coming by. She's trying to keep me out of trouble."

Roy turned his chunky head toward Thorn, settled those bronze eyes on his. This was a man as smart as anyone the island had ever produced. Test score smart, engineering and electronics smart. A stack of *Popular Science* magazines always tumbling out of his school locker. Even with those strikes against him, Roy might have had a gang of friends, for Key Largo was forgiving of its eccentrics, but Roy had a bitter streak. And even now, beneath the sad girdle of inert flesh, Thorn could still see the narrow, wolfish kid who thirty years before had made a career of defying his teachers and mocking anyone who dared to speak to him.

"The police," Roy said with a sour smile. "They think it was somebody drove down from Miami, one of those Santerias. Haitians or whatnot. Some kind of sacrificial bullshit. Voodoo, witchcraft, something like that. Those fucking moron cops."

"And what do you think, Roy?"

"Fuck you, Thorn. I don't need your help. When I get ready, I'll find some more dolphins and start over. So you can just butt out, okay?"

Thorn watched three white-haired ladies power-walking down the street. They slowed as they passed by the dolphin pens and murmured fervently.

"The other day I noticed a guy. He was watching you, Roy, keeping an eye on you as you went through your routines. He didn't seem very interested in the dolphins or the people swimming with them. But he seemed very interested in you. Red baseball cap, aviator shades. Tall with a potbelly. I saw him here twice."

From inside the house Roy's mother called his

name. Roy looked off toward the street and said nothing. A moment later a burst of cackling laughter broke from the back window. Sounded like one of those joke-store gadgets—battery-operated hilarity.

"You believe this shit?" Roy swung around and glared at the house. "I took away all her handbells. Calling me all the time like I'm a fucking maid. Now she uses that goddamn thing. I can't get it away from her."

Thorn could see the dolphin blood on the sides of the cement tanks, spattered like crude graffiti.

"You have an idea who did this, don't you, Roy?"

He flicked away another bead of sweat heading down his gut. He looked at Thorn, then looked back at the horror of the tanks.

"That guy you saw," said Roy. "He was probably one of those Free Willy fuckers."

"What?"

"Goddamn dolphin radicals. They been campaigning to shut me down last couple of years. They don't want captive dolphins of any kind. Doesn't matter how much good comes out of swimming with them, if a dolphin's in a cage, then it's a crime as far as those fucks are concerned."

"Come on, Roy. Dolphin nuts aren't going to massacre the animals they're trying to save."

"Fuck that, those people are crazy. Like those assholes out in Oregon trying to save the owls. They'll booby-trap trees, kill lumberjacks, they don't care. Fucking madmen'll do anything to get their way."

He sat up and glared at Thorn. There was booze on his breath and his eyes were clouded with it. A couple of Cuba libres with his Wheaties. A snarl momentarily reshaped Roy's lips, then he swallowed deeply and let the anger go and a look surfaced that Thorn had never seen on his face before. Roy Everly's eyes welled and his mouth softened into a melancholy mess. He hiccoughed once and it seemed to Thorn that he was about to break into an uncontrollable blubber when his mother once again called out his name and a moment afterward that piercing synthetic laughter sounded again and again from deep in the house. Roy's face hardened again.

"The fuckers had to be cutting on them for a couple of hours."

"What?"

"The way the blood was tracked around. You can see the goddamn footprints. They went down there, climbed back out, went down there again. They were cutting on them, taking breaks, sitting around, having a smoke, then cutting some more. Having a good old time. Nice long evening of torture. While I was lying in there not more than fifty feet away, dead to the world."

Roy waved at the decking on the edge of the nearest tank.

"Go look for yourself."

Thorn went over and stared at the footprints. One large set, one smaller. And it was like Roy said. They'd taken their time. Sat around in bloody clothes and watched the dolphins bleeding. The smell was bad, growing worse as the sun had its way. Thorn went back over to Roy.

"See what I mean?"

Thorn nodded.

"The fuckers cut out their spines. That sound like Santeria to you?"

"Their spines?"

"Shit, yeah. Spines, brains. They knew what the fuck

they were doing. They hacked on the bodies, made a real mess, but these fuckers had a purpose. Some kind of plan.''

Thorn tried to swallow away the lump of nausea rising in his throat.

Roy turned his head, glared at him.

''So what'm I supposed to do, write you a retainer check, Thorn? That how it works? You got some kind of fee? Hundred dollars a day plus expenses, like on TV?'' Roy knew better, of course. He was just angry, trying to goad Thorn to the same place he was.

''You find out anything else,'' Thorn said, ''you know where I am.''

''Yeah, I know. Up in the trees with the birdies and the bees.''

Roy rose to his feet. He glanced once at the empty tanks, then padded toward the horrors in that house.

One suitcase sat by the front door. The other was on the bamboo rug, half closed, Monica sitting on top of it. She'd managed to lock one of the latches, but the other one wouldn't catch.

She got up, opened the suitcase again, looked inside, then flung a couple of blouses onto the bed, and closed it again. This time both latches caught and she stood up, breathing hard. She was wearing black jeans and a black-and-white checked sleeveless blouse, sandals.

It was nearly twelve-thirty. She was on her lunch break. They gave her an hour, but today she was going to take longer than that. She was going to take forever.

Hitting the road again. Change her name, find a job scrubbing somebody's pots. What the hell difference did it make? The fever was on her. The rapid breathing, failure to focus, the jangle in her veins. Love deficit disorder. Alarms bells ringing. Fly, run. Go.

She'd saved two hundred and twelve dollars this time. Enough for gas and tossed salads for a thousand miles or so. Get to Louisiana, maybe make it into Texas. She'd never been to Texas, but she was sure there were people out there who needed their pots scrubbed.

She was gone. Already out on the road, the throb of the Impala's big guzzler vibrating through her bones. The wind, the radio, the daze. She'd done it before and it had brought her here; now it was time again. Find a new self down the highway somewhere. Start over. Do a better job this time. Stay vigilant and tough. Keep the trip wires strung tight around the perimeters of her heart.

Thorn had inched too close. Squirmed past all the land mines, wriggled beneath the barbed wire, then scaled the high ramparts of Monica's walled city, and now he was stalking the hallways, circling toward the inner sanctum. There was not a second to spare. It was time to pry open the escape hatch, flee. Yes, it was cruel. It was mean and cold and pathetic. Monica, poor, stupid girl. Afraid of Thorn, of what she felt for him. Panic firing her blood. He had drawn so close. Just outside the door. She could hear him breathing. A flower opening inside her, exposing her again. God help her, she had to run.

She carried both bags out into the gravel drive. A sunny day, the breeze off the water full of spicy island smells. She opened the trunk, put them inside, slammed it shut, walked back into the apartment to see if she'd forgotten anything crucial. Just leaving behind a few clothes and some drawings she'd done recently.

She guessed she was leaving them for Thorn, a parting gift. She glanced around hurriedly, saw nothing. For the thousandth time she considered a note. He deserved a note. He'd worry, get frantic, maybe even waste time trying to track her. She stared at the far wall, a drawing of Rover sitting on the end of Thorn's dock, then she turned and went back out the door.

Roy Everly was standing beside the car. Red thong, black baseball hat, dark glasses.

"You off?"

"Hello, Roy." She dug the ignition key out of her pocket.

"I saw the suitcases."

"I'm paid through the end of the month, right?"

"Did Thorn hurt you? Do something to you?"

"No."

"You moving in with him?"

"I'm leaving, Roy. Going on a trip."

He nodded and kept on nodding like she'd said something weighty.

"I'm just feeling . . . I don't know. But I need to get out of here."

"I can relate. Life on the rock drives you batshit. No two ways about it."

She stepped close and kissed him on the cheek. He'd been into the rum again.

"I guess you wouldn't want to take me with you. It's always been a fantasy of mine, take a road trip with a beautiful woman."

She sighed, wiped the sweat off her cheek.

"I need to go, Roy."

"I'm not trying to stop you."

Monica let her gaze drift out to a sliver of the bright

Atlantic visible through the mangroves. Her vision was getting blurry.

"I imagine it's a little scary being with a guy like Thorn. That crazy fuck."

"It's not that," she said. "He's fine. He deserves better."

"He was just by, not more than fifteen minutes ago. He's investigating the dolphin thing."

"Yeah," she said. "I thought he might."

Roy looked past her toward his house. Gulls were diving in the canal near the dolphin tanks, squawking with excitement over a school of bait fish.

"I think about running away," Roy said. "I think about it every single day. Getting in the car, pointing it somewhere, going. But like they say, there's never any escape. Wherever you go, there you are."

Monica gripped the ignition key tight in her fist.

"Well, you have a safe journey then. Write when you get work."

Monica watched him walk back to his house, go inside, shut the door. She stood there feeling the key bite into her palm.

CHAPTER

6

Dr. Bean Wilson was the oldest medical man in Key Largo. Thorn estimated him to be around eighty-five, though some claimed he was older. As a youngster Thorn got his first inoculations from the man and he'd seemed pretty damn old even then. Over the years he'd visited Wilson dozens of times—a couple of broken bones, well over a hundred stitches, a fishhook embedded in his calf, another snagged in his earlobe: errant casts by a couple of novice anglers back in Thorn's guiding days. It had even been Dr. Wilson who'd cleaned and closed that gunshot wound in his shoulder.

In all those years, Thorn had watched the doctor's thick hair turn brighter and brighter white, but other than that the man had not aged. Just an inch or two over five feet, Dr. Wilson was trim and limber and his cucumber-green eyes still had the wry spark of a young man who found the world wondrous and outlandish. As a kid Thorn had been buddies with the doctor's only son, Bean junior, thrown together at first because their parents socialized, but gradually becoming inseparable. Four of them. Sugarman, Gaeton Richards,

Thorn, and Bean junior. Exploring the serpentine mangrove canals and the flats, learning every rock and twist of elkhorn coral below the surface on the Atlantic side, and the secret lives of every fish that hid in their crevices.

The Wilsons and Thorn's adoptive parents had vacationed together several summers, trips to Florida's panhandle. Thorn and Bean junior spent those long sunny days wrestling atop the dunes and tumbling down them, or out on a little johnboat with their poles, searching the marshes for redfish and snapper. They'd been blood brothers until their junior year, when Bean junior was shipped off to some fancy prep school in the Northeast, and though Thorn had answered every one of Bean's homesick letters, eventually the mail ceased and they lost touch. He'd heard that Bean went into the military, and had been badly wounded in Vietnam, but he'd never heard the details. The few times Thorn asked Dr. Wilson about him, the old man grew subdued and changed the subject. Bean junior was a doctor now himself. An anesthesiologist. He had a practice down in Key West, a couple of hours away, but he never visited.

Old Dr. Wilson worked out of a small CBS building wedged between a propeller shop and an Ace Hardware. Two decades back, when he purchased the place, it was a one-seat barbershop, the red-white-and-blue pole swirling away out front. Shortly after he moved in, the doctor and a couple of his friends were painting the walls of what would become his examining rooms, when a Yankee tourist bustled in and demanded a haircut. Said he had an important business engagement back in Manhattan early the next day and needed to look sharp for it. Damn sharp.

Dr. Bean Wilson tried to explain that he wasn't qualified for such a challenging assignment, but the New Yorker would have none of it and plunked himself down in the barber chair that Bean had not yet removed. While his friends stood around grinning, Doc Wilson proceeded to cut the Yankee's hair, and afterward the man proclaimed it to be the best goddamn haircut he'd ever had the pleasure of receiving and said that Bean Wilson's hands were the absolute softest, kindest, most intelligent hands that had ever touched his sorry scalp. He tipped Dr. Wilson twenty dollars and Bean mounted it on the wall next to a couple of lunker trout he'd landed years earlier. Inspired by the event, Wilson took the necessary tests for a barber's license, telling his patients he needed a backup plan in case one day everyone on Key Largo had a long healthy spell.

Thorn parked the VW in front of the propeller shop just in case Monica drove by and questioned him later. The story was, he'd been shopping for a new prop for the Chris-Craft—spending the extra loot he was raking in from his Crazy Marys. He promised himself he'd go into the propeller shop after visiting Bean Wilson, look around, see what they had, just so it wouldn't be a lie.

There was a CLOSED sign on the front door of Dr. Wilson's office, but his yellow Coupe de Ville was in the lot, parked next to a white Ford Fairlane with government tags. Thorn tried the door, found it open, and stepped inside.

Bean's waiting room was dark; a dozen mismatched chairs ringed the room. The pane of opaque glass was pulled across the receptionist's window. In the center of the room the barber chair sat like some nutty throne, and that Yankee's twenty-dollar bill was still hanging beside the fish mounts. Everything was exactly as it had been on Thorn's last visit three or four years back. Probably the same *Reader's Digest*s and *Field and Stream*s.

Thorn punched the call button and waited. He didn't hear the buzzer ring, but he could make out voices coming from the back, low and serious. After a minute he mashed the bell again and still heard no response, so he pushed through the door into the narrow hallway that led to Dr. Wilson's office and the four examining rooms.

He followed the voices to the last room on the left.

He'd never seen Dr. Wilson's lab before. It was a brightly lit twenty-by-twenty cubicle lined with metal storage racks. In the center of the room was a long stainless-steel table covered with beakers and plastic boxes, a microscope and some other equipment he couldn't identify. The room smelled of caustic chemicals with a pungent undercurrent of disinfectant. The two men were leaning against the table with their backs to Thorn. The other man had dark black hair that he wore in a rigid flattop. Even through his blue pinstriped banker's suit, Thorn could see this guy was keeping his gym card punched. Wide shoulders tapered to a narrow waist.

Thorn cleared his throat and both men swung around. After a moment's puzzlement, a smile formed on Dr. Wilson's lips.

"Sorry to interrupt."

"What brings you around, Thorny? Got a gash needs sewing up?"

"No, sir. I'm not bleeding this time. Not that I've noticed."

"One of those rare moments in the annals of modern medicine," Dr. Wilson said. "Thorn completely intact. Leaking nary a bodily fluid."

"Brad Madison," the big man said, and stepped forward and offered his hand.

"I'm sorry," Bean said. "Where'd my manners get off to? This is Thorn, and this is Brad Madison. And what a treat. Two of my favorite people meeting at last."

"You're the fishing guide Bean keeps threatening to set me up with."

"I do some fishing, yeah."

"Brad's got a little problem with relaxation," the doctor said. "I was hoping to get the two of you together someday. Drink a little beer, catch some fish, bring his blood pressure down a few notches."

"Now, there's what I like about Doc Wilson," Thorn said. "Always up on the latest medical advances. Beer and fishing. Real cutting-edge stuff."

The men chuckled.

"And I hear you're something of an amateur detective."

"No, not really. Just had a couple of run-ins with some quarrelsome people, misunderstandings I had to straighten out."

"Quarrelsome heavily armed people," the doctor said.

Everyone had another polite chuckle and Wilson led them to his office and poured himself a mug of coffee and offered the pot around. Thorn declined. He was wired already, still picturing those bloody footprints, hearing the echo of that battery-operated cackle coming from inside the dark Everly house.

"Brad's with the DEA, Thorn. Head man, as a matter of fact. Special agent in charge."

"Is that right?"

"You remember the Grassy Key Massacre?" Wilson said. "That drug bust that went bad?"

Thorn nodded. "Four dead, six wounded. And those were just the good guys."

"Those numbers would've been different," Brad said, "if it weren't for Doc Wilson. I sure as hell would've gone from the wounded column to the other one."

"Just doing my job," Wilson said. "Got called into the emergency room that night. Right place, right time, that's all."

Brad was standing stiffly in the doorway, a man who wanted to stay but needed to go. His gray eyes seemed preoccupied, as if he were adding long columns of figures in his head, trying to keep a running total while he carried on a civil conversation.

"I came by to ask you about the dolphin thing," said Thorn.

Wilson set his cup down, leaned back in his leather chair. He eyed Thorn thoughtfully. Today he had on a yellow button-down shirt with a blue polka-dot bow tie, khaki slacks. Although his wife had died thirty years earlier, Bean Wilson still sported his heavy gold wedding band.

"What dolphin thing is that?" Brad reached up to reshape the perfect Windsor knot at his throat. It took him a second or two, but somehow he made it even more perfect.

"Other night at the dolphin research center. Eleven of them hacked up. You didn't hear about it?"

"Oh, that, yeah," Brad said. "Christ, just when you think there isn't any way we'll ever top ourselves—way to go, South Florida."

Dr. Wilson straightened his ink blotter, rubbed a line of dust off his desk.

"I thought since you were working over there, Doc, you might've heard something."

"You work with the dolphins, Bean? I didn't know that."

"Oh, I draw blood, run some tests. Nothing much beyond that."

Brad Madison rubbed at the deep creases in his forehead.

"So what's your interest, Thorn?" Wilson said. "Somebody hire Sugarman to investigate? You helping him out?"

"Sugar's away on vacation. I'm just curious, that's all. It's nothing."

"Every time Thorn gets curious, I have to get out my sutures." Dr. Wilson smiled at Brad. "So what do you need to know, son?"

"Well, for one thing, the dolphins' spines were taken, and maybe their brains as well. There some kind of market I don't know about? New Chinese aphrodisiac or something?"

Wilson wiped away the same line of dust. His smile flickered briefly, then came back full strength.

"The police are pursuing a line of inquiry, I understand," he said. "Roy tells me they think there's a Santeria connection."

Brad chuckled.

"Oh, now, there's some silly horseshit. Santeria is goats and chickens, for godsakes. What're they thinking about?"

"I was wondering about your research, Dr. Wilson. If you might've come across anything that would make dolphins valuable to somebody."

"They're valuable alive," Wilson said. "But dead, I can't imagine how they would be."

He turned his eyes down and studied his ink blotter carefully, as though it were a chessboard ripe with possibilities.

"Who's the research for?" Thorn said. "The blood you're drawing, all that?"

Wilson clicked his eyes back to Thorn. He seemed confused for a moment, his forehead deeply crinkled, as if Thorn had accused him of some obscure misdemeanor.

"I help out various groups," Wilson said. "A professor from FIU who's doing psychological studies on dolphins; another group out in California."

"That's it?"

"And Bean junior, for some research he's doing. It's just simple work, drawing blood, some lab reports. Nothing secretive about it."

"Bean junior?"

"He's working with wounded military vets down in Key West. Pain management. He sends them up here every week to swim with the dolphins. He's studying the biological changes the patients are going through."

"Last you told me, Bean was doing anesthesia. Operating room stuff."

"Oh, he quit that a few years back. Now he runs a small clinic."

Brad Madison was shifting his eyes back and forth between the doctor and Thorn.

"Anything else I can help you with?" the doctor said.

"They tortured the animals. That's what it looks like.

They were there for a long time, hacking on them while they were still alive. Could that have any significance? I mean, medically?"

Wilson smiled patiently.

"I didn't hear about any torture," Wilson said. "But no, I have no idea why anyone would do such a thing. It's horrible, that's all. Horrible."

"Sounds like crazies to me," Brad said. "Teenagers sitting in a dark room too long, maybe some angel dust floating around. They played some records backward or whatever they do nowadays, and got a wild hair going about dolphins. Bang, it happens. Random chaos. With those kinds of kids, looking for some logical reason for this or that is a waste of time. Pure waste."

Thorn looked around at the diplomas on the wall, the mahogany plaques and citations from local civic groups. The doc had been a lifelong volunteer.

"Yeah," Thorn said. "Too long in a dark room. That'll do it."

"I can call Bean junior," Dr. Wilson said, "and the professor I work with at FIU, see what they might be able to contribute to your investigation."

"I'm not investigating."

Brad Madison and the doctor looked at each other and smiled.

"So what exactly do you call it, Thorn?" Brad said.

"Sniffing around."

Brad's smile deepened.

Running a hand through his thick hair, Dr. Wilson lifted his eyebrows and stared at Thorn over the rims of his glasses.

"Anything else?"

"I guess not," Thorn said. "But if you'd make those

calls, I'd be interested in anything Bean or the professor might have to say."

"Investigating," Brad said. "Say it, Thorn. Feel it in your mouth."

"Sniffing around," Thorn said. "Sniff, sniff."

After a minute more of aimless chat, Thorn thanked Wilson for his time, apologized again for interrupting. Brad Madison said he had to get going, had an appointment farther down in the Keys. He walked Thorn outside.

In the lot Brad unlocked his Fairlane, took off his jacket and draped it over the passenger seat. His Glock was harnessed tight against his ribs.

"You have some kind of problem with Doc Wilson, Thorn?"

"What do you mean?"

"Sounded to me like you were cross-examining him. Going after him pretty damn hard."

Thorn looked out at the cloud of gravel dust swirling up from the wake of passing trucks. A shirtless man on an ancient bicycle cruised by on the rutted bike path.

"I just asked a couple of questions."

"Then maybe you need to work on your technique. Seemed to me you were manhandling him for no good reason."

"Well, I'm sorry. That's not how I meant it."

Brad gave him a long, hard look, one he'd probably perfected in dungeon-room interrogations.

"I'd hate to see anything hurt that man," Brad said. "All he's done for me."

Thorn nodded.

"I'd really hate that, Thorn."

After Brad pulled out onto the highway, Thorn

walked across the lot to the propeller shop and went inside to see what kind of deals they might have on high performance three-bladers. You never knew when you might need a little more propulsion.

CHAPTER

7

Pepper's starched white nurse's uniform was half soaked by the time she reached Mallory docks. A northwest wind had kicked up early that morning and Key West harbor was as frothy as a ten-dollar milkshake. Banging hard all the way across from out beyond Christmas Tree Island, the Zodiac inflatable almost bucked her out twice.

Pepper tied up the raft, tucked it under the dock behind Ocean Key House, and walked across the square to the little parking lot behind the sandal shop. She unlocked the hearse, got in, and spent half a minute touching up her hair in the rearview mirror: put on her apricot lipstick, got a little terra-cotta blush onto her cheeks. When she was satisfied, she opened her purse and took out one of the Japanese hot claws that were the current selection in the Chili of the Month Club. Pepper had been a loyal member since high school, when one of her boyfriends signed her up as a joke. Right off, she found she loved the things and she'd been keeping her membership paid up ever since, even during that terrible time after her daddy had his fatal heart attack and money was scarce.

When she'd finished her hot claw breakfast, she cranked up the V-8 and pulled out of her spot and took Whitehead up toward Eaton. The hearse was candy-apple red with a mirror shine and a soft grumbling engine. It had thick white sidewalls and seventeen coats of paint and it could get up over a hundred before you could take a deep breath. Like it did every time she sat in the thing, the car gave her a few extra beats in her heart. Riding along, she was inside and outside the car at once, out there on the sidewalk watching herself slide past while she sat high and happy behind that wheel, feeling all those stallions trembling at the bit, waiting for her command.

Running late that morning because of the long ride across the harbor, and damned if a block up Whitehead, Pepper didn't get stuck behind a car with Michigan plates, creeping along at two miles an hour, five old ladies stuffed in there, gawking at all the Key West weirdness. For two blocks she hovered behind the Oldsmobile, staring at all that fluffy white Michigan hair.

After another block she couldn't take it anymore and coasted up close to their rear bumper, slipped the shifter into neutral, then flattened the accelerator to let the Yankee shit-for-brains hear her silky engine with all that power, the rumble of its glass packs. She worked the accelerator, louder and louder until finally the three biddies in the backseat turned and glared at her, and Pepper smiled her prettiest and reached under the dash and flipped the pneumatic lifter switch on and off, which sent that big car's front end flying three feet up in the air. Slamming back down so hard, the steering wheel popped out of her hands.

She just did it that once, the old ladies still looking,

their eyes as big and white as boiled eggs. Then she saw them yammer to their friends in the front seat, all five of them turning around to stare. And Pepper slipped the car into gear, swung out and roared up Whitehead, going so fast she missed her turn.

A year had passed since the doctor gave her the ten thousand dollars and told her to go buy a used van. Something to haul the patients in. Pick them up at the airport or bus station and taxi them back to the clinic. Shuttle them up to swim with the dolphins once a week, or up to Miami for this or that medical test.

A van was what the doc wanted, with room for wheelchairs and baggage, maybe even a stretcher now and then. But on the first car lot she came to out on Roosevelt Boulevard, Pepper saw that gorgeous hearse. She wound up talking the salesman down to ninety-five hundred. The doc wasn't pleased, but over time he'd adjusted. Like her daddy used to say: You want to do something, go on, do it. Don't ask nobody first. It's easier to get forgiveness than permission.

Now, after a year of handing over every spare dime to Scooter Jackson, head mechanic at the Truman Gulf station, Pepper had herself a showstopping lowrider. Green and red and purple neon tubes on the undercarriage, chrome-plated hopping shocks with Fenner pumps, and Hydro-Aire dumps. Scooter had just finished putting in a Bose sound system that could crush your skull if you twisted it up to full volume.

The way she had it rigged, Pepper could lower the Caddy's body down to an inch clearance of the roadway or use the hopping shocks to make that big car do a Fred Astaire tap dance or send it bucking three feet up in the air like some kind of wild goddamn stallion. Ten switches for a multitude of moves, a half dozen speakers, all the switches concealed under the dash, so nobody on earth could tell what that car could do unless Pepper Tremaine decided she wanted them to know.

As Pepper came to the light at Truman, she reached under the dash and flicked on the undercarriage neon. Nobody could see it in the bright daylight, of course, but Pepper Tremaine knew it was on and that was all that mattered. She goosed the big V-8 and whooped as the tires burned around the corner. By god, she could sense that neon down there rippling along the asphalt like her own incredible aura chasing after her, trying to keep up.

At the clinic, Pepper ducked her head into the TV room to say hey. A few of the vets looked up, gave Pepper a quick hello, then went back to whatever book or bottle or card game they had in front of them. She could hear the weight machines grinding away on the big sunporch they used as a rehab room and she could smell the smog of sweat filtering out.

Doc Wilson was some kind of genius at tapping into government grant money. He had all the best rehab equipment, best Nautilus machines, best whirlpool baths; he had physical therapist nurses coming from the naval hospital every day to work with the vets, and he'd gotten the government to pay for close to two dozen spinal pumps in the two years he'd been running the clinic. Twenty-odd pumps at twenty-five thousand a pop. A goddamn genius.

As she walked down the hallway, she could hear the doctor on the office phone, talking the way he did when he was mad and trying not to show it. His fizz all shaken up, cork about to fire. Only this time it was worse than she'd ever heard. Staying calm, nice and polite, but his voice box about to rupture from the strain.

Pepper pushed open the door, sat down on the padded chair across from him. Bean looked up at her, face red, forehead clenched, then he lowered his head, took his eyes out of gear, and listened for a moment or two more to the voice in his ear.

"Yes, Dad, okay, yes, I'll be happy to look into it. I'll call around and get back to you. I promise. Yes. I know. It's an awful thing. We're all shocked and horrified."

His voice might've sounded calm enough to someone passing by, but Pepper could hear the awful tremble in it, the sound the air makes just before a crash of thunder. With a quick good-bye he set the phone down in the cradle, and leaned back in his chair and laced his fingers behind his head. He smiled at Pepper, but it wasn't a smile that meant anything good.

"Your dad again?"

"How clairvoyant of you."

"What is it this time?"

"Well, as a matter of fact it has to do with you, Pepper."

"Me? What'd I do?"

"Someone was in my father's office a little while ago, asking him about the dolphins that were slaughtered. Imagine that."

"The police?"

"The police are idiots. We don't have to worry about them."

"Well, who?"

"A man by the name of Thorn."

"Is that bad?"

"Well, you be the judge, Pepper. He wanted to know

why anyone would torture the animals before killing them. He wanted to know about their spines and brains.''

"We chopped them up in little pieces. Made a mess. Just like you said.''

"I repeat, he wanted to know about what value their spines and brains might have. Why anyone would torture them. Dad thought I might know the answer to that so he could pass the information on to Thorn.''

Pepper felt the stir in the air. She shifted her butt against the chair, getting ready for the lightning strike, the explosion of thunder.

"This is perfect,'' he said, "just fucking perfect.'' Bean's laugh was full of broken glass. "Of all the goddamn people in the world to get excited about those dolphins, it just had to be Thorn. Goddamn self-righteous pit bull.''

He leaned forward, stared down at his shiny desktop for several moments. Pepper reached into the pocket of her white dress for another Japanese hot claw and watched Bean Wilson's mind crank. Gorgeous man with white skin and thick golden hair. Wearing an expensive green T-shirt and tan chinos. When he lifted his head there was a crafty light in his eyes. His lips spread slowly into a dangerous smile.

"Pepper, my dear. Do you recall where you put that key my father gave us last year?''

"Hanging on the board in the kitchen with the rest of the keys.''

Bean's smile widened. He lay both hands flat on the desk before him like he might be about to make it rise into the air. Pepper believed he could accomplish it if he tried. He was that kind of man, the air always buzzing around him like he was surrounded by a halo of stray electrons.

"So who is this guy Thorn, anyway?"

He lifted his smile to her.

"He's an old friend of mine," Bean said. "An old friend who is about to have a very nasty accident."

CHAPTER

8

Thorn spent the rest of the afternoon bent double belowdecks on the *Heart Pounder*. He was so cramped, he could barely draw a breath. His spine felt like it was bent an inch past the breaking point, his chin pinned to his chest, the crown of his skull grinding against an overhead joist.

After an hour that way he was still three or four complete turns from getting the final nut tightened down on the starter motor. At his current rate, three turns would take another week. With his right arm crooked around the exhaust manifold and cylinder head cover, his left twisted and going numb, he had leaned into the crevice as far as he could, and still he couldn't see the steel plate where the rear housing was mounted, so he was doing this job by feel because apparently the Chris-Craft engineers hadn't planned on the starter unit failing within the normal lifetime of the boat. They'd almost been right.

It had taken nearly forty years for the small electrical motor to give out. Built to last, like things in the first half of the century had been, before planned obsolescence began to afflict even the marine industry. For the last month Thorn had been forced to let the *Heart Pounder* sit idle while he located someone who could fabricate a new field coil and brushes to fit the old housing. Charlie Peacock, an eighty-year-old conch who was the head mechanic over at Performance Marine, charged him nearly double what it would have cost to replace the whole damn unit with an off-the-shelf model. But Thorn went ahead and did it, plundering the last of his savings because he considered it his meager tribute to the gods of his ancestors, trying to live up to their high standards. Not to mention the fact that he sure as hell didn't want to jinx the old tub by doing a crucial repair with some shabby Taiwanese part, then a month later find the power plant dead thirty miles offshore while a tanker bore down on him.

With his knuckles bloodied, his legs dead, Thorn was wedged into the only posture the Chris-Craft designers had seen fit to allow for this particular chore, some kind of tenth-degree yoga move. The Mangled Monkey Pose.

When Monica called his name from out on the dock, Thorn knew he was still at least two full turns away from snugging the starter motor down and would probably be too goddamn stiff to regain the necessary position for another day or two, but he sucked in a breath, pried his right arm out of the narrow cavity, untangled the rest of his body, set down his open-end wrench, and dragged himself out onto the sunny deck.

Impossible as it seemed, in the five months he'd known Monica Sampson, she'd grown even more beautiful. The buzz cut she'd worn when he first met her had lengthened nicely and was starting to tickle the tops of her ears. And the few pounds she'd put on lately had settled into highly sensuous locations. All in all, she seemed to be coming down with a serious case of the Keys disease. Definitely showing the softened features and lazy eyes of the deeply afflicted. As her pulse slowed and her veins relaxed, even the three tense crinkles between her eyebrows had smoothed over as though the years were gradually melting from her body.

"Christ, Thorn, you look like you've been dipped in hot tar."

He groaned as he stepped across the gunwale onto the dock. The parts of his body that weren't asleep were throbbing. From the knees down, his legs were as numb as if he'd been fishing in a Montana stream all afternoon. And a hard fist was tightening around the base of his spine.

"And you look swell too."

He leaned forward to kiss her, but she waved him off.

"Maybe after you've been steam cleaned."

She had on a black sleeveless blouse, black jeans, and white running shoes. Still dressed from work. Not much use for her artistic talents in the Keys. Only job she could find that used any of her skills was art director at the local paper, which sounded better than it was. What it meant was that Monica did the layouts and paste-ups, scissors and glue, some basic computer graphics.

"In that outfit you could take a major smudge, no-body'd notice."

"Don't get fresh with me, sailor."

"Might be fun," he said, "we could roll around, get greasy, then steam clean each other."

"I came over to make you supper."

"The two things aren't mutually exclusive."

"Supper first," she said. "Then we'll see."

They stood for a moment gazing out at the bay, silvered by a declining sun. A hundred yards out a great blue heron skimmed a foot off the surface, its large, ungainly body reshaped for flight, its wide wings moving with gawky grace. Miles to the west the string of mangrove islands was black against the purpling sky as if someone had stenciled a low mountain range into the horizon.

He took her hand in his, gave it a squeeze, but she didn't squeeze back. He looked at her.

"Something wrong?"

She kept her eyes on the horizon.

"What do you mean?"

"I feel something," he said. "Joking around, but with a shadowy undercurrent."

She turned her head, eyed him for a moment, then looked back at the colorful sky.

"Shadowy undercurrent?"

"Yeah."

"It's nothing," she said. "There's no undercurrent, shadowy or otherwise. I had a rough day, that's all. It'll pass."

She gave his hand a perfunctory squeeze and let it go.

He saw the muscles strain in her neck as if she were struggling to breathe.

Eyes still on the bruised light, she said, "So what were you up to all day?"

"Usual. Tied some flies. Spent the last couple of hours trying to get that starter motor in."

Monica made a noise in her throat as if her polygraph were twitching.

"Last I looked," Thorn hurried on, "all I had was a

jar of crunchy peanut butter with some purple fuzz growing on it and a couple of dubious avocados, a stale loaf of rye bread. But I *do* have some wine.''

"I brought groceries," she said. "I lit the coals. You should start getting cleaned up if you want a glass of wine before supper. Yellowtail is marinating. It'll be ready to grill in another fifteen, twenty minutes."

"You've been here awhile."

"I didn't want to disturb you. Sounded like you were having such fun under there."

Thorn stepped around to face her.

"You put the paper to bed? Or is there more work after supper?"

She tilted her head to one side and studied him, her lips hinting at a smile. In her eyes, the cloud shadowing the sun had moved on, a slow brightening.

"What you mean is, can I stay the night?"

"I didn't want to be crude."

"Let's just see how the yellowtail turns out," she said. "I'm sure as hell not sleeping with some guy who can't even cook."

She led him back down the dock toward his wood stilthouse. She walked with one foot in front of the other, normal in every respect, except there was some kind of whispery sway in her hips.

"You walk nice."

She gave a subtle flounce on his behalf.

"Sophomore elective. Sashaying 201. Only useful course I ever took."

Thorn showered, used the pumice soap to rub himself red. His legs were tingling now. Only his toes still numb. He toweled off quickly, stepped into a pair of clean shorts and found his last fresh shirt, a white Hawaiian printed with pink hula girls and simmering volcanoes. The shirt was older than Monica—a relic from his high school years. He'd stored it at the bottom of his drawer because the cotton had worn as thin as woodsmoke. One good fingernail across the back would rip it in half. That's how busy he'd been lately, between the boat repairs, fly-tying, and Monica, not even enough time for a Laundromat run.

When he came out, she was sitting serenely on the sofa, her gold hair backlit by the dwindling sun. Paging through a magazine she'd brought, she hummed along to a song that played softly on her portable CD player —smoky saxophones, a woman's haunting ballad. She had positioned her stereo on the round oak dining table across the room so that it was directed toward the bedroom. Thorn smiled. The tension had eased in her face. Unless he charred the yellowtail or dropped the damn thing into the coals, there would be music tonight.

He stood across from her, the low coffee table between them. He'd constructed the table from wood he salvaged when one of his ironwoods was knocked down in last summer's brush with a hurricane. He'd finished the planks with his finest-grain sandpaper, then waxed it till it was buttery slick. No nails, everything tongue and grooved, dovetailed. It took him two weeks of steady labor to get it done and shave away the wobbles, though a real carpenter would have finished it in half the time.

On the cypress walls behind the couch Thorn had hung a half dozen of Monica's framed drawings. Simple pen-and-inks on white parchment. Dock lines coiled up neatly against rough pine planks. A wicker basket full of fishing reels. Some studies of Thorn's yellow Lab, Rover—the dog sleeping in different positions; one of him paddling across the bay, a stick gripped in his teeth, his head held high; another with him sitting upright, head tipped to one side, eyes attentive as if he might be listening outside the bedroom door to indescribable pleasures within.

Lately Thorn had been spending a lot of time looking at the drawings, trying to figure out how in so few strokes she could give the common images of island life such an uncommon glow. A year earlier he would've said such a thing was impossible. He had lived on Key Largo all his life, but apparently there was much he hadn't noticed. Much he'd failed to fully appreciate.

Monica's head was bowed. She was intent on her magazine—one of those weekly rags she had a weakness for. It was filled with photographs of people—the latest crop of Hollywood brats out on the town, mugging for the paparazzi, and there were always photographs of a few normal folks who'd done some abnormal thing. He found himself staring across at her for several moments, entranced by the cowlick at the back of her head, a corkscrew of untamable hair. He'd had other lovers with far more common ground. There was the woman he'd known since childhood who could outfish him, outdrink him, outsmart him at everything that mattered. But Darcy Richards was years dead now and Thorn knew better than to search for her double.

Monica's nature was harder to define. An artist who could take apart a complicated object and put it back together greatly simplified. Whose drawings weren't so much detailed renderings as they were the object itself stripped of irrelevancies.

Thorn had watched her on several afternoons as she explored his weedy five acres beside Blackwater Sound with her sketch pad in hand. She had the quiet intensity, the resolute focus of a naturalist making field notes in a newly discovered corner of the jungle. He'd seen her squatting in the grass, staring at the flaky bark of a gumbo-limbo, rapt, as if she were taking the tree's deepest pulse. Last week she'd picked up a dead butterfly off the planks of the dock and held it up to the sky, tilted it, rotated it until Thorn saw the microscopic whorls of felt on its wings, the odd hieroglyphs that had been invisible before. Then she rubbed her finger against the burgundy down and sent a weird snow into the air. Monica Sampson surprised him, scared him a little, kept him off balance. He hadn't felt so alert, so invigorated in years.

As she turned the page of her magazine, he sensed the words rising up from his diaphragm, the place where they said great opera singers and orators find their richest tones. The words had been hovering inside him for the last month, so, even though he'd made no conscious decision to speak them at this moment, it could hardly be considered blurting.

"Would you marry me?"

She hesitated a second or two, then brought her face up slowly, peering at him for several more uneasy heartbeats. Then she broke into a deep-throated laugh that sent two doves roosted outside the west window exploding into flight.

"Jesus," Thorn said. "Thanks a lot."

She raised a palm while she struggled for breath.

"It's not some goddamn joke. I'm dead serious. I want to marry you."

She flicked her eyes up to his, then back down. She sighed, then carefully she set her magazine on the coffee table, stared at its cover for a moment as if to clear her head. There were red flecks in the sunlight streaming through the window. A butterfly battled at the screen. With a hand pressed against her chest, she lifted her eyes and met his. The smile was gone. But he didn't much like what had replaced it.

"I'd get down on my knees," he said, "but my back is too sore. I don't think I could get up."

She looked over at Rover curled in the corner by the rack that held Thorn's fishing rods. She shook her head and waved her hand at the room.

"You and me, Rover, a regular glass of wine, this isn't enough for you? You're unhappy the way we are?"

"I'm very happy," Thorn said. "That's the point."

"Thorn, Thorn, Thorn. For godsakes, you don't even have a social security card, a driver's license, and all of a sudden you want to get on a first-name basis with the state of Florida? You got to have some legal stamp on this."

"I want to marry you. I want you to live here with me, for us to have something stable. I'm not the kind of guy who goes from one woman to the next all his life. That's not who I am."

"But that's who you've been."

Her skin shone like translucent porcelain with a rosy light inside.

"Yeah, well, I don't want to be that guy anymore. I want to get married."

"Oh, so some alarm went off inside you, now you've decided you've got to get married and Monica Sampson happened to be walking by at the time. Well, lucky me."

"Come on. It's not that way. I'm serious."

"You're serious." She looked into his eyes, then took a breath and shifted her gaze out the side window where a palm frond was feathering against the screen in the lightest of breezes.

"Yeah," he said. "Damn serious."

"Okay, all right. Then I'll think about it." There was a sharp distance in her voice, as if she'd been half-expecting such an outrage from him and was torn between relief and disappointment that it had finally happened.

"It's because of the age thing, isn't it? That's the problem. You think, twenty years from now you'll still be young, I'll be hobbling around, I can't remember where I put my false teeth. That's what's bothering you."

"No."

"Well, it shouldn't. Because I'm going to be a tough old coot. It's a Key Largo thing. We eat so much fish, breathe all this clean air, it takes years off the clock. Believe me, you see it all the time around the island, guys in their eighties, eyes as bright as any twenty-year-old."

She was staring across the room at Rover. He'd lifted his head from his mat and was giving them a wary look, as if he heard a resonance in their voices that signaled some approaching upheaval.

"Look, Thorn. That's the best I can do at the moment. I'll think about it, okay? I'll think about it and we'll talk again later."

"Okay, that's fine. I'll take that. Not-a-no is fine. No pressure. No hurry, none of that."

"Yeah, right," she said, forcing out a smile. "No pressure. None at all."

He came around the coffee table, bent down, and with a hand against her cheek, he kissed her on the lips. It took a moment or two, but finally she relaxed and the kiss ripened and she rose to her feet and fit into his arms. When the kiss was done, still in the embrace, she rested her head on his shoulder. She made a fist and beat it softly against his back between his shoulder blades. Damn you, damn you.

"There's rice on the stove," she said.

"Let it cook."

The saxophones were mingling with guitars, the woman's rich contralto flushed the air.

"The coals will go out."

"Let's damn well hope so."

As they began to move toward the bedroom, Rover released a long sigh and let his head drop back to the mat.

Thorn and Monica had discovered that particular position a month or two earlier, no Kama Sutra contortion, just a pleasant arrangement, he on his back, pillow under his hips, she astride, knees bent under her so she could control the pressure, the angle, the timing. Ride 'em, cowgirl.

The music played in the living room, the woman's lush voice rising like an excited pulse. Before Monica, Thorn had never played music while making love. He preferred the natural accompaniment of jays and ospreys, the boat traffic across Blackwater Sound, or just human grunts and moans to guide the rhythm—not some Motown metronome. But what the hell. Monica was twenty years younger, from a more musically dependent generation. And Thorn was willing to learn.

Lately, he'd been learning a hell of a lot from this young woman, feeling himself loosen out of his strict habits. Almost from day one she'd made fun of him— his narrow focus, his rigid ceremonies. Every day was the same for Thorn. Up at sunrise, tying bonefish flies all morning, bright iridescent morsels he sold for a few dollars a pop. Then later in the afternoon he took his skiff out to test his latest creations along the shallows at the mouth of Snake Creek or deep in the backcountry. By sunset he was usually grilling whatever edible catch he'd snagged. After a glass or two of wine as the darkness thickened, he stretched out in the teak chaise and read his book of the week until the mosquitoes or sand fleas drove him inside. Then he read another chapter or two in bed before sleep dragged him off. Ten o'clock, ten-thirty the latest.

What a stick in the mud, Monica said, their first week together.

No, no. You don't get it. His was a life of ritual—a much higher order of things than mere unthinking routine. Thorn claimed he was as flexible as the next guy. It was just that his idea of innovation was trying out a new snapper recipe or some fresh concoction of fur and feathers in one of his flies. There was no good reason to tamper with the big stuff, not if it was working fine already.

Bullshit, she said. You're calcified. You got cobwebs growing all over you. Mushrooms, mold, mildew.

I believe in austerity, simplicity, the unembellished life.

An old fart, Monica said. Dead before your time. Rut, rut, rut.

It was after midnight one night when they rolled up for the first time into that equine position, she astraddle him, smiling, liking it immediately, the view from up there. Arching back, hands behind her, gripping Thorn's ankles, Thorn sliding his own hands beneath his butt, cocking his hips up on his elbows for more thrust. And that first time when they were finished, lying back, chasing their breaths, she said, "See. See what happens when you stay up past midnight."

"If I'd only known sooner."

Now on the wood wall beside the bed the late afternoon sun had printed the silhouettes of palm fronds, and as Thorn watched them, a sudden breeze broke the shadows apart and sent the fragments skittering across the wall like a flock of nervous angels.

Monica moved above him, her eyes open, staring up at the rafters, riding with him and apart from him. Thorn more conscious of it all than usual, seeing her, watching her move, feeling the raspy slippage of their joined parts, Monica rocking one way, he rocking the other, pushing himself up, bowing his aching spine, as a thick clot of heat in his chest radiated outward. She reached out her left hand and Thorn laced his fingers through hers. Holding on, holding on.

Until the moment came when she began to fade away above him, her face softening, losing its angular grace, its sharp-edged polish, becoming a blurred generic face, a loose look, as the first spasm of pleasure shook her, and she came down hard against his thighs, lunged back up immediately and then slammed back down as if they were riding together through a tumultuous sea. Her voice rose in its familiar spiral of exhilaration, then she lurched back, bearing down against his groin, staying there, grinding with the smallest movements until Thorn reached the same airless place where she was.

Afterward, gasping and sweaty, they eased back down to the mattress, set their curves against each other and fell asleep with the music still playing.

CHAPTER

9

It was dark when Thorn woke. Monica snuffled beside him, her elegant version of a snore. The music was played out, and in the stillness beyond the bedroom door Thorn heard Rover's low and insistent growl.

He rose quickly, stepped into his canvas shorts, and edged into the living room. Moonlight was swimming through the open porch door. Enough light for Thorn to see the dog wasn't curled up in his usual spot below the west window. Probably he'd cornered a toad on the stairs outside, or perhaps had spied one of the possums that lived in the woods next door tightroping through the canopy of vines and limbs.

Then he heard the dog again, a different noise, one Thorn didn't recognize. Part snarl, part yelp. His back went prickly. Some scent in the air seemed off. He considered taking out the Colt .38 he kept in his fly-tying desk, but it seemed like overkill for an encounter with possums. And he had a quick flash of Monica standing behind him asking him quietly why he was aiming a pistol at a frog.

Rover was not on the upstairs porch and Thorn moved out to the railing, scanned the yard below. The seedpods on the poinciana were rattling in the uneasy night air. Out by the dock the Chris-Craft and the skiff gleamed brightly, as if they'd absorbed all the available light. He was about to go back inside, crawl into that warm pocket beside Monica, when he heard Rover whimper from below the house.

He was down the stairs in seconds, across a patch of grass, taking a couple of sandspurs in his naked sole. Monica's Impala was parked in the dark shadows of the stilthouse. His VW was nearby in its usual spot below the tamarind tree. He stood below the porch and peered into the dark.

"Rover?"

The dog whined again, somewhere off to his right behind one of the ancient telephone poles that supported the house. Thorn breathed in the creosote and the foul decay of shrimp left in the bottom of Monica's bait bucket. Sliding between the Impala and a heap of outboard parts, he followed Rover's moan to the rear bumper of the Chevrolet.

The dog was lying on his side in the sand. When he saw Thorn he struggled to haul himself upright, but he couldn't seem to get his rear legs under him. Thorn stooped over the dog. And Rover lifted his head and looked past Thorn, wrinkled his muzzle and growled. Thorn straightened and swung around in time to glimpse the shadow man, his arm a blur. In his hand a chunk of stone.

The night was even quieter when Thorn came back to consciousness. No breeze or crickets. No distant hum of traffic. He was lying on his back, pressed flat to the sand, while the neat parallel lines of the floorboards and planking above him were blurred. Beside him

Rover was lying on his side. He panted quietly and stared out at the bay with a desolate look.

Thorn concentrated on breathing, a sip at a time. A spoonful of oxygen, then another. His eyeballs had grown a size too large for his sockets. A lump on the back of his head throbbed. He didn't need to touch it to know it was the size and hardness of a Key lime.

Somewhere through the dizzy haze he heard Monica calling out his name—her voice full of the bluesy roughness of sleep. Rover tipped his head and peered up at her bare feet through the planks of the porch. Twenty feet away the tall grass rustled as if Thorn's attacker was still out there, deciding between fight and flight.

Thorn dragged in a breath and tried to yell a warning to her, but it came out as a useless croak. As he watched her feet pad slowly down the stairs, he struggled to lever himself up to a sitting position. But something like a cramp froze him where he lay. He sucked down a breath, cocked his elbows under him, readied himself, then heaved a second time. And nearly fainted from the bolt of pain.

A rush of air filled his throat and Thorn flattened himself carefully in the sand. He had known pain. The list of his injuries was long. But this was different. This pain was out there on the distant edges of endurance.

He held himself as still as possible for a moment, then very carefully he tried to move his legs. And that was when he knew with excruciating certainty that things had altered as irrevocably as if he'd staggered into the middle of US 1 and been broadsided by a truck full of bricks.

Some wrenching of the delicate alignment in his vertebrae had occurred, some invisible boundary had been breached, and now all his body's resilience, tested by years of high school sports, a handful of unavoidable fistfights, and a thousand jolts across choppy seas, all that limberness and flexibility and bounce, was gone, and the neurons that had been flowing in orderly formation for decades, running their messages neatly up and down the staircase of his spine, now were screaming in helter-skelter turmoil.

Thorn could not move his legs. He had no sensation from his waist down. And his spinal cord was hot and wet and very wrong.

Strapped tight to the stretcher, Thorn stared up at that Yankee's framed twenty-dollar bill. The two guys from the volunteer ambulance crew were joking around outside in the gravel lot while Monica spoke to Dr. Wilson, not making much sense as far as Thorn could tell. Going into the whole episode in what seemed like unnecessary detail, describing where she found him, how she tried to help him sit up, his howl. The bloody limestone rock beneath his spine. She had the rock out in her car in case Dr. Wilson wanted to see it.

Wilson waited till she'd had her say, then nodded soberly and stooped over the stretcher. He was wearing blue pajama tops and a pair of baggy gray jeans. His dense white hair badly rumpled.

Behind a penlight he peered into Thorn's eyes.

"Well, you certainly took a hit," he said. "Hammer, gun butt. We'll have to x-ray that damn skull of yours again, add to my collection."

Wilson flicked the light off.

"And you've got no feeling in your legs?"

Thorn told him no, none at all. He tried to stretch his back, twist against the gurney's restraints in a grim effort to unkink whatever it was that was crimping his nerves. Only an hour or two earlier he and Monica had been afloat in the thin atmosphere of sensuality. Part of him had not made the transition to this cold fluorescent room. It seemed like some nightmarish high school play, Act Two jarringly unrelated to Act One. And Thorn had staggered out into the bright footlights without a script or a moment's rehearsal. Everyone playing their parts around him with dramatic flourish, but Thorn without a goddamn idea what the story line was.

"How's Rover?"

Monica said Rover was fine. Whoever clubbed Thorn must have kicked the dog in the ribs, stunned him. By the time the ambulance came, Rover was walking around, wagging his tail.

"Good," Thorn said. "That's good. But you need to watch him, Monica. There could be internal injuries. Check his poop for blood."

"I'll take care of the dog, Thorn. Don't worry about the goddamn dog."

Dr. Wilson rolled the gurney into the narrow hallway. Monica marched alongside, her hand on Thorn's shoulder as they entered one of the small examining rooms. After Wilson cleaned and stitched the wound at the base of his spine, he stepped out of Thorn's line of sight, opened a drawer, and pawed through what sounded like a tangle of surgical hardware. A moment or two later he was back huddling over Thorn's bare feet.

"How about this? Feel anything?"

Monica flinched and turned away.

"No," Thorn said. "Nothing."

A moment later Wilson rose and dabbed a cotton

swab across the sole of Thorn's foot, then wiped a dot of blood from the sharp tip of what looked like a dentist's probe.

"I stuck you, son. Stuck it in, wiggled it around. In your big toe, in the arch of your right foot."

"Shit."

"Yeah," Dr. Wilson said. "*Shit's* the word that comes to mind."

"Can you do anything?" Monica was at his shoulder. "Is it serious?"

Bean Wilson seemed not to have heard. He ran a hand through his white mane, staring at Thorn's legs with a look that seemed to wander off to another time and place.

"What is it, Doc?"

Dr. Wilson blinked hard, came back to the moment.

"You got any kind of pain, son, in your legs or the feet maybe, base of your spine? A throb, a burn, a little tingle, anything at all?"

"No. I feel cold is all."

Dr. Wilson patted Thorn's shoulder lightly.

"Ninety-nine percent of the time I'm working to take away somebody's pain. This is the one percent where pain would be a blessing."

"It can't be that serious," Thorn said. "I just banged something when I fell. Like a stinger in football. You get hit, your hands go numb for a minute or two. Like that."

The doctor nodded, but he wasn't buying it.

"Missy," he said to Monica. "You better go out and tell that driver not to leave just yet. Looks like he's got himself a fare up to Miami."

"You can't do anything for him?"

"Oh, I could do things, sure. Dose him up with steroids, hope it's just swelling in the spinal cord. But he needs more than a country doctor's educated guess. He needs a bright young thing with all the shiny tools. I'll make a couple of calls. I know some good people up there."

Monica touched Thorn on the shoulder, then turned and hurried out.

"It's bad, huh?"

"Bad?" the doctor said. "Well, now, I've seen a ten-year-old boy, he dives into a swimming pool, goes directly to the bottom, smacks his head, everything from his chin down goes dead. Gotta live like that the rest of his days. Puff in a plastic tube to steer his chair. I've seen that happen twice."

"There's always something shittier, isn't there?"

"You bet there is," the doctor said. "From the day you're born till you ride in the hearse, nothing's so bad it couldn't be worse."

Thorn tried a smile. There wasn't much vitality behind it and he could feel it dissolve quickly.

"That's a pretty woman you got there, my friend."

"She is that."

"She love you?"

The smile came back.

"I believe she does. Yes."

"Well," Dr. Wilson said. "You're about to find out for sure."

CHAPTER

10

Just after midnight, Brad Madison was sitting behind the wheel of the white Fairlane, parked on Eaton Street in Key West, sweating heavily. He'd been sweating all day. His mouth was dry. He had a vicious headache. He might be about to die from dehydration, for all he knew. Fine. That was just fine. Bring it on, just hurry up with it.

"Maybe you got the day wrong," Echeverria said.

"It was today. Wednesday. Three o'clock in the afternoon." Brad Madison kept his eyes straight ahead, staring at the front door of the pain clinic.

"Well, hell, she's only nine hours late. Give her time."

Echeverria was finishing up his double cheeseburger in the front seat of the Fairlane parked a couple of houses down from the Eaton Street clinic. Brad Madison's first look at the place. A big Victorian gone to seed. Four stories, with dormers, widow's walk, tin roof, lots of gingerbread curlicues. Maybe white, maybe yellow, it was hard to tell which of the peeling paints was the last one applied. Rusty iron fence outside with arrowhead spikes, a long wooden wheelchair ramp up to the front door. Vines covered the yard and cobwebbed a couple of the smaller trees. A television still played in the front room, its gray light flickering. A couple of the upstairs rooms were lit too. The insomniacs trading war stories.

Brad was immobilized. First time in his career. Sitting in the front seat of the Fairlane all afternoon waiting for Greta to show. Enduring Echeverria's asinine play-by-play of every person walking down Eaton. Old ladies. Gays. Men with their dogs. Echeverria had something to say about all of them. Their clothes, their walk, body types. Most of it was sophomoric, all of it crude.

Three o'clock came and went and an hour or so later it was clear Greta wasn't going to show, but still Brad couldn't rouse himself. Feeling a noose slowly tightening at his collar. His twenty-year career dropping out from under him like the hangman's trapdoor.

Echeverria was eating his third double cheese of the evening. Brad about to retch from the odor.

Echeverria, between bites, was saying, "They could do it if they wanted to. Put the good cholesterol into donuts, pizza, whatever, but they don't."

Brad Madison stared across Eaton at the pain clinic.

Echeverria said, "The AMA, they wouldn't stand for it, curing heart disease. Don't even want to make a serious dent. Where the hell would they be without their three open hearts a day? They'd have to get a regular job.

"Bet your ass they could do it. Extract the good cholesterol from broccoli, cauliflower, all the shit nobody eats. Infuse it into pizzas and Egg McMuffins. The technology's there.

"Same with the corporations. Goodyear's got rubber

never wears out, GM has engines that run on seawater. But they're hiding it from us. Same way with the cholesterol thing. Not that we were meant to live past thirty anyway. That's all we're designed for, thirty, forty years. Old enough to fuck once or twice, have children, feed them a few years, then we're supposed to die. Whole damn thing about living longer, eat the good cholesterol, avoid the bad, stay out of the sun, do this, don't do that, it's contrary to nature. It's totally unnatural to get old.''

Echeverria gulped down the rest of his burger and wadded the papers up and dropped them in the sack.

Brad felt his breakfast inch upward. Nothing to eat in sixteen hours. Maybe he'd never eat again. Wither up and crumble to powder like last year's leaves. It was becoming a distinct possibility.

"You planning on staying out here all night?"

Brad stared out the windshield.

"Why not just walk in?"

"That how you'd handle it, Carlos? Walk in, flash your shield, go poke around in all the closets? Blow whatever cover we still might have?"

Echeverria wiped the ketchup off his fingers with a napkin.

"Well, I gotta say, I'm sorry she didn't show. I was looking forward to seeing Greta again. Only got a look at her once or twice around the office before her accident, but the lady's an impression-maker. A body would've made Liberace sit up straight."

"Shut up, Carlos. Just shut the fuck up for a while, can you?"

Echeverria chuckled. He patted his mouth with the napkin, tossed it over the seat.

"Sorry, boss. Didn't mean to offend."

Brad watched one of the upstairs lights switch off. The wind was stirring the oaks and palms along Eaton, playing dizzy games with the streetlights.

"You know, it's funny," Echeverria said. "The knowledge I have of recent events, if I wanted, I could pick up the phone, make a single phone call, I could put a turd in your file you'd never clean out. You wouldn't be able to get a federal job licking the men's room floor. And here I am apologizing for offending you, playing that same old role. Step'n fetch it. Whatever you want, Mr. Special Agent in Charge."

Brad kept his eyes on the house. He'd known this was coming. Expected it all day. A little surprised it had taken Echeverria so long to get around to it.

"Riiiiing, riiiiing," Echeverria said. "Riiiiing."

Brad turned his head and looked at the man. Echeverria held up an imaginary phone to the side of his head. Eyes on Brad as he chirped into the receiver.

"Yes, Madam Attorney General, I know it's hard to believe. One of your most decorated agents, such a breach of professional ethics. Oh, yes, ma'am, it's hard for all of us. But there it is. Last six weeks, unbeknownst to anyone, Special Agent in Charge Brad Madison was running a little undercover operation totally off the books. Only problem is, he was using a real live DEA agent. And now this agent has turned up missing. Poof.

"Yes, ma'am. You're welcome, ma'am, I was just doing my duty. Can't really take much credit, totally accidental. Mother of the female agent calls up yesterday, wants to know when she can expect her daughter back in town, and the DEA operators route her call to me, 'cause of the way Greta's mom explained the case, it sounded to them like a Diversion issue. I mean, yes, even the lowly telephone operators knew whose turf it belonged on. They knew who to refer the lady to. So I take her call, go to my computer and look up Greta Masterson, and find out she's on medical leave. What? There's no record of any current assignment. No undercover operations running in Key West. And I look a little further, trying to be a good soldier, see where the screwup is, so that kind of thing won't happen again, and lo and behold, all the threads lead to the same place. Brad Madison. Special agent in charge. Our illustrious leader has been playing footsie with some doctor down in Key West. Putting an agent at risk—a crippled agent, I might add. All to what end? Is there some kind of personal vendetta going on here? Is this the ugly face of extortion? Well, no, ma'am, I don't know the answers to those questions yet. And yes, ma'am, I'm sure you're pissed and disappointed. We all are. Oh yes.''

Echeverria set the phone down in the imaginary cradle in his lap.

Brad was looking at him through the dim light. Big man with a potbelly. Bald with a handful of wispy hairs standing straight up from his scalp like electrified spittle. Echeverria had a wide and bloated face with the deepset, glistening eyes of a much smaller man. His cheeks were laced with bright red exploded veins as if the tiny vines that once grew on his flesh had recently been stripped away.

Echeverria was an ungifted agent whose early career had been on the streets of Liberty City and Overtown back at the height of the drug war. But the number of allegations by crack dealers started mounting until they couldn't be ignored anymore. All the stories with the same pattern. Echeverria had ripped off their stash and left them broken and bleeding. Internal Affairs investigated, but found no hard evidence. Insufficient cause to dismiss. So it was decided Echeverria should take a break from the street, and he was transferred to Diversion. It was the program within the agency that targeted doctors and pharmacists who might be diverting drugs for their own use or profit. Not the sexy side of things. Diversion agents were not even allowed to carry weapons or work undercover. Strictly white collar, office work. Like getting sent down to the minors. Usually a street agent who was shipped to Diversion resigned the agency within a few months. Echeverria stayed. Outlasted all the quitters, stayed and stayed until he bobbed to the top spot.

It was one of the main reasons Brad plucked the Eaton Street case file out of the flow and recruited Greta Masterson. He wasn't about to let a detestable son of a bitch like Carlos Echeverria decide the fate of Dr. Bean Wilson's son. All he owed that old man.

"So where do you want to bed down, boss? Pier House or the Casa Marina? Personally, I prefer the Casa. Sit out there at the bar on the big lawn, get out my nightscope, watch all the blowjobs on the beach."

"I'm going in," Brad said.

"Now? Fucking midnight, the place is probably locked up."

"You stay here."

"Sure, sure. Whatever you say, General."

Brad pushed open the car door. Overhead the coconut palms rattled in a breeze that was thick with the scents of overindulgence. The tang of marijuana and stale booze, the luscious essence of sex. Probably more illegal shit going down on that island at the moment than any other patch of dirt on the planet.

* * *

"She's gone," a young blond woman in a wheelchair said. "Left first thing this morning. By Greyhound, I think she said."

"Did you see her leave?"

"My name's Ginny, what's yours, handsome?"

"Did you see Greta leave?"

"I don't think so," the girl said. "You see Greta leave, Billy?"

The man lying on the couch didn't answer.

"So who are you, good-looking, Greta's sugar daddy?"

"I'm the man looking for Greta."

Ginny smiled at his amazing wit.

"Well, you could try talking to Randy. He's been in Greta's room all day, went back there as soon as she left so he could sniff her sheets."

A Japanese movie was on the television, some nuclear radiated insect was knocking down Tokyo. The military flamethrowers were having little effect. On the tattered couch a legless man in his sixties snored, gripping a bottle of rum to his chest.

"You wouldn't know it to look at me," Ginny said quietly, "but I still got complete sexual function."

"Which room is hers?"

Ginny's coquettish smile dissolved.

"Last one on the right."

The hallway was lit by two nightlights plugged in along the baseboards. Underfoot the oak floor squeaked and cracked and seemed about to cave in. A radio was playing salsa upstairs. He passed an open elevator compartment just big enough for one wheelchair, passed the door to the kitchen and a darkened office that looked like the doctor's, then a cramped treatment room with a surgical table gleaming in the middle and several monitors standing silently around it. The smell of urine and dead insects soured the air, and there was a faint undercurrent of talcum-scented air freshener. The place was supposed to be a halfway house for vets moving out of the VA hospital system back into the mainstream, but it felt more like halfway down a steep skid into hell.

His heart was fluttering, legs losing their blood supply. He wasn't supposed to be here. Head man of the Florida DEA walking down the dark hallway of some pissant pain clinic. A little spin of vertigo swirled in his chest as if all the tethers connecting him to earth were coming undone. Brad Madison, the hot air balloon, was circling off into the heavenly void.

The plan had been so simple, come down, pick her up, have her back in Miami by suppertime. Maybe share dinner together while he debriefed her. Maybe the beginning of more. He'd been thinking of her these last few weeks. Got out her file, unclipped her photo, kept it in his desk drawer, took it home with him once and brought it back, carrying it around like a schoolboy. He was wondering what she'd say if he broached the subject of a personal relationship. Careful not to hit on her, just raising it as a theoretical, give her lots of room to maneuver, to back off. After this mission was done, was she planning to stay with the agency? Of course, he'd only go forward if she said she was leaving the job. If she stayed, there was no way. Nepotism, sexual harassment. If she wanted to keep working, he'd just have to cool his feelings.

Scrupulous Brad, always playing by the book. Religiously abiding by the boundaries. That's who he was, who he'd always been. Not out of fear of disapproval, or to be a good little Boy Scout, not even because he particularly believed in the wisdom of the rules. But because it was a hell of a lot more interesting to find solutions to insoluble problems while staying within the lines. The net on the tennis court, the basketball rim at exactly ten feet. You lower the rim or take down the tennis net, ignore the lines, you lost the pleasure, the challenge. Picture that pro football receiver running flat out down the sidelines, a wild man, legs churning, the ball coming fast and just out of reach, and the receiver leaping up over a defender, pirouetting, finding some new spectacular arrangement of bones and muscle, a spontaneous ballet in the air, all so he could haul in the pigskin and stay in bounds. That was the beauty of rules.

You ignored them, things turned to chaos. Once you started screwing with magnetic north, you were lost. You wound up like Echeverria. A guy with the moral discipline of a tapeworm.

That's where the vertigo was coming from, the nausea. Brad was outside the lines now. Way outside them. Not sure how to get back. Lost in a trackless territory with a wildly spinning compass.

And Christ, all of it coming unwound so quickly. Echeverria stalking into his office late yesterday, knowing everything. About Greta, the pain clinic. All of it. Knew Greta was scheduled to return the next day. Smiling at Brad, laying it all out. What do you want? Brad asked him. I want in, he said. There's nothing to be in. I want in anyway, Echeverria said. You're on my turf, Diversion, I'm your new partner. Like it or fucking not. Unless, that is, you want me to go public, make a formal complaint.

So Echeverria had flown down that afternoon, Brad

drove. Stopped by to give his respects to Dr. Wilson.
The whole time feeling the earth tilting away under his
feet. A maggot like Echeverria had him by the short
and curlies and obviously relished the feeling. Jesus
God. And now Greta was missing. Greta Masterson had
disappeared.

Brad stopped outside the last door on the right. He
rolled up the sleeves of his white shirt, loosened his tie
another notch. Sitting out in the Fairlane all afternoon
he'd sweated through the cotton shirt several times,
then had to start the car to dry out in the air-condition-
ing. He smelled like he'd been wrestling with a goat.

He tapped lightly on the door and got no response.
He tapped harder without result. Swallowing the lump
that was hardening in his throat, he twisted the knob
and stepped into the dark room.

Shades pulled down, a little light leaking around the
edges. He patted the wall for a switch but couldn't find
it. A choking stench in the room.

"Greta?"

He took a step toward the window. Get the shade up,
let a little light in. Then all at once there was a shadow
looming in front of him. A very tall shadow. Brad's
hands shot up, he dropped into a crouch. The tall
man's head was bent forward and he seemed to be
tracking in a slow circle.

"I'm looking for someone," Brad said. "I mean no
harm."

The man continued his slow spin like a pitcher
about to unleash his fastball. Brad stiffened, then
thought he saw the man feint forward, so he lunged,
tackled the man around the midsection, drove him
backward a few feet and stumbled over a chair.

He came up slowly. The shadow man was rocking

wildly from side to side. Brad took two steps to the window and opened the paper shade.

"Jesus."

Brad sank down onto the single bed. When he'd recaptured his breath, he reached over and snapped on the bedside lamp.

The naked man had no arms. Short stumps jutted out at rigid right angles to his body. He was not more than forty, with shoulder-length black hair and a small goatee and a Marine Corps tattoo on his white and hairless chest. A bra dangled over his head, one of the cups partially hiding his eyes.

He'd used an electrical cord, tying it to the base of the Hunter fan in the ceiling. The noose knot was carefully made, as if he'd practiced it for years.

A chair was toppled beneath him, and next to it was a mound of shit, some of it smeared across the wood floor. One at a time Brad lifted his cordovans. It was his left shoe that was coated thick with the dead man's shit, his last offering to that grim world.

"You find Randy?" Ginny said as Brad passed through the TV room.

"You need to call 911."

"Why?" she said. "They got drugs for that now, bringing people back from the dead?"

Ginny gave him a flirty smile and turned back to the endless destruction of Tokyo.

CHAPTER

11

Thorn spent Thursday and Friday at Baptist Hospital in Miami, sliding in and out of tight metal tubes, high-tech chrome caskets that permitted the bright young doctors to shine magnetic lights through his body. All the nurses complimented him on how well he stayed still.

"It's one of my few skills," he told them. "I'm a slow-twitch kind of guy. Years of bone fishing."

Lying in his room between tests, he exhausted himself trying to send signals to the muscles in his legs. Move, move, move. Twitch, wiggle, anything, goddamn it. Lying there, sweating as he strained to fire even the faintest nerve impulses through the old pathways. But everything was dead, switched off. His lower body was as dark and empty as the cold depths of the sea.

Monica was there for all of it. A brave smile as she massaged his inert legs, his cold empty toes. He watched her fingers digging into his body as if his flesh were putty she was trying to keep from hardening.

Dr. Wilson came the first day and got Thorn's permission to insert a catheter into the base of his spine to make it easier to inject the twice daily dose of steroids, methylprednisolone. He returned Thursday night and Friday morning to administer the drug himself. Thorn lay still, feeling no pain, just that strange vacant coolness of flesh.

Something about Bean Wilson's boyish bow ties, his ramrod carriage, and his shy smile was deeply soothing in that frantic hospital. Wilson had been a devout widower for almost thirty years. Thorn imagined him still having cheerful conversations with his dead wife, discussing his daily encounters around the island. Maybe it was those regular visits to the spirit world of his departed lover that kept him youthful—his romantic heart had not aged.

Mrs. Wilson was an elegant and cultivated woman. A lady who read poetry and arranged flowers and wore lacy dresses in a town where cutoff jeans and bikini tops were considered formal wear. The two of them had been so passionate for each other, it was sometimes embarrassing to be around them. Their devotion for each other left them little time for Bean junior. Thorn always assumed Bean junior was a late-in-life mistake—a kid whose major boyhood challenge was to find ways to insert himself into his parents' fierce love affair.

Though he'd been a widower for nearly thirty years, as far as Thorn knew, Wilson had never come close to remarrying. On the surface he seemed available enough, no moody griever, no hermit. Out and about at the local restaurants and social events, tirelessly amiable. In the small society of Key Largo, he drove the widows crazy—such a catch, so elusive. Thorn suspected Wilson considered himself still married, ever faithful to the woman who had shown him a brand of love he must have believed he'd never duplicate. It would be dishonest of such a man to become betrothed again—nothing less than bigamy.

All day Thursday and Friday a steady stream of specialists came and went from Thorn's hospital room. Many of them knew Bean Wilson, shared a joke with him out of earshot, but no one gave Thorn any words to hang on to. He watched their poker faces as they stared at the X-rays, checked his chart.

Through both afternoons, Monica massaged his legs while Thorn practiced breathing. At times he found himself floating a few hundred yards above, watching somebody else's body getting a nice loving massage. The play was into a third act, heading for a fourth, but Thorn's mind was still vacant, as if the blow to his spine had numbed his emotions as well, allowing only the vaguest sense of dread to seep through. He had been snatched from his life, dropped into a body not his own, lying on a white bed in a foreign room. He heard the strange voice coming from his throat, he felt the air entering and leaving his alien lungs, the unfamiliar rhythms of the heart beating in his chest. This was not Thorn. Thorn was back in Key Largo tying flies, or poling his skiff across the dazzling flats. But this nameless creature lying half paralyzed in a hospital room in Miami was someone else entirely. Someone with a dull, blank, empty mind. A senseless hunk of beef who was doing a very bad impersonation of a shiftless but engaging fellow that everyone knew as Thorn.

One of the neurologists, a handsome black woman named Roosevelt, had been there from the moment he'd first arrived. After taking his blood pressure late Friday afternoon, she lingered to ask if his legs were in any pain.

"I wish," Thorn said.

She patted him on the thigh and told him not to worry, they were getting there.

"Where is that?" Thorn said.

"Finish line, honey. We're almost done."

"So, you know what it is?" Monica said.

"I didn't say that."

"Then how the hell can you say you're almost finished?"

"Because"—the doctor rested a hand on Monica's shoulder—"we're running out of tests."

"And you still don't have an idea? How can that be?"

"We know Mr. Thorn has a ding on his spinal cord."

"A ding!" Monica balled her hands, shrugged away from the doctor's touch.

"Bull riders get them, rodeo people, and football players. We see a lot of wide receivers. Dolphins, Hurricanes. Those hard tackles."

"A ding," Thorn said. "Is there maybe another word for it? Something a little fancier?"

"A bruise, a swelling."

"But it's temporary. Right?" Monica was at the doctor's shoulder. She looked like she might do something physical if the doctor responded incorrectly. The woman took a half step back.

"When all the tests are completed, Dr. Wilson will sit down and explain everything."

"And in the meantime," Monica said, "we're waiting here, nobody's telling us anything. People coming and going, doing all this shit, everybody with their mouths shut. This is outrageous."

Thorn cleared his throat.

"Well, at least now we know it's a ding."

The doctor squeezed out a smile, then headed for the door. She gave them both a look she must have intended to be sympathetic, then eased the door shut behind her.

"D minus on bedside manner," Thorn said.

"I want to shoot these goddamn people."

"That's liable to be counterproductive."

"I mean it, Thorn. This is shit. Wilson says these are the best in Miami. Neurologists, orthopedists. And look at them. They're walking around, hands over their asses, not going to make a mistake. No, sir. Playing it very goddamn cool. Don't want to stir up the malpractice gremlins."

"How much is this costing, Monica?"

"Don't worry about it."

"I can't let you do this."

"You have any medical insurance, Thorn?"

He looked at her blankly.

"Okay," she said. "So you damn well have to let me do this. We're in this together, you idiot. This is our problem." She blinked, eyes turning hazy.

She walked over to the window, squinted out into the bright sunlight. She'd been wearing the same pair of jeans and long-sleeve white T-shirt for the last two days. Thrown it on as the Keys ambulance pulled down his drive. One of the three outfits of hers hanging in his closet. She hadn't had a shower, as far as Thorn knew. Hadn't slept more than an hour or two. In the middle of the night he had woken several times to find her bent over him, kneading his legs with hushed ferocity.

"This is your father's money? Your inheritance?"

"Yes," she said. "Good riddance."

He watched her stare out into the bright daylight,

breathing through her mouth. The room at Baptist Hospital was on the fifth floor. Beside his bed a window looked out at Kendall Drive. He had spent a few hours watching the endless flow of traffic, all that quiet desperation locked in aluminum. And the joggers making their steady circuits around the lake, the ducks on parade.

The walls of his room were a buttery yellow and there was an imitation Monet on the wall across from him. He'd had lots of time to study the painting. Two women in bonnets and parasols walking through a field of blue and green wildflowers. It looked like a mother and her twenty-something daughter. Thorn wasn't sure why, but he thought they were on a Sunday stroll, the men left behind at home with their cigars, brandy, and ribald talk while the women walked through the shadows of late afternoon in what looked like early spring somewhere in the northern hemisphere. A mother and daughter discussing some deeply personal issue. The mother's sadness or boredom, the daughter's approaching marriage. In their long dresses with many petticoats, they seemed to be floating a few inches above the field of wildflowers, an effortless glide across the beautiful earth. It was not a painting any new paralytic should be forced to study.

But Thorn was holding on. There was no pain. Only the dull absence of what should have been there. A coolness below the waist as if he were lolling in a tub of bathwater that was steadily losing its heat.

The worst thing had been the nights. He'd been dreaming of running. Loping down hard-packed beaches, flushing seagulls into flight, an effortless glide, his legs churning beneath him, carrying him lightly and quickly across the earth. Not running away from anything or toward anything, just racing along, limitless energy flowing. Both times he'd awoken breathless and sweating, his legs still dead beneath the sheets.

Monica coughed, turned from the harsh light, drew in a chestful of air.

"What's going on with you, Thorn?"

"How do you mean?"

"I mean, what's going on with you? Level with me."

"What? You think I'm faking?" He smiled. "Like I secretly wiggle my toes when everybody is looking the other way?"

"I mean the way you're taking this."

"What way is that?"

"You're not reacting. You're holding it in. Joking around."

"Well, hey. I haven't had much practice yet. Maybe a few more days, I'll figure out how a good paralytic acts."

She swung away as if he'd cursed her.

"Monica, look, it's okay. This is temporary. It has to be. Any second those steroids are going to shrink my spinal cord back to normal, I'll be up and going full speed. Find the asshole who did this."

When she turned back her eyes were muddy. A single sleek trail wandered down her right cheek. She took a breath, got control of her mouth.

"It wasn't any prowler, was it? All that bullshit you told the sheriff. You don't believe that, do you? Come on, Thorn. Somebody breaking in to steal what? Fishing flies?"

"I didn't see who it was."

"But you're thinking about it. You've got some idea."

"Maybe those muscle guys from Sundowners, the comedy troupe."

"Stop it, Thorn. The flippant bullshit."

"What do you want me to say?"

She nailed him with a look, then returned to the view out the window.

"I know what you were doing Wednesday."

Thorn looked up at the white ceiling.

"I bumped into Roy and he told me you stopped by. That you were investigating the dolphin thing. That's the word he used. *Investigating*. So tell me, Thorn, maybe I should know for my own safety. What else did you poke around in?"

He hauled himself an inch or two higher against the pillows.

While Monica hugged herself tight and kept her eyes on the view, Thorn told her about his day on Wednesday. He described the dolphin pools, told her what Roy had said about the torture, the spines and brains. He repeated his questions to Dr. Wilson and Wilson's answers. That there was no value to dolphin carcasses that he knew. His promise to look into it further. Even Brad Madison's warning to him out in the parking lot.

Her voice blank, Monica said, "Goddamn it. What's going on?"

"Look, I poked around a little. I found out next to nothing, and on the same night somebody comes around to see what they can rip off. I walk outside and the guy knocks me out. As I fall I hit my spine against a rock. Before he can do anything more, you come outside, he hears your voice and runs off. That's all it is. A stupid goddamn set of coincidences. Random chaos. Bad luck."

"But you don't believe that. You don't believe in random chaos, do you?"

She held his eyes, wouldn't let him look away.

"Sure I do."

She shook her head.

"You're a shitty liar, Thorn."

"All I know is someone attacked me and you came out at the right time before he had a chance to do anything more. You probably saved my life."

"Maybe," she said. Then she said, "I tried Sugarman again."

Thorn's closest friend was island-hopping in the Caribbean—a final fling before he and Jeannie became parents. Jeannie was five months pregnant with twins. Two boys, the ultrasound had told them.

She said, "Apparently they're not following their itinerary. Nevis, Anguilla, I've left messages everywhere."

"It's okay. There isn't anything he could do here anyway. We'd interrupt their vacation for nothing. How about Rover?"

"Janine from work is feeding him. He's fine. His poop is fine too."

She glanced at him, then back out the window. She swallowed.

"Is there anything I can get you? Anything you need?"

Thorn said no, there wasn't.

She'd asked the same thing a dozen times and he'd manufactured a handful of assignments to allow her some escape from that room. He'd sent her on missions for magazines and ice cream and was considering asking her to drive back down to Key Largo and fetch his fly-tying gear. Not that he really cared about any of it, or needed any distractions. He was plenty busy going over and over it in his head, trying to re-create that Wednesday night, his walk down the stairs, the final millisecond after Rover's growl as Thorn spun around to confront his attacker. He'd glimpsed something, but wasn't sure what. Something yellow or gold. A cap perhaps, a shaggy wig. The image wouldn't coalesce.

He'd also been hard at work picturing a future in a wheelchair. He knew a couple of people who lived in them, who adapted to their new conditions. A special boat ramp, a customized platform on their skiffs. One of his old high school friends down in Lower Matecumbe had come home from Vietnam a quadriplegic, but that wasn't keeping the guy from trying like hell to break the light tackle record for tarpon, using a special rod he'd designed that was operated by blowing in a tube.

Thorn had been very busy conceiving that new life, fitting a wheelchair into his old habits, keeping his mind on the technical problems of adapting his house and boat. When he grew tired of that, he'd been spending the empty hours staring at the painting on the far wall, or watching Monica, or listening to the never-ending squeaks and gongs and voices of the hospital. He damn well didn't want to drift. Didn't want to start asking the long unanswerable questions. The ones with *why*. He wouldn't even let his mind form the words. He knew the questions were in there lurking, hungering for voice, but he was all too acquainted with the rush of chemicals those considerations released. He'd wallowed in the caustic bath of mourning and despair before, knew how deep and airless the gloom could grow, what an immeasurable weight it could lay on his chest. So he was keeping his eyes focused on the tangible world—on the shadows and slashes of light that played on the far wall, on the eyes and timbre of voice of the nurses, on the topography of the sheets that covered him. He was not cheerful, but he refused to go the other way. He'd been down there, seen how little that world had to offer.

At eight that evening Dr. Wilson returned to give another steroid injection. He was wearing a pink shirt and white cotton trousers and a dark green bow tie with tiny red fish printed on it. He looked like he was about to pledge to a fraternity.

"How's our patient?" He opened his small medical bag and took out the vial of steroids and filled his syringe.

Thorn said he was fine. Thinking of going for a jog a little later.

Doc Wilson smiled politely. Monica helped Thorn sit up and bend forward. It took only a few seconds for Dr. Wilson to fill his catheter with the solution.

"Feel good enough to visit with an old friend?"

"Oh, Christ." Thorn frowned. "Don't tell me I ruined Sugarman's vacation."

"No, you ruined mine."

It took Thorn a few awkward seconds to recognize the man who stepped into the room. He was just under six feet, trim, with skin so fresh and untanned it looked like he'd been marinating in milk. His hair was as thick as it had been thirty years ago and as blond, though now he obviously paid someone with an expensive education to cut it. He wore dark unpressed corduroy jeans and a blousy white casual shirt with a very uncasual red and gold crest on the left breast.

He stood for a moment basking in Thorn's confu-

sion, then walked over to the edge of the bed in the
stiff-legged gait of a man with steel rods holding his
spine together. Thorn wasn't sure about the steel rods,
but it was clear that something catastrophic had happened to Bean junior's body. The calamity was also in
his eyes. They were still the innocent blue of his youth,
but Thorn could see in the quick flick of attention he
gave Monica, and the peripheral awareness he had of
his own father, that Bean's eyes were far busier than
they'd once been. Thorn had seen eyes like that before
in men who'd once been ambushed, and never, by
god, were going to be ambushed again.

"Bean, Bean, good for the heart, the more you see
him the more you fart."

"Spare me, please, the taunts of our youth."

Bean junior smiled and put out his hand and Thorn
took it in his own. He'd learned long ago not to put
too much stock in the revelations of character transmit-
ted by handshakes. So he tried to discount Bean's cool,
dry skin, the quick squeeze and release, the limp with-
drawal.

"Great to see you. But you didn't need to come all
this way."

"Oh, yes, I did." Bean glanced at his father, gave
him a curt nod. "I had to rescue you from this old fool
before he left you permanently disabled." Bean junior
let it float there for a second, then tried to smile it
away.

"My son is convinced that modern science has
passed me by."

"Like a bullet train, Dad. Like the Concorde with a
tailwind."

Thorn raised his hand, motioned for Monica. He
could see she'd formed a quick harsh opinion of the

young doctor. She looked like she couldn't decide whether to flee the room or throw herself at Bean junior's throat.

Bean followed Thorn's look, turned to Monica, read her expression.

"Oh, please. We're just joking around. Doctor talk. Good-natured sparring. Right, Dad?"

"Been perfecting it for forty-odd years."

"Forty very odd years," Bean said.

"Bean, I'd like you to meet Monica Sampson."

He pivoted awkwardly and smiled at Monica. With businesslike cool she extended her hand and he took hold of it in both of his as if he intended to smother it in kisses.

"Ah, yes, the new lady in Thorn's life."

"I'm not his new lady," Monica announced. "I'm his fiancée."

Thorn smoothed the sheets that lay across his numb legs. A twist in his gut tightened. She took her hand away from Bean, stepped over to the foot of the bed, and gripped the foot rail as if Thorn might sail off somewhere without her. She stared at him, her back straight, mouth defiant.

Doc Wilson was consulting the back of his right hand.

"Well, well. Thorn, I didn't know. Congratulations."

"Oh, it's all a little sudden," said Thorn. "We haven't even had our announcements printed yet."

He smiled back at Monica, took a swallow of air, and another.

CHAPTER

12

"You going to tell him, Dad, or should I?"

Bean junior turned and circled behind Monica. Thorn caught his quick appraising glance of her backside. Bean eased around the bed to stand next to his father. For a second or two the old man studied the far wall, then he brought his eyes to Thorn's.

"They're dismissing you tomorrow."

Monica stared at him.

"I've done what I could to get them to prolong your stay until we have a better understanding of what's going on, a more definitive diagnosis, but the administration is firm. After reviewing all the pictures and tests, it's been determined that your injury isn't serious enough to warrant further use of hospital resources. They were going to send a social worker up, have her sketch out your options, but I said no, I'd do it."

"They're kicking him out?" Monica took a step his way. "For godsakes, he's paralyzed."

"I don't get it," Thorn said. "If it's not serious, why can't I move? What's going on?"

"I wish I knew," Doc Wilson said. "We're all bewildered. I've gone over and over this with specialists here at Baptist. I went over to Jackson, talked to the top spinal-injury people in Miami, some of the highest and mightiest in the whole country, and no one can account for this, Thorn.

"We know there's no tear in the cord itself, no separation. We're certain there's no rupturing in the disk, no breakage or crushing. The spinal cord is bruised, and there's some minimal swelling, but there's absolutely nothing to account for the paralysis. I've talked to a dozen people and no one's suggested anything other than the same regimen of steroids you're already on, the methylprednisolone."

"That's been standard practice for years," Bean junior said. "There are some new nonsteroidal anti-inflammatories that cut down on the side effects, but if the pred's not working, the nonsteroids wouldn't either."

"You're losing me," Thorn said.

"We're baffled," said the old doctor. "You don't seem to be seriously injured. Nothing shows up. We've followed standard procedures, but you're simply not responding."

Thorn gazed across at the painting, those women in the vibrant field, green, red, blue flowers spread around them. They were making no progress. Walking and walking, discussing some weighty matter, but getting nowhere. Exactly where they'd always been, exactly where they'd always be.

Thorn looked at Monica just as she closed her eyes and bowed her head. The gesture lasted for only half a second, then she took an exhausted breath and looked back up, but in that snap of time Thorn caught a glimpse of the toll this was taking on her. Days without sleep; his injury putting a heavy slump in her shoul-

ders, as if this young, bright, artistic woman had just
realized with dreadful certainty that she would have to
bear Thorn's deadweight on her back for the rest of
her days.

"May I, Dad?" Bean junior moved away from the
bed, glancing at the dark window as if checking his
reflection. Then he positioned himself in the room's
one chair. Squaring his legs up in front of him, with
both hands cupped together on his lap like some kind
of Buddhist pose. When he was certain they were all
watching, he formed a careful smile and let a second
or two more pass before he spoke.

"Your MRI and scans show your spinal canal to be a
fraction more narrow than it should be. That would
mean there is less range of motion possible without
some impinging on the cord. It's a condition known as
spinal stenosis, narrowing of the subarachnoid space.
Fairly common. In addition, you've got some bony
growth along the vertebrae, something we see in a
good percentage of athletic men. All those years of
high school football and wrestling catching up to you.
The bony protuberances complicate the stenosis,
which makes you an excellent candidate for back problems."

Thorn looked up at old Doc Wilson. The man was
standing very erect, gazing across at his son with a peculiar wincing smile that seemed to be a blend of affection and something else that looked a lot like grief.

"It's true we don't know exactly what's causing your
current paralysis," Bean junior said. "But these things
happen sometimes, an injury that defies all our high-
tech imaging systems. What we do know with some certainty is that the longer your legs stay paralyzed, the

more atrophy, the more peripheral damage, to the rest of your central nervous system. Don't you agree, Dad?"

"I agree, yes."

"And now, since you have to leave the hospital, and since adequate home care would be extremely expensive if not totally impossible to find in Key Largo, I propose you come down to my clinic in Key West."

"Key West?" Monica said.

"That's right."

"What the hell is he going to do down there, sit around and smoke dope, watch the sun set?"

Bean cut his eyes to her, smiled blankly, and looked back at Thorn.

"My clinic has a very complete, very sophisticated rehab center. The latest equipment, a highly trained staff. I think the sooner we get you working your legs in a controlled situation with professional guidance, the sooner your recovery can begin."

"If there is a recovery," Thorn said.

Bean nodded. It was understood.

Monica had balled her hands. Something new was in her face. A strain beyond what she'd been showing. A sour smile twisting her lips. Thorn thought he could see desperate words building in her throat. Things spinning ahead too quickly for her, decisions being made without her involvement.

"Dr. Wilson?" Thorn looked up at the man. "Is this what you think? Key West?"

Wilson touched a hand to the side of his mane of white hair, patted down an errant strand. He looked pale and old. A deep sadness in his eyes, as if he had just discovered that his lifetime of accumulated wisdom was of little use.

"Bean's an excellent doctor," he said. "And I've

seen the clinic. Their equipment is superb, their staff is very strong. Of course, we can always discuss other possibilities if you like, but I can't think of anywhere you would be more likely to get that kind of hands-on care."

"I don't know," Thorn said. "I guess I need to think about it."

"You can check my board certification, if you like. All my papers are in pretty good order, I believe." Bean junior smiled at each one of them in turn.

"Bean's an excellent doctor," Doc Wilson repeated.

Monica looked down at the floor.

After a moment, Doc Wilson stepped over to her side, put his arm around her shoulder, and hugged her with fatherly affection, but Monica didn't seem to notice.

Thorn glanced at the painting again. He saw it now. In his weakened condition he'd been making too much of the damn thing. The painting was nothing more than a cheap rip-off of something real. Probably mass-produced in some warehouse in Tijuana for hospitals and hotels and rental condos. Muzak in a frame. All the stories he'd been reading into the thing had been springing from his needy, overactive mind.

"So from what you've seen of my X rays and MRIs," Thorn said, "you think there's hope my legs will come back?"

"Will I put a number on it, you mean?" Bean junior glanced at the window, then back at Thorn.

"Hey," Thorn said. "I'd settle for one in a million at this point."

"There aren't any guarantees, Thorn. But if you decided to come down to Key West, I think it'll be as good a chance as you'll get."

"When can I go?"

"If you feel up to it," Bean junior said, "we can drive down tomorrow morning."

Monica was looking grimly at Thorn.

"I'll do whatever it takes to get my legs back," Thorn said, trying for a smile. "Even if it means going to Key West."

"Just like that, no discussion with me. Just, yeah, sure, okay, I'll go down there, switch doctors."

Thorn said nothing, staring over at the empty chair.

Dr. Wilson and Bean junior had gone. Monica was boiling. As mad as she ever remembered being. Mad and hurt and terrified. There was a constriction in her throat, the air passages tightening down.

An hour earlier she'd as much as promised to marry this man, made a public statement. A couple of days earlier she'd packed her bags and was ready to run from this difficult, monkish guy who she loved and cared for but couldn't imagine living with. His silences, his lifelong habits; a man so self-sufficient he could probably live on a naked mountaintop, snag gnats for food, not feel deprived. But she'd spoken the words. Saying it in front of those men, "I'm his fiancée." And yes, she said it partly out of embarrassment and anger.

But after they finally left, she and Thorn didn't discuss marriage or engagements or any of that. Just Thorn saying he was tired, his eyes sliding off hers, embarrassed, guilty. Could she go back down to Key Largo, please, pick up a few things for him? A little packing. Of course, she said quietly, whatever you want. She would need to go to the laundry, do a few loads. Did he want to take some of his fly-tying stuff? Yeah, that might be good.

She fetched for something more to say, but all the words deserted her. This guy she barely knew. A few months together. Great fun. Monica feeling secure with him, feeling challenged by his calmness, his orderly world, a long list of things he loved to do.

Then just this week getting very edgy that she was feeling too much for Thorn, too quick. Old love injuries coming back to her, the men who'd fooled her in the past. Not trusting her own reactions. Which was why she'd packed, loaded her car. Going to kidnap the foolish young woman who was in love but didn't want to be. Cart her off somewhere where she could chill down, come to her senses.

Another moment of silence, then Thorn reached out a hand for her and Monica stepped forward and took it. Strong and warm, familiar.

"I meant what I said. About being your fiancée."

Thorn looked at her, then stared across at the empty chair.

"Not like this."

"What?"

"The way I am. Paralyzed. It changes things."

"You're going to get better. You're going down there, work your butt off, and you'll be walking again in no time."

"What if I don't?"

"You're going to get better, goddamn it."

"I wouldn't have asked you to marry me if this had happened first."

"What's that mean? You're taking it back?"

"Yes," he said. "I'm taking it back. You're off the hook."

"You think I said what I did just now because I feel sorry for you? Is that it?"

"It wouldn't be fair. I'm not the same person I was last week."

"Sure you are."

"Monica, believe me, I'm not. I may not be that person again, even if I do get better."

"Oh, so you get a bump on your spine and that makes you a new person. And this new person doesn't love me anymore. Is that what you're saying?"

"I don't love anything at the moment."

"Thorn, goddamn it, you're going to get better."

He swallowed, found a breath. His eyes weren't his. They were on loan from some grieving, brokenhearted fool.

"Maybe I'll get better, maybe I won't. Either way, I won't let you throw away your life because you feel bad about what's happened to me. If we went ahead with it, neither of us would know for sure why you said yes. And that doubt would always be there, poisoning things."

"I'm not some schoolkid. I know what I'm doing."

"Look, Monica, I don't have any energy right now for candlelight and champagne. I'd just kill it, whatever we have."

"Christ, you don't have to woo me, Thorn. I love you. I'm going to stand by you no matter what. Sickness or health."

"No," he said. "It won't work."

"You mean you won't let it work."

"Go on home, Monica. Leave me alone."

She closed her eyes for a moment, watched the white bursts of exploding cells. When she opened them again, he was still there, eyes hard on hers.

"Just like that. Push me away. Slam the door in my face."

"Just like that," he said.

"Well, fuck you, Thorn. Fuck you, fuck you, fuck you."

He nodded, agreeing. And without another word, Monica turned and stalked from the room, found her way out of the hospital, tracked down her car in the huge lot. In a gray daze she drove back to Key Largo, collected his clothes, drove down US 1 to the Laundromat, separated the whites and colors, did his wash, took it out, dropped the quarters into the dryer, sat and watched his clothes tumble and tumble.

She folded everything neatly. Got the creases straighter than she ever had. All of it very important, that his underwear be just right. She kept her mind focused on the precision of underwear, the geometry of creasing, folding his shirts, each of them exactly the same, shaking them out, starting over for the smallest flaw. Driving back to the house, she shifted gears meticulously.

She went inside, located a gym bag, packed the clothes, selected a few feathers, some bits of fur, Mylar threads, his favorite set of pliers. She got his bathroom things and two pairs of shoes.

By midnight she was finished, the bag packed, sitting by the door. A perfect folding job, perfect packing. Monica poured herself a jelly glass of red wine, went out on the porch, looked up at the heavens, dense with stars. A clear night, the last coolness before summer closed in.

She drank the wine, poured another. She fed the dog, talked to him for a while. He listened to her woes and somehow knew better than to wag his tail. When she'd finished telling Rover everything that had happened, everything that was on her mind, she stood up, stepped out to the edge of the porch, gripped the railing, leaned out toward the black shimmer of the bay, and she sobbed.

CHAPTER

13

"You sure do like your sleep," Pepper said.

She stood in the narrow doorway of Greta's stateroom chewing on a sleek green chili pepper that resembled the toe of a giant frog. Tonight Pepper wore a sequined T-shirt and electric-blue shorts, black high heels—fitted out like the main event at a two-dollar strip club.

Greta closed her eyes and settled her head against the pillow. She'd been drifting all day inside the morphine fog. Maybe two days. She wasn't sure anymore. The drug had slowed her respiration and pulse to almost a flatline, and behind her closed lids she watched the bright pings of what surely were dying brain cells. All day she'd been slipping deeper inside her body, down through the hazy shadows of lassitude. It was as if she were fading back into her very cells and molecules, second by second, dwindling to some baseline biological unit, prehuman. Mind still tracking sensations, but barely.

"Doc's got your pump set a little high," Pepper said. "Couple hundred milligrams in your bolus, then a maintenance dose after that. He didn't want you to be screaming and carrying on, making a disturbance. Not that anybody would hear, anchored as far out as we are. But he had to play it safe, considering you're a federal agent and all.''

In the dim light of the cabin, Greta stared across at the thin girl. Her shoulder-length hair was auburn and so fine that the tips of both ears peeked through. Framing her face were two strands of bleached hair, the color of rancid margarine. Once, a couple of weeks earlier, Pepper had shown Greta her high school homecoming portrait. In a tight yellow chiffon gown, Pepper Tremaine, princess in waiting, stood stiff and uncertain on an outdoor stage. Either the poor girl's father had bribed the judges or it had been a very small, very unfortunate class at Key West High.

Tonight Pepper had tried to redraw the map of her face with raspberry lipstick and eyebrow pencil and heavy smudges of blush. Maybe across the room in some hazy midnight Duval Street bar her heavy jaw and muscular face might be mistaken for attractive, but out in the daylight her smile was mulish and vacant. A grin that recalled another Greta had seen years before during her brief stint as a schoolteacher. One morning at recess she'd approached a group of her third graders who'd gathered around an older girl on the far edge of the playground. The girl was huddled over a scrawny stray dog that had haunted the schoolyard for weeks. As Greta stepped close she saw the girl had her knee pressed hard to the dog's throat and was training a laser of sunlight through her magnifying glass, sizzling the mutt's right eye, a thin ribbon of smoke rising. When the girl swung around and faced Greta, she wore the same sickly grin that was on Pepper's face.

Pepper was one of four nurses working in the clinic.

The other three had regular duties at the naval hospital but were loaned out to the pain clinic on a weekly rotation. Pepper was a local girl Bean Wilson had selected himself. Because of that, Pepper considered herself the office manager and routinely ordered the other nurses around. Greta heard plenty of grumbling from them, but the doctor always seemed to side with Pepper. In her six weeks at the clinic, Greta tried several times to befriend Pepper, but the woman was alternately remote and rude. Greta was fairly sure it was territorial, another woman trespassing in her lair. Spreading her scent.

"You got about an hour before your next bolus. You should be about as clearheaded right now as you're going to be all day."

"I'm awake."

"You think you can stay that way long enough to get up and pee and do your other bathroom business?"

"I need help."

"I know you do, honey. That's why I came by. To get you in there before you shit the sheets."

"I can get you immunity. You testify against him, you won't serve any time. I can promise you that."

"Immunity? What the hell would I want with that? I had every vaccination there is. You name it, I'm immune to it."

She cocked a hip and grinned.

"Pepper, I'm a federal agent. They're not going to stop looking for me. You're going to do some heavy time for this if you don't cooperate."

"They can send in the army and navy and the Green Berets if they want. I'm not deserting Bean. He's getting close. He's almost there. Going to be the biggest damn scientific breakthrough of the twentieth century.

Biggest thing since penicillin. If a couple of federal agents have to disappear in the meantime, well, I don't think that's much price to pay."

"What breakthrough?"

"The drug he's working on. Reason you're here."

Pepper came over to the V-berth and scooped Greta up in her arms, grunting and complaining that Greta was a hell of a lot heavier than she looked, and she carried her into the tiny head just beyond the door to the forward stateroom. Greta got only a quick look at the sights beyond her door. The narrow hallway was paneled in dark mahogany and the carpets were burgundy. There appeared to be two other cabins beside Greta's narrow wedge of space in the bow of the boat. It was one of those old mahogany yachts from forty or fifty years earlier. Fitted out in the sumptuous and dreary style of mid-twentieth-century funeral parlors. Heavy brass fixtures, lamps with golden shades, meant to honey the light. The carpet smelled of terminal mildew and there were constant creaks and moans in the timbers of the ship—even tonight, when the sea outside was perfectly calm.

Pepper positioned her on the toilet, helped rearrange her blue surgical scrub and pull down her panties.

"You're not going to fall off now, are you?"

"There's nowhere to fall."

"Look," Pepper said. "I been meaning to ask you something. I noticed you around the clinic, how you did your face, your makeup I mean, and I was wondering if, you know, you could show me how you do a couple of things. Like girl to girl."

Greta stared at her.

"I mean, I know some of the basics, and I'm getting

good advice from a girl at the cosmetics counter out at Searstown, but I thought, if you didn't mind, maybe you could go over one or two problem issues with me."

Greta took a breath. She studied Pepper's face in the mirror. The girl seemed sincere, the first vulnerable note she'd heard in her voice.

"What do you want to know?"

"Like the way my eyes are now. Start there. Any suggestions you might have. Something's not right, but I can't figure out what."

Greta took a breath.

"A good craftsman leaves no traces."

"What?"

"You're being a little heavy-handed, Pepper. Scooping it on."

"But you want them to see it, right? What's the use of putting it on, if they can't see it?"

"You want them to notice *you,* not your eyeliner."

After a moment's pout, Pepper turned to the lavatory mirror, stared at herself for a moment, then turned on the water and began to wash her face. When she'd dried herself, she set out her array of sponges, velour puffs, brushes.

For the next hour Greta helped her define her eyes, feather her foundation, plump her lips. They experimented with different blends of colors, harder lines, softer ones, Pepper peering into the mirror while Greta talked her through it.

At one stage, after an arduous ten minutes of work, Pepper swung around from the mirror to show Greta two completely different eyes, one tiny, one huge.

"I look like one of those goddamn Dick Tracy freaks."

Pepper stood there for a few seconds, the look on her face impossible to decipher.

"Yes," Greta said. "You do."

Pepper's lips quivered as though she were about to bawl, then at the last second she settled on a smile, and before Greta could stop herself she laughed. Pepper hesitated, staring at her sternly, then her mouth relaxed and she chuckled back. Greta and this woman who was holding her hostage, who'd helped implant a spinal pump in her belly, giggling like schoolgirls.

Finally, with Greta doing a good deal of the detail work, Pepper got her face on. And to Greta's amazement, she looked better. No one was going to mistake her for a runway beauty, but the sluttish air had vanished and a more innocent, appealing young woman was showing through. Pepper smiled.

"Hell, that's pretty good. Only problem is, I'll never be able to do it again."

"It takes practice, that's all."

Pepper moved to the bathroom door.

"Well, your suppositories are there on the sink," she said. "Everything else you need's right there. When you get done, you just crawl on back into the bedroom."

"What?"

"I have to go," Pepper said, smiling mischievously. "Got a hot date. Hot and hung."

"Don't, Pepper. Don't do this."

"You sleep tight now, Agent Masterson. And thanks for the help."

"Don't go. Please, we need to talk."

"Now what do you think, just because you helped me with my makeup, I'm supposed to let you go free? That what you had in mind, is it? Well, I hate to disappoint. But night-night. I'll see you in the morning, 'cause right now I gotta go see about smudging this lipstick.''

She shut the door and a minute or two later Greta heard the outboard crank to life. It idled for a moment, then roared away into the distance.

"Shit, shit, shit."

Greta rocked back against the toilet tank. She took a long breath, blew it out. So much for female bonding. The woman wasn't as malleable as she seemed. And not nearly as dumb.

As near as Greta could figure, it was Friday night. Nine-thirty according to the green glow of the digital clock sitting on a bare white shelf across from her. Less than an hour till she heard again that noise she'd come to dread, the quiet hum of the pump embedded in her body delivering its powerful spurt of morphine.

She knew a good deal about these pumps. During her first weeks in the clinic she'd considered having the surgery. She'd examined a couple of the units she'd found on Wilson's shelves, silver devices as small as a baby's fist. The pump had a collapsible drug reservoir, microprocessor circuitry, a lithium battery, a tiny antenna. It could run for a couple of years on that battery, and with the antenna the doctor could reprogram the pump to deliver more or less drug at variable intervals. He simply held a black plastic transmitter wand over the patient's belly and typed a few coded instructions into a laptop computer wired to the wand, and, lo and behold, the pump received a new set of commands, invisibly and magically through the flesh. *Noninvasively programmable,* the literature said. Acoustic transducer, peristaltic pump, bacterial retentive filter, and fill port with self-sealing septum and needle stop. All of which meant that the spinal pump could be refilled with a long thin needle, a delicate injection through the belly of the patient.

Also on his shelves Greta had seen the complicated catheter arrangement, the same unit that now curled beneath the flesh at the edge of her rib cage and looped up to the top of her spinal column, where the drug seeped out of a six-hole spout. All that was inside her now. A pound of hardware, maybe slightly more. And though she could feel a vague dulling of the pain in her arthritic elbow, the drug had almost no effect on her phantom pain, the searing burn in her legs and feet. The fire continued to boil her flesh every waking second without relief. Even in her sleep she could feel the nerve fibers smolder.

A few weeks back Greta had gotten to know Harry Crowell, a Desert Storm vet, a young black man who for years had been suffering from the effects of a brutal tank collision on the sands of Iraq. In the course of two years Harry had four back operations but was still in constant, racking pain. His condition was known as sympathetic dystrophy. His legs were bright crimson, viciously inflamed, the flesh peeling away in flakes as big as potato chips. The skin so agonizing to the touch that Harry spent all his waking hours propped on his bed, naked. Even the air moving against his flesh was a torment.

Greta had been in the treatment room when Bean Wilson met Harry the morning after his morphine pump had been installed and asked him if he was feeling any pain.

"Shit yeah, Doc, my legs still hurt like hell," Harry said. "Only now I don't care."

But Greta still cared. The morphine had not

changed that. In fact, she cared more than ever. They could flood her veins with any drug they wanted, it wouldn't matter. The fire was still raging in her legs, but she had converted it now. Turned the pain to fuel, powering her anger.

When her bowels were clear and she was cleaned up again, she took a deep breath, spent a moment analyzing the physics of her situation, then grabbed the lip of the sink and hauled herself forward until she toppled from the toilet seat. For a moment or two she sprawled on the cramped floor, her chin on the carpet just beyond the doorway. She gathered her breath again, pried herself up on her elbows, and started the slow, impossible crawl down the twenty-foot passageway toward the breezy darkness and the stars.

It took ten minutes, maybe fifteen, to make those six or seven steps. And ten more to scratch and scuff her way up the four stairs to the outer deck. By the time she was out in the night air, her right wrist was bleeding from a carpet nail and two of her fingernails were broken to the quick. But she was outside now and none of her pain mattered. The sparkling sky, the clank of distant halyards.

She scooted across the teak deck, stopped, looked around the cockpit, saw the white box against the transom wall. She crawled over to it, lifted the lid, pulled out one of the orange life jackets and wrestled into it.

Speeding up her pace, she crawled over to the starboard side, then, balancing on her senseless knees, she used a cleat to pull herself up to the gunwale.

A mile or two to the north was the ivory phosphorescence of Key West, and another half mile to the west was a scattering of lights out across the dark sea. Other boats at anchor, live-aboards, winter people waiting for the last possible second to head north.

Greta had been a better than average swimmer once. She'd done laps at the university pool one entire year when she was under the impression that boys found swimmers sexy. Her only hesitation in going overboard was the tide.

Many afternoons in the last six weeks she'd wheeled herself down to Mallory Square for the sunset carnival and she'd seen the big rollers the current sometimes produced at the mouth of the harbor. She was certain a changing tide could sweep even the strongest swimmer miles off course before it went slack again.

But there was no time to debate it, no time to gauge the lunar cycles. She had maybe half an hour before her pump drenched her spine again with morphine, and if she was in the water at the time, there was little chance she'd keep herself afloat. The hum would begin and in seconds Greta would sink into the chemical haze. Even the life jacket would not keep her face out of the water.

She dragged her body up to the wide teak gunwale and ducked beneath the chrome rail, took a look at the long drop, then looked out across the harbor, measuring her strength against that watery distance. Then she rolled herself overboard.

Only after she was floundering in the air did she realize she could no longer control her body well enough to dive. She dropped fast and clumsily, the water rushing up, and she landed with a vicious smack on her right side.

She must have sunk a dozen feet, and without the use of her legs she had to churn her arms furiously through the cool, black water, her lungs flaming as she dragged herself upward until finally she broke through to the delicious air.

Treading water, she gasped and splashed, felt the panic clench her gut.

Even with the life jacket, it was all she could do to keep her chin above the slapping sea. She rolled onto her back and it was a mild improvement. Greta hung there for a moment, then tried to swim. Never much of a backstroker, she windmilled vainly for a minute or two, then rolled back on her belly to check her progress. The big white cabin cruiser was still the same few feet behind her.

She took a long, deep drink of air, then on her stomach she began to swim. An Australian crawl, head high out of the water, her eyes locked on the shore.

Picking out a spit of land, a green lamp burning there, a place she'd decided was the closest spot, Greta focused, not letting herself think or feel, not letting herself count the minutes or try to add up how much time she had left before the pump switched on, just reaching out with her left hand, grabbing water, pulling it past her, reaching out with her right.

She swam and her legs trailed behind her. They did not hurt. Nothing hurt. She felt fine, swimming; Greta Masterson swimming to shore on a gorgeous subtropical night. No tide to contend with either, a mile or two, maybe slightly more. Difficult but not impossible, especially with her adrenal gland in hyperdrive. Swimming through the dark water without fear of sharks or barracuda or jellyfish, confident now, just feeling the good rhythm of her arms. Those arms and shoulders that were far stronger than they'd been before her fall. All the rehab work she'd done, the miles she'd put on her wheelchair, those strong arms picking up the slack of her legs. Strong, strong arms. Greta with one thought. Holding to that green light burning on the spit of land, finding a nice cadence in her stroke and her breath, keeping her head high. The water smooth. Thinking of Suzy. Her daughter. Suzy and the green light.

Then she heard the noise approaching from behind her, an outboard engine. And she stopped, swiveled to peer back into the dark at the rubber raft, a person standing up behind the console, swinging a flashlight back and forth before them. The yellow light washed over the water. One of those flashlights boaters used with half a million candlepower. A little patch of noon.

Panting hard, Greta turned back to the green light. She held her head up and resumed her stroke. Quieter now, careful to slice her arms neatly into the water, careful to dig as much water as possible past her with each pull. Fast but without splashing. She swam and saw the spotlight lay a path to her right, begin a sweep in her direction. Then it halted and swung the other way. She heard the outboard motor muttering closer.

One stroke after another, Greta swam as fast and noiselessly as she could. Figuring a backup plan. The closer she was to shore, the more likely someone was to hear her scream. She was cold inside, quiet, secure. The panic had burned itself out and now she was strong and fast, her arms powerful and warm and efficient.

She swam closer to shore, closer and closer as the inflatable zigzagged behind her, the spotlight straying close to her once or twice but missing her. She was maybe two hundred yards from the green light when she felt the quiet whir in her belly. The pulse of morphine had begun to move beneath her flesh, snaking back to her spinal canal. A minute, two minutes, no more than that until the dense cloud descended.

Greta focused on the shape of her stroke, made each one count. She could see the shadowy forms of people walking along the seawall. She would get a few yards closer, then use her last seconds to scream for help. A perfect stroke, another one, gliding across the surface of the black water, the dense aroma of seaweed all around her and the harsh rumble of a motorcycle accelerating up Duval. Greta's mind flooding with ethereal light.

But it was no motorcycle. And it was not the light of ecstasy.

It was the raft, the spotlight. She felt the vibration of the prop churning through the sea, was blinded by the half-million candles. She halted, treaded water, ducked her eyes away from the painful glare. Too breathless to scream, too drugged to lift her arms for another stroke.

The light switched off and a moment later a round life buoy splashed a yard in front of her. She hesitated a moment, but the morphine had begun to saturate her spine, and the muscles in her shoulders were melting. She nudged forward and hooked her arm through the buoy and a second later felt her body tugged back toward the raft.

"Nice night for a swim."

It wasn't Pepper. It was a man's voice. A voice she couldn't place. Not Bean Wilson's, she knew that much. Some stranger hearing her thrash across the bay, noticing her dire condition, had done what any good sailor would do. She was saved. Drawn back into the civilized world where laws ruled, where people of good will rescued others in danger. The world where good doctors could undo what bad doctors had done. She was alive. Drenched and weak, but safe.

The man hauled her close to the raft, then knelt at the edge, took hold of her armpits, and dragged her up over the rubber sides.

Greta flopped onto the floor of the raft and stared up at the stars. A million of them tonight, as if all the dirty layers of the atmosphere had been peeled away to reveal the heavens in splendid clarity.

"You need to see a doctor," the man said. "You look terrible."

The outboard roared to life and the raft swung in a wide arc and the wind was cold over Greta's wet surgical scrub. She lifted her head and scooted backward, propping her shoulders against the rubber sides. In the glow of the console lights she could barely make out the man's face. For a moment she couldn't put a name to him. Sure she knew the guy, but not certain which time, which place. The morphine swirling it all together.

"Good to see you again, Greta. I gotta say, for looking so bad, you look pretty good."

Yes, now she knew. It was that other life. Greta on two legs. Greta marching through the offices of the DEA on her way to meet her first supervisor. The remarks ricocheting around her as she walked. This one was the worst offender. Carlos Echeverria. "Hey, man, I want to work undercover with that broad. Strip search, strip search." Worse than an adolescent.

She stared at the tall, potbellied man, and she forgave him everything. None of that mattered. The insinuating looks, the salacious quips. Carlos Echeverria had saved her. Her colleague had pulled her from the dark sea of troubles and was whisking her back to safety. From this moment on the man had her unending permission to stare at her breasts.

"Jesus," she said. "Am I glad to see you."

Echeverria gave her the wolfish smile.

Greta pushed herself higher and looked out across the water.

"Brad's been real worried about you. He's got me searching all over Key West, talking to Greyhound bus drivers, see if they remember picking you up, people at the airport, taxi drivers. Even got me following the nurses from the pain clinic back to wherever they live, poking around in their houses. I mean, I been busting my ass trying to find you, Greta."

"They got me on drugs, Carlos. I need to get to a doctor quick."

"Tonight Brad's watching the doc's comings and goings. Got me doing the shit detail. Shadowing Pepper Tremaine, see what I might be able to dig up on her."

Greta swung around, got her bearings. They were headed out to sea.

"Where're we going?"

Carlos kept his hand on the throttle, rolling the chrome wheel to the right.

"Brad's very worked up over you, Greta. Not thinking too straight these days. Kind of strikes me as odd how involved he is in this case. Like maybe there's something personal going on here, something more than just a professional interest in your welfare. I've gotten that feeling."

"Carlos, what's happening? Where're we headed?"

He smiled at her, backing off on the throttle.

Then she saw the old wooden cabin cruiser looming in the dark.

Miss Begotten.

"Echeverria! Goddamn it, talk to me."

"Truth is, I been having some interesting personal thoughts about you myself. Remembering that week you started at DEA, how you were around the office, nose way up in the air, all haughty in those suits, Miss Ultra Professional. Well-pressed dark suits, but always careful to show just a teensy peek of cleavage. Which always struck me as odd. Like it's fine if you wanted to wave your nookie around in the air, get some mileage out of being sexy, but it wasn't fine for us to notice."

"What're you doing, Echeverria? What the fuck do you think you're doing?"

He drew the inflatable up to the rear platform of the cruiser.

"You women, it pisses me off sometimes how you get to have it both ways. You make a career out of wagging your goodies in our faces, but the second somebody takes the bait, makes a comment, a little friendly pat, hey, you're all righteous and insulted, yelling for the harassment squad to come nail our ass, like you hadn't just spent an hour before work getting your tits all set up so they look like they're about to spill out of your fucking blouse. I say that sucks. That's what I say. I say that's a fucking big-time double standard."

He idled close, cut the engine, then leaned out and lashed the starboard line to one of the cabin cruiser's stern cleats.

"Imagine my surprise," Echeverria said, turning back to her. "Pepper hands off the raft, I come tooling out here to spend a quiet evening of guard duty, and my captive is gone. Imagine my shock and dismay. Who would've thought in the time it takes to get a raft to shore and back, a cripple like you would've jumped ship and gotten halfway to land. Christ, was I ever crazed there for a second.

"I mean, the doc is already pissed at me, ready to cut off my rations. Two years, getting a nice steady retainer, all I have to do is alert him to any heat coming down from DEA, and then look what happened. Greta Masterson, working undercover for the big man himself. Jesus, the very thing I'm supposed to keep from happening. And if it hadn't been for your sweet little old mother, we would never have known."

"What about my mother?"

"She called. Looking for her little girl. The call got routed to me. Now, there's a lucky twist of fate, wouldn't you say, Greta? Fucking lucky indeed. Otherwise, today we'd all be out of a job."

"This won't work, Carlos. Brad's going to find me. You know he will. The best thing you could do right now is take me to shore. Maybe Brad can find some way to keep this off your record."

"Best thing you could do right now, Greta, my girl, is shut the fuck up."

With the raft rocking in a mild swell, Echeverria wobbled over to the side and stepped across to the dive platform.

"Now you scoot over here, young lady. I'll get you dried off and into a new nightie. If you're good, I'll read you a bedtime story. And if you're real, real good, well, I might even introduce you to the frightful hog I keep in my shorts."

Grinning, Echeverria leaned over the side of the raft for her and Greta pivoted on the floor, swung herself up as high as she could manage, and screamed, then screamed again, aiming her voice at the nearest lights, a sailboat several hundred yards to the east.

And though her voice was ripped apart by the breeze and blew in useless tatters out across the dark harbor, she continued to scream until his heavy hand clamped over her lips and he wrenched her backward and pulled her up into his meaty arms.

While Greta continued to warn and threaten him, Echeverria carried her onto the boat and maneuvered her down the narrow passage to her cabin. He lay her on the bunk and stood above her staring at her breasts.

"You're in enough trouble already, Echeverria. Get it out of your mind. It isn't going to happen."

"Sure it is," Echeverria said. He reached out and ran his fingers over the damp fabric of her surgical scrub, outlining her right breast. She slapped his hand away. "All right, then," he said. And he cocked his arm and clipped her hard against the temple.

In a black dazzle, she pushed herself upright and tried to jab him in the groin, but he easily swatted her groggy punch away.

"It's gonna happen, Greta. Fight all you want, it just makes me harder."

For a moment she stared into the twisted fire of his eyes. Then she lay back on the mattress. The morphine had begun to work, drawing her down into its humid chemical embrace. She closed her eyes and watched a thousand tiny stars explode in the black sky.

CHAPTER

14

Key West had never been Thorn's idea of paradise. Going there was always problematic, like visiting a black sheep uncle. Some charming bachelor who leered at all the ladies and their daughters and had a long history of sophomoric pranks. A fascinating but vulgar man, who only children and lunatics adored because somehow they managed to overlook his dark self-loathing and saw only his exuberant hijinks.

There was always something new and gorgeous missing from Key West, some landmark drenched in history destroyed by the very men who should have been its staunchest guardians. It was a town that flaunted its obsessions, exaggerated and mocked every craze it embraced. Its endless celebration of the perverse was tiresome and shallow. Even its most exquisite parts were flawed, as more and more of the stately Victorian mansions that made up the island's charming core suffered from the dry rot of absentee ownership. Some eccentric tycoon's fourth home, closed up for eleven and a half months of the year.

Yet despite all that, despite the tawdry vendors, the throbbing all-night bars, the steady onslaught of bulldozers, rapacious politicians, the endless supply of grabbers and takers, the island still had a powerful allure. Its blend of watery light and cinnamon breezes, its banyan-shaded streets clogged with clunky bicycles and rented mopeds and red Harley choppers piloted by grandmothers in bikinis, its iguanas with diamond chokers, its happy, raunchy, thumb-in-your-eye parade of goofiness always cheered Thorn, gave him hope that the string of islands he called home, at least for a little while longer, had not been tamed.

With only a quick stop in Key Largo to pick up his gym bag of clothes, Bean junior and Thorn made it all the way to Key West before noon. Bean drove with nervous care, as if he wasn't used to handling the large red hearse with white leather seats—a car in such gaudy bad taste that almost anywhere else but the Florida Keys it would have drawn whoops of ridicule.

For much of the three-and-a-half-hour drive, Bean gave a long and detailed summary of the decades since their boyhood days. Thorn asking just enough questions to keep Bean moving ahead. Relieved to sink away into the shape and texture of someone else's life.

Lonely prep school days in Vermont, homesick for the tropical Keys, followed by a grueling four years as a premed major at Harvard and a tour in Vietnam, where he was an intelligence officer. After Bean was badly wounded he was sent to rehab in Bethesda. When he was back on his feet, he returned to Harvard to attend med school. After a stint at Johns Hopkins, he spent the next fifteen years working as an anesthesiologist, bouncing from operating room to operating room around Florida, until just a couple of years ago he'd hooked up with the VA system and now was developing a specialty in the treatment of chronic pain.

Never married, though he'd been close a couple of times, once during med school, once in Orlando. Though these days he considered himself wedded to his career. No time for a social life. And Key West was hardly the best place for a man like him to find an acceptable spouse. He'd only come there because the VA hospital was looking for a head anesthesiologist and he'd been between jobs at the time.

But even after three hours of information, numerous anecdotes about his fiancées, the family backgrounds of his college roommates, the Asian cities he'd visited on R and R, Thorn felt curiously uninformed. As if Bean had given the emotionally sanitized version of his history, a carefully edited concoction that kept the real man safely hidden.

"And you?" Bean junior said as they were cruising down Roosevelt Boulevard, Key West's burger and fries thoroughfare. "How'd you spend the last thirty?"

"Short version or the long one?"

"The long one, of course."

"Fishing," Thorn said. "And tying flies."

Bean junior smiled.

"Ah, yes. The simple life."

"I try."

Thorn was wearing a pair of khaki shorts and a dark green button-down. Once again Bean was dressed in a studiously casual style with drapey white trousers and what looked like a silk T-shirt.

"You're too much, you know that, Thorn? So full of shit."

"You're not the first to notice."

Bean's lips twitched as he wheeled the red hearse sharply into the parking lot of a Jet Ski rental shop and jerked to a stop. He swiveled in his seat, a flush rising into his cheeks. He seemed to be trying hard to swallow back the words that were forming in his mouth.

"Fishing, tying flies. Yeah, right."

"What is it, Bean? What's the problem?"

"No problem." He turned back to the steering wheel, reached for the ignition key, then halted and looked across at Thorn.

"You don't think I've heard about all the shit you've been into?"

Thorn was silent, watching Bean try to fight off the anger, his mouth working like a man chewing taffy for the first time. He sat back in his seat, took a deep breath, but it was no use, the rage was boiling up into his throat.

"You think Dad doesn't tell me every detail he hears about you? Caught this bad guy, brought him to jail, risked your life to save this person or that one. I heard it all, Thorn, every goddamn particular. If you wake up with a sore throat, I know it by noon. You sneeze, I grab for the Kleenex.

"And you sit there, still coming on like you did when we were kids. Mr. Walden Pond. Big-time bird-watcher, student of the clouds, on a first-name basis with every goddamn fish in the sea. Never grew up, not a care in the world. Well, screw that, Thorn, don't try to con me. You might be able to pull that off with your cute young girlfriend. Maybe she buys that Mr. Natural happy horseshit, but it doesn't fool me. I've had my nose rubbed in your life for the last thirty years. And all those years our parents hung out together, who'd they talk about? Who was the kid who got all the airtime? Well, it wasn't me, Thorn. I'll tell you that. It wasn't fucking Bean Wilson, Junior, no sir."

Thorn watched a barefoot young woman in torn

jeans and a red bikini top approaching along the dusty shoulder of the road.

"You been saving that up for a while."

"You're goddamn right I have."

"Well, now you're rid of it."

"If only it were that easy."

"Maybe you should drop me off at the bus station. I can catch a ride back up to Key Largo. This doesn't look like such a great idea."

Bean sat back in his seat and stared ahead out the windshield. The young woman had jet-black hair, which she wore as short as Monica's. She looked like a runaway who'd traveled a few miles too far and had used up the last of her bread crumbs days ago. Thorn felt the cold knot harden in his gut. He was hearing an echo of his words to Monica last night. The bitter tang of them still on his lips. Telling the woman he loved that he didn't love her.

The traffic roared past on Roosevelt, and Thorn looked over at Bean, watched him concentrate on taking a breath and then another one. The anger still glittered in his eyes, but as he continued to breathe carefully, the veins in his temple subsided, the flush drained from his cheeks.

"All right," he said finally, turning back to Thorn. "Look, I'm sorry. I apologize for going off like that. I've got a lot of hostility floating around inside me. But it wasn't fair to unload on you. I'm sorry."

"Listen, Bean, the only goddamn reason I'm here right now is because you and your dad convinced me there was some hope I could get better down here. But if you're as pissed off at me as it sounds, then I sure as hell don't see any reason I should stay. I can find a rehab place in Miami."

"Hey, I said I'm sorry. Really, I apologize. I have a lot of stored-up shit. It's not your fault. I'm not angry with you. I just get all twisted up inside and things fly out of my mouth."

Thorn watched the young woman hesitating a few yards away, sizing up the situation.

"Can you forgive me, Thorn?"

Thorn blew out a breath.

"Sure," he said. "It's okay. Forget it."

The young woman approached Thorn's window. She stooped down and mouthed some words through the glass, then rubbed a hungry hand across her belly. Her face and arms were covered with raw patches, as though she'd been dragged along the highway behind somebody's car.

"You got a dollar? All I have is my last twenty."

But Bean didn't seem to hear. He reached for the ignition key and Thorn saw his hand stutter in the air. Then he stiffened and sucked in a loud breath, fumbled the keys and they spilled to the floor. While Thorn stared, Bean's back went rigid and his face crumpled as if some harsh spark of voltage had just shot up his spine.

"Hey, you okay?"

Bean tried to speak, but he bit the word in half as he lurched forward and slammed his forehead into the steering wheel. Thorn grabbed for his shoulder.

"Bean. Hey, what the hell!"

Small barks of torment came from deep in his throat. Panting hard, he seemed to gain control for a moment and lifted his head from the wheel, blood seeping from a cut at his hairline.

Then it took him again, harder this time. It seemed to clutch him by the front of his shirt and shake him from side to side. Bean gasped, yelped as he tore the seat belt loose, and swung around toward Thorn, moving with the fury of a man on fire. Shivering violently, he flattened his back against his door and took hold of his right knee and wrenched the leg up and smacked down his heavy white tennis shoe in Thorn's lap.

"Leg," he groaned. "Rub it. Leg."

Quickly Thorn rolled Bean's pants leg up. He reached out, but his hands froze in the air.

Gold rivets ran up Bean's shinline. The leg was made of white plastic.

"Rub it, goddamn you. Rub the fucking thing!"

Thorn gripped the plastic, cold and unyielding, and began to massage.

Grinding the back of his head against his window, Bean clenched his eyes against the welling tears while a series of small wet whimpers escaped from his throat. At the window the girl stood transfixed, watching Thorn knead the hard, white, artificial leg.

"Hold still, damn it," Pepper said.

Pepper and Tran van Hung were standing in the bathroom in front of the mirror, both of them naked. Pepper was applying chocolate lip liner to Tran's narrow mouth. When she was done she was going to fill it in with a dark chocolate shade with plum undertones. Very chic, the cosmetics girl at Sears had told her.

She had the bathroom shade open for the light. A gorgeous view out the Bahama shutters—the patio and central gardens of the Marquesa Hotel, a big coconut palm with its fronds trickling in the breeze, rich tourists lazing glamorously around the beautiful pool. Best hotel in Key West, she'd been told, and she believed it now.

"I look like a geisha girl," Tran said.

"No, you don't. You look fine. Now hold still."

"Geisha girls are okay," Tran said. "That was a compliment."

"You men don't know how hard it is. You think we just look this way without any work. But hell, you've got to get a steady hand, got to know all kinds of things about complementing your coloring, adjusting your skin tones, shading, about foundation and blush and highlighters and contours. A woman's got to be a goddamn artist just to get by."

"You're pretty any way. Paint or no paint."

"It'd be easier," Pepper said, "if you and me had the same skin tones. But you're more a deep autumn color and I'm warm autumn. You got bronze tones, olive, and I'm more ivory and beige. If I were doing you for real, I'd have to go out and buy cinnamon blush. But you'll just have to settle for my salmon."

She held his chin in her hand while she finished outlining his lips.

Working on her own face in the mirror was so damn hard, she'd thought maybe if she experimented on Tran, tried a few things, she could get a little control over her hands and things would go easier in the future.

Tran was willing. He was never pushy or shy like most men. If Pepper wanted to do something, fine, he'd go along no matter what it was. Not like the boys she was used to dating, guys who always had to be in control. She wasn't sure how old Tran was. Maybe a few years younger than she, maybe thirty years older. In bed Tran was as limber as boiled linguini, double-jointed, maybe even triple. The things he could do, Christ, a regular contortionist.

"When you finish, I will kiss you all over with my new lips."

Pepper laughed. She was never sure if Tran was trying to be funny or not, but he made her laugh a lot. She couldn't even tell if he was smiling or scowling. Reading his face was like trying to read a turtle's. His mouth hardly moved, even when he talked.

"Do you find me inscrutable, Pepper?"

"What?"

"Inscrutable," Tran said. "It is how Westerners sometimes characterize Asians."

"No," Pepper said. "I find you very scrutable."

Tran laughed and tilted his head for a kiss.

"Shall we have sex again now?"

"No," Pepper said. "I'm sore. No sex until tomorrow. At least."

"Soar, like a bird?" Tran smiled. His English was as good as hers. Maybe better. He'd learned it in school, then got a lot of practice using it during the war.

"Sore like hurt," Pepper said.

"I will make you soar like a bird. We can fly together to the moon."

Pepper laughed again.

"If you marry me, pretty Pepper, I'll make you laugh every day. Every hour."

"I'm not marrying you, Tran. I got my sights set on something else."

She finished filling in his lips, wiped off a couple of smeared places, then she started on his eyes.

"You want to marry the doctor. I know. Have blond children."

"Yes, that's right. Lots of blond children."

"The doctor's a bad man. He kills people."

"Hey," Pepper said. "He's doing it 'cause you're paying him to."

"I'm paying him to develop the drug, not to kill people."

"He doesn't mean to kill them. He's trying to do good. It just doesn't always turn out right."

"If you marry me, I'll make you a rich woman. I'll buy you all the blond children you want. I know where to get them cheap."

"You're not my type."

"And what's your type?"

"I like blond hair, blue eyes, the way the doctor dresses."

"Blond is just a color. I have money, charm, an education. That's more important than color, don't you think?"

"I like blond."

"You think I'm ugly? You don't like Oriental men?"

"You're very handsome, Tran. Just hold still, don't blink till I finish this."

Tran watched Pepper in the mirror as she brushed on the metallic eyeshadow, a champagne color with mossy-green highlights.

"You think if you put these colors on your face, the doctor will marry you?"

"I'm not some dimwit. I don't think that. No. I'm just trying to catch up, is all. I didn't have a mother or sisters showing me how this makeup stuff works. No girlfriends. Just boys, and generally they don't know eyeshadow from mullet chum. So I'm educating myself, that's all."

"I like you the way you are, right out of the shower."

"Aren't you sweet." She stepped back and peered at Tran's eyes. She'd drawn the eyeshadow out too wide.

He looked like some kind of bird you'd see on a travel show.

"Anyway, it's the women I'm worried about, Tran, not the men. The wives of the other doctors, like the ones I used to talk to over at the hospital. Bunch of snooty ladies. But if I'm going to be Bean's wife, I'm going to have to entertain those ladies and their husbands, and go over to their houses and talk to them at parties, formal dinners. Women notice this makeup shit. They judge you. They whisper about you if you're using the wrong colors. Putting on your blush too heavy. Women will eat you alive, Tran, if your nails clash with your lips. So I damn well gotta get this right."

Pepper worked in silence, dabbing the eyeshadow back into shape. She reshaped Tran's eyebrows with her liner pencil, gave them a thicker look. Then went to work on his lashes, coiling them out, lengthening them with her teensy Estée Lauder mascara comb.

She stepped back from him, turned him away from the mirror toward the window light.

"How do I look? Good enough to eat?"

"You look ridiculous."

Tran examined himself in the mirror.

"Yes," he said. "I look like a drag queen with a terminal disease."

Tran's hair was so short and close to his skull, it looked painted on. He had a very good body. Trim and limber. The sex was the best she'd ever had. He'd found some places on her body she'd never known existed. He knew how to turn her inside out. Tran swung away from the mirror and stared at her.

"Maybe you should try painting the doctor's face, see how good he looks."

"He'd never sit still for something like that."

"That's my point exactly. I'm good to you. The doctor isn't."

"It's no use," she said. "I'll never learn this stuff."

Tran turned on the water in the sink and scooped up a handful and started rubbing his face clean. Pepper stared out the window at the women lying around the pool. Even from that far away she could see that most of them knew more about the fine art of makeup than she ever would.

Tran was staring at her when she looked back. He shook his head.

"I don't like Dr. Bean Wilson."

"You're just jealous, Tran."

"I saved his life in Vietnam, and this is how he repays me."

"You didn't save his life. You were the enemy."

"No, no. I worked with the South Vietnamese. I was assigned to Bean Wilson, helping him with his translations. When he was injured, I was the one who found him. I carried him back up the hill during an artillery barrage. I won a medal for it. And now this is how Bean treats me. Brings me all this way with promises. Arranges for my company to loan him money for his project, but refuses to discuss the details of his experiments. Tries to conceal from me that he is killing people."

"You saved Bean Wilson's life?"

"That's a true story, yes. He was bleeding to death."

"Wow. You were a war hero."

"But I will tell you this much. If that man fucks up one more time, he's finished. No more money, no more work. I'll go back to Vietnam. Deal's off. My people are not happy with all the fuckups."

"He's getting close. Don't worry about it."

"One more fuckup, I'm going home. You should know this, Pepper. The next one works, or I'm going back."

"You like Key West. What's your hurry?"

"Key West is okay. But the doctor has already spent a great deal of cash. Next time or else."

"Oh, it'll work next time. He's just got to get the proportions of the ingredients right."

"You got more *habanero*?"

"I got one more in my purse, I think."

"Rub it on me. I have a pain in my weenie."

Pepper had taught him the word. She'd told him *weenie* was the dirtiest utterance in the English language. Right up there with *motherfuck*. Tran had a weakness for dirty words.

Pepper followed Tran back into the bedroom. He lay his body lengthwise across the bed, his heavy penis flopping across his left thigh.

Pepper got the #15 scalpel and the last *habanero* out of her purse. She stood over Tran and watched his expression tense as she cut the chili in two and then stooped over him to smear one half, then the other, up and down the length of his organ.

"You're so good, Pepper," he said, his eyes beginning to water. "I'll marry you and make you a very rich girl. Give you rich blond babies. All the babies you want. Take you back to my country, you'll be a queen there. Big tall woman like you."

"I'm spoken for."

"I'll take care of you. You can buy all the lip liner you want. Every color on earth."

She rubbed the chili up and back, up and back, careful to smear the acid juice onto the soft round head, giving him pain and soothing him at the same time. That miraculous power of chili peppers.

Tran closed his eyes and moaned.

Bean was gripping the steering wheel fiercely with both hands, his arms locked straight, shoving his back hard against the seat like an astronaut struggling against staggering g-forces. He stared directly ahead out the windshield. In front of the Jet Ski shop the girl was sitting at a picnic table. She was staring at the car, not sure what she'd just seen. Some radical new form of Key West perversity. A few feet away the traffic clamored along Roosevelt. It was a bright, airless day. A few whiskery clouds were crawling up the western sky.

"What was that? A seizure?"

Bean filled his lungs slowly. His voice was hoarse.

"That, Thorn, was a little telegram from hell. It goes by the incredible misnomer 'phantom pain.' "

"You lost your leg in the war?"

Bean turned his head and looked at Thorn.

"Both legs."

"Jesus, I'm sorry. I didn't know."

"How would you?"

Bean gave a rueful chuckle and swept a hand through his hair.

"I get angry or upset, it seems to set off an episode."

"Christ, it scared the shit out of me."

"It's the only damn thing that works, having somebody rub my prosthesis. It's crazy. Makes no logical sense, I know. But it works. Fools the brain somehow."

"Phantom pain. I don't know anything about it."

"You will," Bean said. "Everybody in the clinic has it to some degree or another. Amputees, paraplegics. You'll be the only one that doesn't."

"Oh, joy."

The blond girl sitting at the picnic table was talking to a guy with long tangled hair and a bedroll roped to his back. Just hitched into town. He was rolling her a smoke, smiling, talking. The girl brushed her bangs off her forehead and listened to his rap.

Bean bent forward to pick up the ignition key from the floor. And he stayed down there, craning his head up to peer at the underside of the dash.

"What the hell?"

Thorn twisted forward and saw the row of silver toggle switches Bean was looking at.

Bean nudged one of them and a small electric motor sounded and the rear of the hearse began to tilt upward. Thorn slid a few inches forward on the leather seat, then caught himself with a hand against the glove box.

"Goddamn, Pepper," Bean said. "Redneck bitch."

Bean flipped the switch again, and with a groan of gears the car leveled back out. He tried another toggle and the front end of that big car suddenly launched a yard up into the air and slammed back down.

"Holy shit!"

"That idiot," Bean said. "That fucking cracker."

Thorn looked over at the two drifters who'd been watching from the safety of the picnic table. They were on their feet now, getting the hell back up the highway. Key West was turning out to be a little too weird for fainthearted folks like them.

CHAPTER

15

"I know what's going on, Monica. I figured it out. About the dolphins."

Saturday noonish, Roy Everly was hovering over her desk in a red, green, and yellow flowered shirt. Enough material to cover two couches. White tennis shorts and a pair of unlaced work boots without socks. The other four members of the *Key Largo News* staff had stopped what they were doing to listen. Minnie Johnson, the owner and official grande dame of gossip for the island; Jimmy Bob Johnson, her gay son, the managing editor; and Sally and Steve Marcus, the husband-and-wife reporting team who regularly reminded anyone who'd listen that they were way too professional for such a small-town rag. Monica could imagine the headlines next week. ROY EVERLY SEEN WEARING SHIRT. A major scoop by Key Largo standards.

"I'm really not interested, Roy. I'm sorry, but I'm not the person you should be talking to."

"I'm interested," Sally Marcus said.

"Fuck you, lady."

"What!"

Roy swung toward the Marcuses.

"You goddamn people—a bunch of leeches and hye- nas. Fucking journalists, you write ten words, five of them are lies, the other five are factually wrong. If Jesus Christ gave you an interview you'd find some way to make him sound like a goddamn moron or else a crook. So just stay the fuck away from me."

"Hey," Steve Marcus said. "Who the hell do you think you are?"

"Maybe we should go outside, Roy," Monica said.

Monica led Roy around the Marcuses' desk to the front door. She smiled back at their matching scowls.

"Want to borrow my steno pad, Monica?" called Jimmy Bob.

She shut the door behind them and Roy followed her over to the picnic table in the shade of a jacaranda. The traffic boomed on US 1, people squealing in and out of the Winn-Dixie shopping center across the road. Monica looked over at the small white *Key Largo News* building and saw Minnie peering out her office win- dow as if she were going to attempt some lipreading.

"I know why they tortured the dolphins before they killed them."

"Sit down, Roy. Relax."

"I didn't know who else to tell."

"Have you been drinking, Roy?"

"I've been at the computer for the last two days, running through databases, posting queries on bulle- tin boards all over the Internet, shooting E-mail to peo- ple I know. This morning, I put it all together. I haven't had time for a goddamn drink."

Steve Marcus came out the front door and glanced over, shook out a cigarette, lit it, and blew his first plume of smoke in their direction.

"It's about endorphins," Roy said. "The spines, the brains, the torture. It's all about endorphins."

"Slow down, Roy. Please. I'll listen. You can walk me through it. But calm down."

Roy took a deep breath and straddled the wooden bench across from her. He bowed his head and ran his finger through the groove of a heart someone had gouged into the wood long ago. Two sets of initials linked inside the heart.

"I kept going over and over it. Spines and brains. Torture. It didn't make any sense. The torture sounds like crazies. The mess they made, all that hacking and slicing, blood everywhere, that looks like somebody was high on drugs, some kind of fucking maniac. But that was all a cover. The hacking came first. Then cutting them into small pieces came after they were finished."

"How do you know that?"

"Whoever killed my dolphins knew exactly what they were doing, exactly what they wanted. It's not easy breaking open the cranial cavity of a dolphin. And they had to do some very careful, very precise surgery to get the entire spinal column out."

Monica's gaze strayed across the highway. Mothers and their children rolling shopping carts across the asphalt lot toward the grocery. The weekly errands, the endless cycle of routine. A world anchored in comforting regularity.

"Dolphins produce endorphins just like people do," Roy said.

"Endorphins. The runner's high."

"Runner's high, yeah. Endorphins are the body's pain suppression chemical. You hammer a thumb, the adrenal gland secretes some into the bloodstream. You keep hammering the same thumb, more endorphins spurt out. That's what the fuckers were doing. They were torturing the dolphins, cutting on them, hurting them so they'd produce maximum quantities of endorphins. Much more potent than human beta-endorphin. Same chemical structure up to a point, but much more powerful. It's because the average dolphin is exposed to a lot more pain second by second, day after day, than human beings are. They need a better pain suppression system. From what I've read so far, human beta-endorphin versus dolphin's is like the difference between aspirin and morphine.''

''I don't see it, Roy. Somebody mutilated the dolphins, why does it have to be about endorphins, of all things?''

''Because they took the spines and brains. The two body parts that would be saturated in endorphins after the animals were tortured. That's the connection.''

''That's quite a leap.''

''The more they cut, the more endorphins produced. They cut, they wait, they cut some more, then when they're pretty sure they've maxed out, they kill the animals and remove the spines and brains. I've talked to people, Monica. People I've met on the 'Net, on the phone, experts, people that've spent their whole lives studying dolphins. I've thrown out this scenario and asked what possible logical connection there could be between torture and brains and spines. Everyone is stumped. I get nothing but silence for the last couple of days, then some fifteen-year-old kid in Seattle E-mails me, he's figured it out. Just that one word in his message. *Endorphins*. And bang, I knew he was right. That's the only thing that makes any sense.''

''What about random chaos?''

''This wasn't random.''

"Just because they took the brains and spines?"

"No," Roy said. He stared over at Steve Marcus. The man had finished his cigarette but was still standing on the porch, glaring in their direction.

"Go on, Roy."

"It's happened before. This same exact situation. Three times before. Once up in Orlando, one time in north Florida, a little dolphin center near Jacksonville, and once over in St. Pete. Somebody broke into their dolphin tanks, tortured and killed a few dolphins, harvested their spines and brains. Chopped them up in pieces afterward. Identical scenario."

The sun was printing the shadow of Monica's head on the table. She looked down at it, her dark other half. The side of her that had wanted to go on another road trip, take another stab at reinventing herself. The side she probably should have listened to.

"Where'd you find all this out? About the other dolphins."

"Database," he said. "All the newspapers and magazines in America. I did a word search, typed in *dolphin* plus *slaughter* and those three articles popped up. I got on the phone, called the places, talked to a couple of the owners. Two went out of business right after it happened, the other one finally got hold of some cast-off navy dolphins and that place is up and running again. All of them said the same thing. Tortured and killed."

"Why hasn't anybody else seen the same pattern?"

"Who would? And even if they did, who would care?"

She looked over at Steve Marcus, and trilled her fingers at him. He swung around and stalked back into the newspaper building.

"A journalist," she said. "How come a newspaper person didn't pick up on this?"

"If one of them thought they could win a prize or get a raise from writing about some little tourist dolphin place, they'd do it. Or if one of the Kennedys was involved somehow. But hey, fucking journalists don't get a lot of points for writing about the Roy Everlys of the world."

"Okay, let's say it's so. Just for the sake of argument. Then who the hell would want dolphin endorphins? What for?"

"Drug company, maybe. Someplace with scientists who know their way around a chemistry lab, looking for a cure for something. They send some lowlife out to get their raw ingredients. They can't get legal permission to trap and kill dolphins for their experiments, so they go where the dolphins are easy to steal."

"I don't know, Roy. Even if all that were true, how the hell would you find out who's doing it?"

"I got my feelers out. I should hear something the next couple of days."

"What kind of feelers?"

"Don't worry about it, Monica. This is my problem. I'm sorry I even came over here, bothered you with it. I just thought Thorn might want to know. That when you see him you could pass it on to him."

He started to stand, but Monica put her hand on his and he settled back onto the bench.

"You're being cautious, aren't you, Roy?"

"Sure I am."

"All this stuff on the Internet, thrashing around in public like that."

"Hey, Monica. I'm no dummy. I've been playing with computers since before you were born. I can talk to people all over the world and stay anonymous. Don't worry about it."

She stared out at the traffic.

"I don't like it. Somebody who'd kill dolphins like that, they aren't going to take kindly to some guy sniffing their trail. They hear you gaining on them, they could turn around, shoot you through the heart."

"Hey, let 'em shoot. What the fuck do I care?"

"Roy."

"It's not like I'm putting it up on a billboard, Monica. But I need to talk to specialists. I'm using my connections to find out what research companies might be doing work in that area, have some interest in that kind of drug. That's all. Harmless as that. Last piece of the puzzle."

"Maybe you should be talking to the police."

"A couple more days, I'll hear back from my contacts. If they know of any research going on out there, dolphins and endorphins, then I'll talk to the cops. Give them something solid, not a lot of speculation. So don't worry. I'm being very circumspect. I've thought this through. Only people I called were the ones I've already worked with a lot. People I know, friends, like."

"Who?"

"That professor at FIU and Dr. Wilson down in Key West. They're closer to the hard science end of things than I am. They study the research, know who's doing what with dolphins; they deal with the drug companies all the time. One of them'll come up with something, I'm sure of it."

"Just be careful, Roy. Promise me you won't take any chances."

"You worry too much, Monica. You're the one needs to calm down."

She stared at her shadow.

"Yeah, you're right," she said. "You're absolutely right."

CHAPTER

16

After Thorn stowed his clothes in his stark and gloomy room on the first floor of the pain clinic, he took the one-man elevator up to the third floor. Bean was waiting for him when the doors slid back to reveal a spacious and sunny set of rooms. Bean had rinsed his face, slicked back his thick blond hair, and put a small bandage on the cut on his forehead. Once again he had the scrubbed and well-tended look of prep school aristocracy. He'd changed into a fresh white polo shirt and faded jeans, and wore the same tennis shoes he'd had on earlier.

"I'm afraid you'll be displeased with your accommodations after you've seen mine. But actually it was more a question of money than pampering myself. I began restoring the house from the top down. Funds simply haven't permitted finishing the work. I've had to devote a good deal of my own capital to getting the clinic up and running."

His oak floors were freshly refinished and glowed golden. There were window seats in several of the windows, the cushions upholstered in lush tropical prints, Oriental rugs and simple furniture fashioned out of thick planks of pine. Over the windows were gauzy white drapes that swayed in the breeze and gave the light a soft and faintly luxurious feel. But it was the photographs on the walls that dominated the room.

There must have been over a hundred framed black-and-white snapshots. Some had been blown up to more prominent sizes, but most were the blurry five-by-nines of ancient Kodak box cameras. And as Thorn rolled forward into the room he saw his own face everywhere. He and young Bean together.

Thorn and Bean in a skiff that had long ago rotted; Thorn and Bean at thirteen or fourteen, their snorkels and masks cocked up on their foreheads, both holding up matching lobsters while they treaded water miles offshore; Thorn and Bean scooched down in a pair of rattan chairs, with their heads bent over Hardy Boys mysteries. Another shot of the two boys shirtless with cutoff jeans hanging low on their hips as they wrestled atop a sand dune, a prairie of sea oats waving behind them.

Thorn circled the room and felt the soft, dizzy swirl of his boyhood arrayed before him, a hundred vivid moments in the sun. A hundred plucks on the tight string in his chest. Moments he barely recalled, the film in his own memory bleached to white. But here it was, the complete and unabridged edition of Thorn and Bean. The boys on water skis pulled in tandem behind Bean senior's old teak runabout. Another shot of them proudly holding up fish, Thorn's yellowtail a few inches smaller than Bean's hog snapper. Another crisp and sunny shot of Bean standing next to a hefty sailfish hanging at the docks at Bud and Mary's. A smiling Thorn on the other side of the fish, gripping the gaff he'd used to help land Bean's fish.

A hundred blinks of time framed and glassed in and pickled in silver—preserved far better than Thorn's brain had saved them. But as he stared at each of the photographs, the scene beyond the frames glimmered to life. Other friends, Thorn's adoptive parents, Bean's mother and father, all of them cropped out of this specialized collection. It was as though Bean and Thorn had lived alone on some desert island of boyhood, undisturbed by adults or rival chums. Bean and Thorn, Bean and Thorn. Two blond boys who wore the uniform of the Keys' perpetual summertime, torn shorts, shoeless, their bare backs and shoulders burned coffee dark, hair scorched and tousled. At ten or eleven the two of them had nearly identical bodies, but as time passed in the photographs on the wall, Thorn's body bulked up while Bean stayed slim and sinewy. Bean had never been a team-sport man. He had no use for weights and running, skipping rope, isometrics, the hundred grueling high school exertions Thorn's coaches had demanded. Thorn's muscles ripened, gaining at least twenty pounds on Bean as the photographs aged.

At the end of the exhibition on the far wall near the kitchen, there were a few shots in color. The boys were not grinning so readily anymore, a somber distance taking shape between them. There was one of Thorn and Bean about to race the length of Doc Wilson's saltwater pool. Bean with his long lean frame cocked, toes curled over the lip of the pool, setting up for his racing dive, while behind him Thorn aped for the camera, pretending to be about to shove Bean into the water. Bean won that race. As Thorn recalled, Bean had won most of the things they'd competed in. Serious and focused. Determined to prove his athletic skills were the equals of Thorn's or any of his friends who had embraced the silly theatrics of high school sports. And Bean was right. Developed in isolation, cultivated on his own, Bean's strength and speed and agility in all things physical was daunting. But what was absent from those last snapshots, missing in Bean's face and in the rapport between the two of them—in fact, what had started to quietly disappear from Bean's demeanor long before those final color snapshots, was any clear sense of pleasure in the moment. Thorn could see it now, see it with the stark clarity of thirty years' distance —Bean Wilson had always been deadly serious about his fun, and for him, Thorn was never as much a friend as a rival.

"You probably don't remember most of these."

"This is weird, Bean. This is very weird."

"It's what Dad did instead of parenting. He took photographs. I believe he thought the two of us were brothers."

Bean offered Thorn a drink, which he declined. He was looking at one of the final color shots, the summer before Bean went off to that New England private school. The two of them were target shooting at a range in a palmetto scrub field that was now the parking lot of a Publix grocery store. Bean had been a poor shot. It was the only sporting endeavor he didn't excel in. Something about the noise, the kick of the pistol, the anticipation of that violent blast made him wince at the trigger pull, send his shot high again and again. Or maybe it was what he pictured down range, the target's concentric circles coalescing into some familiar face he could not bear to fire upon.

"By all outward signs," Bean said, "we had a fairly happy childhood. I look at these photographs and in a second I can travel back there. I'm on that skiff, on that sand dune. It's all still very alive for me."

Thorn nodded.

"Having the photographs on the wall seems to preserve it. My youth isn't gone. I don't have to grieve, be nostalgic, any of that. It's all right there, black and white, flesh and blood. None of it lost. I know that sounds demented, but I've found it's important to keep that time alive somehow. It's the golden place I go back to when things seem overwhelmingly bleak in the here and now."

"We had some fun."

"But then we had some pain as well, I suppose."

"Yes. There's always that."

Thorn rolled himself into a patch of sun, looked out the west window into the luminescent green depths of a banyan tree.

"You know a little about pain, don't you, Thorn?"

"I've been to the dentist," he said. "If that's what you mean."

"Now you're doing it again. You're treating me like I don't know you. Like my father hasn't been sharing every medical emergency you've suffered for the last twenty years. No, no, Thorn. I know about every cut, every gunshot, each of your concussions. I know how many stitches you've had. You have some considerable experience with pain. Don't pretend otherwise."

"How many is it? Stitches."

"A hundred and five at last count."

Thorn shook his head, staring across at Bean. After a few moments he said, "Sure, I've been hurt a few times. I don't know that I've learned anything very important from it."

"Okay, that's good. That's better."

Bean eased himself down onto the couch and rubbed at his knees.

"I didn't realize it years ago when I started out in medicine, but that's always been my interest, my driving concern. The study of pain."

Thorn rolled away from the window and looked over at Bean. He was gazing across at the photograph of the two boys target shooting.

"What I came to learn, at least medically, is that pain treatment is an incredibly complex area to master," he said. "Partly because there's no meter you can use to register someone's pain, no X-rays. All we have is the patient's own descriptions. We give them questionnaires. It's called the McGill test. Circle one, two, three, or four. Does your pain flicker, shoot, stab, crush, scald, or sting? Is it a temporal sensation, a spatial one; is it a puncture, an incisive pressure; is it thermal or does it have brightness?"

"Gotta say the right word before you get the right shot."

"Exactly," Bean said. "That's the problem. You need people to tell you what they're feeling, describe it accurately. And you need for them to tell the truth. Naturally, you'd think they would do that willingly. They're in pain, they should want help. But you'd be surprised how many people, even those in acute distress, will underplay what they're feeling. As if they're ashamed of it. Or that by trivializing it, they've diminished its power over them."

"Stiff upper lip."

"Well, that's part of it. But the other part is that people simply have different thresholds, different attitudes toward their pain. Generational differences, regional ones too. Our parents are more likely to deny their pain than we are, and if they're from northern Europe, they deny it even more. Mediterranean cultures have lower thresholds, Scandinavians have higher. An Italian will cringe at a needle prick. A Brit or Swede is more likely to take a serious wound without much outward show of distress. Put two people side by side, what's tolerable to one can be unbearable to the other.

"Christ, there are even cultures where women practice couvade, in which the female in childbirth shows virtually no sign of distress. She will work in the fields until the onset of labor, then give birth and be back in the fields in the afternoon. While she's delivering her child, her husband crawls into a bed nearby and screams and moans as though he is in great pain while his wife bears the child. Then after the delivery the man will stay in bed with the newborn to recover while the wife goes back to her manual labor.

"For these women, pain simply doesn't play the same role in their experience as the childbirth pain of an American woman. All of which suggests that pain is at least as psychological as it is physical."

"What isn't?" Thorn said.

Through the bedroom door he could see an oak chest of drawers, and lying on the rug beside it were two prosthetic legs with white tennis shoes fixed on the feet. His extra pair.

"Every generation has different attitudes toward pain," Bean said. "Ours, for instance, has been incredibly spoiled. Pampered and protected, coddled. We've had it so goddamn easy, most of us. Nothing like the stresses and physical discomfort of our grandparents' era. Add to that the fact that our generation also learned a great deal about drugs, discovered there are some pretty good sensations available with the right ones. Some pleasures. We're not as frightened of drugs as our parents were, or their parents. We're a watershed generation in that sense. We've experimented and found there are a whole host of virtues to chemically induced experiences, and the risk of addiction is not nearly as great as we'd been warned. We've smoked our share of dope and not gotten hooked, so our suspicion of drugs in general has been mitigated by that knowledge.

"But the big difference between us and all the generations before us is that we don't accept pain as a given. We don't see it as character building. Enduring pain doesn't make you a richer human being, a wiser one. We don't even see it as particularly useful for alerting us to the seriousness of an illness. Most of us don't put any value in pain at all. It's purely an aberration, a wrong turn off the highway of happiness and pleasure."

Thorn watched a squirrel pick its way through the branches outside the window, halting and moving ahead with nervous bursts. He was carrying something in his mouth, some ruby-colored morsel of garbage he'd scrounged down on the earth. An anxious twitch of his tail as he hauled the bounty back to the nest. A strawberry.

"Think of it, Thorn. A cavity filled without Novocain. A headache that doesn't stop until it's run its course. And every generation before our parents— thousands of years of human life on this planet without any real relief from the agony of broken bones, war wounds, rotten teeth, the daily savagery and brutality of primitive life. Oh, yes, the ancient Greeks had their salicylic acid, a mild aspirin. They made it from the bark of willow trees, as did Native Americans, and they had alcohol and an array of root teas and grass beers. They had opium and cannabis. But it's only been within our lifetime that we've made any real progress in anesthesia. Nitrous oxide—laughing gas, for godsakes. Ether, chloroform. Like using sledgehammers to put a patient out.

"It's a breakthrough time. We're on the threshold of amazing discoveries. Drugs with morphine's clout but without its side effects, electrical stimulation of the spine to interrupt the pain messaging system, spinal implants, a whole new class of antidepressants that can diminish nerve-damage pain. An incredible array of new drugs. And all of this because you and I, Thorn, we don't like to feel bad. We stub a toe and reach for the Tylenol. We wake up with a twinge in our back and we're screaming for a pill, something that will make the world all peachy and perfect again."

Outside the window the squirrel with the berry had stopped, its body hunched awkwardly. As Thorn watched, a flurry of feathers and wings surrounded the squirrel and was gone. The red berry with it. The squirrel rubbed a paw across its face and hurried on.

"That's what's going on, Thorn. That's what I'm a part of. Creating a new world, a world with no pain."

"Sounds like a dreary place. Everybody stoned, smiling at the sun."

Bean smiled tolerantly.

"Oh, yes," he said. "There is that school of thought, that you only know pleasure by contrasting it with pain. Like pain is some kind of exotic spice that makes the stew taste better. But that's idiotic. That's the nonsense of someone who doesn't know chronic pain. Pain that's unremitting."

"Like yours."

"Yes, like mine. I have no legs, but my legs hurt like hell. They hurt every second of every day. The only variation is when they flare up like they did earlier. That's not some minced garlic that flavors the meal. That *is* the meal, Thorn. Second by second, hour by hour, day after day, the legs I no longer have are broiling incessantly."

"And with all these brave new drugs," Thorn said, "there's nothing that helps your pain?"

"That's exactly what I'm working on," he said. "A medication, a cure."

"Well, well, well."

"People with phantom limb pain are not exactly the largest constituency out there. The work being done on finding remedies is practically nonexistent. So I'm contributing what I can, in my own meager way. It may sound selfish to focus my energies on the very condition I suffer from, but Thorn, the truth is, if I were to make a serious dent in my own condition, then there's no pain out there that's not within my reach. None. Chronic, acute, cancer pain, you name it."

Thorn looked out at the oak branch. A monarch butterfly staggering through the breeze landed on the trunk, hesitated a moment, then dragged its feet through the damp remains of the strawberry.

"So what happened in the war, Bean? I know your college roommate's name, but I didn't hear about 'Nam. A big gap there."

"You don't want to know."

"I can see it was bad."

"Listen, Thorn." Bean leaned forward, a sudden sneer twisting his lips. "Just because you've lost the use of your legs, that doesn't make us equals. We're not going to sit around the campfire, swap war stories."

"All right. Fine."

Bean bowed his head, rubbed his face as if trying to rouse himself from sleep. When he tipped his head back up, his mouth was set in a rigid smile.

"I'm sorry," he said. "I keep flying off, don't I?"

"Yes, you do. You're wired pretty tight."

"You want to hear about the war, okay, I'll tell you about the war, but you'll have to get me drunk enough first."

"I suppose I should just shut up and be grateful," Thorn said. "I'm paralyzed, but at least there's no pain."

"Oh, there will be in time," Bean said. "Count on it, my friend."

Thorn held his eye.

"What does that mean?"

Bean shrugged, and broke away from Thorn's stare.

"There's no pretty way to put it," he said. "Long-term, if your condition doesn't improve, there's a high probability of serious and permanent nerve damage. Some very intense discomfort."

"That's the first I've heard of that."

"Dad was coddling you. He couldn't bear to let you know what's in store."

Thorn tried a chuckle but it sounded more like a strangled snort.

"Hell, I should've stayed in bed that night."

Bean brushed some invisible crumbs off his lap.

"But brave Thorn had to defend his castle and his fair maiden."

"The dog was growling. I did what anybody would do."

"And? Have you figured it out? Who was out there, what they wanted? Who did this to you?"

He was peering into Thorn's eyes, intense and prying, as if searching for the boy in the photograph, the kid he'd wrestled down those dunes.

"At the moment," Thorn said, "I don't give two shits who did this or why. I just want to do whatever I can to get my legs working."

Bean sighed and clapped his dry palms together, then pushed himself to his feet.

"Yes, well, then, I suppose we should get started, shouldn't we?"

Thorn nodded. His gaze wandered again to the photographs. To those two blond kids at play in a world that no longer existed, two kids with the asinine confidence of youth, boys who thought their summer sun would never set.

C H A P T E R

17

As they were leaving his apartment, the phone rang. Bean apologized and took the call in the kitchen, his voice going quiet, listening mostly, and when he returned to the room his mouth flickered between a scowl and a smile, as if he was having trouble selecting which mood to counterfeit.

"Well, let's get you going, Thorn. Can't have those fine muscular legs of yours atrophy any more than they have already."

Bean Wilson followed Thorn down to the first floor, rolled him out to the sunporch, introduced him to the other mangled residents, then left him there. Something had come up, a situation he needed to take care of.

None of the other cripples was particularly curious about Thorn. Nobody asked him any questions. Just a couple of nods. Ginny, a paraplegic with shortish blond hair; Hardy Jones, who was missing both legs; Pepper Tremaine, the head nurse. A couple of others whose names he didn't catch.

On three sides of the sunporch there were jalousie windows that looked out on an untidy side yard. A couple of small oaks were choked with vines and beyond them was a ragged hedge. The grass had not been mowed for months and there were several mattresses and broken pieces of furniture piled up next to a small ramshackle building that looked like a one-seat outhouse. If medical centers could be condemned for bad landscaping, the Eaton Street clinic should've been out of business long ago.

But inside the rehab room, all the equipment was new and well maintained, and the room was full of the expensive whirs and nicely meshing hums that only the latest Japanese machinery seemed to produce. Several Nautilus machines, four sets of waist-high parallel bars, what looked like a double-wide massage table, and several other pieces of highly polished equipment Thorn couldn't identify. The room had the feel of a high-tech torture chamber and there was a sour bite in the air that tasted like the sweat of frightened animals.

Pepper wore a blue smock and white pants and silver running shoes. She was tall and had the sunken cheeks and rawboned limbs of a coal miner's wife. A woman brawny enough to sling a bushel of potatoes over one shoulder and Thorn over the other and tote them both a few miles up the highway if the whim took her.

"A little exercise?" Pepper motioned at the large table.

"Sure," he said. "I came all this way."

Using a wood slat that looked like a sawed-off fraternity paddle, she showed Thorn how to lever himself out of his chair and onto the table. It took a half dozen fumbling attempts before he could manage the move with a minimum of help from Pepper, and by then the muscles in his arms were quivering on the verge of failure.

Once Thorn was on the table, Pepper rearranged his
useless legs and settled him flat on his back, then began to push his knees up toward his chest, first one
then the other, pumping them as though he were riding a bike a few sizes too small. Thorn watched his legs
work—a brisk ride around the park—his strong,
healthy appendages pushing the speedometer up to
twenty miles an hour while Thorn felt nothing except a
small rhythmic jarring in his belly.

After fifteen minutes he was light-headed and
drenched with sweat. Pepper lay his legs flat and suggested he rest for a while, then maybe he could consider taking a turn on the walking course. It was a blue
foam mat twenty feet long with a harness suspended
from a pulley system in the ceiling. Pepper helped
Thorn resettle in his wheelchair, where he watched
Ginny try the course, twisting and cursing as she struggled to muscle the aluminum walker ahead.

"Just happened, huh?"

Hardy Jones drew his wheelchair up next to Thorn's
as he watched Ginny inch down the mat. Hardy's chair
had flame decals on the side, an old raccoon tail hanging limply from one of the grips. All he needed was an
ah-ooo-ga horn.

The man's wiry black hair was liberally flecked with
gray and was gathered into a ponytail. He had on white
fingerless gloves and a weight belt cinched at his waist.
His gray T-shirt had a Marine Corps logo stamped on
the breast and the sleeves were torn away to reveal his
massive arms. On the smooth ends of both his stumps
were crude tattoos that had the look of jailhouse art. A
naked Oriental woman on the right stump, a blond
and buxom beauty on the left.

"Your legs," Hardy said. "You just got gorked."

"Gorked?"

"Paralyzed."

"Yeah," Thorn said. "Wednesday. Gorked."

"You haven't withered yet, but that'll happen pretty quick. A month, two months, you'll be a bone man before you know it. One of the happy skeletons."

He looked into Hardy's faded green eyes. Thorn was tired. Irritable from the long car ride, from the pain lecture, from sitting in that goddamn chair.

"Let me tell you something, friend, you can get the freaking nurses to manipulate your legs from now till the apocalypse, your muscles are still going to disappear. Only thing that'll do you any good is the upper body shit. Got to build up your lats and triceps so you can haul your broken ass around. Work the bars, man, that's the only way. Lots of dips and chins. That's all you fucking got anymore is your arms. Sooner you get your head wrapped around that, the better off you'll be. All you are is arms."

"I'm focusing on the legs."

"You are, are you?"

"The doctors don't know what's wrong with me. There's a good chance I'll be walking again soon."

The man grinned.

"Sure thing, partner. Whatever you say."

"They looked at the MRIs, all the X-rays, they don't see anything wrong. It may just be a short-term thing. Bruised spinal cord or something."

"That's the bullshit now, is it? Their new motivational tool? A short-term thing."

Thorn stared at the man. Something lurched in Thorn's chest, a heavy weight tipped off its shelf, started to sink into the mush of his gut. He'd been believing completely in his recovery. Not his usual skeptical self. Wanting so badly to buy into Doc Wilson's happy story of his future.

"Hardy Jones," the man said, putting out his hand, "101st Airborne. Out of Ft. Campbell, Kentucky. Screaming Eagles."

"Thorn," he said. "Out of Key Largo." He shook the man's iron paw.

"Don't believe a word of the shit they tell you. Good, bad. Don't believe any of it. Only thing that's true is what's happening to you right now."

"Okay."

"Where were you based in 'Nam?"

"I wasn't," Thorn said.

"Germany?"

Thorn shook his head.

"Then you're one of the lucky fucks did your tour stateside."

"None of the above."

"Well, you're not old enough for Korea." Hardy backed his wheelchair away to get a different angle on Thorn. "What? Desert Storm?"

"I'm a civilian."

"Civilian?"

"That's right."

"What about 'Nam?"

"Missed it entirely."

"Missed it? What the fuck does that mean?"

"I wasn't invited."

"The fuck you weren't. Everyone was invited."

Thorn watched Ginny rock her upper body back and forth until she got enough momentum to nudge the walker forward a couple of inches. She gave herself an ironic cheer.

"Hey, Ginny. We got us a fucking draft dodger."

Hardy rolled another foot away from Thorn, as if the stench were getting to him. "Burned his goddamn draft card, went off to Woodstock to party with his fellow pussies instead of serving his country. One of those."

With a groan, Ginny sank into the grip of the harness. There were tears in her eyes and she had soaked through her dark T-shirt and bike shorts.

"What're you doing here, draft dodger?" Hardy said. "This place is vets only."

"I'm a friend of the doc's."

"Hear that, Ginny? Our boy Thorn is a draft-dodging pinko peacenik friend of the doc's. That supposed to cut some ice with us, is it?"

"Give it up, Hardy. Fucking war's over."

"No, ma'am. Maybe the one you were in is over. But that other fucking war isn't ever going to be over."

"Don't listen to him, Thorn. He's just a broken-down old asshole. Pisses his bedsheets every night."

Hardy swung his chair around to face her.

"Shut up, Ginny."

"Suck my shorts."

"You goddamn slut. Somebody needs to weld that fucking sarcastic mouth of yours shut once and for all."

"Yeah? Well, come on and try it, needle-dick."

Hardy started for her, and Thorn snapped out a hand and yanked his black ponytail and held on. The man halted, backed up till the pressure was off his hair. Thorn let go and Hardy wheeled himself slowly around.

"Okay, draft dodger," he said. "You want to play, hey, let's do it."

"Just leave the woman alone."

"That's no woman. That's Ginny, queen of the sluts."

"That what they taught you in the 101st, is it? Insult women, knock them around? Skilled warrior like you."

Little strands of muscles winked in Hardy's shoulders as he gripped his armrests.

"You want a bite of my ass, draft dodger? Well, come on."

Hardy cocked his body forward and shot an open-handed slap at the side of Thorn's face. Thorn brushed it off into space.

Hardy grinned.

"Well, well. We got us some martial arts training, do we? Spent a few hours in the gym, paid his money to learn the secrets of the Orient."

"I don't want to fight you, Hardy."

"Course you don't. 'Cause you're a pussy. 'Cause you're a fucking draft-card-burning faggot. 'Cause your country club kung fu isn't worth shit in the real world. Come on, baby, Hardy'll show you a little of what you missed out on. Little basic training exercise."

His next shot was a closed fist, short and hard, aimed at Thorn's chin. He was quick but wild, and Thorn got just enough of his forearm in the way to redirect the punch, taking the glancing shock on the side of his skull.

His eyes went blurry. He backed away a foot. Hardy was breathing fast already. He smiled at Thorn, then torqued himself forward and rammed his footplates into the spokes of Thorn's chair, nearly threw him onto his side. The muscular man wheeled himself backward to make another ram, when Pepper took hold of his chair and put the brakes on.

He swiveled around and cursed her, but Pepper just smiled and held on against his exertion.

"That's enough, boys," Pepper said. "I don't want to have to mop up any blood. End of my shift, time to go home, don't be making any extra work for Pepper now, you hear what I'm saying?"

Hardy glared at Thorn, his arms rippling as he tried to haul himself forward.

"You need to work on that left hand," Thorn said, "if you ever want to hurt anybody."

He wheeled past Hardy, out through the TV room. He rolled onto the front porch, took a few seconds to find his breath, then aimed himself down the wooden ramp and let his chair coast out into the sweltering streets of Key West.

He spent the next hour rolling down Duval and back up Whitehead, reminding himself why he loved and hated this town. The sky was a perfect blend of perfect blues, the temperature in the low eighties, a breeze swept off the water and filtered through the maze of old wood houses and picked up the scents of fried fish and black beans, garlic and rotting meat. The shops were busy, the sidewalks brisk. The windows were full of bright frivolous things only people on vacation would consider buying.

After an hour working his way to the Southernmost Point and halfway back down Whitehead, the muscles in Thorn's arms were cramping. And he still wasn't used to the perspective, moving along at the height of a three-year-old, belt-buckle level. Several times he'd almost been trampled by groups of giddy tourists, all those legs and torsos churning toward him, parting at the last second, a scowl for the idiot in the chair.

He never imagined that sitting down could be so

exhausting. Fighting his way through the steady on-slaught, the bombardment of faces and clothes and stray bits of conversation, the bus fumes and blare of revving hot rods, the endless push and nudge of the crowds, the small potholes in the sidewalk that seemed like impossible canyons. Or maybe what was tiring Thorn so badly were all the pitying looks he was get-ting, the flustered glances, strangers dodging eye con-tact as though the terrible stroke of luck that put him in that wheelchair might be contagious.

On a couple of intersections along Whitehead the city planners had failed to provide cement ramps for people in his condition, and Thorn had to test the laws of physics, easing himself over the enormity of a three-inch drop from sidewalk to street level, then jacking himself over the same dangerous hump on the other side. If it hadn't been for two passing Samaritans he would have tumbled onto his face both times.

With only the twenty-dollar bill in his pocket, he had no idea how he would sustain himself for any length of time in Key West, but by midafternoon all he could think of was drinking as much beer as the twenty would buy.

He cut back over to Duval and selected the first bar he could find whose floor was near sidewalk level, a dark and smoky joint near the corner of Fleming, and cranked himself over to a vacant table by the front win-dow.

A young man wearing a leather vest over his hairless chest marched across to Thorn's table and Thorn or-dered a beer.

"I'm not your waiter, I'm the manager."

There were pimples on his chest and his eyes were yellowed at the edges. He kept standing there staring at Thorn, mouth twitching as if his vocal cords were sending up sounds his lips refused to transmit.

"There a problem?"

"We're not really set up for wheelchairs."

"How's that?"

"The bathroom's downstairs, two steps, no ramp."

"You asking me to leave?"

"I got nothing against cripples, you understand. It's just, you know, sitting here, at the front like this . . . You know what I'm saying."

"It's a bummer, huh? Puts a shadow on the festive mood? Well, that's too goddamn bad, 'cause I'm staying."

"Ah, fuck it," the guy said and stalked back to his station to spread his charm to the next lucky customer.

Thorn's waitress showed up in a while and he ordered a three-dollar Budweiser. After he'd downed it, he was about to leave to search out a cheaper spot when a young woman with straight brown hair down to the middle of her back walked into the bar wearing pink shorts and a white halter top and passed by his table, then swung back around, gave him a regulation happy face and asked if she could join him.

"Only if you buy," he said.

"I saw you sitting there. You looked so lonely."

Thorn tried to return her smile, but he could see by her puzzled look that his smiling apparatus was malfunctioning. He let his mouth go slack.

"I would be honored and thrilled if you'd join me," Thorn said.

The girl had blue eyes and large white teeth and was attractive in a standard sort of way, as if she'd dropped off the end of a pretty girl assembly line, one of ten thousand identical units produced during the month of June twenty-three years earlier. After she had a sip of what she told Thorn was her fifth margarita of the afternoon, she said her name was Bonnie and that she'd decided Thorn should be fully informed about each of the courses she had just completed in her first semester of law school at Emory. Five courses, only one in which she'd gotten less than an A.

Under normal circumstances Thorn would've strangled the young woman right then and stuffed her body under the table and marched out of there, but on that day, in his condition, he was immeasurably grateful for the dull static of her presence. The law student seemed to be unaware of his wheelchair hidden beneath the tabletop. She seemed to have no idea his legs were dead. She didn't get sorrowful and sympathetic and adjust her speech accordingly. She was simply and resolutely full of youthful pep and mindless ardor for her scholarly life. She talked to Thorn as if he were whole, as if when they were finished talking they would walk off to resume their happy lives in the healthy normalcy of America. And he cherished her for that. Cherished her for her obliviousness, for the next two hours of vapid babble.

As she talked, Thorn watched the manager making his rounds, barking orders at the waitresses, hovering behind them as they served their drinks, stepping in to rearrange the glasses an inch this way or that, or to set down a forgotten coaster. As he circled the room the guy helped himself on the sly to drinks left on abandoned tables. Thorn watched him sneak down the dregs of two beers and a whiskey sour.

When Bonnie finally decided she must be on her way, it was late afternoon and most of the bar's tourist trade had swarmed off to Mallory Square for the sunset silliness. Thorn finished the last of his beer without her.

He could feel the pressure in his external bladder; the plastic bag strapped around his waist was tight, probably about to overflow. He looked around and smiled at the man paying the check at the table next to him, then waited till that gang had cleared out before he unzipped himself beneath the table, whisked one of Bonnie's margarita glasses out of sight, and refilled it with his own frothy elixir. He half-filled his beer glass too, a parting gift for his thirsty host, and with a pleasant nod to the bare-chested manager, Thorn rolled out onto the sidewalk and headed back toward the clinic.

He was an hour past tipsy and for the next block he coasted along, blissfully unaware of his paralysis. The muscles in his arm had recovered, and now he simply stroked his wheelchair forward with the effortless ease of a man long accustomed to such conveyance.

Just as he was about to cross Eaton, he saw the man coming toward him. Shambling along in dark pants, white shirt, shiny black shoes. Tall, with that potbelly shaped like the helmet of a Hun. Thorn backed away from the curb and stared at the man. He knew he was drunk, knew the heavy doses of steroids he'd been getting had heated his blood to a feverish boil, but he would have recognized that man through the thickest haze.

Just to be double certain, he set a red baseball cap on the man's head, tipped it down low, then pressed the aviator sunglasses with the gold frames against his eyes. It was a perfect fit.

As if Thorn might need more proof, at that moment the man stepped out into Eaton and dug his thumbnail

between his two front teeth and gouged loose a parti-
cle of food and flicked it into the street.

The man from the dolphin pools was crossing the
intersection of Eaton and Duval, coming directly
toward him, and following a half step behind, in a pair
of neatly pressed blue Bermudas and a yellow tennis
shirt, was old Doc Wilson's good friend, Brad Madison.

CHAPTER

18

"You're drunk."

"Damn right," Thorn said. "You would be too."

"I guess I would be," Brad said. "Christ, I'm sorry, Thorn. What's happened to you, it's a terrible thing."

"Yeah, tell me about it."

They were sitting in the rooftop bar at the La Concha Hotel. Tallest building in downtown Key West, a three-sixty view of the island and surrounding waters. From up there you could keep tabs on the great wall of condos and hotels that had almost finished circling the island, the same wall of concrete that was moving mile by mile to ring the entire state, blocking the water from the riffraff. Soon, if they wanted to walk the beaches of their state, they'd damn well have to rent a two-hundred-dollar room for the privilege.

Thorn was nursing a tall frosted glass of seltzer water. Across the small round table, the man named Echeverria was munching the second of three cherries from his cherry Coke. Behind him the sunset was a major disappointment. Mostly grays, just a single horizontal band of red along the horizon, which was slowly dissolving into a purple splotch. A sunburned woman at the table next to them had given the sunset a C minus. She said she was going to ask for her money back. From whom? one of her tablemates asked. From God, she said. And there was a round of dizzy laughter.

"I just got off the cell phone with Doc Wilson," Brad said. "He told me what happened to you. Must've gone down right after I saw you the other day."

"That same night," Thorn said. "A prowler."

Echeverria had big hands, long thick fingers, nails chewed to the quick. His cheeks were spiderwebbed with tiny veins and his jowls had the loose and oily look of a man who had not been eating his vegetables. He seemed monumentally uninterested in Thorn, and his small eyes kept moving around the outdoor bar as if he were awaiting the arrival of a very hot date.

"When we saw you come out of the clinic in the wheelchair, I was stunned. So I called Wilson to find out what was going on."

"You saw me come out of the clinic?"

"We have it under surveillance," growled Echeverria, his eyes following the hypnotic gait of one of the waitresses.

"What is this?" Thorn said.

"Maybe we should wait till he's sobered up." Echeverria sucked the last of the cherries off the stem, dropped the stem on the floor.

"We're in a bad situation here, Thorn."

"He's drunk, Brad. Guy can barely keep his chin off his chest."

Thorn turned his head and stared into Echeverria's eyes.

"I may be drunk," he said. "But I know who you are, asshole."

"What?"

"I know who you are and what you've been doing," Thorn said. "I just don't know why yet. But I will."

"What the fuck're you talking about, you wacko? I've never seen you before in my life."

"Thorn?" Brad reached across the table and gripped his arm. "Hey, what the hell is this?"

Thorn kept his hold on Echeverria's eyes until the big man tried to swallow away the lump of worry growing in his throat, then Thorn broke off and turned to Brad.

"Sorry," he said. "Must be these drugs. I'm getting twitchy, all the shit they've been pumping into me."

He looked back at Echeverria and smiled.

"This guy's out of it, Brad. Forget him."

"Thorn, listen. We could use your help. We're in a very difficult posture at the moment, and just by the sheerest piece of luck you're in a position, you could be an enormous assistance. I have to get up to Washington tonight for a meeting I absolutely can't miss. But Carlos is staying here at the Casa Marina Hotel. He'll be acting as your contact until Tuesday when I can get back down."

"My contact? You're getting a little ahead of yourself, aren't you?"

Thorn took a sip of his seltzer. He was dead sober. Give him a white line to tightrope. Order him to close his eyes, touch a finger to his nose. Hell, he could build a house of cards standing on one hand, count backward from ten thousand. Every time he took another look at Echeverria he got a few degrees more sober.

"Look, Thorn," Brad said. "I'm not going to plead with you, but we need some eyes and ears inside that clinic. And we need them bad. You could do it. Doc Wilson told me about some of the things you've been into in the past. I think you're just what we need."

"I'm still listening."

He smiled again at Echeverria. He liked smiling at the man. It was the most fun he'd had in months, smiling at the guy that had something to do with slaughtering the Key Largo dolphins. And it wasn't too much of a stretch to guess he might also be smiling at a guy who also had a little something to do with putting him in that aluminum chair.

"It's a long story," Brad said.

"If you're buying the seltzer," Thorn said, "I've got the time."

Ten minutes later Thorn was fully informed of the situation and he was more sober than he'd been in years. A woman named Greta Masterson was missing. She was a DEA agent and had been investigating Dr. Bean Wilson, Jr., for possible diversion of narcotics. All this was an off-the-books DEA operation. Brad had wanted to protect Doc Wilson's son from a major scandal, possibly losing his license. If the suspicions proved true, he'd been planning to sit down with Bean, lay out the evidence, maybe bring Bean senior in on it, shame the boy into going straight. It had sounded easy, humane. The right thing to do. But then Greta disappeared. And now it was at a whole different level of seriousness.

"What do you think, Thorn? Will you help us, be our eyes and ears? Talk to Bean, see if something he says might give us a direction."

Thorn sat back in his chair and looked around the outdoor bar. The woman who'd wanted her money back from God had left too soon, missing an off-the-chart sunset.

Half the sky had ripened to a flawless crimson that was only produced when sufficient pollution was floating in the atmosphere, enough to absorb the blander wavelengths. Unmuted by blues and yellows, that brilliant cherry light had stolen up from the sea and seemed to be blistering the air.

Thorn had spent much of his life on the sunset side of Key Largo and had watched the sky light up over Blackwater Sound for so many years that by now he had as many words for red as Eskimos had for snow. But the best sunsets were more than color, they were topographic displays, three-dimensional maps of the heavenly terrain. And that night's clouds were a wild collection—a dozen shapes and textures set against the backdrop of scarlet corrugations like some gigantic plowed field of blood that reached high overhead and faded off to the north and south into purplish clumps of ripe bougainvillea blossoms. Along the horizon a few scarlet barracuda were schooling among the twists and swirls of vaporous crimson coral fans. There were patches here and there with the texture of crushed velvet, and other swatches as slick and glossy as puddles of oil paint. It was the kind of sunset Monica and he would stare at wordlessly. Daunting and huge and impossible to absorb.

Echeverria glanced at the sky and looked away. Brad turned his eyes that way and took a breath and let it go as if it were the first time he'd remembered to breathe that day.

"Sure, I'll help you," Thorn said, turning his grin on Echeverria. "If it means I get to hang with my old pal here."

He lay a hand on Echeverria's and the big man jerked away from his touch.

While Thorn continued to beam at Echeverria, Brad thanked him. After a few minutes of strained silence, Brad paid the check, shook Thorn's hand, told him that they'd be in touch, to just keep his eyes open, don't go snooping, don't bring up Greta's name, anything like that. Thorn said sure, he could be tactful, no need to worry about him. A last grin for his pal, the dolphin killer. And the two men left him there with the fizzless remains of his seltzer.

When they were gone, Thorn looked back at the sky, still rippling with rosy light, and the harp string that was strung tight through the center of his chest plucked itself and a triple note, deep and resonant, thrummed through his gut. Monica.

He had spent the day not thinking about her. He had been doing a damn good job of it. It was something he'd trained at for a long, long while. Blocking out difficult thoughts, holding emotions at bay. It was one of his great talents. Olympic-class repressor. A necessary ability for a man who cycled through women at the rate he'd been doing lately.

Although, of course, his were always serious relationships. Only a handful of one-night hoot-and-hollers. It was how he preserved his self-respect, how he'd made the saga work on his behalf, a tragic tale of Thorn's failed attempts at love. Always something tripping him up. Some boomerang sailing in from offstage upsetting his best intentions. And that's what had happened with Monica as well. A crack on the head, a crack on the spine, and he'd martyred himself to this new condition, told her good-bye, kissed her off.

But he didn't believe it for a second. Get enough booze circling his veins and the *veritas* was impossible to ignore. The only boomerangs doing any damage in Thorn's life were the ones he'd tossed himself. Maybe there was some fraction of random chaos in the events of any moment, but not enough to let anybody off the hook. The undoing of his affair with Monica was his own doing. There were no quarks or radio waves or pulsars beaming down from some control booth out in the dark heavens. Thorn had thrown the curved wood into the air and it had spun and tilted and looped back to knock him in the spine.

He'd punched Dingo the body builder. But Dingo was no boomerang, no midnight prowler. He was the kind who sailed off in his own peculiar trajectory of self-absorption. By now he was in a gym somewhere studying his body in the full-length mirror, pumping the barbells, perfecting the symmetry of his grotesque physique. The memory of Thorn, just one more goad.

Thorn had a sip of his dead seltzer and set it down on the glass-top table. The sunset watchers had gone. Now it was only Thorn and the serious drunks. A lot of *veritas* floating around that rooftop.

If he had it right and the world was truly stitched together with a million cobweb threads, and every jiggle here caused a jaggle there, every hop and skip produced somewhere along the network of entanglements a mirror duplicate skip and hop, then Thorn had only himself to blame for anything that happened. He'd done this to himself, paralyzed his own body because he'd tripped the tripwire that he himself had hidden in the grass. He had asked Doc Bean to look into the connection between torturing dolphins and their brains and spines and later that night the boomerang he'd sailed into the atmosphere spun back and gorked him. Doc Wilson had called his son and told him of Thorn's questions, and that same night Thorn was attacked.

Goddamn Bean, with his half a body and his lifelong hurt and his obsessive photographs. Those snapshots lining his walls told a far more bitter story than the one Thorn remembered from their shared youth. But that's the way it went. No matter how bound together two people were, no matter how many shared afternoons and mornings and midnights there were between them, every memory was edited by the heart. Each snapshot pasted on the endless walls of memory was cropped and tinted and arranged in an order that tried to tell their private story, make some small sense of their chaos and hurt.

"Anything else?" the Jamaican waiter asked him.

"I need to get her back."

"What?"

"A woman," Thorn said. "I told her I didn't love her, but I do."

The waiter looked at him for a moment.

"Well, then," he said. "She's got every right to despise and revile you."

"Yes, she does."

"What you need to do, you need to fall on your worthless knees and beg her to forgive you. Tell her you love her madly. You always loved her. And for once in your puny, worthless life, you should mean it."

Thorn looked out at the darkening sky.

"Thanks."

"Can I get you anything else?" the waiter asked him.

"No," Thorn said. "I believe I have everything."

"Right on, brother."

Thorn watched the darkness eat away at the edges of the sunset until the rooftop bar was nearly empty and the sky was completely drained of light.

CHAPTER

19

An hour past midnight, Pepper was driving the hearse north on US 1. The black sky out over the water pulsed with strokes of lightning as they passed through Sugarloaf Key, heading back up to Key Largo—Pepper and her favorite traveling companion, the tall guy with the belly. Finally took his sunglasses off and his baseball cap, showed her his bald head, and finally told her his name. Echeverria.

"What is that, Cuban?"

"It's Basque."

"What the hell's that?"

"In the north of Spain, industrial. Basques are the supermen of Spaniards."

"You're a superman?"

"I can be," he said. "If the situation arises."

"I had a Cuban boyfriend once," she said. "Only way he'd have sex was from behind. Didn't want to look at me. Now, what kind of thing is that, you're making love with a guy, he can't stand to see your face."

"I don't like women who talk like that."

"Like what?"

"Dirty. Gutter shit."

"I don't care if you like me or not. I was making conversation. We're in the car together like this, it kills the time driving along. We got two hours, and what, we're supposed to look out the window the whole time? Whistle songs?"

"Did you like it when he fucked you from behind?"

"I liked it fine."

"Then what're you complaining about?"

"It's not normal. The guy didn't like kissing or anything from the front. I couldn't even suck him. I never met a guy didn't like getting sucked. Except this Cuban."

Echeverria looked out his window. She thought she saw a bulge growing in his pants. For a guy who didn't like girls who talked dirty, he seemed to be liking her just fine.

Pepper had never considered herself highly sexed. Just a normal woman, normal appetites. But in the month she'd spent hanging out with Tran van Hung she'd gotten seriously revved. Tran wanted it all the time, day, night, afternoon, standing up, in the shower, slopping around in the tub, in the car, at restaurant bathrooms. Soon as he finished one session, he was looking for a way to start the next. And Pepper must've caught the fever. The way the guy wrapped himself around her until she couldn't tell them apart, she'd be looking at an arm or a leg in the dark while they were humping and would have to reach out and pinch it to see if it was hers or his. A couple of snakes.

"So what do you know about this guy Thorn?"

"Thorn?"

She glanced over at him.

"Yeah, you know anything about him?"

"Not much," Pepper said. "He's some kind of old friend of Bean's or something. Apparently he just had a nasty accident."

"Well, if you ask me," Echeverria said, "it wasn't nasty enough."

"How do you mean?"

"I met him this afternoon, it was like he recognized me from somewhere. Going after me like he knew something he shouldn't."

"A trained professional like you," Pepper said. "Hard to imagine anybody'd have any dirt on you."

"I don't like it," Echeverria said. "It's too cute. The doc brings this guy into the clinic, knowing he's been snooping around about the dolphin thing. It's like some bullshit spy movie. Trying to be too clever, buddy up to your enemy. So now Brad Madison recruits this guy to sniff around with the other patients. Does that bother Bean? Not a bit. Now the doc gets the bright idea he can feed Brad info through Thorn, send him off in the wrong direction. Tell him Greta was having a fling with one of the vets, some crap like that. They ran off together. Another bullshit story stacked on top of a Leaning Tower of Bullshit. But we don't need any of that. It just makes things more complicated. It's stupid. The way a civilian thinks."

"Bean's a smart man. He wouldn't do it if it wasn't going to pay off."

"It's all getting fucked up," Echeverria said. "It's taking a weird turn."

"Doesn't seem weird to me."

"It doesn't strike you as strange, this guy Thorn is the same one in all the photographs on Bean's wall?"

"Thorn? He's that kid in the pictures?"

"That's right. I thought I recognized him, and I

asked Bean about it tonight and he said yes. Same guy."

"Wow."

"So, I ask you, what the fuck's going on here? Our guy Bean some kind of fairy or something? He got a thing for this guy Thorn, or what?"

"Shit no, he's no queer. He's straight as a chalk line."

"You know that, do you? You know that for a fact."

"Damn right I know it."

"So what's he doing with all those pictures on his fucking walls? Some kind of fixation bullshit. One of those things, you can't get something out of your head. It drives you crazy. That's what it looks like to me. Bean's crazy about this guy Thorn. Faggot or not—you ask me, it amounts to the same thing."

"Bean's not gay. He's absolutely not."

"Then he's crazy."

"Well, what if he is? Crazy isn't bad. Everybody's a little crazy."

Echeverria grumbled. He watched the lightning for a few minutes, then he turned and looked at her.

"You carrying a gun?"

"Smith three fifty-seven," she said. "Why? You want to fondle it?"

"I was just asking."

"Maybe you wanted to shoot me, but you had to see if I was armed first."

"If I wanted to shoot you, I would've done it by now."

Pepper slowed for a car turning off the highway.

"I had another boyfriend, a French guy. Talked real nasal like he had a head cold all the time. So, you know, I'd heard how Frenchmen could do things to women, make them come over and over. All this great stuff that only Frenchmen knew.''

"But not this guy, huh?''

"Oh, yeah. He made me come a lot.''

"So? What's the damn story?''

"That's it. I was telling you about a French guy who made me come a lot. You got to the end of the story faster than I was planning on getting there, so now it's over.''

"Jesus, you're some kind of dumb.''

Pepper let that pass, watching the road, a Winnebago from Tennessee in front of her.

"You met Tran van Hung yet? The guy paying your salary?''

Echeverria grunted. Pepper saw him touch the bulge in his pants with a finger, shift his dick around a little. She had him going now. Wearing a tight black turtleneck tonight, black jeans. Knowing she looked cute in black, brought out the olive in her eyes.

"The Vietnamese guy. You met him?''

"I've seen him.''

"Well, now, there's a guy who knows about sex. A man you could learn something from, Echeverria. Teach you how to screw from the front for a change, teach you a lot more than that. This guy, he takes those monkey gland shots or something, keeps his pecker stiff for hours.''

"I don't want to hear this.''

"Yeah, we've got this thing we do with hot chili peppers. You know, like the one I dripped on your arm. Burned the shit out of you.''

"This is sick.''

"I dribble it on his dick to cool him off. That's how hot this guy is.''

"Keep your eyes on the road, would you?"

"A couple of nights ago we're in his hotel room going at it, neither of us could get enough. An hour in, maybe two or three, who knows, somebody starts knocking on the wall. We thought we were being too loud, so we slow down and listen, get real quiet and then we can hear, Christ, it's the headboard in the next room. Like there's something in the air, sex pollen or something, it's infecting everybody around us. Somebody banging away over there too. So we go back to it; a few minutes later, there's more banging. We stop and listen again, and now the banging's in stereo. Both sides of us, bang, bang, bang. Nice, expensive hotel like that, full of rich people. All of them fucking like crazy. Little shrieks over there on the new side, come on, come on, harder, harder. Like a goddamn porno movie going on all around us. So we just stopped and listened. And you know what?"

Echeverria looked over at her.

"What?"

"It was better than doing it, listening to somebody else doing it. Just hearing them through the wall like that, it made me weak inside. The woman moaning, rooting her guy on, the man huffing like a bull. And it was like I could see them, a vision like, how they looked, how they felt about each other, the way their love was. And then after a minute or two of that, Tran reached over in the dark and touched me on the breast, just a hand stroking across my nipple, very light, almost like a puff of wind, touching me like he'd done a bunch of times already, and just like that, all at once, a wave of goose chills raced up my back and my heart exploded. I had an orgasm, Echeverria. A major, class-twelve orgasm. Just that one touch and I melted. Now, that's weird."

She looked over at him.

Echeverria was staring out his window.

"If you're nice," Pepper said, "I can tell you sex stories all the way to Key Largo. Okay? You listening to me, Echeverria? You big, dumb, come-from-behind Cuban."

"Basque," he said.

"You like my stories, you big Basque?"

"They're all right."

"Well, you let me know if I get too dirty for you, okay? You tell me, and Pepper will just shut her mouth and we'll whistle old songs or shoot our guns out the window to kill the time. Okay? You'll tell me when to quit, and I'll quit. Okay?"

"Okay."

So Pepper talked all the way to Key Largo. And she talked all the way down the street where the dolphin tanks were, and past them, and kept talking even for a little while after she'd found a nearby street without houses on it and parked. After she stopped, they sat there a few more minutes to let the air cool off. Two hours talking and she hadn't even gotten through half the men she'd been in bed with. Describing the things she'd done, all the little tricks she'd picked up over the years, things men liked, things that drove even the quietest guys out of their heads.

"That was better than our last trip together, wouldn't you agree?"

He made a noise in his throat. He agreed.

"So you ready to do this thing now?"

Echeverria grunted.

He'd been rubbing that pointing finger back and

forth against the length of his dick for the last hour while Pepper told her stories. Doing it real sly like she wouldn't notice. She knew his face was hot. She believed he'd finally had some kind of little orgasm about a mile or two back in Tavernier. Groaning quietly, pressing back into the leather seat. She bet his heart rate was about double what it was an hour ago.

Pepper had found it was a pretty reliable rule of thumb—somebody said they didn't like to hear dirty talk, it was usually because they knew they liked it a little too much.

"You got a wife, Echeverria?"

"Yeah."

"You have sex with her?"

"Not so you'd notice."

"Then where do you get your fun?"

"I'm not real big on fun."

He looked ahead out the windshield down the long, empty street. A tall white bird with orange legs was standing down there in a pool of streetlight like he was lost.

"That why you raped Greta?" she said. "You so horny you have to use a cripple to get off?"

He looked over at her.

"Maybe you should quit now," he said. "While you're ahead."

"If I were to tell Bean about you raping her, you'd be a dead man. You know that? She's his next experimental subject. They're hard to come by and he doesn't like them getting hurt, not even a little bit. It can throw everything out of whack. All her chemical balances, everything. He'd kill you if he knew. Kill you in a second."

"I'm not afraid of that legless twit."

"It wouldn't be him who'd do the work. It'd be me."

"Oh, boy, now I'm really scared."

"You raped her a couple of times, didn't you? That's what she said."

"I might have. I didn't count."

"If I told him, you'd be dead by morning, riding the outgoing tide. He gives me an order, it doesn't matter what I think about it, I have to do it."

"But you're not going to tell him, are you?"

"I don't know," she said. "I haven't decided yet."

Echeverria slid lower in the seat.

"All right then," he said. "What exactly do you want from me?"

"I don't know that yet either. But when I do, you'll be the first to know."

He looked over, shook his head, a tired smile came to his lips.

"You're a piece of work, Pepper. A piece of fucking work."

"Glad you noticed finally. You big dumb Basque."

CHAPTER

20

"Dr. Wilson told us to come talk to you, Roy. But we can't talk to you if you're asleep."

The huge man was sitting on the side of his bed. He wore cotton pajamas, pale pink with booties. Booties like a ten-year-old. On the chest of his long-sleeve pajama top a half dozen white lambs were lined up waiting to jump a wood fence. Roy was hunched forward and kept rubbing his eyes, sniffing like he'd been crying in his sleep. Face all bloated. Must've weighed over three hundred pounds. Pepper hated to think how many trigger pulls it would take to bring this one down and keep him there.

Echeverria had jiggered open the front door, and they'd walked right into the dark house that smelled of VapoRub, mildew, and piss. And they'd found his bedroom right away from following the sound of frog croaks and cricket noises and the loud rumble of a mountain stream running over rocks. A little machine beside his bed was making the racket. First thing Echeverria did was walk over and shut the thing off.

Roy was flinching against the bright lights, massaging his face. Echeverria had walked around the room and turned on each and every light. Even the one in the bathroom, and another in the closet. An air-conditioner rumbled in one of the windows.

"Frogs help you sleep, do they?" Pepper said.

"Who the fuck are you?"

"Dr. Wilson's research assistants," Echeverria said. "He told us to come speak with you, said you were curious about something and we should explain it to you."

"He sent you here? Bean junior?"

"That's right," Echeverria said.

"Frogs would keep me awake," Pepper said. "Crickets and all that water noise. I like it quiet when I sleep. Just the sloshing of the waves against the hull is enough for me."

She was looking around at Roy's room. Posters taped to the walls, rock bands she'd never heard of. Guys with lots of vampire makeup and tattoos. Another poster of Donnie and Marie Osmond from before Pepper was born. Stuff a big dumb kid would listen to. There were stacks of magazines bundled in one corner, and a black computer on his wicker desk and a small television mounted on a swivel rack in the ceiling. Roy could lie in bed, head on the pillow, and watch his favorite cartoons. In another corner of the room there was a little white refrigerator so he didn't even have to hike to the kitchen when he wanted a cold one.

"You're research assistants?"

"Yeah," Pepper said. "We're here to fill you in, whatever you need to know."

"You came in the middle of the goddamn night. Broke into my house."

"Front door was open," Echeverria said. "We tried

to make it during regular business hours, but we've been real busy, this was the only time we could fit you in.''

Pepper was studying a photograph in a cheap black frame cocked up on his dresser. Taken a long time ago when this guy was a kid, geeky as hell in a white dress shirt and shiny black pants, black graduation robe and mortarboard. Some big blond woman stood beside him out in the sun, a woman who looked like his mother. Roy was holding up his high school diploma very stiffly, like he was making fun of how the photographer was trying to pose him. Neither mother nor son was smiling. Looked like they'd just had a fight and wanted to kill each other at that moment, waiting till the photographer was finished to get back to it.

"Listen," she said. "You wanted to know about dolphin endorphins, right?"

"Yeah, that's right."

"And you thought the doc might be able to help you out."

"Yeah."

"Why'd you think that?"

Roy was looking up at her, his moon face all red and rashy looking.

" 'Cause Bean junior does research on dolphins, I thought he might've heard something, you know, through his connections with drug companies."

Echeverria stepped closer to the bed. There was a dark stain near his zipper. A credit to Pepper's story-telling ability.

Echeverria said, "Where'd you get this interest, Roy, dolphin endorphins—you dream that up yourself, did you?"

"Myself, yeah."

"Nobody else?"

"Whatta you mean?"

"He means, do you have a partner, a group of friends or something, you sit around and talk about these things with?"

"No, I'm alone."

"Alone, Roy?"

"Me and my mother, that's all. I don't tell her anything."

"You believe him?"

"No," Echeverria said.

"You aren't research assistants. Who are you?"

"Sure we are," Pepper said. She glanced around the room again, used both hands to sweep the hair back off her face. "You ever hear of the rat-tail crush test, Roy? It's the way we research assistants test out new local anesthetics, see how well they're working. You shoot your experimental painkiller into the rat's tail, then you put the tail in a precision vise and start clamping down little by little, all very measured, you keep cranking until the rat squeals. That's how you know how well the drug's working. Sounds primitive, I know, but that's the way we do it. Research assistants like us."

Echeverria was staring at her.

"What're you talking about?"

"I'm explaining to Mr. Everly that we're not some weirdos walked in off the street. We're scientists, digging around for the truth."

Echeverria shook his head and sat down on the bed beside Roy. Pepper saw the butt of his Colt sticking out under his sport coat.

"So, Roy. You call the authorities, tell them about your concerns, did you?"

"I'm not talking anymore. Get out of here."

Roy wouldn't look at Echeverria. If he turned his head to the right they'd be touching noses, but Roy was staring at the door, probably trying to figure how many gunshots he'd have to take before he could make it out of the room.

Echeverria reached back and pulled out his Colt and rested it on his knee. Long silver noise suppressor screwed on the end of the barrel.

Roy tipped his head to the side and peeked at it sitting there.

"You're the fuckers who killed my dolphins."

Pepper was opening her mouth to reply, when a loud cackle of laughter came from beyond the door. Echeverria lurched to his feet and stepped away from Roy and lifted the pistol. The laughter came again like somebody'd turned on the TV too loud in another part of the house.

"What's that?" Echeverria said.

Roy kept his mouth clamped.

"Go see what it is," Echeverria said.

"She doesn't know anything. I swear. I don't tell her a goddamn thing about my business. She's just a dotty old woman."

Pepper went to the door and opened it onto the dark house and the laughter sounded again. She followed it down the hallway to the last room. She drew out her pistol, pushed open the door, and the haw-haw-haw was even louder.

After waiting a few seconds, Pepper stepped into the darkness. The room smelled worse than the rest of the house. Like the windows had never been opened and the sheets hadn't been changed in a year, or the bedpan, or the cat litter. Down in a crouch, the pistol out in front of her, Pepper felt around on the wall for the light switch and flipped it on.

An old woman sat in the wingback chair beside the bed. She was dressed in a pink chiffon party dress with a big red sash and bow around her waist. The dress came only to her knees and there was a rhinestone-studded clutch bag sitting in her lap. She was barefoot, but on her head was the mortarboard from the photograph on Roy's dresser.

"You the mother?"

The woman lifted a small plastic box shaped like a set of dentures and she aimed it at Pepper and mashed a button on the thing and the cackling laughter sounded again. Only this time the laughter was running out of juice and trailed off into just a little buzz.

"Need new batteries," the woman said.

"I'll say you do."

The woman lifted the laughing box again and pressed the button, but this time only a last little snicker made it out before it died.

"Your son dress you like that?"

"Roy," the woman said. "Where's Roy?"

"Roy's been making fun of you, lady. The clothes he's got you wearing."

There were too quick pops from the other room. If Pepper hadn't known better, she would've thought they were opening champagne over there. Getting the party started.

"Well, I guess it's time to go," Pepper said. "It was real nice meeting you."

She walked out into the hall, then stopped, turned around, and came back in. A whole lot of people were depending on Bean and his research. There were people sobbing in pain every hour of the day waiting for him to get the formula right. It was a hell of a responsibility. You couldn't be too careful.

Pepper went back into the room. She set the Smith on a dresser top and took out the Flaming Canary chili pepper she'd carried along for a snack, and her #15 scalpel.

"So, Granny, you familiar with the miraculous effects of capsaicin?"

The old woman aimed the dentures at her like a raygun and pressed the useless button.

"Capsaicin is the chemical in chili peppers that burns so bad. It's what they use in arthritis creams these days. You know about that?"

Pepper moved closer to the woman. She stared at Pepper, at the scalpel and the small green pepper.

"What happens is, capsaicin hits the nerve endings and burns like hell, and all that burning depletes the Substance P, that's the neuropeptide that transmits pain signals to the brain. All the Substance P gets used up dealing with the pepper juice, which then reduces the sensation of pain in that area. You use pain to make pain stop. That's how it works. You overload the receptors and they get tired and quit."

The woman reached her free hand out as if she wanted to touch Pepper, see if maybe she was a ghost.

"You've had a long life," Pepper said. "And here you are still learning things right up to your last day. Now, that's pretty unusual, wouldn't you say? That's something to be grateful for."

"Where's Roy?" the woman said.

Pepper capped the Flaming Canary and reached out with it and pressed the juicy side to the old woman's soft, wrinkled throat.

"Now there'll be a little burn, but it'll go away."

The woman touched Pepper's arm.

"See, what I'm doing is, I'm making this as painless as possible. You got that burn, and it's already starting to subside, then I'm making the cut right behind it, which you shouldn't feel at all."

Pepper raised the woman's chin so she could get a better shot at her vein. The mortarboard fell to the floor. She made the cut, quick and deep. Her patients had bragged for years about Pepper's gentle touch. She could find a vein, draw blood without even the twitchiest patient knowing she was under way.

"Now there, that's done. All you should feel now is a little sleepy. The blood will just start leaking out of you. Get your dress messy, maybe, but hey, who cares about that at a time like this? From now on, every heartbeat is going to pump a little more blood out of you until you just sort of coast off to sleep."

"My boy," she said. "He's unhappy with me."

"Oh, no, I'm sure Roy loves his mom. He's just been getting back at you a little. Taking advantage, that's all. Can't blame him for that. Probably has some leftover childhood things going on in his head."

"Roy," the woman said, and lifted the laughing box again, but her arm sagged and the box fell from her hand.

Pepper stayed with her for a little while longer, a minute, not much more than that. Till the front of her dress was dark and damp and her head was slumped over. She'd had a long life, and a pretty easy way to die. Damn sight better than most people could say.

Pepper closed the door softly behind her and went back down the hall.

Roy Everly was sprawled on the floor. He looked bigger dead. Like a rhino had charged into the room and collapsed. Enough meat on that carcass to throw a neighborhood barbecue every day for a month.

"He tell you anything?"

"Yeah, he blubbered out a name."

"How'd you get him to talk?"

"I'm a trained professional," Echeverria said. "You keep forgetting."

"Somebody else he told about the endorphins?"

"A neighbor," Echeverria said. "Some friend of his named Monica."

"You think to ask him where Monica lives before you sent him off?"

"I told you. I'm a professional."

Pepper brushed the hair off her face, tucked her pistol in her waistband.

"I'm starting to like you, Echeverria."

"Don't do me any favors."

"If you weren't such a dumb, ugly Cuban, I might entertain serious sexual possibilities with you."

"I thought you had the hots for the doc."

"A woman's got to keep in shape," she said. "When the Prince finally shows up at the door, invites you to the ball, you want to be in peak condition, ready for action."

Echeverria started for the door, then stopped.

"Greta had it coming," he said. "Way she dressed, her attitude. Flaunting her body all the time. One of those haughty bitches that used her tits and ass to get where she was, then she turns around and shoots anyone down who pays any attention to them."

"Short skirts, tits falling out, like that?"

"Exactly," Echeverria said. "And anyway, she enjoyed it. Don't tell me she didn't. I saw it in her face, lying there, enjoying the hell out of it."

"Doesn't matter if she fell in love with you, Echeverria, wants to get married, have your children. The second Bean finds out what you did to her, you're one stone dead buckaroo."

CHAPTER

21

Monica knew she was only having a nightmare, but that didn't calm her any. Same thing happened with movies and books. She'd be scared out of her mind, and she'd force herself to look up, glance around at where she was, put the book down, stretch, yawn, blink, but she'd still be scared shitless. Or she'd be in the dark theater, heart wild with fright, she'd make herself have another handful of popcorn, munch it, remind herself for the dozenth time that it was only a movie, but it wouldn't matter. Her heart would still be thrashing around like an injured bird in the cage of her ribs.

She knew Thorn was safe, not locked up beneath the deck of his Chris-Craft, she knew that, though in the crazy logic of the dream it seemed true, truer than what her mind knew standing just outside the borders of the dream watching it happen, knowing it was all false, a script her unconscious had written for its own arcane purposes. Just her mind sorting things out, putting things in order, filing away the day's problems and images. She knew that. She knew she was dreaming, lying in bed, the pillow rolled up under her neck. She could even feel Rover sleeping on her feet, not letting her roll over if she wanted to, not letting her escape from the dream.

Thorn was locked below the deck of the *Heart Pounder* and the boat was sinking out in the Gulf Stream. On either side of them other boats paraded past. Monica sat out on the deck in the sun, her drawing pad in her lap, doing the most exquisite rendering of Rover that she'd ever managed. Complicated and rich and densely made. Nothing like her real drawings. An artistic breakthrough. A new Monica being created as she created the drawing, as she created the dream and watched herself create it and knew it was wrong for her to be sitting there doing such a frivolous thing when Thorn was in danger belowdecks, the boat sinking, both of them in danger, and even though she knew Thorn was about to die, Monica still had to finish her drawing.

She could hear him tapping on the floor. She could hear Rover growling, but the dog continued to sit perfectly still for his portrait, because he was a good dog, a well-behaved, happy, healthy dog, and she loved him. She could feel that love for the dog, feel it pour into her arms and her hands and feel it pour into the drawing she was doing. Focused on that page, on that white empty paper, filling it with fast beautiful lines as the water filled the spaces belowdecks and the boat sank slowly way out at sea with so many people around she could easily call for help, but she didn't because she was absorbed with the drawing, pushing herself to this new place, a revelation of major proportions, a seismic shift inside her, seeing the possibilities of art as greater than anything she'd imagined before. A great flowering. Everything making sense, finally making sense.

Monica hated it when people talked like that. A

great flowering. All that artsy-fartsy bullshit. That kind of talk didn't help you draw. Drawing was just a wordless act that you either got better at or didn't. And she also hated it when people bored you with their dreams. Like you cared. Like anyone could possibly be interested in the secret code of another person's unconscious, even a person you liked or loved. And she really hated it when movies and books and dreams scared her and she couldn't break free of their grasp. She hated being a sucker, giving herself over to someone else's mind, to their visions of savagery and violence and the grotesque. Like watching someone you loved drown slowly beneath the deck of his own ship, hearing each glub, watching each bubble drift slowly upward as the water filled his lungs, while the one he loved, the one he counted on to save him, completed her breakthrough drawing on the upper deck.

Knowing it wasn't real only made the terror worse. Dreams were scarier than real life because they had stronger magic. Like this mind had figured out all the escape routes and blocked them, a mind that made you fall in love with someone, then killed them before your eyes, a mind that outsmarted you at every twist, one step ahead, always a surprise, always a heart-stopping race against the second hand, or in a dream, a mind that was your own mind, a part of you that was smarter than all of you. A mind that you didn't know even though it was living within your own mind. That could dream up terrors worse than any you could ever dream up, whispering in your ear, telling you a story about a sinking boat and you and your loved one going down, and you oblivious of the danger, while he drowned, while you drew, while all of it sank beneath the dark surface of the magical sea.

Rover barked. Footsteps crunched through the gravel outside. And Monica was awake, sitting up in bed. Terrified.

"You don't know what goddamn lip liner is? You gotta be kidding me."

"I don't care what lip liner is."

"How about an eye blender brush?"

"Cut it out," he said.

"You're no fun, Echeverria. No fun at all. I bet you wouldn't let me put makeup on you, would you?"

"You're goddamn right I wouldn't."

A dog yipped from inside the little downstairs apartment. Echeverria had his pistol out, holding it down by his leg. She had hers out too. They were standing in the gravel drive looking at the door of the apartment.

"There was something else I was supposed to do on this trip," Pepper said. "Another job Bean gave me, but I can't remember what the hell it was. You ever have that, Echeverria? You have a thought one second, it's clear as day, then you turn around, zap, it's gone. Something important you gotta do, you can't remember what."

Echeverria was staring at the apartment. He kept swallowing.

"What I found," Pepper said, "best thing you can do is get on with whatever you were doing, and the thought'll come to you then. But you try to remember it, the thing just squinches down and hides inside a brain cell."

The big man wasn't moving.

"You okay, Echeverria?"

"Shut up for once, would you?"

"You got the look of a man about to spew his cookies."

She stood beside him as they listened to the dog bark inside the apartment. There was a rustle at the curtains, someone staring out at these two figures in the driveway.

"Was that your first kill, cowboy? That what this is?"

His chest rose and fell.

"That's the look you got. Like it's starting to hit you, what you've done. Got that seasick thing going on in your face, the ground starting to feel rocky underfoot. Is that what it is? 'Cause if it is, tell me now, and I'll go in and do this one. I wouldn't want you to choke on your spit, have to call an ambulance. That'd be hard to explain. My friend got some gray matter spattered on his shoes and it's made him a little woozy. No, that wouldn't sound too good."

Echeverria walked up to the door and tapped on it twice with the butt of his Colt. He kept tapping till the overhead light came on and a voice sounded through the door.

"What?"

"There's been a problem, ma'am. Mr. Everly is hurt, we need to use a phone."

"Mr. Everly?"

"Your neighbor, Mr. Everly. Hurt bad. Please, ma'am. We have to act fast."

The door swung open and a woman stepped out holding a little black-and-white terrier in her arms. She wore a yellow silk nightie and her hair was in curlers under a net. There was white war paint on her face. She was six hundred years old, and still doing everything she could to look four hundred.

Echeverria stepped back from her, a safe shooting distance.

"You a friend of Roy Everly?"

"Who you want?" The woman had Cuban mush in her mouth.

"Is your name Monica?"

"Monica?" The woman saw the pistol. "No, you make mistake."

"I don't think so," Echeverria said.

"I no Monica. She young girl. Live there, in house. Blond *chica*."

She raised her arm, pointing at a house across the canal, while she clutched the dog tight against her breast with the other arm. Echeverria lifted his pistol and shot the woman in the face. She fell backward and the dog spilled out and his nails spun on the cement as he charged. Echeverria shot it too. Took two slugs to stop the thing from yipping.

"You sure that was her?"

Echeverria was still pointing the pistol at the terrier.

"It's what Everly said. The house next door. You see another one?"

"Maybe you should check her ID, make sure."

"You don't think it's her, then *you* check her ID."

"All right, all right. Let's get out of here. That's about all the fun I can stand for one night."

"Aw, fuck, maybe you're right," Echeverria said. "We should check that house, the one she was pointing at."

Monica watched the tall man and woman stride back down Sandpiper Drive. From her window she could see Mrs. Benitez and Pepito lying side by side on the cement floor of the carport just across the canal.

Monica didn't have a phone. No one in the world to call but Thorn and he didn't have one, so she hadn't bothered. She stood at the window and tried to think. She knew what she'd just seen was no dream. Happening with all the sloppy, helter-skelter rhythm of a normal event. Brutal and quick and ugly.

Monica stood at the window and watched the moonlight spread like the golden sheen of a swelling tide, rising up the gravel drive until it lapped near the two fallen bodies. A minute, two. Trying to breathe. Trying to reconstruct what she'd seen. The woman dressed in black, the tall man with the potbelly showing through his white shirt. The man shooting Mrs. Benitez, then Pepito, then turning around and walking away. All of it, twenty, thirty yards away across the narrow canal. That close.

Trying to put it together, what she should do, her brain was buzzing with static.

Rover whined at her leg, wanting to go out.

Monica went over to the door and swung it open. She was wearing her cotton pajama shorts and a white T-shirt and the night air felt suddenly cool on her flesh. She reached back into the apartment and grabbed her purse and keys from the desk and walked out to the Impala.

She could drive over to Roy's, try to rouse him, use his phone, or she could drive to the Food Spot, call the police from there.

Rover jumped into the front seat, wagging his tail hard, sensing her edginess.

She started the car and the noise and vibration of the big V-8 finished waking her. She slid the car into gear, backed out, turned up Alamanda Lane toward the main entrance road, and her headlights lit them up. The tall girl in black and the bald man in a white shirt and black trousers striding down the middle of the street. Like they were going house to house, shooting whoever they found.

They halted, the woman saying something to the man, the man waving her away.

Monica shoved Rover to the floor and told him to stay. Stamping the high beam button, she flattened the accelerator, let go of the clutch, and fishtailed toward the two killers.

The woman jumped aside, but the big man held his position and lifted his pistol with one hand and fired twice. She saw both spits of flame from his barrel and felt the spray of windshield glass against her cheek, but she kept the wheels burning down the asphalt, swerving a little but holding the big car on the street, flashing past them, hearing another two sharp pops as she passed and feeling an icy numbness at the back of her neck. She skidded left onto Poinciana and raced toward the highway.

After only a second or two the warmth began to seep back into her neck, while something even warmer spread down her back. But she didn't reach around to probe the wound. She knew she was in shock, feeling no pain; the golden glow of numbness might last the fifteen minutes it would take her to drive to Mariners Hospital. Let the emergency room people call the police. First things first, get down the road, get some medical attention, stop the bleeding. Her eyes were clear, she was thinking straight. She'd just been grazed. It was only fifteen minutes to the hospital, twenty max. She'd make it, no worry.

She was out on the highway, a half mile down, cruising at eighty through Rock Harbor when she leaned over and saw Rover on the passenger floor. She took her foot off the accelerator.

"Rover," she said. "Rover."

A bullet had gouged through the car just behind the wheel well and there was a bloody scoop gone from the top of the dog's skull, his head cocked against the carpet at a hopeless angle. His mouth was open and his teeth were bared as if even in his last seconds he had been doing what he could to protect her.

CHAPTER

22

Sunday morning at eight o'clock Thorn parked his wheelchair across the street from the Casa Marina Hotel. It was a palatial Mediterranean structure, a Marriott update of a building where in an earlier incarnation congressmen and Hollywood rogues and rumrunners and lobstermen had swapped lies. Piazzas, loggias, black cypress ceilings, a full orchestra playing on the lawn. All those indispensable features of a 1920s resort, built by Henry Flagler, the man who single-handedly concocted Florida and made it safe for millionaires.

The Marriott people had decided the thick stucco walls of Flagler's old beauty should be replastered and dabbed with hipper colors, fitted out with flimsy brass lamps and cutely painted Mexican tile. And they had continued to veneer and paint and tile with all the trendiest materials until by now every vestige of the graceful original had been concealed by a series of slapdash contractors who'd apparently served their apprenticeships decorating wedding cakes and Mardi Gras floats.

Thorn was waiting for Echeverria to appear. He was

going to follow the son of a bitch through his Sunday routine, spy on the spier. See if he tried to butcher any more dolphins. And if the occasion presented itself, Thorn had decided to test the limits of his own physical condition, see if he could blindside the bastard, knock him into a side street, throttle him until he bleated out the truth. And if truth was not forthcoming, just keep throttling him till he was senseless.

That's how he'd awoken this morning. Angry. Angry at the sky, angry at the trees and air and sidewalk. Angry at the people walking on two legs, angry at the joggers, angry at the cars and the dogs and cats, angry at the clouds and the herons and ibis and gulls, angry at the men hosing off the sidewalks outside the bars, angry at the paper cups tumbling in the wind up Duval Street, and especially angry, uniquely and particularly angry, at the two legs attached to his body. The two stupid, useless, empty reminders of the careless life he'd been leading, the healthy, vigorous body he'd been taking for goddamn granted.

Across from the Casa Marina, Thorn rolled his chair into the shade of a royal palm, and watched a series of taxis and Mercedeses and BMWs come and go, noting each of the walkers, the runners, the early morning golfers heading out for their play. Not a single Echeverria among them.

For the third time that morning he reached into the pocket of his blue work shirt and drew out the snapshot he'd found in the desk drawer of his room. A handsome blond woman was squatting beside an eight- or nine-year-old girl who looked very much like the woman's daughter, both of them laughing wildly as a silvery wave crested above them, about to crash onto their backs. The woman was wearing a black one-piece and her daughter was in a polka-dot skirted two-piece. Blond pigtails on the girl, a cute nose, a splash of freckles across her forehead. Mother with beautifully muscled legs.

Thorn had decided it was Greta Masterson, the woman who'd preceded him in that dark narrow room at the Eaton Street clinic. The woman who Brad Madison had sent to get the goods on Bean, the same woman Brad had now lost contact with. Thorn promised Brad he would sniff around among the other patients in as quiet a way as he could to see if any of them knew what had become of the woman. He'd sworn to be extremely careful, agreed to relay everything he learned, no matter how trivial it might seem, vowed not to freelance this in any way.

Brad and he had shaken hands on the bargain. Thorn, suddenly a deputized DEA agent. But already he'd violated his oath. He'd found the photograph of the woman he believed to be Greta, and he'd told no one about it, nor did he intend to. He'd rolled out of the clinic this morning as soon as he'd received his steroid injection from the morning nurse, without questioning a single other patient. And now here he was, positioned outside the Casa Marina, determined to freelance the hell out of the situation.

For the next half hour he watched the hotel and took occasional peeks at the photograph. There was something haunting about the beach scene that kept bringing his eyes back. The woman was beautiful, but that was only part of it. She had the delicately balanced features and immaculate skin Thorn associated with Alpine milkmaids. All the elegant angles of her face were measured out with the classic precision of a Swiss watch. But there was something complicated about her exuberance in the shadow of the crashing wave, her arm locked securely around the shoulders of her child, as if she were trying to show the young girl how to defy the ocean's strength without losing sight of its danger.

Brad had told him almost nothing personal about Greta Masterson, but what he saw in that photograph he liked a great deal. This was a woman for whom surrender was not an option. And it struck him now, that most likely she was also a woman with sufficient foresight not to have left behind such a snapshot unless her departure was sudden and unforeseen.

"Cute, huh?"

Thorn jerked to his right and there was Ginny, the young blond woman from the clinic. She was wearing gray leggings, purple running shorts, a halter top with a Nike logo, and a black baseball cap.

"That's Greta Masterson," she said. "But I guess you knew that already."

"I found it in my room."

"Yeah, that was Greta's room. Till she left."

Ginny smiled at him, and repositioned her wheelchair so she was in the sunlight. A man walking a rottweiler down the sidewalk had to step into the street to get around them. He looked away as if he expected them to try to hit him up for a dollar.

"I'm taking my morning roll. You too?"

Thorn nodded.

"Want to learn how to do a wheelie?" Ginny said. "It's harder than it looks. Helps build up your arms."

She tipped herself backward, got her footplates up in the air, and held the wheelchair steady with tiny movements of her push rim.

"Maybe later," Thorn said. "At the moment I got my hands full just rolling along, point A to point B."

"What're you doing out here?"

"Taking a breather."

"Waiting for somebody?"

"Just a breather," Thorn said.

"Bet you're waiting for your contact."

Thorn looked at her.

"Contact," she said. "As in pharmaceuticals."

"No," he said. "I'm not waiting for my contact."

"I got a pretty good connection myself, if you're interested. Just grass, but it's good shit. Hydroponic stuff. I can give you a joint, see if you're interested."

"My drug days are long gone."

"Don't be so sure," she said. "Drugs are the name of the game around here."

Wearing blue jeans and a white button-down shirt, Echeverria came striding out the double front doors of the hotel and walked briskly down the driveway. Thorn swung his chair out of Echeverria's line of sight, and backpedaled behind the shrub.

"Hey," Ginny said. "Where you going?"

Thorn waited till the big man turned the corner and started down a side street, then he rolled forward and out across the broad avenue. Ginny tagged along.

"I lied when I said I was out for my morning stroll. Actually, I been following you since you left the clinic. You interest me, Thorn. You're not like those other guys."

There was no ramp on the opposite sidewalk, so Thorn stayed on the edge of the street, a few inches out of the gutter.

"Truth is," she said, "I got a thing about older guys."

"I'm not interested, Ginny. Drugs, romance, any of it."

"What I find is, older guys take their time. They're more appreciative. They don't have so much to prove. Of course, I like younger guys too. They have their virtues. And then there are guys my own age, they aren't all that bad either. In general, I guess you could say I just like guys."

Echeverria turned the next corner and headed toward Louie's Backyard and the Reach, Waddell Avenue, a shady street that was rank with mildew and expensive garbage.

"You gay, Thorn?"

"No."

"Whew," she said. "In this town, that makes you eligible for minority status. You can park in the special zones. But then, you can park there anyway, what with the fucking wheelchair, right?"

Losing sight of Echeverria around the next corner, Thorn wheeled himself faster. Ginny stayed with him.

"So you're not a vet, huh?"

"No."

"You got the phantom pain?"

"No."

"Wow, a lucky guy."

Echeverria halted at the corner of South Street and Vernon. He stood for a moment staring down South. A moment or two later a red Cadillac swung to the curb and Echeverria got inside. Unless there was a candy-apple red hearse dealership in Key West, it was the same car he and Bean had been driving in the day before.

"That was nice, what you did yesterday."

"Forget it."

"I bet that's the kind of guy you are. Find a bird with

a broken wing, you stop what you're doing, take it somewhere to get it fixed. I bet you're like that, huh?''

"Not usually."

"No, really. It was nice. Above and beyond the call. Hardy can be one mean son of a bitch. If Pepper hadn't stepped in, man, I wouldn't want to see the mess you two would've made. I don't care what kind of kung fu you know. Hardy's got some heavy-duty hours in that chair, and he knows how to fight. I've seen him take on two guys at once, two healthy guys. Beat the ever-loving fecal matter out of them.''

A shirtless guy on a rickety red bike was coming down Vernon. Big blue milk crate fastened onto the back of the bike, a white terrier riding inside it. Thorn rolled forward down the incline and into the street and the guy on the bike steered wide around him.

"I need a ride," Thorn called out to the guy. "It's an emergency." He had long reddish hair and a scraggly Chinese mystic's beard that looked like he'd been working on it for years. He brought the bike to a squeaking stop a few feet away and looked back. Thorn rolled over to him.

"What kind of emergency?"

"Catch up to that car, the red hearse.''

"What car?"

"Just go," Thorn said. "Take this right, then the first left. Come on, we're losing him.''

He gripped the blue basket. And the guy shook his head and made a little sigh like he'd been waylaid like this a few times before—price you paid for living in paradise. He stood up on the pedals and muscled the bike forward. Skinny guy, looked like he might be surviving on one grain of rice a day. As they picked up speed, the white terrier stared at Thorn's fingers curled over his blue basket. The bike weaving a little from the strain of pulling the wheelchair.

"Left here," Thorn said. "Left, left."

The guy wheeled the bike onto Simonton. He was breathing hard, still standing up on the pedals. The wheelchair bumped over a couple of smallish potholes and Thorn nearly lost his grip.

"We're losing him," Thorn said. "Come on, man, pump. You can do it."

The terrier was licking Thorn's fingers, brown bulging eyes fastened to Thorn's as if maybe he liked the way Thorn tasted so much, he was toying with the idea of switching masters.

Thorn saw the hearse turn left a half dozen blocks ahead.

"Faster, man, faster."

The guy was working now, sweat running down his bare back. The dog rested his chin on Thorn's knuckles. Thorn didn't see it coming and neither did the guy: a big limb in the street, a couple of feet long, probably fell off somebody's lawn service truck. The front wheel hit it and the bike veered hard to the left into an oncoming station wagon. The skinny guy sailed right, tucking and rolling onto the grass beside the sidewalk, and Thorn kept on going straight for about ten feet, tilting up on one wheel, then slamming back down before he brought the chair to a halt.

On the roof of the station wagon, the terrier was barking furiously at the young girl in a white uniform who stood beside her door looking at Thorn, at the bicycle, and at the bearded guy in the grass.

Thorn stared down Southard, the hearse long gone. If he was going to tail Echeverria, he was going to have to get a turbocharger for his goddamn chair. He rolled over to the guy in the grass and asked him if he was okay, and the guy mumbled that he was fine, Jimmy crack corn, fine and dandy. He didn't seem to be bleeding, no bones poking through, so Thorn left him there and rolled back into the street.

"Lost him, huh? The guy you were shadowing."

Ginny rolled up next to him. Only took her half a minute to catch up. Not even out of breath.

Thorn sighed.

"Yeah," he said. "I lost him."

"With a little practice, you can crank it along fast enough, just about stay up with cars. I'll show you some tricks if you want. How to get maximum horsepower out of these things." She patted the side of her chair. "Like most things, it's all technique."

He rolled ahead a few feet, then stopped. The woman in the station wagon was trying to get the terrier off her roof, but it was dodging away from her.

"You're not the friendliest guy I ever met," Ginny said. "Which is fine. I've always had a special fondness for unfriendly guys."

Thorn rolled ahead a few more yards and stopped in the shade of a poinciana. He swiveled around to face Ginny.

"What do you know about Greta Masterson?"

Ginny made a scornful smile.

"Man, you bozos. You're all tuned to the same damn channel, aren't you? Greta, Greta, Greta. Big breasts, Christ, all they are is some extra fat cells gooped together in the same sack of flesh, but you guys don't care. You can't get enough of that breast shit."

Ginny wasn't more than twenty-five. Monica's age. But she had the shadows and puffiness around the eyes of someone twice that. Living hard, not counting her fat grams anymore. Not counting much of anything.

"I'm not interested in her breasts. I was wondering why she left the clinic."

"Who knows?" Ginny cranked herself around Thorn and headed slowly up Southard. Thorn caught her at the corner.

"Did she have the phantom pain?"

"All of us do," Ginny said. "It's required for membership in our happy little club."

An empty Old Town Trolley passed by, heading toward Duval to start its daily tourist rounds. Shuffling toward them a barefoot man in cutoff jeans and a ragged T-shirt grinned and halted briefly, bleary eyes loose in their sockets. He seemed to be ready to ask them for a handout, but he took a second look at Ginny and headed off. The long-haired bicyclist retrieved his terrier from the roof of the car, picked up his bike, and pedaled off.

"Did you know Bean Wilson suffers from phantom pain too?"

"Doesn't surprise me," she said.

"Has he done you any good, eased your pain at all?"

"Not a fucking bit. My legs burn twenty-four hours a day. Never quit."

"So whatever Bean's doing doesn't work."

"Not yet, but hey, the guy's trying. That's a shitload more than I can say for the other twelve doctors I had. Those worthless assholes told me it was all in my head."

"And Greta? Was hers particularly bad?"

"Chronics don't talk about the pain. It's there, you can see it in somebody's face if you know what to look for, but we don't talk about it."

"You're all vets, you all have phantom limb pain. There anything else?"

"Else what?"

"Anything else you all have in common?"

"Besides all of us being cripples, you mean?"

Thorn nodded.

"Well, we're all fans of Jack Daniel's, Robert Mitchum, and Dire Straits. That's about it, far as I know."

Ginny watched a black German shepherd work his way up the block, lifting his leg at every tree. The dog eyed the guy in cutoffs on the opposite sidewalk, sizing him up as a breakfast possibility. The guy noticed and hurried on.

"Oh, yeah, and we're all castaways," she said. "If that's what you mean."

"Castaways?"

For the first time since he'd met her, the sneer disappeared from Ginny's face.

"Loners, outcasts, however you want to put it. No friends, no family. Bunch of sad fucking lepers. Two rungs down from the hoboes. No phone calls, nobody gets any mail, nothing. Only friends we got are right there on Eaton Street. One of us were to die, you could toss the carcass in the nearest Dumpster, nobody in the world would care."

"You don't have a mother, a father?"

"People like me and Hardy, we died a long time ago. Only people know we exist is the other losers in the clinic. And they're so shitfaced, they can't remember my name half the time."

Thorn started forward, but Ginny blocked his way.

"So what's this bullshit about? Who the hell are you?"

"My name is Thorn."

"What's with the questions?"

"I'm trying to figure things out," he said. "Why I'm here. Why I was invited to the party."

She snorted.

"You're some kind of innocent, aren't you?"

"First time anyone's called me that."

"You don't know what's going on around the clinic?"

"I've been there a day. I know what I've seen so far."

She shook her head and started back down South-ard.

Thorn caught up, grabbed hold of her chair and stopped her.

"What is it, Ginny? What do you want to tell me?"

She kept her face away from him.

"You'll figure it out. Just stick around."

"Talk to me, Ginny."

"It's not my place. I don't even know who the hell you are. You might not even be paralyzed, for all I know. Those legs you got, they look fine to me."

"Try me," he said.

Ginny looked at him and grinned. She drew close. Peered up and down the empty street. Then she reached out, slid her hand up the bottom edge of his shorts, and took a pinch of the hairs on his inner thigh and twisted. She pulled her hand out, held up the clus-ter of blond hairs. A dab of blood on the roots.

"Satisfied?"

"You could just be good at not flinching."

"What do I have to do, cut off a toe?"

She took another look down the street and reached her hand up the leg of his shorts again. Thorn looked down at his indifferent crotch as her hand groped. She drew herself closer and kept her hand inside his shorts for half a minute. Enjoying herself.

"Now, there's a fucking shame," she said as she pulled her hand out. "Goddamn fucking shame."

"You're telling me."

She rolled back from him.

"Do I pass?"

She swiveled her chair around, took a careful look at Thorn.

"You're not a cop?"

"Not now, never have been."

She sighed and shook her head. The sun was up now, coming over the oaks along Southard, starting its slow burn. Sky still pure blue, weeks and weeks of perfect days that anywhere else in the world would be called a drought. But in South Florida the tourist board had outlawed such terms.

A couple of loud-talking female joggers passed by. Across the street an old man was walking his tiny black poodle. Ginny gazed up the street at a bakery truck double-parked outside a small motel restaurant.

"What's going on, Ginny? Talk to me."

"We're the chimps," she said.

"What?"

"The chimps. The experimental subjects."

Thorn said nothing.

"You ever realize the big drug companies do some of their testing in third world countries?"

"No, I hadn't heard that."

"Apparently, what's happened, it's gotten too complicated and too damn expensive to go through all the bullshit rigmarole to get approval in the U.S., so some of the pharmaceutical companies go down to Ecuador, Colombia, into the barrio, they find people with whatever illness they're working on, and they give them the latest drug. They can rationalize it by saying this is the only way these poor people would ever get drugs of this type, but the assholes aren't down there to do charity work. They want to know the side effects, so they find a group of people nobody gives a shit about.

"Way the laws are, it's easier to get permission from the Ecuadorian government to run drug trials on its citizens than it is to get permission in the U.S. to use goddamn chimps, so they go down there to do their trials. It's legal. Just one country using another country as its own special primates. No big deal. And looking at it from the sick people's point of view, it's okay too. Is it better to take the risk of some side effect to get a pill that maybe cures your illness, than just to stay sick the rest of your goddamn life?"

"That's what he's doing? Bean's running drug trials on you?"

She looked at him. Her sneer came and went. She shook her head.

"The doc's your friend, and he hasn't told you any of this?"

"He used to be my friend. When we were kids."

"And he didn't hint at it or anything?"

"No."

Ginny shrugged. She rolled herself up into a wheelie again, balancing there in a slab of sunlight.

"That's the reason why Hardy got so mad at you yesterday. It wasn't just the Vietnam stuff. He saw you coming in there, legs not even atrophied yet, Doc Bean's buddy, and he thought you were there to cut in line ahead of him. Way we figure it, Hardy's next at bat. He's got seniority. Been in the clinic the longest of anybody."

The street was splashed with green shadows. A Baltimore oriole fluttered down from the oaks to peck at something in the dirt. Behind it a large black cat with white paws and white ascot came out of the tall grass. It crouched and began to stalk the orange bird.

"What Bean's doing, it's no big deal," Ginny said. "Whole goddamn country is one big drug trial. Everybody's taking pharmaceuticals left and right, nobody knows what anything's going to do to you, not really. Not long-term. Even the water, even the food."

"You're telling me that everybody in the clinic knows what's going on? He's got your permission?"

"Sure," she said. "We don't talk about it. But we know. Pepper's in on it. The doc. I don't think the other nurses know."

"And Greta? Did she know?"

"She should have. It's all there, out in the open. But then, she was a little like you, sweet and innocent. And the doc had her conned pretty good. He can be convincing as hell when he wants to be. Turn the charm on and off like a Palm Beach hooker."

"So where is she now?"

"I don't know. Probably still wherever he does the procedure. He's got a place."

"Upstairs in the clinic?"

"No, the good shit happens somewhere else. Not in the house."

"You ever see anybody afterward? Anybody come back and tell you how it went?"

"No."

The muscles in Ginny's arms twitched and wriggled as she held her front wheels off the ground.

"So maybe the drugs aren't working," Thorn said.

"It's a trial, remember? If it's not working yet, then

maybe he'll have it right by the time he gets to me. That's the way I look at it. That's how Hardy sees it too."

"And if the drugs are killing your friends from the clinic?"

"So what?" she said. "That's supposed to get me spooked? I might get killed?"

Thorn reached out and pressed hard on the arm of her wheelchair and brought her down from her balancing act.

"Doesn't bother you, huh? Dead, alive, it's all the same?"

"The fucking pain in my legs bothers me. But being dead, no, I don't think that would be a big bother."

"That's how it is? The doc could be killing your friends, you don't give a shit. Hardy's next in line, and he's pissed at me 'cause I may be cutting in front of him to get killed? That doesn't make any sense, Ginny. None at all."

She gave him a sour smile.

"That's 'cause you don't have the pain, Thorn. And if you don't have the pain, then you don't know what the fuck you're talking about."

CHAPTER

23

Monica spent the early morning hours Sunday at the Tavernier police department. She told a female officer and two deputies everything she'd seen. Told them again. Told a different set of people and then another set after that. Five times, six times, like they were trying to trip her up, find inconsistencies, like she was a suspect. After a couple of hours she even started feeling that way, vague guilt, like maybe there was something she should have done, some shout of warning to Mrs. Benitez. She tried to explain why she didn't have a phone. Feeling guiltier each time she went over it. The sheriff's people looking at her silently. No one helping.

Then the sheriff arrived from Key West and she repeated it all again. She'd seen two people. A tall man with a potbelly, a tall woman, brown hair. She hadn't seen their faces. No, she had no idea why anyone would want to kill Mrs. Benitez and her dog. No, she had no idea whatsoever. She barely knew the woman, nodded to her only in passing as the old woman walked the terrier around the neighborhood. And she had no idea why they would fire on her. Probably just surprised them with her headlights and that frightened them into firing.

At dawn they let her go. Dazed, she drove to Thorn's, lay Rover's body near the butterfly garden where he'd spent so much time stalking those fluttering yellow frustrations. She watched the sunlight take the sky.

She hadn't slept. Might never sleep again. She lay the dog's body on his right side near a clump of lantana blooming yellow and red. The dirt was soft and rich there. She'd planted some roses last month, so she knew. She stood for a while and watched Blackwater Sound lose its leaden glaze, turn pale blue and glossy.

She went into the house, got her drawing pad and pens and came back down and squatted in the grass a few feet from Rover, and she opened the pad to a blank page.

She'd doodled all through high school, then majored in art in college, and had drawn ever since. But the fact was, she'd never had any compelling reason to draw. A distraction, a way to minimize the world, bring it down to some manageable size, have some small margin of control. But Monica had never tested her craft with a subject of any heft. She had drawn what interested her eye, but her heart had stayed clear. At best she was a craftsman. She'd never pretended to be an artist, had no philosophy of art, wanted none. It was a hobby, a habit, not even close to a need.

But that morning she drew in a different way than she'd drawn before. She drew because she had to, because there was no choice. And what she saw was different. Rover lying there. Every blade of grass, every flicker of shadow, the matted fur, the crust at his eyes, the complicated arrangement of his paws. The flesh sinking against his ribs, his muzzle dancing with flies.

This time she sketched in every line and angle. Everything she saw she put on the page. And even more than she saw. This time she put in the things that were not there but needed to be there to make the other things real.

She drew it all and she drew it to save herself and defend herself and because she needed to draw it and because she didn't believe she was good enough for such a subject, a dead dog in the grass, because it seemed a challenge beyond anything she had prepared herself for, and she drew it because someone had tried to kill her a few hours earlier and that could be her lying in the grass, and because Thorn was not there and Rover was his dog and he would want to know what happened and so the drawing damn well better be real.

And all of that only made her draw harder, see more clearly, work and work in the early morning light until the page was filled until finally what was out there on the lawn was not out there anymore. All of the death and all of the grief and all of the fear and desperation and doubt were on the page of her pad.

Sunday morning, the seventh of April, almost noon when she was finished and set the pad aside. And she was different now. She knew she had made herself different. She had changed the way her brain was wired, changed the way she breathed, the way the blood pressured in her veins, changed the way the goddamn light weighed on her skin.

Rover was dead. Someone had tried to kill her. And Monica Sampson was there, sitting in Thorn's yard. She had prepared herself for years to draw the picture that lay on the grass before her, and now she had drawn it.

Brad Madison listened to the phone ring in Echeverria's hotel room. Ten times, fifteen. Fourth call he'd made this morning. Starting at 8:30. He knew Echeverria was no early riser. But the guy wasn't in. Hadn't been in his room all night.

Brad was in the Georgetown Sheraton. First buds of spring coming up in the park across the street. Usually a fun trip, the yearly SAC meeting. All the special agents in charge gathering to vie for the year's awards, next year's funds. Brad always came out near the top on both. One of the advantages of living in South Florida. Business was always booming.

The meeting was mandatory. SACs came sick. They got rolled in on stretchers fresh from surgery. No one skipped. No one even tried. A career breaker if you didn't show. But at the moment Brad was a half-second from grabbing the rip cord, bailing.

He put the phone down and called Echeverria's home phone and got a Cuban woman saying "talk to me." He tried, but the two of them quickly figured out that his Spanish wasn't as good as her English. They met in the middle and Brad Madison asked her if she'd heard from her husband in the last twenty-four hours. Echeverria's wife shouted a few Spanish curses that Brad was intimate with. No, he hadn't been home. He hadn't called home. And she didn't care if he ever did again. She hung up.

He called the Casa Marina again and asked the operator to leave another message. Urgent. The last one said urgent too, the operator said. Will he be able to tell the difference? Okay, then make this one very urgent, no, extremely urgent. Yeah, she said. That's good. Maybe next time you can try stupendously urgent.

Brad hung up and stared out at the flowers across the street.

The image went through his head, quick but vivid, of going across the street and picking every single one of those flowers and jumping on the next plane to Key West and giving them all to Greta Masterson.

If he only knew where the hell to find her.

Greta felt a faint yaw in the big boat, a quiet creak as Pepper stepped from the dive platform to the rubber raft. Greta had spent the last four days listening to every tick and twitter of that old yacht. It was all she had now; whatever knowledge she could accumulate about her surroundings was her only advantage. And now she was as certain of Pepper's departure as if the young woman had cranked up the outboard and roared away.

They were taking precautions. Now Pepper would probably paddle the raft well out of earshot before starting the engine. And they had attached restraining straps to the bed frame and tightened them across Greta's ankles and breasts. They'd seen what she was capable of, swimming almost to shore.

But Greta had solved the straps. Some nearly forgotten Nancy Drew lore from her youth—puffing herself up as her captor cinched the belts, taking a slow, deep breath, clenching the muscles in her arm, inflating, pressing up against the tethers, all the while keeping her face as serene as possible.

Now, when she was certain Pepper was well away, it took Greta only a few minutes to wriggle one arm free, work the hasp loose, sit up and unbind her feet. Then she was out of the bed and on the floor, squirming down the passageway and once again working herself up those six steps to the upper deck. Same journey, only this time in daylight. Sunday midday.

She dragged herself up to the transom, brought her head above the gunwale, and surveyed the surrounding waters. Greta groaned and fell away. It must have happened late at night while the morphine had been occupying Greta's full attention. They'd moved the boat to a new anchorage. The city of Key West was barely visible to the east. Six miles of gray choppy water, maybe more. Absolutely no hope she could cross such a distance.

Greta flattened herself on her back for a few moments, staring up at the clouds, their endless shaping and reshaping. She blinked back the tears that grew warm at the back of her eyes. And at that moment, watching the busy sky, the pump in her belly began its morning buzz.

Almost immediately, as it had done the night before, the mechanism shut down. No morphine was left in its reservoir. So there would be no bleary hour as the drug trickled onto her spinal cord. That, at least, was some small reason for thanks.

Greta Masterson lay on the deck and inhaled the ocean scents and watched the clouds cruise past in neat squadrons of threes and fours. She followed the darting gulls and terns, and for a while she studied a black frigate bird hanging in place from the dome of the sky like some dark angel gazing down on its handiwork.

Greta Masterson was okay. Echeverria had not returned since Friday night. After he'd gone, she'd examined her body with a mirror and had found no bleeding, no outward signs of harm. The rape itself had been grim but painless. The first time since her fall she'd been grateful that everything below her navel was numb. And Echeverria had been mercifully quick —apparently an experienced premature ejaculator. Even his second time, he'd come in less than a minute, four or five hard humps and he was done. He hadn't struck her, had even stayed mercifully silent after getting her aboard. Going about his carnal business with flat and empty eyes, as if he were living out some twisted reverie he had nursed since youth.

As for psychic trauma, yes, perhaps some emotional time bomb might detonate a year from now. But for the moment, it was nothing she couldn't handle, certainly a lesser horror than the one she'd already suffered at Bean's hands. An even more gruesome foreign body inside her own, metal and cold, with a silicon mind.

She lay back and took the early morning sun, let her eyes drift closed, relishing as much as she could, the freshening breeze.

Moments later Greta roused herself. Dark splotches of sweat had begun to stain her blue scrub. She was squandering time. This was not the moment to sunbathe, no time to mellow.

She rolled onto her belly and crawled over to the lower deck console. As she'd expected, the VHF radio had been removed, hidden away somewhere on board. And naturally the ignition key was also gone.

Greta wormed back to the companionway steps and bumped down them. Belowdecks, she made the arduous crawl down the narrow corridor, lifting herself up to try each door along the way. Coming first to a cramped head with a tiny shower, and then a small cabin that was apparently used for storage—the narrow berth stacked with engine parts and cans of oil, tarps and tools.

The cabin two doors aft of Greta's was Pepper's stateroom, twice the size of Greta's and exceedingly tidy. She'd tacked a poster of a cluster of red chili peppers on one wall and a bare-chested Brando on the other. Her bunk had hospital corners, the top blanket rigid enough to bounce a quarter. Her hanging locker was tight with clothes, blouses and hot pants and skirts all organized by color, from white to yellow to blue to green to red and finally to black.

Greta opened each of the drawers in the built-in cabinet and found that Pepper was just as fanatical with her underwear and slips and socks. Everything folded and organized by hue. An entire drawer devoted to black lingerie, as if she felt some ghostly parent were hovering near, grading her performance, watching her deportment for the slightest flaw.

Greta patted through the rayon and silk and cotton things, careful not to ruffle Pepper's fastidious system. But she found nothing hidden beneath the underthings.

Across the cabin there was a small mahogany linen locker fixed high above the bulkhead, clearly beyond her reach. Greta stared at it for a moment, then turned and crawled to the cabin door and drew it open.

In the passageway she halted. It wasn't like her to give up so easily, to abandon the cabin half-searched. Perhaps she was worn down by the drugs, more dispirited by the rape and the captivity than she'd known. But that wasn't her way. That was the habit of a flincher, someone who planted the seeds of their own defeat—who did a half-assed job, then whined about half-assed results.

She twisted around, and on her belly she studied the geometry of the narrow cabin. The single bunk was butted up against the bulkhead and just beyond the edge of the wall, the linen locker door was positioned within easy reach of the sink. A perfect storage spot for washcloths, hand towels, and night creams. There was no chair to crawl onto, no ladder, no stool. But by kneeling on the bed, a cripple might still have a shot at opening that interesting door.

Greta hauled herself to the bunk and muscled the deadweight of her body up over the edge of the bed frame. She rolled the single pillow into a hard cylinder, positioned her knees on the pad, and taking a handhold on a small shelf fixed to the bulkhead, she swiveled around and levered her body upright, flattening her right cheek against the bulkhead, straightening her arm overhead as she reached for the locker door. Arm and shoulder lengthening to their maximum like some overzealous schoolgirl pleading to be called on.

After a second or two of struggle, she could see the knob to the locker was an inch or two beyond her fingertips, so she shifted her hand to the right, crooked it at a better angle around the edge of the bulkhead, and managed to hook a fingernail into the bottom edge of the cabinet door.

She pried the door forward, but the wood was swollen from the constant humidity and was tight in its frame. She continued to tug at it, bending her fingernail back and back, edging the door open, a half inch, another, until finally the fingernail snapped off at the quick.

She sucked in a breath, clenched her eyes, cursed

quietly. After another moment she shook it off, reset her knees, then used her second finger and pried the door the rest of the way open.

She had to come down from the pillow and back away to the foot of the bed to get a glimpse inside the closet. And from there she saw what she had not even allowed herself to hope for. She had been looking for the VHF radio, the boat keys, or maybe even a mirror she could use to flash Morse code back to shore. But what she saw was the silver butt of a pistol resting on the edge of the single shelf—a very substantial pistol.

When she heard the outboard motor roar up to the hull of the *Miss Begotten,* and felt the big yacht sway in its following wake, Greta was a few feet from her cabin door.

The pistol was a stainless steel .357 Smith & Wesson with a four-inch barrel and a rubber grip. It was loaded with Magnum hollow-point shells so powerful, they would be able to tear a hole through the side of that old mahogany yacht big enough for Greta to squeeze her head out, scream for help.

She squirmed through the door, hauled herself back into her bunk, and settled against the mattress. The plan took shape quickly in her imagination. When Pepper walked in, came over to the bed, stood close, Greta would show her the pistol. Freeze her, give her slow, careful instructions, then she would follow Pepper down the hallway again, out to the deck, and supervise the navigation back to shore.

It had to go something like that, a close-quarters ambush. Anything else and Pepper might bolt before Greta could even use the weapon. Duck away behind the cabin door, get back up to the top deck, radio for reinforcements. Once Pepper had eluded her, there was no way Greta could chase her around the yacht. No, it had to be done at close range.

Greta tucked the pistol out of sight beneath her hip. She was running the scenario another time, checking it for flaws, when she felt their weight settle on the stern of the yacht and heard their voices arguing. Bean, Echeverria, another man she didn't recognize, and Pepper, all coming aboard together.

"Three people, Echeverria. Jesus Christ. Two old women. A dog, for christsakes. A goddamn dog. What the hell were you thinking about?"

"Hey, you told us to plug the leak. I never heard anything about having a quota. Two, three, four, what the fuck difference does it make at this point?"

"And you, Pepper. That ridiculous fucking car."

"The car?"

"You know what I'm talking about. All that preposterous bullshit you've been doing to the hearse."

"Oh."

"That goddamn car almost broke my back yesterday."

Tran van Hung said something to Pepper in Vietnamese. Probably another plea of love like he'd been making for days.

They were on the stern deck, Pepper in nice black walking shorts, a yellow sleeveless top. Trying out some new makeup she'd bought yesterday. Plum lip gloss, a white silvery eyeshadow, Pro-glide mascara that separated and defined each lash. She'd even torn out a perfume strip from her latest copy of *Cosmo* and dabbed it on her wrists and throat. Seventy-five dollars a bottle stuff.

Dr. Bean Wilson was wearing a handsome pair of gray linen trousers and a burgundy long-sleeve polo shirt and his heavy white tennis shoes. His hair was perfect and his eyes were dense with excitement.

Pepper could feel her heart working. Knowing she looked especially alluring today, thinking this was the day, if things went the way she hoped, it was time to say something personal to Bean, some nudge or enticing look that would get things tilted in the right direction.

But then all the way out on the Zodiac, Bean had been giving Echeverria a load of shit, and her too, in a roundabout way. Complaining about the mess they'd made in Key Largo, three dead. The police in an uproar, the Miami papers and TV stations sending their best people down to cover it. Three dead.

"So fire me," Echeverria said. "Try that, why don't you? Or pull out your six-gun and take me down."

"Don't fucking tempt me."

"This is all wrong," Tran van Hung said. "Arguing like thieves. This is not good. Big day like this, it's a bad omen to bitch and moan like bunch of ridiculous weenies."

"He's right," Pepper said. "We should all just back off a little, take a few deep breaths of this nice fresh ocean air."

Bean stared at her, standing in the passageway down to the cabins, giving her a twisted, ugly look like his mouth was melting in the heat.

"I've surrounded myself with morons. An enterprise as momentous as this and I've got idiots and rednecks working for me. What the hell was I thinking?"

He turned and stumped down the stairs, waited for Pepper to join him in the narrow corridor.

"And that other thing," he snarled at her. "My father's office. Tell me, at least, you did that the way I asked.''

Something gassy bubbled in her belly. Pepper was about to lie, give him a slick story, how she had completed the task exactly as he'd instructed, how everything had gone smoothly, make up some funny incident that happened going into his father's office or back out. But Bean read the lie in her eyes before she had the chance to mouth the words.

''You moron. You forgot! You forgot to do it!''

''In all the excitement, I knew there was something else, but I couldn't remember what.''

Bean struck her hard across the face, knocked her to the floor, blurred her vision, stung her cheek and jaw. Stung it all the way down to the bone. Deeper even than that. She sat up, opened her mouth, heard a click in the bone. Something out of line, the smooth hinge warped.

''All right, it's Sunday,'' Bean said. ''The old man's not in the office today, so you're going back ashore. Echeverria will take you in. Then you and you alone will drive that idiotic hearse up to Key Largo and you'll do what I told you to do last night. No fuckups, no embellishments, just do it. Get it done. Is that understood?''

She looked up at him. She climbed slowly to her feet, staying out of range.

''I can't stay just a little while longer, see how this turns out with Greta? Just a few minutes? We're so close.''

He stepped forward, his right hand closing into a fist

''All right, all right,'' she said. ''I'm on my way. I'll do it. I promise. I'll do it right.''

CHAPTER

24

Greta tucked the pistol farther below her hip, rearranged her blue scrub over it. Against four of them the odds clearly weren't in her favor for any kind of full-fledged shoot-out, even with the element of surprise and her excellent aim.

She listened to them talking in the passageway. As she was wedging her arm beneath the strap she heard the outboard roaring off. And before she could get to the pistol again, her cabin door swung open.

Bean had a mock smile ready for her as he came into the cabin. Following him was a small Asian man in shiny silver shorts and a matching shirt. The man glanced at her, then took a seat on a plastic chair across from the bunk. Sitting primly, hands on his thighs, mouth pursed in a wrinkled frown.

Bean set his leather medical bag on the bedside table and drew back the blue plaid curtains from both portholes.

"You've been sweating," he said. "Are you all right? Any kind of fever?"

She remained silent.

"I need to know if you've been having side effects

with the morphine. Pepper said no, just drowsiness, which is normal enough, of course, but look at you, you're soaking."

Greta stared into his eyes and said nothing.

"Now, now," he said. "I know you're very angry with me, Greta. I know you feel deceived and ill-used. And I'm sorry for that, I truly am. But you must realize this is for your own good. It doesn't matter that you're a DEA agent, that you were investigating me. None of that's relevant to our common interest. Getting rid of your pain supersedes everything, your role in law enforcement, your temporary discomfort here, don't you agree?"

"Enough talk," the Asian man said. "Give her the shot, get on with it."

Bean turned to the small man in silver foil.

"Greta, I'd like you to meet Tran van Hung. Tran is an old war buddy from my Vietnam days. He's representing a group of investors over there who are looking for a marketable painkiller that they might make a few billion dollars from. Tran, the money man, as Pepper likes to refer to him."

"This is taking too long. All this talk is not necessary. Give her the shot, we'll see if you fucked up again."

Bean turned back to Greta and smiled.

"Tran doesn't fully appreciate the medical formalities I must complete before I can refill your pump. I need to know a few things from you, Greta, otherwise our data isn't complete. And our experiment doesn't have the scientific credibility it requires. Sooner or later we will have to run our trials in the light of day. Face the scrutiny of the FDA, the AMA, all that. So it behooves us to stay within strict medical guidelines as closely as we can even at this early stage."

Tran huffed and crossed his legs. He reached in his shirt pocket for a box of cigarettes and shook one out, set it in his mouth and was clicking a small gold lighter when Bean wheeled and snatched the cigarette away, dropped it to the deck and crushed it with his shoe.

Greta inched her right hand to her hip, touched a finger to the steel.

Tran protested in a burst of Vietnamese and Bean spewed something back that sounded like the man's native tongue. Tran closed his eyes and took a breath, then opened them and gave Bean an owlish look. He reached into his shirt pocket and this time drew out a tiny green chili pepper.

"Is this okay, Doctor? Is it okay if I munch a hot pepper?"

"Help yourself, little man."

When Bean turned back around, Greta had the pistol out. She cocked the hammer and kept the aim steady on Bean's midsection. Tran van Hung spit out the green pepper and stood up.

"Oh, shit," he said. "You fucking weenie. Where'd she get a gun?"

Bean's eyes were calm. He canted his head to the side, looking past the pistol at Greta's face.

"Come now, Agent Masterson," he said. "This isn't necessary."

"Put your hands up, both of you."

"What're you going to do, Greta? Shoot us, take the boat in to shore yourself? Is that what you think?"

"In the air," she said. "Your hands where I can see them."

"Is that what you want, Greta? Are you sure? Do you really want to spend the rest of your life in misery? Chronic torment, acute episodes that at any time could send your heart into an arrhythmia. Don't you want a chance at a better life than that, Greta? Doesn't Suzy deserve that? A real mother, a mother who can take care of her, be there for her. Wouldn't Suzy want your pain to go away? If she were here, if you could ask her now?"

She felt the pistol waver.

"Oh, yes," Bean said. "We know about Suzy, we know she's staying with your mother. Echeverria is on his way at this moment to pick up your daughter, bring her down here."

"You're lying."

"Oh, yes, Greta. He's on his way as we speak. He'll go to the door, flash his badge, tell Granny he's come for her, come to take her to her mother."

"Bullshit. You had no reason to abduct her. You didn't know I'd give you any trouble."

"Are you going to risk that?"

She steadied the pistol.

"Okay, Bean, turn around, both of you, and walk over to the door. I'm going to follow you upstairs. We're going to go very slowly back to the upper deck, and we're going to take this goddamn boat into Key West. If I have to kill you both, I don't really care at this point."

Bean moved to his medical bag.

"Not another step!" Greta shouted.

He opened the bag and took out a plastic Baggie that contained a syringe and a small vial.

"Here it is, Greta. Here's the end of your pain. No one has to get hurt. I can give you the injection, fill your pump. You can hold on to your pistol the whole time. I don't care. When it's finished, you decide if you can forgive me for inconveniencing you this way. You can shoot me or you can sing my praises, whatever you think is right. I'll take that chance.''

"Inconveniencing me? Is that what you call this?"

Tran van Hung had made several small steps toward the passageway. He was a half second from lunging to safety when Greta aimed the pistol at him and ordered him to move the hell back into the cabin. Tran hesitated a moment, staring at the barrel, then he muttered something and stepped back over to his chair.

"You're going to be sorry for this, Bean Wilson. There's no more money after today. After this fuckup."

Bean smiled to himself as he filled the syringe from the glass vial.

"Tran keeps threatening me," he said. "But at this point it hardly matters. If his people don't want to market our drug, Greta, there'll be a long line of others who will."

"That's enough, Bean. Put it down. Put it down now and turn around and go to the door."

"You see how confident I am, Greta. I know there are two sides warring in you right now. Greta the DEA agent, and Greta the woman and mother. Should you do your duty and risk serving out your life sentence of excruciating pain, or should you put all that aside for a while and save your own flesh and blood, give your daughter back her mother. Should you destroy me, or should you be part of the medical breakthrough of our age? Those are the options, Greta, and I know you'll agree with me. Your duty is important, yes; I know about duty. But ridding yourself of torment is far and away your more important responsibility."

"There's no debate going on in my head. Another fucking step and you're dead."

Bean smiled and took that step.

She shot him in the leg, shot him a second time in the other leg. The explosions were immense in that tiny cabin. Bean was knocked back against the door. He howled and cursed, but after only a few seconds he was back on his feet, sagging to one side but upright. Tran lay flat on his belly on the floor, low noises coming from his throat as if he were cycling through a chant.

Greta stared, her heart churning.

Bean's pants legs were ripped just below both knees, but there was no gore, no wound of any kind. With a groan, he stooped and retrieved the syringe and held it up to the light, and made a long sigh of relief. Greta stared at his legs, her mind whirling with the crazy sight before her, splinters and wire. Two fist size gouges in the gray fabric of his pants. But no blood.

"Prosthetics," he said, setting the syringe on the table near his bag. Then he swung his head to the side and shouted at the Asian man. "Tran, no, no, don't do it!"

Greta jerked her aim to the left but the man in silver clothes was still on the floor. Before she could swing back to Bean, he'd lunged for the pistol and had torn it from her grip. He stepped away and held her eye.

"Now, Greta, we'll have to wait a few minutes till your blood pressure drops back to normal."

He set the pistol on a shelf across the cabin.

"And Tran, after you've pulled yourself together sufficiently, do you think you can help me tighten up these straps?"

There was something bad wrong with Pepper's jaw. She could open and close her mouth, but when she tried to touch her teeth together, they didn't mesh, and worse than that, they ached, all her teeth at once. Every single one, right down to the roots and below.

She sobbed for the first twenty miles, then got it down to a whimper by the time she made Bahia Honda and was just sniffling a little as she passed through Marathon. By the time she hit Islamorada her eyes were clear and there was a hornet buzzing in the big vein in her neck. And her teeth were throbbing worse than they had before.

She knew exactly what was wrong. Bean had broken her jaw. Which meant she would have to get her mouth wired shut for six weeks, and for that month and a half she'd have to drink all her meals, milkshakes with raw eggs, hot soup, which she hated. She wouldn't be able to brush, no yawning, no French kissing, no hot peppers, nothing solid in her mouth at all, animal, vegetable, or human. And worse, she'd have to start carrying a pair of wire clippers in her purse everywhere she went in case she got sick. With your mouth wired shut, you didn't want to be doing a whole lot of vomiting.

At noon, as she pulled into the gravel drive of Dr. Bean Wilson's office, she didn't have a single drip left in her tear ducts and she could feel the blood in her chest getting sludgy and hot. Nobody'd ever hit her before. Not even her daddy. Not even when she'd called him vile names, spit on him, tried to claw out his eyes. Not once. He'd treated her with respect and kindness even when she'd attempted to bite the end of his dick off that first time he slipped it in her mouth when she was half asleep. Ten years old and clamping down on her daddy's meaty pecker like it was a drumstick, sinking her teeth deep into the blood of it. But not even then did he hit her. And not later, when she bad-

mouthed him in front of his boat bum buddies. Calling
him sex names she'd heard her girlfriends use on their
boyfriends. Pencil dick, nutless wonder. Embarrassing
him, making him angry, but even then he didn't swat
her, didn't say an unkind word to her. Just came in
later and asked her if she meant those things and she
said no, not really, and that was all there was to that.
He'd been Pepper's husband from the age of ten till
the year she turned twenty-one, when he died. He'd
asked for her hand that first year of sex together. One
night lying next to her in the dark after they'd finished, asking her if she'd rather be his daughter or his
wife. She didn't need to think that one over. His wife,
she'd said, of course, his wife. And afterward he'd always been a good husband, showing her how to do
things in the bedroom, how to please him and how to
please herself. Three or four sexual things were all he
knew to teach her. Nothing like the knowledge Pepper
had acquired with other boys since her daddy died.

Her daddy was always polite, apologetic even. Born
on Key West of a mean sponge-fishing father, raised
with courtly conch manners and strong family discipline, her daddy would kiss her on the forehead or on
the temple, but never on the lips, even when he was
riding along above her groaning and sweating. He
wouldn't do that and she understood why, because
even though Pepper was his wife, he treated her like a
lady, because it would've made everything too personal, too intimate if they'd touched tongues, slob-
bered on each other's faces. Even when she told her
guidance counselor at school she was married to her
daddy and later that night the sheriff and two of his
men came to the boat and woke him up and questioned him and then questioned her too, and took her

daddy away to the jail to question him some more. Even after he came back the next morning, let go for lack of evidence, he didn't hit her. He just said he understood she was mad at him and that was all right, 'cause from time to time women got mad at their men, it didn't matter how good the man was to the woman, there'd just necessarily have to come that moment when she couldn't stand the sight or smell of him and she'd get mad. From time to time it was perfectly natural that she should hate him. His only request was that when the next time came, and the terrible anger heated her blood, would she please stay away from the frying pans and the long kitchen knives. His head was still ringing, he said, from a conking Pepper's mother had given him twenty years before.

In Dr. Bean Wilson's parking lot there was a yellow Coupe de Ville and another car, a little black Japanese convertible parked beside it. She got out, peeked into the convertible, and saw a couple of tennis rackets and a wire basket full of Day-Glo yellow balls.

She got the key to the office door out of her pocketbook and went over to the front door. She slipped the key in the lock but the door was already open, so she pushed on inside.

There were voices coming from down the hall. Bean's father doing a little Sunday morning consultation. Pepper drew the #15 scalpel from the pocket of her shorts. You never knew when you might have to make a quick incision. She slid through the door back to the examining rooms.

"Still nothing?" she heard the old doctor say.

Pepper'd met him twice before when he'd visited the Eaton Street clinic in the last couple of years. Nice old gentleman who smiled a lot and had good Southern manners like he thought every woman was a lady and every man a gentleman until proven otherwise.

"Numb as a hunk of roast beef," another man replied.

Pepper edged down the hallway to the room with light coming from it.

"Jesus, Eddie, I don't know what it is," the old doctor said. "But there's something wrong here. I simply don't understand this."

"I'll say there's something wrong. Christ, maybe you used the wrong stuff."

Pepper snuck a quick look around the edge of the door. The old doctor had his drug cabinet open and was fumbling around inside it. A tall thin man with a bald head was sitting on the examining table. He wore white tennis shorts and a white T-shirt.

"I'm going to have to call for an ambulance, Eddie, get you into the hospital. I'm sorry, but I don't see any other choice."

"Shit, Bean, it's just tennis elbow. What the hell's going on? I walk in here, I'm fine. What is this, some kind of heart attack?"

"No, no. I need you to calm down, Eddie. I'll get that ambulance down here and we'll sort all of this out at the hospital."

"Jesus Christ, Bean, it's the club mixed doubles tournament. There's going to be some very pissed-off people if I don't show."

"Blame me," the old doc said. "It's all my fault."

Pepper ducked across the hall into a dark examining room and listened to the doctor walk back to his office and call 911. Four or five minutes later the ambulance was outside and the two of them left, Eddie still bitching about his arm.

Pepper went into the examining room where they'd been, opened the drug cabinet, and took out the four remaining vials. She was back in the hearse a minute later and on her way back to Key West.

As she drove, every few seconds she'd forget and touch her teeth together and there'd be another explosion of splintered light in the back of her brain. That bastard had broken her jaw and she wasn't going to be right again for a long time. There wasn't any brand of love she knew that could stand up to something like that. Pepper sure as hell wasn't one of those women with self-esteem problems. Some brute of a husband beating the shit out of her in the morning and the woman all dressed up in her frilly things with his favorite supper on the table by evening time, greeting him at the door with a gooey hello. No, sir, she wasn't one of those. Her daddy'd taught her about love, and though she knew the world considered their marriage perverted, at least her daddy had never once hit her, never once done anything but praise her efforts, no matter how paltry they'd been. Didn't matter he was a child molester. Give her one of those any day instead of a bastard who broke the jaw of the woman whose only fault was loving him.

As she drove through Lower Matecumbe, Pepper minced up a hot claw on the back of a folded-up road map, then pinched the crumbly pieces into her mouth one dab at a time and sucked their juices. In no time her mouth was filled with dazzling fire, her eyes watering furiously, then the numbness began to seep into her gums and after that everything was fine for a little while.

CHAPTER

25

At noon Thorn called the offices of the *Key Largo News*, though he knew Monica would not be there. It was Sunday after all, day of rest. Not like the *Herald* up in Miami, where it took every hour of every day to cover the unceasing parade of outrages. In Key Largo you could miss a day or two, nobody'd notice, maybe a month. He was just going to leave a message on the answering machine, ask Monica to call him first thing on Monday. Then maybe slip in another discreet sentence or two, tell her he loved her, say he was sorry for how he'd acted last week, pushing her away like he'd done, leave it at that for the time being.

He was getting the words right in his head when the phone was snapped up on the first ring and a man barked an impatient hello. When Thorn hesitated, the man snarled hello again.

"Is Monica there?"

"Who is this?"

"Who is *this*?" Thorn said back to him.

"Monica's not here."

"I want to leave a message for her."

"Who is this?" the man repeated. Thorn was forming a picture of the guy. A square head with tiny ears and small weak eyes. A phone bully—all those safe miles of cable between them.

"My name is Thorn."

The guy took a three- or four-second break to think that over.

"You're the boyfriend."

"That's right. The boyfriend."

"Well, she's not coming into the office today."

"I know. I just want to get a message to her. I want her to call me."

"So you heard about what happened?"

Thorn didn't like his tone. Ominous and gloating.

"No," Thorn said. "Why don't you tell me."

"Three dead. Two by gunshot, one with her throat slashed."

Thorn lost the air in his lungs.

"They did Roy Everly execution style, two bullets through the temple, and his mother had her throat cut, then some old woman across the street was shot in the face."

"And Monica!"

"She got grazed on her neck. No big deal. Innocent bystander."

Thorn gripped the phone harder.

"No big deal," Thorn said.

"That's right."

"You ever been grazed by a bullet?"

"Fuck you, Jack. I don't have time for this."

"Where's Monica now?"

"Home, I think. Or over at your place. She had to bury the pooch."

"What?"

"Her dog. It got shot too. Lots of bullets flying."

Thorn closed his eyes. Worked on his breathing for a few seconds.

"Listen," Thorn said. "Whatever the fuck your name is. Get your self-important ass up right now, and drive over there and tell her to call me."

"Can't do it, lover boy. *Herald*'s bringing me on board to do some interviewing on this. I don't have time to be running messages. This is my shot."

"You're going to go over there," Thorn said. "And you're going to tell Monica to call me."

"Wrong," the guy said, and hung up.

Thorn stared at the dead phone in his hand. He was losing it. Couldn't even intimidate a guy over the phone—like the asshole knew Thorn was crippled, stuck in an aluminum chair, his threats without weight.

He dialed the Key Largo sheriff's department, worked his way past the receptionist to Jennifer Bell, head cheerleader back in Thorn's football days. Pert and blond and full of serious pep. Captain Bell now. No-nonsense Captain Bell. Her school devotion had turned civic.

"She's fine, Thorn. We talked to her a good part of the night. Upset, of course, discombobulated, but okay. She's probably sleeping it off now."

"Is anybody watching her?"

"What? You mean like protecting her?"

"That's exactly what I mean."

"This wasn't about her, Thorn. She was just an eyewitness to the event and got herself between the shooters and their escape vehicle and they took a couple of potshots at her. That's the way we read it."

"You're sure of that?"

"If we thought she was in the least danger, there'd be somebody over there, Thorn. Believe it."

"Can you get a message to her, Jen? I need to talk to her."

"When I get a minute, yeah, I'll send someone over. It's kind of crazy around here at the moment. Three dead, that's a year's worth for us. But I'll send somebody when I can. Okay?"

It wasn't okay, but it was the best he could arrange so far from home with Sugarman off on vacation.

All afternoon he waited for the phone to ring, exercising in the rehab room, doing dips on the parallel bars, and working his useless legs. As the hours drifted by, he felt the anger swelling at the bottom of his gut like a tumor that seemed to double in mass with every breath.

The clinic's phone was silent all afternoon, and after his workout, a long shower didn't cool him down, and the rum and Coke he accepted from Ginny only gave his frustration a brittle edge. At six o'clock he made himself a grilled cheese sandwich and a simple salad from the paltry supplies in the kitchen, and a while later he submitted to his second steroid injection of the day at the hands of Nurse Jankowitz, a humorless woman with an impenetrable Slavic accent who untaped the adhesive strip that covered the catheter tip at the base of his spine, flooded his spinal cord with the useless steroids, then retaped the spout, all with the soft-handed tenderness of a meat packer.

Back in his airless room, Thorn sat and stared at the bleak wall, watching the daylight die. He was trapped in someone else's failed body. The ice in his legs had rooted itself deep in his marrow, and again and again as he tried to work a single toe, tilt his ankle, pass even the faintest signal to the dark mass of his legs, nothing made it through. Tipping up his foot a quarter of an

inch was as far beyond his abilities as levitating a gran-
ite boulder. His mind throbbed from the effort, and
the anger snapped through his veins like the tattered
claws of flame.

At ten that evening he used Bean's office phone to
call the sheriff's department again, but Jennifer Bell
had gone home for the day. She'd left no messages for
anyone named Thorn. He slapped the phone down,
then raked the thing off the desk onto the floor.

Afterward, he took the elevator up to Bean's darkened apartment and stationed himself beside one of
the windows. While he waited, the anger grew, its heat
radiating up into Thorn's chest, down into his deadened legs, a glow of warmth that seemed to give some
small nourishment to the cold empty spaces below his
waist. As though he could heal himself with this anger,
regenerate the nerves and fibers that relayed the elec-
tronic pulses from brain to toes. As if anger alone
could do it, anger becoming rage, rage becoming fury,
fury becoming miraculous cure.

It felt like he was breathing in darkness and exhaling
fire. Little by little filling the room with the heat of his
impotence and frustration, packing it tight, pumping
more and more pressure into the room until soon he
would reach the critical moment when the door would
explode, the walls blow away.

Out the window where he sat a heavy wash of stars
was visible above the electric haze of Key West. For the
next hour he stared at the Big Dipper, forcing himself
to muse about the unknowable distances between
those bright dots, trying to picture the immense journey starlight made to the earth—all the old reliable
metaphysical gymnastics he'd used since childhood to

put his trivial affairs in perspective. Against the night sky his worries never seemed so goddamn important.

But on that night it wasn't working. Not even close.

If he'd had a Higher Power, it was the perfect moment to beseech him. Make a deal, maybe swap his soul for the use of his legs. But Thorn was no foxhole convert. He'd laid no religious groundwork and was not tempted to mouth the name of the one or two gods he was acquainted with to see if the dark air shuddered and answered back. If those stars didn't do the trick, nothing would. Religion was all self-hypnosis anyway. Placebo effect. What you trusted deeply enough might get you through. And what Thorn had always relied on even more than the stars, more than the healing power of an easterly breeze off the Atlantic or perfect days of fishing or tying flies or any other of the constellation of natural pleasures, what had gotten him up one shit creek after another was the white knot of gristle at his stubborn core.

Whatever it cost, he was going to finish his pursuit, find out who struck him down and why, then he would find Monica no matter where she'd fled, and plead with her to forgive him for his stupid show of pride. He would tell her the truth, that he had pushed her away because his feelings for her frightened him to his core. But he loved her, and wanted to marry her and live with her till the end. And she would demand to know why he was frightened, and then Thorn would have to tell her the truth. That somewhere in the last few weeks he had finally admitted to himself that Monica was the only woman he'd ever loved who needed him less than he needed her.

That's where he was just after midnight, feeling a soul-splitting wail taking shape inside him, when a crack of light widened at the door, and Bean came thumping through the darkness, hit the switch, saw Thorn and nearly toppled over.

"Jesus God, you scared the red-hot devil out of me."

Bean circled the room, turning on the rest of the lights. His pants were torn and his prosthetics looked badly mangled. He tottered on them as unsteadily as a tightrope walker in a hard wind.

Without another word, Bean stalked into his bedroom and shut the door. He was gone five minutes and when he returned he wore a pair of faded designer jeans and a white silk T-shirt that clung to his tightly muscled body. His hair was wet and raked back off his face and his eyes were fired up. As he headed for the kitchen, Thorn saw his gait was back to its normal stiffness.

"Join me in a drink, Thorn? I'm breaking out the Cristal."

"What is it, Bean? You make some progress with your wonder drug?"

He halted and turned around slowly. A smile crawled across his face.

"Well, well. You've been investigating again, haven't you? You just can't seem to stop doing that."

"Call me crazy." Thorn rolled forward, left the Big Dipper to empty itself. "But whenever someone knocks me on the head and paralyzes me, I just get this itch to find out why."

Bean's smile soured and the glitter in his eyes sharpened.

"And you think I had something to do with your injury?"

"Of course you did."

"I see," he said. Then he smiled. "Well, all the more reason for that drink."

He opened the champagne, presented Thorn a glass, foamed it to the brim. Thorn held the glass by its fragile stem, staring into Bean's eyes. Bean nodded and clinked his glass against Thorn's and went back to the couch and sat.

"Tell me something, old buddy."

"No," Thorn said. "You're going to tell me something. A lot of things."

Bean smiled again, all pleasantness and good cheer.

"Ah yes, one of our old familiar standoffs."

Thorn had a bit of the fizzy wine, then in a swift unthinking motion he tipped up the drink and swallowed it. Bean got up and refilled his glass and topped off his own.

"Okay, then how about a truth swap? Tit for tat." Bean turned to Thorn and scratched a finger against the raspy bristles on his chin. "And since I'm the host and providing the refreshments, it seems only right I begin. Because there's something I've always wanted to know, Thorn. That's been eating at me for almost thirty years."

"Name it."

"Why didn't you go to the war? Vietnam."

"I wasn't drafted."

"There was a lottery, Thorn. It was based on birthdays, and yours was in the top fifty. I know, because the second after I looked at my number, I looked at yours. They called everybody in the top hundred numbers. What do you think happened to you? Did they lose your name? Couldn't find your address?"

"I don't know. I was never called."

Bean stared down at his drink.

"Did you realize that back then my father was on the Monroe County draft board?"

"No."

"I've always been deeply curious about that." Bean had a careful sip and set his glass down on the wicker side table. "I wonder if perhaps he might have swayed things to your advantage somehow, playing favorites. Because, you see, my lottery number was higher than yours. I was in the nineties. But I was called and you weren't. I went and you didn't. What do you think, Thorn? Is it possible my father gave you a pass but didn't give his own son one?"

"I never got a notice, Bean. I would've gone if I'd gotten one. It wasn't anything I cared about one way or the other, but I would've gone."

"Oh, yes, yes. Because you're a good citizen. Because you always do your duty. Yes, isn't that nice? Isn't that all morally admirable and noble."

Thorn drank down half his second glass and set it on the window sill.

"Why does it matter, Bean? It's gone, it's over. What difference does it make now?"

"What difference does it make? Oh, that's good. That's just like you, Thorn. Immanently practical. Get on with it. Do what's in front of you, forget the past. Yes, yes, that's very enlightened, a very wise way to live, I'm sure."

"This isn't about you and me, Bean. This is about you and your father."

Bean lifted his eyes, fastened them on Thorn.

"What about my father?"

"You should ask him what happened on the draft board, hear what he has to say."

"Oh, it's all so simple, isn't it? The world according

to Thorn. An uncomplicated place. Just ask and hear the answer. Oh, yes, so easy. Well, listen to me, Thorn. You think you can drop out of the world and go about your merry business and it has no effect on anyone. Well, I'll tell you what, that's not how the universe works. When you drop out, someone else has to take your place. And in the case of Vietnam, that someone was me, Thorn, me. You stayed home, played with your navel, and I went to war. I lost my legs. I live with that every fucking day. The torment.''

"And that's my fault?''

"You got a pass, Thorn. I didn't. So what do you think? Is it your fault? In the larger scheme of things?''

Bean stared into his eyes for a long moment, then let his gaze drift back to the photos on the wall.

"So is it my turn yet?''

"Of course,'' Bean said. "Fire at will.''

"How many people have you murdered already?''

He flinched but recovered quickly. He turned his head and peered again at Thorn.

"I suppose you're referring to my experiments?''

"That's right.''

"Well, I don't want to quibble over semantics,'' he said. "But there's a considerable difference, legally, ethically, in every way I can think of, between murder and assisted suicide. Wouldn't you agree?''

"So that's how you work it out, is it? You find vets who're so desperate, they've stopped caring if they live or die, they're happy to let you exploit them. That makes it okay to kill them.''

Bean's smile withered. A dark crease appeared in his forehead. When he spoke, his voice was as dull and rigid as iron.

"To answer your question, Thorn, yes, unfortunately

we've lost some volunteers, but all of them were fully aware of the risks of the experiment and each of them accepted those risks willingly. I even have signed documents, witnessed and notarized, if that matters to you. They all knew exactly what the dangers were and they all clamored for the chance to be next."

"And Greta Masterson? Did she clamor?"

Bean chuckled and had another sip of champagne and studied Thorn above the rim of his glass.

"You've been a busy little do-bee, haven't you? Sticking your nose into every crevice you could find."

"Is Greta dead?"

"Oh, quite the contrary. Greta Masterson is in excellent health, doing very fine indeed. In fact, Greta is the cause for our celebration tonight. Because as you correctly surmised, the drug is working. Her pain has been totally and completely neutralized. She's clearheaded, blood pressure normal, heart rate at 62. She's sleeping under a nurse's care right now and doing fine. Just fine."

"Pepper is her nurse?"

"That's right. Pepper Tremaine."

"Where are they?"

"Now, *that* I can't tell you. It might create something of a problem if you were inclined to contact the police or something of that sort."

"You're going to take me to see her, Bean."

A sputter of laughter broke from his lips.

"I am! And why the hell would I do that?"

"Because I'm the one you want to prove this to."

"What the hell are you talking about?"

Bean wiped his hands on his pants legs and sat back against the couch. He swallowed, drew in a long breath through his nose. As close to fidgeting as this controlled man would allow.

Thorn said, "You're dying to let the world know what you've discovered. But you can't do that yet. You need more time to get everything all in place, make sure you can stand up to the public scrutiny. But the yearning is still there. You want to go up on the rooftop and scream the news. But I'm the best you've got, Bean. I'm the one you want to impress, anyway. Next to your dad, I'm the one who counts the most."

"You arrogant asshole. Fuck you, Thorn."

"Come on, Bean. Admit it. You're dying to show me what you've done. How smart you are. Rub my face in your triumph."

Bean finished off his glass and poured another. He held up the bottle to Thorn but Thorn waved it off.

"You and me alone, is that what you're saying?"

"Just the two of us, yes."

"You think I'm half-witted, Thorn? What's to keep you from calling the police, the DEA, having them follow us? Why should I trust you?"

"You know who I am, Bean. You more than anybody. If I say this is between you and me alone, then that's what it is."

Bean's eyes relaxed, a sly smile rose to the surface of his lips.

On some rare angling expeditions, there was a moment right after a powerful fish smacked the bait, a second or two into the first sizzling run, when Thorn could tell with utter certainty that the hook was set deep and true and all the knots would hold and the line was strong enough. Most fishing was filled with uncertainty. Even after a long fight, with the fish floundering helplessly at the boat, the angler reaching down with the net or a hand, there was always a tremor of anxiety that the fish would at that last possible second explode, shake the hook, snap the frayed line, run free. That uncertainty, the fragile, flitting link between hunter and prey, was one of the agonizing pleasures of fishing.

But with those deeply hooked catches there was something almost sad and tragic about the act, too effortless, an unseemly conquest. He cranked the reel, brought the fish close, scooped him up. A mechanical exercise. And that's how it felt with Bean. So easy. Appealing to his vanity. Watching him gulp down the morsel, the hook cutting deep into his gullet. A man so starved for any trifle of praise, he was willing to risk his kingdom for a handful of fool's gold.

Bean sat forward on the couch, the smile maturing into a self-satisfied smirk.

"All right. I'll tell you what, old friend. I'll carry you out there. I'll let you see the results of my labors, let you draw your own conclusions. You deserve that much, all the trouble you've gone to investigating me so diligently. I suppose I should be honored, really, you spending your valuable time looking into my affairs.

"Tomorrow morning, first thing. How's that? And afterward, if you think I should be punished, if you think I should serve the rest of my life in jail, face the electric chair, then okay, do what you have to do. But before you decide, you need to talk to Greta. You need to hear from her how she felt a day ago, what her pain was like, and you need to hear how she feels now, and then you'll have to ask yourself if the man who found the cure for her pain and the pain of millions of others should be punished for the methods he used in reaching that goal."

"Why don't we go right now?"

"Oh, no, she needs her rest. And I need mine. It's been a long and difficult day."

"You had those dolphins killed, didn't you? Echeverria is working for you, and he killed them."

"My, my, such an impressive demonstration of ratiocination. If I ever need to hire a private eye, I'll certainly know where to go."

Thorn rolled his wheelchair across the room, picked up the bottle of champagne, and rolled back to his place by the window. He poured himself another glass and gulped half of it down.

"Tell me something, Thorn. Are you familiar with the smell of burning shit?"

Thorn looked over at him.

"I haven't smelled any lately."

"No, I guess you wouldn't have. Because, you see, the smell of shit burning in diesel oil, that's the smell of Vietnam. The smell of that particular holocaust. Those were our latrines, you see, fifty-gallon drums partially filled with fuel oil. Set ablaze every morning to purify them, the fire tended by some unlucky grunt. But then, you're not interested in war stories, are you? That's not what you're after."

"If it explains anything, I'm listening."

Bean scowled. He finished the champagne in his glass and settled back into the couch and stared across at one of the photographs on the wall. Thorn and he were racing on a white strand of beach up in the panhandle. Their feet splashed through the sheen of an incoming tide and a shower of sparkles flashed at their ankles. Bean was leading the race, pumping his elbows, his mouth set, neck straining. Thorn was trying hard too, his hair was long and streamed back. One of them was always winning, the other always losing. And Doc Wilson was the official record keeper, peering at them through the viewfinder of that old Kodak. Thorn's memory told him that Bean had won far more than his share of those contests, but it was clear now that those were not the triumphs Bean had longed for, and winning those races had done nothing to satisfy the hunger that burned in his eyes back then and was burning even now.

Thorn had heard others' war stories in midnight bars. Men his age who had scarred some vital muscle that would never heal. Men who were still lost in nightmare jungles on the other side of the planet, unable to distinguish friend from foe, savior from killer. Men who still heard shards of lead whizzing by their faces like insane bees. He'd listened to their stories, watched their eyes turn inward as the room where they sat dissolved around them and re-formed dense with vines and thickets and the steady drizzle of equatorial rain.

And all the war stories he'd heard sounded the same. The Ancient Mariner determined to tell his tale to any stranger he could snag. Stories recited with mechanical precision, as if it were some school assignment the old soldier had composed long ago and committed to memory and now was retrieving, phrase by well-honed phrase. They always had the feel of narratives told too easily and too often, so that long before that night's telling they'd lost their hold on the teller, lost their power to mend the wounds they described.

But Bean's story was nothing like those.

It was clear that his had never been recounted before. Rendered in ungainly sentences and halting cadence, the story had been lying dormant for thirty years in the sludge of memory, and now, as he drew it to light in all its squalor, he seemed surprised by how raw and unpolished it sounded aloud. The crude power of catharsis. But he slogged ahead anyway, his eyes feasting on Thorn, as though this crippled man who sat across from him, this man who was Bean's oldest friend and most despised enemy, was precisely the audience he'd been waiting for all these years.

C H A P T E R

26

At nineteen Bean knew he was going to be drafted. Convinced he could cut a better deal if he enlisted, he put himself in the hands of a Miami recruiter who assured him that with test scores as high as his, Bean would train for intelligence work, which meant any assignment he got would place him well outside the war zone.

After basic training and a stint in language school, where he picked up some rudimentary Vietnamese, he was assigned to the 404th Radio Research Detachment, attached to the 173rd Airborne Brigade in the U.S. Army. He was stationed with this brigade throughout the war, but his mission was covert, so he reported directly to the larger Radio Research Group in Nha Trang.

The recruiter was a stooge, a paid liar, for he had to know that in Vietnam there was no place beyond the reach of the war. Bean was assigned to Landing Zone English just outside the small town of Bong Son in the province of Binh Dinh, about five kilometers from the coast.

LZ English was in a valley with mountains of dense

rain forest to the north and west and rice paddies and plains to the south and east, toward the South China Sea. The LZ was strategically placed a few hundred yards from VN 1, the major north-south highway that ran the entire length of the country. While most of the land was lush with palms and rain forest vegetation, there were many defoliated areas—bald patches of red clay.

English was a landing zone for helicopters, and the constant takeoffs and arrivals whipped up that red clay, coating everything he owned. The fine dust permeated his clothes, glued his eyes shut at night. Seeped into his nostrils, his asshole, and his pores. Hueys and Cobras and Chinooks, the whap-whap of their rotors every hour of the day and night. And the other noises, bursts of automatic arms fire or the distant rumbling of Phantom jets working out on nearby hillsides. And there was the constant music from the 8-track cartridge players. Jefferson Airplane, Santana, Blood, Sweat & Tears, Eric Burden, the Last Poets.

"Imagine it, Thorn. Imagine that unremitting noise. The hellish hullabaloo. While you spent those same hours in Key Largo beside the quiet bay, stalking bonefish in the shallows. I thought of you a great deal back then, imagining your life. I used to wonder if I ever passed through your thoughts, if you had any idea what I was suffering on the other side of the world. But no, you didn't, did you? You don't need to answer. I can see it. I know. I was nothing to you."

Just ten kilometers south of LZ English and in plain view of the highway was a singular, very high peak, three thousand feet or so, with a bald top. It was called the Hawk's Nest. That's where Bean was airlifted every few weeks to serve his time on the barren crest. Only a few bunkers dug into the top, eight-by-eight holes with timbers to support the flat roof of tin and sandbags four feet thick for walls; with a one-foot-high opening around the top for light and viewing. Inside the bunkers it was dark and dank with a dirt floor and four cots.

Below the perimeter of the peak there was about a hundred yards of barren ground defoliated by Agent Orange, then about four hundred yards of dead trees, timbers, and earth parched from napalm. This area was crisscrossed with row after row of concertina barbed wire, and interspersed through the fallen trees were small land mines, grenades with trip wires, and claymores. All for protection against the Viet Cong sappers who would try to crawl into the camps at night and do their murderous work.

The peak was circular and about 150 feet in diameter. Ten to fifteen American soldiers and a half dozen South Vietnamese were camped there as well for security, part of the 173rd. Those soldiers were assigned to protect Bean Wilson.

For Bean was a Vietnamese interpreter, a voice intercept operator and code breaker. On his sojourns on the mountaintop he would set up his ground-plane antennas and listen to radio signals, scanning the frequencies all night and day for tactical Vietnamese voice traffic. He used a PRC 25 radio, a precursor to modern CB's; or for longer range communication, the VR 744.

When he stumbled onto voice traffic, he would tape-record it and also try to transcribe it by hand. Usually the traffic he was looking for was a series of binary numbers: 43 17, 54 19, 65 27. Each group of two would indicate a certain cell on a 10-by-10 matrix, with a word, letter, or phrase in that cell. The matrix was the

crude encoding device used in the field by the VC and
NVA. Because the Americans had acquired all the ma-
trices, it was a fairly easy process to break the code and
translate the message into English.

Normally he received messages about rice, stating
when and where rich harvests or shipments would be
picked up. Rice pickups were the VC's form of taxa-
tion. Occasionally Bean would intercept a message indicating the location of a machine-gun emplacement
set up for an ambush. Then he would contact his major
at the 173rd by scrambled radio message and give a
tactical report. The major would authorize the necessary troop movement to avoid the ambush or eradicate
the machine gun. All very mechanical and distant.

Except that's not how Bean was experiencing it. He
never mastered the skill that so many of his fellow
soldiers had, disconnecting from their grim assignments. Dick Scherer, Larry Mowrey, Allen Chambers,
Al Carrs, Stony Castanias, Rick Burke. The men he remembered from that time. Men who returned from
their murderous expeditions with dead eyes and a
deep thirst for booze and ganja. Men whose brushes
with combat gave weight to their words, purpose to
their sprees of inebriation. But Bean was not one of
them. An outsider, uninitiated in the violence that was
occurring all around him.

And because he'd witnessed no fighting directly, he
found himself picturing everything. As the weeks
passed and he grew more and more isolated from the
men in his group, his imagination grew wild, winging
him away to machine-gun emplacements he had exposed, to the bodies blown to bloody fragments because of Bean's decoded message. He saw the slaughter
in his nervous sleep, or in the long, hallucinatory vi-

sions he suffered through the endless weeks of monsoons.

Every distant burst of machine-gun fire was linked to him, the result of some fragmentary message he'd stolen from the sky. Each jet rumbling off to the north was on a mission of death directed to its target by Bean's eavesdropping. On his peak he began to feel like a deranged god, with the power of life and death over his subjects below. Throwing thunderbolts at whomever he pleased. He hated it. Hiding himself in his hooch, he wept for hours. He trembled from a cold that was not there. At night, beneath his blankets, he would scratch the edge of a razor blade across his wrist, not cutting deep, but taking practice swipes for that moment when he summoned sufficient courage. In the meantime, he continued to do his job, his madness growing deeper with every passing day. Night after night intercepting the radio signals, listening in on the traffic of human affairs. Decoding the numbers, deciding who should die, who might be granted a reprieve. An unbearable weight.

Then late in the spring of his first year, Bean Wilson intercepted a message that sappers had been deployed to attack the Hawk's Nest at midnight. For a while Bean sat at his post and stared at his handwritten notes. It was suppertime, only a few hours before the scheduled assault. There was plenty of time to call in artillery support, have his security force aim their mortars downhill, enough time to dispatch *Puff the Magic Dragon*, one of the Huey gunships, a Duster from a neighboring fire base. But Bean simply ate his supper with the other men, chatted, joked, walked among them like a ghost among his brethren. And he felt an almost religious liberation, released from the guilty burden that had been growing heavier in his bones for those last months.

At eleven that night, filled with his terrible, secret joy, Bean Wilson ambled down the hill, snuck past the watch post, crossing over into the barren patch of earth. He waited there, looking up at the sky, saying his final prayers. Liberated from his grief and turmoil, he wept and fell to his knees. Bowing his head, he presented himself to the savage gods of that devastated country. An offering.

"You dropped out, Thorn, and I took your place. That should have been you on that hillside. It was your ticket I was riding."

But the sappers didn't get him. Instead, precisely at midnight flares lit up the sky, a Huey gunship roared over the peak behind him. Mortar shells began to pound the hillside. Evidently, on another hill like his, one of his fellow decoders had intercepted the same message and had called in the artillery.

But Bean did not flee his position.

And soon, only a few feet from where he stood, a shell landed, debris spraying into the night sky. Incredibly, Bean was unhurt, but only a few feet away from his position, several sappers screamed. And almost immediately, more fire was directed toward their wailing.

He did not move. It hardly mattered anymore if he was cut down by friendly fire or the Viet Cong. Climbing to his feet, Bean watched as another set of flares reddened the sky, the air shimmering with rosy phosphorescence, as if God himself had awakened from his ten-thousand-year sleep and his angry breath was pulsing through the dark.

And in that eerie incandescence, Bean Wilson squinted out to see, five feet before him, a small Asian boy about thirteen years old. The child hesitated a moment, his arms and face bloodied by the concertina wire, his mouth a terrified slash, then the boy lifted his rifle and aimed it unsteadily at this interloper on a hillside of his native land. And Bean did not cringe, did not duck or try to flee. With perfect calm, he stood before his executioner. The boy lay his cheek against the stock, curled his finger against the trigger, but instead of the rifle shell hammering into Bean's chest, there was an awesome thunderclap and Bean was blinded by a crimson flash, and a few feet before him the earth erupted in a great geyser of dust, sending him tumbling backward through the air, clutching in his arms the warm flesh of what he took to be the boy. Bean flew backward through a dark endless sky, embracing that boy, flying and flying until long impossible moments later he crashed in the tangled brush, opened his eyes briefly and saw his arms locked around one of his own severed legs.

Trotting down the hill through the blaze of automatic fire and the thunderous artillery bursts came Bean's South Vietnamese language advisor. Seventeen at the time, a weakling not even half Bean's height, he risked his life racing down the hillside, scooped Bean into his arms and trudged back up the steep incline with the mountain erupting all around him.

Bean came to consciousness long enough to stare into the eyes of Tran van Hung. Then he shut his eyes again and resumed his flight, lofting through a black and empty sky until he woke days and days later in a suffocating room, as large as heaven, a warehouse of white, where flies clung to the sluggish fan blades and slow nurses floated through the labyrinthine rows of beds, and all around him were the cries of fatherless children lost in a maze without exit.

And that's when the ceaseless burn of his phantom pain began.

"I don't have a passport."

"It doesn't matter," Tran said. "We'll take the boat to Cuba, fly from there. You won't need a passport. This is how I came to Key West. How I'll go back."

"I don't know," Pepper said. "It sounds shaky."

Pepper was in his hotel room again. The smell of their sex clung to the curtains and the rug and the bedspread. The good people at the Marquesa Hotel would have to call the sex fumigators when Tran finally checked out, exterminate all the carnal cooties roosting in the crevices if they were ever going to make the room safe for the next lucky visitors.

Several of Tran's bags were packed, sitting by the door. It was one o'clock in the morning, quiet out in the patio and gardens except for a couple of drunk guests stumbling back to their rooms, shushing each other and laughing.

Pepper's jaw ached. Worst pain she'd ever had. It hurt to breathe, it hurt to swallow, it hurt to talk, and it hurt just to stand there in Tran's room watching the slender little man pack his toiletries in a leather shaving kit and slide it into one of his big gold bags. The worst hurt, though, was in her chest, where her heart had once been rooted.

"You want me to kill Bean Wilson before we go? Or I can send a man later and kill him then?"

"Whatever you think," Pepper said. "Now or later, I don't care."

"So why have you chosen me? You stopped loving

your blond doctor? He hit you once and that's the end of your love affair for him?"

"You bet your ass."

"The man is a giant weenie. I think, yes, we shall kill him now. Let you see him die on the floor like an animal, so you will never think of him again in your future life with Tran."

"If it's easy to do, no risk, that's fine. I don't care. I don't need to see him die. He's dead now, far as I'm concerned."

"You want one more sexual activity in our love nest before we begin our travels?"

"No," she said. "My fucking jaw hurts. Hurts to blink my eyes."

"Sexual activity will take your mind off your pain. That's what it is for."

"Oh, that's what it's for, is it? Well, good, now I know. And there I was, thinking it had something to do with making babies."

"I will give you a baby, if you want a baby. I give you a hundred babies."

She went over to him and opened her arms and Tran van Hung stepped into her embrace. Short little guy, his ear only came to her breasts, the man pressing his head there, listening to where her heart used to be.

Short, yes, but that was okay. Short was fine. So what if he was a midget? So what if he was from the other side of the planet, and warbled and screeched like an inflated balloon squeezed in your fingertips, and his face was pinched and slitty? That didn't matter. He didn't strike her, he worshipped her body, and he was going to be a very rich man. Their sex was great, and Pepper was going to be a queen over there. A giant woman in a land of runts. Her head so high in the air she'd never have to use makeup again. That was fine. A huge change of plans, and happening awful fast, but it was fine. She was going with it. She was going to have a different life than she'd imagined, but what the hell, what the fucking hell?

"You want me to write down the formula for you, before we go?"

"What?"

Tran stepped out of the embrace. He cocked his head and looked into her eyes. The lights were low in the room and the incense of their sex was strong. She could feel the clenching in her stomach, wanting him inside her. Even with her jaw the way it was.

"Formula. Ingredients and numbers. You know what I'm saying. You want me to write down the formula so you can see it?"

"No," Tran said. "You don't need to write it down. You have it in your head. That's good enough."

"You're sure? I mean, I might decide to run off and sell the formula to someone else and make myself rich. Or some foreign agent could kidnap me, whisk me away somewhere, give me sodium pentothal to make me confess the formula."

"You should not worry about these things, Miss Pepper. I will keep you safe. You are secure with Tran. You have nothing to fear. I will give you all the blond babies you want. Diamonds and rubies too, what every girl wants, I give you. You are Tran's queen. You will wear beautiful dresses, a different one every day of the year. All the lipstick and eyeshadow a girl could ever want."

"You love me."

"Yes, sure. I love you. I love you completely and ter-
rifically."

"Well, that's the right answer. Yes, sir. You couldn't
come up with a righter answer than that."

Pepper walked over to his luggage and stared at the
gold fabric. She didn't know much about luggage, but
she could see this was expensive stuff. When it came
rolling down the ramp at the baggage claim, everybody
was going to watch it, see who picked it up. The problem was, except for the luggage and a few weeks of sex
with Tran, she didn't have much proof of who he was
and what he was all about. It was a scary step, going off
with him. Scary as hell when you paused a second and
considered it.

Tran came over to her, stood close.

"You think I am lying about love? Is that what you
are saying? You think I only want the formula. You give
me this test, dangle a bait in front of me like I am some
kind of giant weenie person?"

"*Weenie*'s a stupid word, Tran. I just told you that
word to hear you say it all the time. I was goofing on
you, that's all. Anybody who'd use that word has got to
be a major weenie himself."

"You were trying to trick me?"

"Not a trick. More like a joke."

He looked hurt or maybe it was angry. She'd gotten
a little better at reading his expressions than she'd
been at the start, but she still had a long way to go.

"We shall go to the boat now," he said. "Take it to
Cuba, then fly home. Miss Pepper, I don't know what I
need to say to you to convince you of my love. All those
hours we spent together in the sheets of that bed, I
thought this would demonstrate with certainty how I
felt. I would never try to cheat you, Pepper. You are the

woman of my dreams. You are the woman I want always."

She stared at him for a long moment, then reached out and touched her fingertips to his cheek.

"Maybe I've been confused."

"Confused about what?" he said.

"Maybe I didn't know what the word means. I used it a thousand times, but I didn't understand what it was about."

"Which word is that?"

"You know which word, Tran. The word you shouldn't ever say until you paid your dues and you own the thing free and clear."

"I love you, Pepper."

"I know you do."

"Do you love me?"

"I'm working on it. I'm working on it real hard."

He stepped forward and they embraced again and she could've sworn she felt the molecules and atoms and a thousand other microscopic parts of her flowing out through her skin, through her clothes and into Tran and mingling with his microscopic parts, swirling up together, and his parts flowing back across into her. Some kind of magnetic thing or like the acid juices that oysters secrete to glue themselves to the pilings, mingling and joining. And even when she stepped back from the embrace, breathless and weak, she could feel that part of her was gone, passed across to Tran, and that missing part of her had been replaced by an equal part of him. It scared her. Made her dizzy.

She couldn't even look him in the eye.

Swinging toward the door, she said, "On the other hand, maybe we should kill Bean now. Kill him before we leave. That might be a good idea, now that I think about it. We blindside him before he knows what we're up to. Kill him and go."

"All right, then," Tran said. "Whatever my queen wants. We will kill the blond doctor, then go off to Vietnam. My beautiful country."

CHAPTER

27

When Thorn rolled off the lift into the first-floor hallway, Ginny was stationed in front of the elevator door wearing a goofy smile and nothing else. And even through the dim light and the boozy haze, Thorn could see that she had spent a great deal of time shaping her upper body into something taut and formidable. Her breasts were heavy but showed no sign of sag; muscles ridged her stomach. A lot of angry, obsessive dips on those parallel bars. Not trying to sculpt herself into something beautiful, but doing it because it was necessary—because it was all she had now, her upper body.

"I've been waiting for you," she said.

"I see that."

She was holding a bottle of red wine in her lap.

"I thought you'd like to come to my room, I could show you a few things you won't learn in rehab. So you could see it's not as hopeless as you think. There's a lot of pleasures still available."

She held out the wine to him but he shook his head. Then she touched the bottle to her lips and tipped it up. After she'd bubbled down a swallow, she set the bottle on the floor and rolled over next to Thorn.

"You can touch me, if you like. I know you want to."

Slowly, Thorn reached out with his right hand and ran a cautious finger along her sharp jawline. The muscles in her neck relaxed. Her flesh drank him in as if this were the first human touch she'd had in years.

"You're a beautiful woman, Ginny. Very beautiful."

"All right then, no more talk, let's hop to it."

"If I weren't already in love, I'd be there in a second."

She sighed, straightened her head, gave him a long, exhausted look.

"Well, it's a good answer anyway."

"It's the truth."

"You shouldn't kid yourself, you know. If you're in love with somebody, where is she when you need her?"

"I pushed her away. She's not here because I told her to leave me alone."

Ginny rolled back a foot, out of reach.

"But she's a normal woman, right? Legs, arms, completely intact."

"Fairly normal," Thorn said. "But she has her endearing peculiarities."

"How long you think something like that's going to last? Is she going to be able to deal with who you are now? Gorked. Half a man."

"I don't know. But I intend to find out."

She snorted, then reached down for her bottle and swiveled her chair around and headed down the hallway. At the door to her room, she halted.

"There's rumors about where the doc does his procedures."

Thorn pivoted around and faced her.

"On a boat," she said. "He takes them on a cruise to nowhere. That's what I heard. So you'd best take along your life preserver. Dead legs don't float real well."

"Thanks, Ginny."

"Sure," she said, and turned to her door. "Down the road, if you discover you need some pointers on bedroom stuff, the offer stands. I'm not going anywhere. I'll be right here waiting till it's my turn to be the chimp."

The champagne haze evaporated as he rolled into his darkened room. He felt around for the switch, flipped it on, and his heart staggered.

Perched tensely on the edge of the bed, hands folded in her lap, Monica stared into his eyes. Wearing a pair of old jeans and a black mock turtleneck and running shoes that matched his own.

"I was just talking about you."

She put a finger to her lips and shushed him.

"What? What is it?"

In a whisper she said, "You're in danger, Thorn. We've got to get you out of here, right now. Right this second."

"I heard you were wounded. Are you all right, Monica?"

"I'm serious, we have to go now."

"The guy at the paper said you were shot."

"I'm all right. I'm fine." She twisted her head stiffly, pulled aside the turtleneck and displayed the bandage on her neck. "It's nothing."

She stood up and came over to him. Stood there for a few seconds peering into his eyes, then kneeled slowly and embraced him, pressing her cheek against his chest, and after a moment or two a quiet sob shook her, then another. He held her hard until she was still, and after another moment she raised her face, tilted toward him, found his lips, pressed her mouth flush to his, filling his lungs with feverish breath. It was an awkward embrace, a fumbling kiss, the salt of her tears on his lips, but the kiss lasted, neither of them getting enough, teeth clicked, their tongues working, and he felt the hard lump of anger in his chest liquefy and begin to drain away.

Finally Monica pulled away and stood up. She took a long breath, ruffled her short hair. Her eyes roamed the dreary room. Bare walls with dingy white paint, dirty wood floor covered by only a single tattered rag rug. A room where too many people had passed sleepless nights, too many had cried out in torment.

"The policewoman, Jennifer Bell, she came over at suppertime, told me you'd called her, that you needed to speak to me. I was just leaving anyway. I had to come tell you what I found out."

"I heard about Roy and his mother, some other woman."

"All murdered, yes."

"Those fuckers. Those goddamn motherfuckers."

"We need to get out of here. This has something to do with a drug Bean junior's been producing. Dolphin endorphins."

"Endorphins," Thorn said. "That's what he wanted from the dolphins? Some goddamn chemical."

"Yeah, Roy figured it out and he called Bean to help him fill in a few blanks with his research, then later that same night the killers came for him. It had to be Bean, his people."

"And they were coming for you too."

"I don't know that for sure."

"Maybe Roy talked before he died, gave them your name."

"Let's go," she said. "No more discussion."

"I can't, Monica. I've got to stay."

"Didn't you hear me? You're in danger. If they think I know about the dolphin thing, then they have to realize you know too. We have to go to the police, explain what's been going on. Let them handle it."

"It's not as simple as that."

"What?"

"There's a woman, Greta Masterson's her name. It's a very long, very involved story. But Greta's in danger and it looks like I'm the only one who can get her out of it."

Monica stepped away from him.

"Greta Masterson. A woman."

"That's right."

"Someone you knew before me?"

"I've never met her before."

"Never met her? But you've got to save her?"

"She's with the DEA. She was investigating Bean and he took her hostage. He's got her hidden somewhere, using her in his experiment, but he's going to take me to see her tomorrow morning."

"Why can't the goddamn DEA save her? Why do you have to do it?"

"I'm all she's got."

"Wait a minute," she said. "If Bean Wilson is holding this woman hostage, why the hell would he take you to see her?"

"I talked him into it. I preyed on his vanity."

Monica studied him, hands balled on her hips. Her eyes were talcum blue, probing his face for signs of sanity.

"From the first moment I saw that man in your hospital room, I didn't trust him. That bastard's going to try to kill you, Thorn, that's why he's taking you along with him—off to some remote place where he can shoot you in the back."

"He might try."

"Jesus Christ. Listen to you. You're in a wheelchair, for godsakes. This isn't some guy in a bar fight, you with full use of your body. You're not on equal terms with Bean Wilson."

"I think I am."

"Look," she said. "I'm taking you out of here, whether you want to go or not. You make a fuss and we'll both be dead."

She got behind him, took hold of the grips, and muscled him toward the door. She was reaching around him for the knob when someone tapped quietly on the wood frame.

Thorn wheeled away from her, snapped off the lights. He waved Monica into the corner, then rolled over to his gym bag and dug beneath the clothes and got his Colt. As he drew it out, Monica took a sharp breath.

He motioned for her to yank open the door, and after a moment's hesitation she stepped over, got a hand on the knob, and threw it wide. Thorn cocked the Colt and set his aim.

Old Doc Wilson stood stiffly in the doorway. His hair was a mess and his white shirt and khaki pants were badly rumpled. He held his hands up to his shoulders.

"Wait," he whispered hoarsely. "I come in peace."

He stepped inside the room and Monica shut the door behind him and switched on the lights.

Doc Wilson's face was drained of color. His shoulders were rounded, head sagging forward as if both his lungs had collapsed and he was coasting on what little oxygen he had left in his bloodstream.

"I made it as soon as I could."

Monica sat down on the edge of Thorn's cot. She shivered while her eyes wandered the dismal room.

"I may have good news."

"Great. We've been a little low on that lately. Come in, sit down."

He stepped into the room and shut the door.

"The first thing I need to know, Thorn, did you get an injection today?"

"What?"

"The steroids, did you get an injection today? In your catheter."

"Yes."

"How many?"

"One in the morning, one at night. The usual."

He frowned and took a quick look at Monica.

"And since you've been here at the clinic, they've given you the shots regularly? Never missed?"

"Twice a day, same as before."

Doc Wilson stared down at the floor. He tried to arrange his mouth into a smile but failed. He looked around the room, then headed for the cheap desk chair and sat down with a long sigh.

"Hey, you said good news. What's the deal?"

"That's nine injections, by my count. Starting with Wednesday night. Though maybe there were two Wednesday. Your assailant's, then mine. That would make ten. Depending on the strength of that first dose, we might be over already."

"Wait a minute. You're losing me." Thorn rolled back to the bed and slipped the Colt into his gym bag.

He patted Monica on the leg. She swallowed back her frustration and stared across at the door. "Might be over what?"

"God, I'm sorry, Thorn," the doctor said. "This is all my fault. I should have seen this coming. There were signs. For years I tried to ignore his wild swings of emotion. I told myself he was getting better, getting a handle on things. But it was all self-deception. He was sick as a boy, starved for something his mother and I could never seem to provide. And he's only gotten worse with time. And I was always so preoccupied with my patients, their problems, and then when his mother died, with my own grief. My own loss . . ."

He looked up at Thorn. "I'm sorry, forgive me. I'm rambling."

"Good news, remember?" Monica said. "What is it?"

Doc Wilson pressed his palms together and squinted into the middle distance, as if trying to organize his scattered thoughts.

"Okay," he said. "Here's what happened. Eddie Robertson, he was in my office this morning for his weekly shot for tennis elbow. Steroids, methylprednisolone, same thing I was using on you. From the minute you walked into my office, Thursday and Friday at Baptist Hospital. Same supply I used for Eddie's shot this morning. That's when I knew."

His voice trailed off and the doctor gazed at the blank wall, his eyes failing like a man who'd gone without sleep for weeks. Monica cleared her throat. Dr. Wilson blinked and looked at her, then at Thorn.

"It's not steroids that were in those vials," he said. "It's something called marcaine, Thorn. It's an anesthetic. Very new. Cutting edge."

"Marcaine."

"You're not paralyzed. I was injecting an anesthetic into your subarachnoid space since Wednesday night. Every twelve hours, another dose."

Thorn rubbed his thighs.

"He's okay? He's going to be all right?"

"I'm afraid," Doc Wilson said, "there's more to it than that."

"Oh, that old story," Thorn said. "Good news and bad."

"It had to be Bean," Dr. Wilson said. "He attacked you, or had somebody to do it, and he gave you the first injection that night. Then he must have hit you in the spine with the rock to make it look like an accidental fall. Apparently he'd already broken into my office, substituted the marcaine for the steroids. I'd given him a key to my office a year or two ago, just in case something ever happened to me. He knew exactly what drug I'd reach for when you came to my office, and he knew I'd continue to treat you with the same solution."

"He must've gotten a charge out of that," said Thorn. "Making you his unsuspecting accomplice."

"And then," Dr. Wilson said, "when Bean stepped in to offer his services, he took over the shots himself and continued to load you up with anesthetic. His only mistake was leaving behind the vials in my office."

"All right," Monica said. "So what's the bad news?"

"This morning when I took Eddie Robertson to Mariners Hospital to see what had happened to his arm, I carried along the vial I thought was prednisolone. It took most of the day, and a very bright young technician at Mariners, but we were able to analyze the solution, narrow it down. I've never used marcaine before. No one I know has used it. It's a very new application.

Very specialized. A kind of timed-release anesthetic. Polyester microspheres.

"When we were reasonably certain of the chemistry of what we were dealing with, I immediately got on the phone to some of my anesthesiologist friends in Miami. They helped me out, got busy, looked up what literature they could find on long-term dosing of marcaine."

"And?"

"Well, this is the part that's not good. Not good at all."

Monica stood up. She looked around the room, her eyes jittery, as if she'd just noticed the walls were closing in. She moved to the door, eyed the knob.

"Jesus Christ," she said quietly. "There's no lock on this thing. He could walk in right now."

"It's okay, Monica. Let the doctor finish. Whatever it is, we'll deal with it, all right?"

Wilson rose from the chair, ran his hands through his hair. He smiled at Thorn for a moment, then looked away before his smile had a chance to wither.

"There've been only a few studies, rats, dogs, that have tested the prolonged use of regional nerve blockades. But what they suggest is that over time with repeated usage, there is an increasing concentration, a buildup in the spinal canal, so that long-term applications will almost certainly result in neurotoxicity."

"Thorn's been poisoned?"

"Not exactly," Bean said. "Based on the concentration of the marcaine in the solution in my office, and your weight, Thorn, we tried to calculate how many injections you could sustain before the nerve damage begins to be irreversible."

"What? Like a specific number of days or dosages?"

"Yes," he said. "There are variables, intangibles, of course."

"But you have a number, an educated guess."

Dr. Wilson nodded, eyes flicking between Monica and Thorn.

"I faxed your charts, your MRIs, blood tests, your complete workup to the specialists I know—the best neurologists and pain doctors in Miami. They sat down with everything, factored in your weight, your overall physical condition, your medical history. And they put that up against the dosages of marcaine you've been receiving."

"Well?"

"Five days, ten dosages," he said. "Beyond that the damage is irreparable."

"We're there now," Thorn said.

"Yes, and every hour you wait there'll be more motor function loss. Every hour, Thorn, less likelihood you'll regain mobility."

Thorn nodded slowly.

"So come on, goddamn it." Monica moved to the door. "We can get out of here, have him airlifted to Miami, get him to the trauma center, start reversing this thing. Pump out his spine, whatever they have to do. I have money, I can pay whatever it costs."

Dr. Wilson stepped close to Thorn's chair.

"She's right, Thorn. Not about pumping out your spine. But we need to get you to Miami right now. Even under the best-case scenario, there are going to be some serious medical consequences. Spinal headaches, loss of motor function. Nerve damage."

Thorn rolled over to Monica, reached out, and took her hand in his and gave it a squeeze. He swiveled around to face the doctor.

"Tell me something, Doc."

"Yes."

"Were you on the Monroe County draft board once? Back in the sixties."

Wilson flinched, then held his ground in baffled silence.

"Were you?"

The doctor swallowed and his eyes filled with misty light.

"Yes," he said.

"Did you do something to keep me out of the war?"

The wind rattled some seedpods outside the window. Like a mobile of old bones stitched together by threads. The air leaked through the window frame and stirred the yellow shades and brought with it the fertile spice of Key West, that blend of honey and sperm, cinnamon and deep-fat frying.

"Did you, Doc? Did I get special treatment?"

Doc Wilson took a deep breath and let it go. He squared off before Thorn and shook his head.

"You never registered, son. Your name never made it onto the list. And though I noticed it wasn't there, I said nothing. If that was a sin, then I committed it. You were underflying the official radar even back then, Thorn. No driver's license, no social security card. You didn't exist on the social records. Not such an unusual thing back then in the Keys. You were one of many who didn't officially exist, and I saw no reason to bring you or any of the rest of them to anyone's attention."

Monica was shifting her eyes between the two of them. A dialogue she could not decipher and wasn't sure she wanted to. She gave up trying and moved a step toward Thorn.

"No more talk. Now let's go."

"I can't. I've got to go along with Bean tomorrow. Find where he's keeping Greta."

"Are you crazy! And wind up living in a wheelchair forever?"

"I don't have a choice, Monica."

"Of course you do. You don't have to risk everything you have for some stranger you've never met. No one's asking you to do that. No one expects it."

"She risked her life, Monica. She went undercover to investigate Bean. She put herself in danger. If she'd found out what he was doing in time, I wouldn't have wound up like this."

"That was her job, Thorn. She was just doing what she was paid to do. And anyway, she failed at it. Because she failed, you're crippled. Is that the woman you want to risk your life for?"

"I love you, Monica. You know that, don't you?" He rolled toward her, but she stepped away.

"Maybe you do," she said. "But you love yourself more. You love some ridiculous idea of gallantry. Like some little boy in his sandpile, dreaming up adventures with his plastic soldiers, dragons and maidens in distress. That's what you love, Thorn. Some fantasy story you keep trying to get right. It's not about people. Not about anyone you love or care about. You don't even know this woman, but you're going to risk everything you have to play your sandpile game, to get her away from the dragon. That's what this is about, Thorn. Pure and simple."

She crimped her mouth and looked steadily into his eyes. Her words seemed to startle her, as if she'd guarded those thoughts for so long that she'd assumed they'd disappeared.

Wilson said, "It's not my place to tell you what's important, Thorn. But you're playing around with very dangerous stuff here. With what we know right now, we can have Bean arrested.''

Thorn backed away to the bed. He could feel the breeze against his neck. Down the street a car revved to life, a limb scratched against the side of the house like some huge animal that wanted inside, wanted to join the crew and be cured of its relentless pain.

''If we called the police now,'' said Thorn, ''and had Bean arrested, the people who are helping him could get rid of Greta in the meantime, and no one would ever see her again. There's a person out there who's alive and depending on me. She doesn't know me and I don't know her, but from my vantage point, it looks a lot like I'm the only person who can keep her alive. So I'm going to do it.

''I know it's gotta be tearing you up, Doc. Your own son using the cover of his profession to try to cure himself at the expense of anybody that gets in his way. I know that's killing you right now. And you want to rescue me before I turn out to be another of his victims. I appreciate that. I do.

''And I listened to your math. You think I'm teetering on the edge here. Nine injections, ten. But math can't account for everything. You said there were intangibles. Well, I think I can get in there, save this woman's life and get back out alive. Because I believe I can do it, that tips the balance as far as I'm concerned.

''So tomorrow, when I get back, we'll all go on a nice airplane ride to a nice hospital and we'll get my spine all flushed out and my legs working again, and everything will be as close to how it was before as we can get it.

''And maybe you're right, Monica. Maybe I am a kid

in a sandpile playing out his fantasy. Maybe it's stupid and self-indulgent to risk my body for some stranger. But I can't help any of that. It's the fantasy that gets me through. It's the one that works. And anyway, right now there's no backing out. That's how it is. Doctor's orders or not. That's how it's going to be. Idealism, chivalry, whatever bullshit you want to call it, it doesn't really matter at this point. There's something broken and I'm the one who has to fix it. Simple as that."

Monica released a quiet breath, then she walked over to him, held his eyes for a moment, and stooped and kissed him on the cheek. Stood back up, eyes hard on his.

"Thorn, Thorn, Thorn," she said. "You idiot. You utter, complete moron."

He smiled. "Present and accounted for."

"Well, the least we can do," Dr. Wilson said, "is to make sure that no more marcaine reaches your spinal cord."

"There's a way to do that?"

"Yes," he said. "But the trick will be to do it in such a way that Bean won't notice it if he tries to give you another injection tomorrow."

With a pair of tweezers and a sterilized and straightened bobby pin, Dr. Wilson and Monica inserted a tiny wad of absorbent cotton into the catheter and tamped it deep into the tube. When they were done, the catheter taped back into place, Thorn sat up.

"If he notices that thing, he'll realize something's up. The whole thing will blow up in our faces."

"Don't worry. I believe I got it far enough in there, he'll never know. I may be a country doctor, but I can be as devious as any city specialist if the occasion demands it."

"We need a plan," Monica said. "We can't let you go into this by yourself, Thorn."

"All right," he said. "But it's going to involve a boat. Can one of you handle that?"

"Hell, yes," she said. "Just watch me."

After Dr. Wilson left, Thorn asked Monica about Rover. She said nothing, but went over to her purse, drew out a cylinder of paper. She rolled off the rubber band and opened the page and held the edges of the drawing flat against the table so Thorn could see.

Rover lay dead in the grass near the butterfly garden. There was no blood visible, no wound, but somehow it was clear that this was no restful afternoon snooze. The dog was dead. And its death was in every blade of grass. It was in the shadow lying across the right corner and in the single butterfly perched on the stem of a lantana with its wings pressed tightly together. Death was in the empty spaces as well, the white resonance of the sky, the blank distances beyond the foreground.

It was pen-and-ink like all her other drawings, but this was not like anything she'd done before. Things had changed for her, grown darker, flesh was on the bones now, and everything was far more serious than she'd anticipated. There was a dead dog lying in the grass and the drawing showed it without sentimental gush or exaggeration. It was exactly enough, not a line too many, not a line too few.

Afterward, she rolled the drawing up again and put it away, and then without discussion, she helped him out of the chair and onto the bed, and with the slow measured cadence of a dream she disrobed him, then stood beside the mattress and unfastened her own clothes and let them fall. Her skin had the juicy gleam of a peach in late afternoon sunlight, and her body was tight and warm and even from two feet away gave off the aroma of a feast of soft hot breads glowing with butter.

She stood before him for a minute, then another, neither of them speaking. Standing there as if to let her nakedness reignite his pulse. The slender hips that were just generous enough, the lithe waist and tight breasts with their dark raisin centers, the wide shoulders with collarbone shining golden in the fragile light. She had dancers' calves, muscles so sharply hewn they looked to be constantly on the verge of cramping. Her head was cocked a few degrees to the right and her hands were clasped, almost shielding the spun wheat of her pubic hair. Her expression blended amusement with mild consternation, as if she'd tried to rouse herself to anger and had fallen just short. When she finally broke her pose and stepped to the edge of the bed and reached out to touch Thorn's cheek and settled in beside him, the air trembled in the room with the quiet voltage of a summer rainstorm, and his lungs were instantly drunk on her scent of apples and hay with the faint undercurrent of wood smoke.

The door was unlocked and there was a killer two floors above who blamed Thorn for his pain and was dedicated to making Thorn's life mirror his own fucked-up, miserable tragedy. And maybe Bean's hovering presence had something to do with their lovemaking; maybe the danger, the weight of the silence in the house, the vibrations of suffering all around them filtered into the act and gave it a gravity they'd never known.

Or maybe it was simply that Thorn had always depended too much on the half that was missing to define this moment, a half that Monica Sampson showed him now in her long, delicate motions was not necessary at all, perhaps had never been necessary, perhaps had even handicapped him more seriously than he was now. How she knew what to do, the physics and geometry of this new world, he had no idea. It was as if she had been waiting for this moment, storing in reserve the burden of a knowledge greater than she'd been called on to demonstrate. And now she showed him all of it, guided him to junctures of flesh, slow mergings of muscle and blood that lofted him to groggy heights.

Perhaps it was also the blind-man thing, the way deprivation of one sense heightens another. There was only half of Thorn, but the half that was there had never been so receptive. His fingertips reading the Braille of her downy cheek, teasing the subtle fuzz on her wrist. No woman's flesh he'd ever known had been as various or succulent. The shape of her ear, the bristly nap on her calves, the delicacy of her toes. And Monica knew this and led him through the stages of desire, kiss and massage and stroke and counterstroke, until it was clear that Thorn's lost half was a half he could live without, a half that was simply not required for her rapture or his own.

CHAPTER

28

Two in the morning, Monday, Pepper was carrying Tran van Hung's luggage out to the hearse. A trickle of breeze coming from the east, stirring the oak limbs and making the shadows jitter on the pavement of Fleming Street like a gang of hoboes were dancing around their bonfire.

Pepper was having second thoughts, and third and fourth ones too. Not sure she wanted to leave Key West. Promising to go one minute, taking it back in her head the next. The idea of whisking off to the other side of the world, queen or not, it was starting to put a nervous quiver in her pulse. No friends, no one who knew her name. Hell, probably no one over there who could even pronounce her name. Leaving all her earthly possessions behind, her wonderful lowrider hearse, the *Miss Begotten*.

On the other side she had Tran. Very good sex. Excellent sex. And that was important. No question. And he'd never hit her. Never broken a bone. She didn't think he could break one even if he tried, the frail little guy. And the thing she'd felt a few minutes earlier, the electrons or molecules flowing back and forth between them, that was a powerful incentive. That was something new and extreme and important.

But still it was hard, going full blast in one direction then, bam, making a U-turn quick as that. For the last couple of years being in love with Bean Wilson, every day imagining their life together, dinner parties, entertaining the other doctors' wives, setting out her china, crystal, all that, then in a matter of hours, dropping that fantasy and hooking onto a train going flat out in the complete opposite direction. Emotional whiplash.

She was out at the hearse, way off inside her head as she threw the luggage in the rear, when Echeverria came stalking out of the shadows. He was wearing baggy blue jeans that showed his white socks, and he had on a white shirt and black shoes. As usual, dressed like a middle-age dork.

"What're you doing, stalking me?"

"I came by to see you," he said. "I came by to talk."

"Such a sweetheart. So get busy and talk. I'm in a hurry."

"You're going somewhere." Coming up close to her, booze on his breath.

"Yeah, yeah. Tran's going home. The experiment's done, the drug works. So he's leaving."

"Good," Echeverria said. "I don't like that little weasel hanging around you. He's a bad influence."

"Tran's all right. He can't help it he's from the Far East."

Echeverria stood there blocking her way back to the hotel, head slumped over like he was carrying some extra weight in his brain.

"What's chewing your ass, Echeverria?"

"Tomorrow's the day," he said. "The doc told me to come over, make sure you knew. You're supposed to bring the *Miss Begotten* in to dock, and the three of us are going on a little cruise, tie up some loose ends."

"Which loose ends are those? Greta?"

"Her, yeah, and this other guy. Thorn. We're going to take them out, grind them up, feed them to the minnows."

"Okay, so you told me. You can go now."

Echeverria just stood there, mooning at her.

"There's another thing."

Shooting a glance back at the hotel, Pepper said, "Yeah? And what would that be?"

"I wanted to see if you meant what you said the other night. About you and me getting together."

"I said that?"

"Yeah, you made certain sexual remarks. Salacious suggestions."

"That wasn't me. I never used that word before in my life. I don't even know what it means."

"For a couple of hours you talked very intimately to me. You put forth some fairly serious propositions concerning our future together."

"Hey, I was passing the time. That's all that was, Echeverria. Shooting the ever-loving shit."

A black-and-white patrol car idled up. Fleming, the cop bending low, looking over at them. Pepper gave him a small finger-wave and he kept on going down into the capering shadows.

"I want us to try things out," Echeverria said, voice getting lower. "You and me. Give it a shot, see what happens."

"You want to have sex with me, that what you're saying?"

"More than that," he said. "Not just sex. Hell, I can get sex from my fucking wife."

Pepper closed the back of the hearse. She looked down toward Duval. There were still people walking down there, drunks, tourists, trim gay guys, chunky lesbians, yuppies from Miami, Rastafarians, the usual stream of derelict zombies. Probably nobody she knew personally, but still, it was comforting to see them there, everybody having a good time. One long party. One boozy, dopey night after the next.

"Forget it, Echeverria. Get it out of your head. That was just so much jabber, a way to pass the hours, that's all."

"It was more than talk."

"No, it wasn't. It was words, nothing but."

"It was more than that to me. It got me started thinking about things, about what's important. What I been doing with my fucking life. The shit I been missing out on."

"Well, that's fine. You keep thinking about those things, and if you figure out anything important, you write me a nice long letter and mail it to Vietnam." She started around him toward the walkway to the hotel, but Echeverria stepped in her way.

"I'm talking about you and me living together. Maybe someday more than that. Get married or whatever. We've got things in common."

"You got to be shitting me."

"I'm serious. Stone-cold serious."

"What? 'Cause we murdered a couple of people? Got dolphin blood on our hands? That gives us a bond?"

"We have that, yeah," Echeverria said. "We have other things too. We can talk to each other, say anything we want, confess things, all the shit we've done, it wouldn't matter. It wouldn't shock me hearing what you done in your life, and I don't think it would shock you to hear my stories. Hell, I never been able to say shit to my wife. If I was to tell her some of the things I been doing, she'd pick up the phone, have the FBI on my ass in a minute.''

Pepper glanced over at the beautiful Marquesa Hotel, wished Tran would hurry up and get his shriveled ass outside.

''Now look here, Echeverria. A woman doesn't talk to a guy a couple of times and suddenly decide she wants to marry him. There's foundations need to be laid. If I'm going to get serious about somebody, I got to have some surefire, ironclad guarantees. That's how it works. A woman wants to know she's going to be provided for, wants to know her man will keep her safe and protected and worship her. Make a safe place for her babies.

''And what're you, Echeverria? You're some DEA agent who plays both sides of the street. Who could trust a guy like you? What woman would want to marry some bozo, he can't even keep it straight whether he's a good guy or a bad guy? Not me. No, sir. Give me an out-and-out bad guy any day over somebody who jumps back and forth. So now, you just get on out of my way, please. Tran and I got to be moving along.''

''You're going off with that yellow devil. You're running away.''

''Don't get me mad, Echeverria. You don't want to see me mad.''

''You're stealing that formula, running off to cash in with that Jap.''

''He's Vietnamese, Echeverria. There's a big difference.''

''Those people will knife you in the back first chance

they get. That's how they are. Piano wire around your throat till your eyes bulge out."

"Now, that's a racial slur, Echeverria. That's a very stupid, uninformed thing to say. Not all Orientals are like that."

"I'm not letting you go," he said. "I can't let that happen, Pepper. Not for me, not for the doc and his experiment. No, ma'am, that's not going to be what happens here."

Tran came out the front door of the hotel muttering as he dragged the smallest of his gold bags.

Reaching his right hand around to the small of his back, Echeverria pulled out a black automatic and aimed it at Pepper, then at Tran.

"Put the bag down," he said. "And stand over there beside the car."

"Don't worry about him," Pepper said. "He's love-sick is all it is. A silly boy who's been carving hearts in tree trunks, putting my initials inside. Go on, Tran, load up your luggage. Mr. Echeverria isn't going to do anything to you."

Tran hesitated, saying something in Vietnamese, something so pissed-off and angry, she didn't need any translation. Then he came forward and chucked the luggage in the rear and scurried around to the passenger door and got in.

"Now look, Echeverria. I'm just taking Tran to the bus station. Sending him on his way. Tomorrow, I'm taking the boat out like you said. Give me ten minutes, wait right here, I'll be back and we'll talk some more about this."

"Fuck that. Don't try to bullshit me, Pepper. You're running off, I can see what's going on here."

He came around to the front of the hearse and stood

in its path and said, "Get out of the car and get your hands up, both of you sex freaks."

Pepper opened the door and got in behind the wheel.

"One minute you want to marry me, next minute you're going to kill me. You're not convincing me of your mental stability, Echeverria."

"Get out of the fucking car. I'm warning you."

A light came on across Fleming. Some old man stepped out onto his porch wearing pajama bottoms and carrying a white cat in his arms. He stood at the railing of his porch and stroked the cat and watched Echeverria aim through the windshield of the hearse. He had an old bony chest that was yellow and papery in the porchlight.

Pepper cranked up the engine. All the talking she'd been doing had made her jaw ache worse than ever. A tom-tom throbbed in her throat.

Pepper put the car in gear and inched forward toward Echeverria, trying to nudge him out of the way.

He stepped back, stiffened his arms, and the goddamn windshield exploded.

Tran howled and slithered down to the floorboard. There was glass everywhere. In Pepper's hair, a piece embedded in the upholstery next to her shoulder, all over the dashboard. Tran was gabbling and cursing, saying some of the words Pepper had taught him.

"Jesus Christ, Echeverria. Look what you did. You fucked with my car."

The man on his porch was stroking his cat, just standing there, the cat watching too. No big deal, gunfire in the street right outside his house.

Echeverria came closer, right up to the grille, aiming his pistol at Pepper.

"Don't be doing anything else to my car. You hear me, Echeverria?"

"You going to come away with me or what?"

"Those my choices, come away or die?"

"Come away or die, yeah. That's how it is. That's the corner you backed me into, you bitch."

"I think I'll take what's behind door number three," she said, and flipped the switch for the hopping pumps.

The front end of the hearse flew three feet up in the air and knocked the pistol loose and it skittered down the sheet metal hood and slid toward the windshield. Echeverria dove for it, sprawling across the hood. He fumbled around, got hold of the pistol, then lifted his head, looked at Pepper, tried to say something, but before he could get more words out to confuse her further, she tripped the hopping pumps again, left front, then right front, bouncing him from one side of the hood to the other, scrambling his brains a little, then she flipped both together, which threw him off into the street.

When he didn't get up, she switched on the hydraulic lifters and slowly raised the car two feet off the ground.

"What're you doing? What're you doing, Miss Pepper?"

She took a breath. The guy'd just proposed, then tried to shoot her. No reason in the world to be crying, but there were the tears, filling her eyes.

"Don't worry about it, Tran. The guy was trying to kill us, trying to wreck my car. I'm within my rights here, self-defense. It's a cornerstone of our American legal system. The right to defend yourself against rogue

DEA agents trying to murder you 'cause you'd refused their advances.''

The man on his porch was still petting the white cat. But now Pepper saw the cat didn't look right. Its head was crooked to one side, front legs droopy like a beanbag cat. Or a dead one.

Maybe it was time to get out of Key West after all. Men petting their dead cats on their front porches in the middle of the night. Terminal freakiness all around. The whole town rotting away—decaying around her like some old tooth you didn't even know was going bad till all of a sudden one day you bite down on a blackberry seed or something small like that, and the whole thing that's been there all your life and has never hurt and always been invisible, this bone you thought was solid and secure, all of a sudden it just crumbles away, and you have to spit out the pieces of bone into your hand, dark and rotten, and all at once the nerves inside that tooth are exposed to the air and the awful pain begins.

Pepper inched the car forward and when she was fairly sure they were over Echeverria's body she lowered the hearse again, listening to the hum of the pneumatic lifters until they ground to a halt.

Something in her stomach turned over. Her jaw throbbed. There was a man under her car. A big American man with a government job and a pension coming his way eventually. There was a life out there Pepper could have disappeared into. Kids at soccer, grocery shopping on Thursdays, barbecues with the in-laws. Blend in with all the other wives who vacuumed and dusted and taught themselves new recipes every week. A life her daddy had trained her for. Marriage. With a big man moving above her in the dark, drops of his sweat dampening her breasts. A big American man who could share his twisted secrets with her. The bad shit he'd been into.

But Pepper had done that already. Her daddy had shown her all she ever needed to know about that way of doing things. He'd shared his own fucked-up secrets and he'd been good to her and yes, Pepper had enjoyed their time together, but she'd had enough. She had no interest in another turn around that same old racetrack. Not with Echeverria, not with Bean. Not with any of them. It was time to strike out for new territory. Keep her secrets to herself if she wanted, let Tran keep his.

It was a little frightening, sure, going all the way to Vietnam. Being a concubine or whatever Tran had in mind. But then how scary and weird and different could Vietnam be? After all, Pepper had paid her life-long dues at the mecca of weird, that tiny coral island jam-packed with more misfits and degenerates than they'd invented names for yet.

She brushed some of the broken glass off her lap, then very slowly she drove down Fleming into the jittery shadows, hearing the noise of Echeverria's body dragging and scraping along beneath the car. At the next corner, she took a quick look in the rearview mirror to see the trail they were leaving. It was like she and Tran were riding inside some kind of big snail, coasting slow through the two A.M. streets of Key West, leaving behind them the long red slick of an American male.

Greta's pain was gone. Like someone had shut off an alarm bell that had been ringing deep inside her flesh for months. An immense vacuum echoed in her cars.

But the opposite of pain was not pleasure. It was

nothing. No feeling. Just being there. Lying on that bed. And that was what was in her ears now, that was what she felt at the core of her bones. Nothing. Not pleasure, not joy, not the tickle of sensuality. She felt as neutral and colorless as water in a glass. No taste, no smell. A dull peacefulness.

She was awake, alert. Hearing the croaks of the ship, the harsh squeak of the anchor line as it pulled tight against the tide. Greta Masterson lay still and watched the starlight through the porthole across from her. She was the squeaks and the starlight now. That's all she was anymore. Not daughter, not mother, not woman. Just a screen on which were projected the impressions of the moment.

She breathed in the musty wood of her cabin, the stale dust that lined the cracks of the ship. She was alive and without pain, without judgment or regret or longing. She did not miss her daughter. She did not miss her legs, or her freedom to move, to dance, to climb garden walls to clip orchid blossoms. She was alive, in the cabin of a ship anchored offshore a few miles from the southernmost tip of Florida, inhaling the night air, basking in the flicker of ancient starlight, Greta Masterson without worries or wishes.

Whatever Bean Wilson had injected into her pump was by now bathing her spinal cord. Greta Masterson didn't care what it was, didn't care about its name or its history, its source or chemical makeup. She cared about nothing but the blue curtains over the porthole, fluttering, giving shape to the wind. She cared about the wood beams of the decking above her, teak or mahogany. Parallel rows of wood. Parallel lines that could run to infinity and never intersect, unless some man-made error had miscalculated and pigeon-toed them slightly, in which case infinity was plenty of time for them to find each other, to cross for the briefest of moments and begin to move away from each other for another eternity.

Adrift in those airless solar winds, Greta was indifferent—no longer hungry, not thirsty. Her body was the same, but she was a new creature, as if some great knowledge were passing through her wordlessly. Like a conduit carrying a wisdom she couldn't comprehend. Changed by the drug flooding her spine, changed into something with a smooth unbroken history, a connection to the primitive earth more natural and profound than anything human. As though she'd been transfused with the plasma of angels, a dense light saturating her brain and nerves and filaments.

A rising breeze moved through the porthole. Starlight shivered. Insights strobed through her head faster than she could absorb. She felt the weightless presence of knowledge course through her bones. Watching the breeze toss the curtains, listening to the water slap against the hull, the boat's slow undulations. Knowing something she couldn't say.

Maybe she was dying. Maybe that's what this was. Life leaking from her, replaced by this other thing. But even that was all right. It simply no longer mattered. For a short while the world had made a space for Greta Masterson and now that space was closing. She watched the blue curtain flutter, subject to each new impulse of wind.

CHAPTER

29

When Thorn woke before dawn, Monica was gone and the room was as bleak as an Alabama jail cell. Wind gnawed at the edges of the house, the oak creaking.

For the next hour he struggled through his morning routines. Like one of those pommel horse gymnasts, he straight-armed himself from the wheelchair to the wooden straight-backed chair sitting in the shower stall, soaped and rinsed, then hauled his body back to his wheelchair, using his wooden slat as both lever and inclined plane. He was slightly better at the complicated maneuvers than he'd been a couple of days ago, but they weren't skills that came fast.

Lying on the bed, he dried himself with the flimsy towel, then squirmed into a pair of khaki shorts and a blue work shirt and wedged his boat shoes onto his swollen feet. By the time he was done he was out of breath, heart heaving. He lay there for a few minutes watching the first light gather against the pitted walls.

Maybe Monica had been right after all. He should give up the idea of saving Greta, call in the blue suits and let them fumble with it. Maybe this was simply beyond his abilities. If he was pushed to his physical limits just to shower and dress, how in God's name could he expect to take Bean down and maybe a couple of others as well?

It was sunrise and he'd heard no flushing toilets yet, no water running through the noisy pipes. But that wouldn't last long. This was not a house of heavy sleepers. After struggling back into the chair, he rolled out into the hallway, stopped just beyond his door, and listened for signs of activity. When he heard nothing, he moved down to the small supply closet near the TV room. For the last couple of days he'd seen the nurses getting rolls of gauze and fresh linen there. Rubber gloves, ointments.

He opened the door, moved in close to the shelves. Mainly bandages and first-aid materials, a stack of towels and washcloths. He pawed through the boxes and bottles until he found something that might work. A roll of strapping tape, steel filaments running through the sheer plastic wrap.

As he closed the door, behind him the elevator clanked to life and began to rise toward Bean's third-floor apartment. Thorn rolled quickly back to his room and shut his door. He pulled out a length of strapping tape, and with his teeth he tried to rip the piece loose but got nowhere. In his shaving kit he found a pair of nail clippers and rolled back to his bed and began the tedious snipping, a quarter inch at a time till he'd bisected the tape.

As he was finishing, he felt the thud of the elevator settling to the ground floor and heard the clatter of its door opening. There was no time to cut loose a second piece of tape. One would have to hold it.

He snatched the Colt .38 from his gym bag, bent

forward till his chest was hard against his thighs, and he pressed the pistol to the vinyl bottom of his wheelchair seat, and flattened the length of strapping tape across it, mashing the adhesive hard against the underside of his thighs.

Bean didn't knock.

He swung the door open and stood smiling in the doorway as Thorn was coming back up to a sitting position, feeling the blood hot in his face.

"All dressed and ready to roll, are we?"

Bean wore white linen trousers and a crisply pressed French blue sport shirt with a yellow pinstripe, those same heavy tennis shoes. A man about to pilot his yacht around the Bermuda coast, swill martinis in the luxurious shade.

"Sure," Thorn said. "Let's go meet Greta. See how she's holding up."

Bean chuckled dryly and stepped around behind him and guided the wheelchair into the hallway.

"Did we sleep well?"

Thorn played the words back, checked for irony, any hint that Bean had the room wired, maybe a video camera in the light fixture. But no, his tone had been neutral—probably only Thorn's paranoia heating up.

"I slept fine, Bean. Just fine."

"Just one quick stop before we head out. Got to stay with the program, you know."

He rolled Thorn into the small examining room, switched on the lights, and walked over to the medicine cabinet. He unlocked the door with a single key and swung it open. For a moment, as Bean poked the syringe needle through the rubber stopper and drew the solution from the vial, Thorn considered bolting. He might be able to make it out to the sidewalk before

Bean caught up to him, scream for help, draw a crowd. But he didn't move. He watched Bean put away the vial, lock the cabinet, flick the side of the syringe.

Obliging, he pulled his shirt up and bent forward, giving Bean access to the catheter. Bean's hands were gentle and efficient, fingertips cool against Thorn's back. He slid the needle into the spout of the catheter and pressed it to the hilt, then he halted and stepped away.

"You finished?"

"No." Bean's voice strained.

"What's wrong?"

"There's a kink or something. The needle's not going all the way in."

"Same thing the nurse yesterday said. Jankowski, or whatever her name is. A kink in the tube."

"She didn't tell me about it."

"Probably got bent from all the wrestling I've been doing. Or maybe that marathon I ran yesterday."

Bean hummed to himself, then stooped back to the catheter and finished the process.

"There now," he said as he retaped the spout. "Didn't feel a thing, did you?"

"That's the idea, isn't it?"

Bean stepped around and gave Thorn a puzzled smile.

"To feel nothing," Thorn said. "That's what you're after. Your career. Numbness. Deadening the flesh."

Bean's small smile grew to a grin.

"Are you trying to say something, Thorn? Is there a metaphysical point here? A critique of anesthesiology perhaps."

"Nothing so grand as that. Just a small, very personal observation. You've been dedicating your life to doing away with pain, but that's hardly the same thing as curing illness, is it? That's not your concern. That's for other kinds of doctors. Like your dad. What you are is the doper. You put them out, keep them out. Let the other guys worry about fixing what was wrong."

His smile melted away.

"It takes both kinds, Thorn. Those doctors can't do their work until I first do mine."

"Just like the war. You're in control. On your mountaintop. Everybody waiting for you to tell them when to go to work. You whine about it, but you love it, Bean, being the guy who calls the shots."

"How stimulating," he said. "And to think, without any formal education, any systematic study of psychology, you can come up with such penetrating insights into my personality. Someday, when you get a spare minute or two, Thorn, maybe you should try examining your own pattern of behavior. Withdrawing from the world like you've done, shrinking away into your infantile self-absorption. Isn't that your own version of anesthesia? Your way of numbing the pain? Come on, Thorn, face it. Being in the world hurts and you've made a career out of dodging that."

He glared at Thorn, all that hate dammed up, brimming into his eyes.

"Okay, Bean. You win. You crossed the finish line way out ahead. Education, money, prestige. Important social contributions to the world. No doubt about it. You're better in every way. The war's over. I surrender. I'm yours, do with me what you will."

"You bet your ass you're mine. You bet your everloving ass. You've been mine all along. You just didn't realize it until now."

He rolled Thorn outside and down the ramp. Thorn

expected the red hearse, Pepper, Echeverria, hail, hail, the gang's all here. But there was no one on the sidewalk, no sign of the big red car.

Bean pushed him along the walk, rolling across the intersections at Elizabeth, then another block across Simonton and on to Duval. Thorn had to fight off the urge to lean forward, steal a hand below his seat, press the strapping tape tight again, afraid that all the jounces along the sidewalk had loosened it, that the heavy weapon was hanging by a last smudge of adhesive, that any second it would fall and clatter onto the sidewalk. But he held himself still, depending on the generosity of industrial giants, the dollop of stickiness they'd allotted to that single strip of plastic.

Bean whistled quietly to himself, a tuneless ditty in a minor key. Thorn kept his eyes forward, watching shadows knife across the empty street. The wind was fierce, gusting to twenty-five or thirty. A man in an apron was washing down last night's puke from the sidewalks in front of Sloppy Joe's. Ahead of him, at the end of Duval, heavy clouds gathered to the north, packing the horizon. Gorgeous pinks and peaches like the flocking on some extravagant Easter float. Two white-haired joggers shuffled up the center of Duval and some vagrants congregating on the steps of a fast-food shop cheered them, blowing streams of tobacco smoke as they hooted.

These didn't feel like final moments. There was nothing dark or desperate in the creamy light or the hard breeze. Everywhere he looked the signs said business would be very usual today. The customer would be right as always, the flow of cash and the reciprocating flow of beer and tequila would be at its usual Monday volume. The vagrants didn't call out any veiled warn-ings to Thorn, they barely noticed his passing. If treacherous omens were lurking out there anywhere, they were disguising themselves well.

But then, of course, it was possible that Thorn was simply projecting his inner calm. The aftermath of an exceptional night of sensuality and revelation. Perhaps that was why football coaches preached the folklore of abstinence before the big game. You lost some of your enthusiasm for crippling your fellow man when your balls were drained, your ashes hauled, your snake tenderized.

But that was no problem for Thorn. He was calm all right, but his edge was still there, blade honed to a fierce glint. All he had to do was picture those slaughtered dolphins, Roy Everly, his mother, see Rover lying flat in the grass. The buttons were there and they were all hot. It would take a lot more than one extraordinary night of sexual discovery to unclench the muscles in his throat, to relax his veins. All he had to do was look down at his senseless legs and his blood was back at boil.

Brad Madison inched down Duval in the white Ford Fairlane. He watched Thorn and Bean Wilson rolling past a gang of hoboes and then past the Pier House parking lot. He slid the car into an open space and got out. He was still dressed from his travels. Gray pinstriped suit pants, white shirt, cordovans. He'd ditched the tie, the coat, but still he knew he was an eyesore. Even the bankers in Key West wore shorts and sandals to work.

He was skipping out on the annual meeting, all agents in charge assembled to give their reports, a gathering presided over by Madame Attorney General herself, the chair of the Senate Judicial Committee right beside her. Set to begin in an hour or so, Eastern Standard. With seventeen operations in Florida and the Bahamas whose progress he was supposed to update, whose increased funding he was supposed to campaign for, Brad was cutting an assembly no one was ever allowed to miss. Careers were permanently scarred for unexcused absences. And Brad Madison hadn't even filed a report, hadn't called in the feeblest alibi.

All weekend in the Georgetown Sheraton he'd phoned Echeverria's room in the Casa Marina. Nothing. He'd called the Miami office, checked his voice mail, talked to Darlene, his secretary, told her to call him the split second Echeverria checked in. Nothing. And nothing again, followed by more nothing.

He called and called and called and got nowhere until he knew something had come even more unwound than before. Echeverria dead. Echeverria held hostage. The whole island of Key West sinking into the sea. So he caught the Sunday red-eye to Miami, made the twenty-minute very bumpy hop to mile zero, roared over to the Eaton Street clinic first thing, ready to storm the house, gouge that two-bit doctor in the eyes, strangle the breath from him until he told the truth, just standing up into the street, about to shut the Fairlane door and there were the two of them, Bean and Thorn, half a block away in the shade of the big oak trees, rolling down the front ramp, not a word passing between them. Neither of them looking around; focused, intense, headed somewhere. Brad ducked back in the car, breathless. Then slid along behind. His career was over. There was no way to repair the damage. He wasn't acting as an agent of the

Justice Department any longer. Now he was simply
Brad Madison, private citizen, trying to rescue a young
woman he himself had put in jeopardy. Now this was
personal.

Monica rented a fifteen-foot Aquasport with a seventy-
five Evinrude. The rental guy at Garrison Bight Marina
didn't seem to care if she knew how to run a boat or
not. She didn't. But with some help from a woman on
a houseboat two slips away, she got the runabout
started and immediately slammed into one of the pilings and nearly bounced overboard. When she finally
got control, she motored out into the harbor, fighting
the wind and current, and she started toward the markers out to open water.

At the first marker, clear of the land, she turned on
the radio, switched it to their prearranged channel, 68,
and fiddled with the squelch until she'd cleared the
static. Wilson had his own hand-held VHF that he carried in his car. A Key Largo thing. She'd run into a lot
of locals who liked to drive along the highway monitor-
ing the salty banter just offshore. Wilder talk than the
shock-jock radio guys.

"Red Rover, Red Rover, come in."

She guided the boat under the bridge and stayed far
to the right as she navigated the markers out to the
shallow bay north of the navy housing. The radio was
silent. Gulls swooped low in the channel before her,
screaming with greedy delight, plucking minnows that
danced near the surface. Barracuda below, gulls above.
Monica could relate.

"Red Rover, Red Rover," she said. "Come in, Red
Rover."

"Red Rover here," Doc Wilson said. "I hear you, Monica."

"Can you talk, Doc?"

"I'm at Mallory Square," he said. "Where are you?"

"Still in the channel, just out of Garrison Bight. Everything took longer than I thought. The water's very rough. Whitecaps. I'm getting sprayed."

"It's ten minutes to get here," he said. "Over."

"If I don't get lost, you mean. Or capsize."

"The boat's tied up at the dock. *Miss Begotten*. Big Hatteras, mahogany cabin, white trim on its hull. Bean is rolling Thorn aboard at this very moment. You need to hurry, Monica."

Drifting too close to one of the marker pilings, Monica had to jerk the wheel hard left, or port, or whatever the hell it was. Even idling along at fifteen hundred rpms, she couldn't control the goddamn thing—how the hell was she going to be able to do her part of this?

"I'm in a no-wake area," she said. "Manatee zone. Is there a shortcut or something?"

Doc Wilson started to speak, but another voice broke in, some Cuban fisherman out past the reef, cursing the bad fishing. Been out since dawn, hadn't caught shit. Sea getting plenty rough. Might have to come back in.

"Red Rover, repeat please. Repeat."

"They're pulling out, Monica. We're going to lose them. I think the manatees will understand. Flatten the throttle. Hurry, sweetheart. Hurry."

C H A P T E R

30

Pepper Tremaine was standing at the top of the ramp when Thorn came aboard. She wore a cream sweatshirt and navy shorts and was munching on the wrinkled tip of a purplish and evil-looking chili pepper. In the hard wind, her hair snapped around her face, wispy strands snagging on her lips and nose. She made no effort to pull them free.

The wooden ramp was bumpy and Thorn could feel the strapping tape loosen, the pistol beginning to rattle against the backs of his thighs. As Bean muscled him up the last few feet, Pepper stepped away from the gunwale and climbed the ladder to the flybridge, sat down behind the control console and started up the big diesels.

The Hatteras was a few years older than Thorn, probably nearing her first half-century. A fifty-footer with the bulky, inefficient lines of an era of cheap gas and flagrant indulgence. Even with a quick glance he could see that no one had been keeping pace with the relentless attack of salt spray and sun. Rust circled the base of the outriggers and spreaders, reddish trails of it had leaked over the side and stained the white hull. The coaming padding was dried out and the vinyl was split, its stuffing beginning to poke through. Behind the bulkhead, the gin pole was bent and the winch was corroded solid. Bleached almost to white, the teak deck was spattered here and there with what looked like bloody chum.

Most of the wear appeared recent, three or four years old, as though the solemn old lady's husband had recently passed on, and for a few years after his death, his grieving widow had managed to keep herself together, but then little by little she grew dotty and absentminded, completely forgetting the purpose of combs and hairbrushes, soap and shower baths, until by now she was almost at the end of her transformation from dignified lady to derelict.

Those who should have cared for her, who should have been there to see her through these difficult years, bathe her, help her with her toiletries, take her for exercise across her familiar waters, were apparently too busy with their own concerns. And that was a shame, for on land, when people found themselves so completely abandoned, they went down fast, while at sea they went down many times faster.

Bean stationed Thorn near the transom, where an ancient chum grinder was fastened to the gunwale, a pungent musk hovering around it, specks of rotten meat caught in the gears, putrefying in the sun. Bean loosened the sternline and threw it down to the young dockhand, then inched forward and did the same with the line at the bow. In the harbor the water was a dreary gray and pitched with waves. One after the other they rolled in toward shore and buffeted the big Hatteras and ground her starboard side hard against the rubber fenders on the dock.

"Where's Echeverria?" Bean called up to Pepper. "I told him eight o'clock sharp."

"He's not coming. He couldn't make it. Feeling kind of low."

For a moment Pepper grinned into Bean's hard stare, then she turned back to the controls and set about angling them away from the dock, thrusting and counterthrusting until they were heading out into the wind, the broad-beamed lady wallowing across the slop. At the end of a ten-foot towrope, a full-size Zodiac inflatable bounced along in their wake.

Judging by the decay above deck and the ragged sound of her exhaust, those diesels were probably caked and clogged with years of sludge, their valves and cams and pistons mired in oil as thick and unhelpful as honey. In a perfect world overseen by a sparrow-watching God, those engines would be doomed to seize up a few yards offshore and the ship would founder and be thrown back against the seawall and its hull would crack and it would begin taking on water, and while saving all aboard, the authorities would find Greta Masterson and Thorn and the whole rotten plan would be exposed.

But that God was on holiday, had been for some time, as far as Thorn could tell. Sparrows everywhere were on their own. These days it seemed to be Job's God running the show. A guy with a taste for the grotesque, an appetite for torture. Prick them, poke them, wire their privates to electrical outlets, see how much they spasm, turn up the juice, see how long it takes them to call out his almighty name. You didn't pray to that God. You kept your head down, followed his instructions, and no matter what suffering he threw in your path, you stiffened your upper lip, and most important, you didn't take his name in vain. All of which was fine by Thorn. He preferred a God that didn't micro-manage. There was at least some slender hope that folks like Thorn could go unnoticed, free for a time to choose their own calamitous destiny.

Pepper kept them into the wind and the boat rose and dipped across the swells and Thorn had to hold tight to a starboard cleat to keep from breaking free and crashing through the companionway door. Grumbling along with grim resolve, the diesels carried the boat out into the path of the lumbering waves.

For a moment Bean stood at the door to the lower deck, holding Thorn's eye with a wistful smile. Waves splashed high over the sides and sea spray dampened the deck before him. Bean rocked back and forth, gripping the ladder against the steady lurch.

"I'm going below," he said. "See if Greta is ready to join our little tea party. You can interrogate her, Thorn, ask whatever you want. See if she considers herself my victim or my advocate."

"Fine," Thorn said. "Go get her. And don't forget the crumpets."

Bean turned and struggled down the steps.

Up on the flyway, Pepper was smiling down on Thorn as she steered one-handed, taking them out into darker and rougher water.

Capsizing was a distinct possibility. The rollers Monica met when she rounded the backside of Key West and headed into the harbor were so high and unpredictable she almost gave up right there and turned the boat around and headed back to Garrison Bight. If they were five to six feet in the harbor, how big were they outside?

But she took several slow breaths, fought down her panic, and nudged the throttle forward, tried to find the right pace so she could cut as smoothly as possible through the chop.

But there seemed to be no way of outsmarting those waves. Most were rolling in from the west, coming directly into her bow, and when they rammed the land, they rebounded and sent countersurges ricocheting at her from unexpected angles. The boat was lifting and hammering, not holding a steady path, and Monica was drenched. Cold, shivering.

A gray sun was up, air temperature in the high seventies, but she might as well be mushing sled dogs across the arctic steppes. Teeth clicking, she crashed on through the waves, gripping the chrome wheel with one hand, the console rail with the other, leaning out around the smeared windshield to locate her target, the pier at Mallory docks. Dr. Bean Wilson's frail voice coming over the VHF, urging her to hurry, hurry. He was losing sight of the *Miss Begotten,* which appeared to be heading out of the harbor into open seas.

Monica couldn't spare a hand to pick up the microphone and answer him. The boat plowed into the waves, taking great splashes of water over the bow. The deck was covered, water damming up at the scuppers in the rear. She was trying to read the harbor, find the path of least danger across the waves, but she could only manage an occasional glimpse as she mounted the summit of each roller, not enough of a view to make an informed decision.

As the boat slammed down and porpoised through a series of small whitecaps, the outboard sputtered and coughed. With a yelp of dread, Monica jiggled the throttle. If she lost power she'd be finished; floundering around out there, she'd flip the boat for sure, or maybe be driven into the cement seawall thirty, forty feet to her left. Either way, it was the end.

She bent low, tried to read the labels below the several switches and toggles on the console. Looking for the choke that might be engaged, mixing too rich a blend. But she saw nothing, and with a gasp and flutter the engine died.

Wind wailed around the straps of the canvas top, buckles chattered. The VHF antenna was whipping violently from side to side. Twenty feet away a laughing gull beat its wings into the gale but made no progress, so it tilted to the side and let the wind take it where it would.

Monica turned the ignition key but nothing happened, and a wave cast the small boat hard to the left and another lurched it back to the right and she was knocked off balance and banged her hip against the flip-up seat. She reeled, almost went down, but seized the console rail in time and hauled herself upright.

She took a breath, wiped her face, and tried to remember what the woman on the houseboat had showed her when she cranked the engine the first time. Riding high on a swell, Monica slipped the throttle into neutral, then turned the key. The engine spun several times but didn't engage. Probably a damp spark plug or something. She had no idea how outboards operated, what might be wrong.

She held the ignition key on *start*, spun the motor for several moments, and could hear from the slowing spin that the battery was quickly running low. That much she knew. She'd lost car batteries before, wintertime in the tundra of upstate New York. She'd worn out more than one trying to bring a frozen car engine to life.

Caught in a vicious curl of water, the boat pitched hard toward shore, the seawall only twenty feet away, barely enough time to scramble forward and get out the life jacket. But Monica decided she couldn't abandon the ignition key, couldn't give up yet to go dig through the locker.

She turned the key to *off*. Counted the seconds. Letting the swells take the boat where they would. She'd give the battery a chance to think this over, decide if it wanted to rest forever on the bottom of Key West harbor. Peering at the seawall, Monica waited, trying to gauge the right second, hearing the dim echo of some counsel given to her by a mechanic years ago: Let the battery rest so it can renew its vigor.

Ten feet from the seawall, riding in the trough of a strong current, Monica set her feet, chose her moment, and twisted the ignition key hard. The engine turned over twice, faltered, then roared to life.

She jerked her hand to the throttle, eased it forward, and for a moment seemed to make no progress at all, so she pressed it farther, milking some revs from the engine, trying not to stall, while the cement wall came so close she could read the graffiti, white paint, red, initials, hearts, a poem scribbled in yellow. On the roughened cement she could see the tiny crabs scuttling for safety.

Hell with it. She rammed the throttle flat, swung the wheel as far right as it would go, and with a hard bump and rumble and spew of water the boat surfed up out of its ditch, breaking the hold of the wave.

She took a huge breath. Then tried again to find in that chaotic soup a quieter path. But it was all turmoil and upheaval, like a pond bombarded with boulders, nothing resembling a pattern, every route as dire as the next. But she kept looking, laboring to see the larger view. And finally, as she narrowed her eyes to a squint, she saw the course she'd need to take.

She'd been looking out too far or else reacting to the immediate situation before her, but now she saw it, keeping her eyes on a place ten or fifteen feet ahead, the middle way. She steered the boat into a gentle eddy that gave way to a smooth stream, and that led to a short stretch of lazy water. She ducked behind the curl of a roller, rode in its trough for a few moments, then found another mild avenue after that.

Seeing now the topography of the harbor, the patterns and designs that held sway for a moment or two, then passed, she swept the boat ahead, rode it like a steeplechase Thoroughbred, timing her jumps, sliding and swinging around those watery obstacles, one after the other, feeling a bond growing with that rental boat as she dipped and swayed, holding her balance, squinting at the water, reading her way forward, ten feet at a time until he was there, Doc Wilson standing on the Mallory Pier, waving his arms above his head. Waving and pointing.

Monica swung around in the direction he was indicating, peered out to sea and saw it coming in like a mountainous iceberg broken free of its glacier, a great white cruise ship, ten stories tall, arriving at port, ramming the water out of the way, taking an angle that would almost certainly intersect with her own.

She faltered briefly, lost her concentration, and the waves hurled her hard to the left. Staggering, she clipped her knee, had to grab the wheel with both hands to drag herself back up.

Dr. Wilson was waving her away, pointing furiously beyond the cruise ship. His voice on the VHF was shouting at her now, shouting the words over and over. "Forget about me. Follow the boat. Follow Thorn!"

Thank the Lord, Greta's pain was back. Oh, to be hurting again, flesh inflamed, a cramp knotting the calf of her right leg, her toes burning separately as if someone were holding a match to each one. And to be famished, her stomach rumbling from days without a substantial meal. Such a joy. Even the dread and longing for her daughter was a kind of strange comfort. Thank God, thank God, Greta Masterson could feel again.

She rocked on her bunk and listened to the old diesels complaining, felt the yacht grind on through a choppy sea. And then she heard the distinctive thump of his step on the companionway stairs. Bean Wilson coming to check on his patient. The one in torment. Beautiful pain.

Wincing at each hard bounce of the ship, Pepper sucked on a Tokyo Rose, the hottest chili known to man, some genetic freak the Japs had cooked up. Hot as it was, the pepper still wasn't doing her much good. The throb in her jaw was growing worse by the minute. Eyes watering from the chili, she could barely see to keep her daddy's boat in the channel.

Dark clouds were accumulating in the north, like maybe the last cold front of the season was rolling down the state, colliding with all that stale Florida air. Gloomy day. Perfect weather for what they were about to do.

Tran was hiding down in the storage cabin. Ready to dart out when things started taking shape. They didn't have a plan exactly, but they were well armed, which Pepper had come to believe was better than all the plotting in the world.

She steered her daddy's boat out the mouth of the channel. No traffic to speak of today. One or two tourist charters, a dive boat braving the ten- to twelve-foot swells, but all in all a good day to be alone on the ocean, get off by yourself, shoot a few of your nearest and dearest.

Pepper set a course due south, away from the reefs where the diehard fishermen would be, heading out toward the bottomless Gulf Stream. And as they moved past the million-dollar houses of Truman Annex, running along a half mile offshore, the swells began to smooth out, coming high but regular, easy enough for the *Miss Begotten* to slice through.

Pepper sucked on the Tokyo Rose and guided her daddy's boat out to deep water, where the air was fresher, the daylight clearer, and the laws of man didn't apply.

CHAPTER

31

With Bean belowdecks and Pepper piloting them out to sea, Thorn bent forward slowly to peel the Colt from the bottom of his seat. Up on the flybridge, Pepper swung around and asked him what the hell he was doing.

"My morning sit-ups," he said.

"Well, knock it off. Just sit there and don't move or I'll shoot both of you right now."

"Aye, aye, Captain. Whatever you say."

Thorn hadn't seen Pepper's pistol. For all he knew she was unarmed. But it wasn't a chance he could take at the moment. He allowed himself one quick glance backward, but there was only the Zodiac floundering in the big boat's wake, no other boat back there shadowing. Something had gone wrong with that part, but Thorn didn't let himself consider what it might be. He stared instead at the northern sky, where along the horizon thunderheads towered up, gray and translucent as scar tissue. The sunlight was dimmed by half, a suppressing light that stole the blue from the sea and deadened the glitter of the boat's chrome plate.

Pepper looked forward again as Bean appeared at

the top of the steps with a blond woman scooped up in his arms. She had one hand around his shoulders, the other on the overhead rail, helping to steady them against the brutal pitch of the boat. For a moment they looked like drunken newlyweds reeling over the threshold. The bride with a ghastly smile, the groom gripping in his right hand a black automatic.

"Is this a drug bust or what?"

"Just keep your eyes on the road," Brad Madison told the blond kid. Thirty years old, said his name was Tropical Mike. Happy-go-lucky when Brad flashed his badge and jumped aboard, but looking a little grim now as he steered them out past the first markers.

"Channel, you mean. There aren't any roads out here."

"Channel, then," Brad said. And looking over at Doc Wilson, who was staring out the console window, he said, "She'll be fine, Doc. Don't worry. We'll catch up to her, take her with us. She'll be fine."

"So you going to tell me or not?" The kid was smiling uncertainly, getting up in Brad's face like he was nearsighted. Tropical Magoo.

"Tell you what, kid?"

"A drug bust? Is that what this is?"

"Yeah," Brad said. "Exactly. A drug bust."

"Marijuana or cocaine?"

"Neither."

"What? Roofies, angel dust, what?"

"What're you, a junior G-man or something?"

"I've got a quizzical nature, that's all. Hey, you commandeered my goddamn boat, least you could do is tell me what kind of drug we're looking for."

"Dolphin endorphins," Dr. Wilson said.

Brad gave him a look. The old man's eyes were murky and his face bloated as if he'd spent the night sobbing. Might be on the verge of it still.

"It's a long story," the doc said. "I'll fill you in later. But maybe you should get on the radio now, call for a helicopter. We're going to need to airlift Thorn out of here the second this is over. If it's not already too late."

Brad nodded, reached for the microphone. His last official act with the DEA. Tomorrow he was sure to get the phone call—an invitation up to D.C. for a skull session with Madame Attorney General. His skull against her mallet. Negotiate his severance package, a cement parachute.

"Which way?" Tropical Mike said, waving toward the end of the channel. "North or south?"

Brad leaned out from behind the cockpit windshield. The wind was fierce, ten- to twelve-foot seas. No boats in sight.

"Which way would you go, Tropical?"

"What, to do a drug deal?"

"Let's say you wanted to murder somebody, be alone when you did it."

"Murder?"

"That's right."

"Okay, well, that's easy enough. All the killing gets done out in the Gulf Stream, south. Throw the bodies overboard, they float away, ride the current north, wash ashore in Daytona Beach or wherever. If the sharks don't get them first. Drug deals are north, in the backcountry."

"Drugs north, murders south, I like that," Brad said. "A good system, neat and efficient."

"I mean, but, hey, I can't promise anything," Tropical Mike said, getting the boat up on plane, opening it up. "It's a big ocean."

"So, I've heard," Brad said. "Let's take a look."

Bean set Greta in the fighting chair and rested his hand on her shoulder. She was wearing a blue surgical gown and her blond hair was tied back in a ponytail, looked like it hadn't been washed in weeks. As haggard and dazed as she seemed, the photograph hadn't done her justice. Her skin was as creamy as a ten-year-old's, eyes a deeper and more resonant blue than the snapshot had shown. But behind that elegant symmetry and the flawless skin of a Swiss milkmaid, there was a diamond-hard fierceness flickering, a woman who'd trusted one too many men, once too often, and by god, was never going to make those mistakes again.

"Hello, Greta," he said.

"Who the hell are you?"

"Excuse my manners," Bean said. "This is Thorn, he's come to rescue you, Greta. That's what he does, a hobby of his when he isn't holed up in his cave, showing his back to the world—he goes out and saves women. Preferably beautiful ones."

Greta tilted her head and studied Thorn critically, as if he were the fish she'd been reeling in for days and this was her first look at him up close—a much less impressive specimen than she'd been hoping for.

"I thought all the heroes had found better-paying jobs."

"Oh, no, Thorn works for free," Bean said. "The genuine article. Newly crippled but still thinks he can go hand to hand with any fire-breathing monster that steps in his path. Isn't that right, Thorn?"

"How you feeling, Greta?"

Thorn rolled forward. He held his wheels steady against the toss and sway of the waves.

Bean was gripping his automatic in one hand while his other still rested on Greta's shoulder. On the flybridge Pepper kept the yacht plowing out to sea, holding a speed that smoothed out the giant swells as much as that was possible. Her head turned to the side, eavesdropping and keeping them in her peripheral sight.

"I'm feeling good," Greta said. "Better every second."

"So now you see, Thorn. You were wrong as usual. You came all this way for nothing. There's no one here you need to save. Except possibly yourself."

Off their starboard, a single ibis, as gawky and fragile as a creature made from chopsticks and tissue paper, toiled into the heavy wind. On a course for shore, the bird was clearly not taking the quickest route, but following a path that must have been scripted in its blood, some ancient stubbornness that told it where to build its nest, the precise branch where its young would be born. To hell with the wind, to hell with the obstacles —you did what you were designed to do.

"I found this," Thorn said. "You left it behind in your room. I guess you must have been in a hurry to leave."

With one hand still holding himself in place, Thorn drew out the snapshot of Greta and her daughter at the beach, then he let go of his hold and rolled forward and handed it to the woman. She studied it for a while, then looked up and a cautious smile spread her lips. She held his eyes for several moments, as if trying to read his thoughts or transmit her own.

"Thank you," she said. "Thank you, very much."

"Did Bean tell you," Thorn said, "where he gets the ingredients for the drug he used on you?"

She shook her head.

"Dr. Wilson and I haven't been communicating very successfully of late."

"He slaughters dolphins, hacks them up, then he takes a spoonful or two of some chemical from the leftovers."

"I see."

"So tell us, Bean. How much pain have you relieved by killing those eleven dolphins?"

A swell crashed the boat broadside and a spume of seawater rained down on them. Thorn backed away to his corner near the transom.

Bean wiped the moisture from his face. They were four or five miles offshore, Key West a hazy silhouette.

"Oh, here we go," Bean said. "Thorn's going to do the math, figure out how much prison time I should serve. His own little moral formula."

Behind Bean, coming up the stairway, was a small Asian man in droopy yellow shorts and a shirt as green and shiny as a lizard's new skin. He paused at the head of the stairs and craned his head up as if trying to see Pepper on the flybridge.

"From what I saw," said Thorn, "those eleven dolphins were making hundreds of people feel better, a little at a time. Lessening their pain, making some pretty shitty lives tolerable. How do you work it out in your head, Bean, that the pain in your missing legs is more important than all that?"

"I don't try. That's for assholes like you. People trying to score points with God."

"How about you, Greta? You think that's a fair swap, eleven dolphins to make your pain go away?"

"It didn't go away," she said.

"What?" Bean stepped around in front of her, putting his back to Thorn.

"It subsided for a day, but the drug wore off and now the pain's as bad as it was before. Maybe worse."

"You're lying. You little bitch, don't try to jerk me around. It won't work."

Thorn watched a swell roll toward them and held hard to the cleat during the steep ride up and over the wave.

"It's true," she said. "I was in some kind of swoon overnight, but now that it's over, I feel all the pain I felt before. And then some."

Bean rocked toward her, a tremble coming into the hand holding the pistol. Thorn looked out to the west and saw the next big roller heading toward them. Timing its approach, he reset his butt against the seat, took a hard grip on his wheels.

"You lying cunt. Don't play your fucking games with me."

Bean raised his hand as if he meant to pistol-whip the truth from her and Thorn delayed a half second more till the big wave rocked beneath the boat and tipped the deck severely, giving him a downhill angle on Bean. As Bean swung the pistol toward Greta's jaw, Thorn cranked the chair forward, accelerated down the steep incline, and slammed hard into the back of Bean's legs.

Bean crumpled sideways to the deck, and as he was falling Thorn lunged for his wrist, fumbled for a second, then got it, wrenched the automatic from his hand and with a backhanded flick he sailed the pistol overboard.

Thorn twisted out of his chair, let his deadweight fall

on top of Bean. He squirmed onto his belly, chest to chest with Bean. And he grabbed hold of Bean's ears and slammed his head back against the deck, slammed it a second time and once more until his old friend's eyes rolled back. Thorn rolled off, heaving for breath.

He hauled himself back to his chair, and elbowed up into his seat again.

"The big man has done our work for us. Many thanks, sir."

Smiling, the Asian man stepped forward and showed the group his shiny pistol. He held it at eye level, rocking it from side to side as though he were waving a flag at a political rally. Then he waggled the revolver at Thorn, backing him off. The man wore a pair of bright yellow shorts that drooped below his knees.

Pepper climbed down from the flybridge.

"You didn't need to hurt Bean. Nobody told you to do that. He didn't do anything to you."

Thorn said, "Turn us around, Pepper, take us back in. You do it now, it's going to go lighter on you."

"Yeah, right. We're going to take you back to shore. Of course we are. Whatever you say, weenie breath."

"People know we're out here. They're coming for us now."

"They are, are they?" Pepper gazed around at the rocking seas. "And where would they be, these people?"

Bean groaned but stayed down. There was blood on the deck where Thorn had slammed his head.

"They're invisible," Thorn said. "They paint themselves black, the blackest black there is. No light reflects off them. You won't see them till they're on top of you."

Pepper gave Thorn a long smile. "Hey, Tran, we got invisible people after us."

"This man is crazy. Maybe we should put him out of his misery now."

"A color so dark no light reflects? Is that possible, you think? There a black that's that dark?"

Tran spit out something in Vietnamese.

Stalling was about all Thorn could manage. Even if his pistol was within easy reach, the odds weren't on his side. Nothing to do but wait and delay, hope that Monica and Doc Wilson had not lost track of the *Miss Begotten* in the rough seas.

The Asian man stepped over to Bean and gave him a miserable smile. With a savage cry, Tran kicked him in the ribs and Bean jerked away and hugged his chest.

"The drug doesn't work. You hear that, Pepper? This whole goddamn thing was a big waste. You Americans, you are nothing but a bunch of children playing games. Bunch of fools.

"It is no wonder to me you lost the war. I see it now. All the shit you waste, the money, the time, and food. Spoiled Americans. If Vietnam had all you have, a little country like mine would be the strongest in the world. You Americans get some extra money, you stay drunk until your money is gone. Party, party, party. You lost the war because you are weak, because all you want is to have a good time."

"Hell, that's just Key West, Tran," Pepper said. "It's not America. You got it wrong. Don't be bad-mouthing my country, okay? You don't know what you're saying."

He aimed the gun at Bean, then focused it on Thorn.

"It's okay, Tran." Pepper stepped over to him, looped an arm through his. "We'll just go ahead like we planned. Give the formula to your science people, let them fiddle with it till the thing works.''

"And these weenies?''

"Like we discussed,'' Pepper said. "No reason to change anything.''

Tran sighed.

"It doesn't matter. Not really. I am taking something home with me better than any miracle painkiller. Pepper, my queen.''

"You're a sweet man. Very sweet.''

Tran's finger was curled hard against the trigger, pointing his weapon halfway between Thorn and Greta. At best Thorn would surprise them, duck down, get his pistol, roll out of the chair, maybe get off one free shot, go for Tran, but if his first wasn't fatal, he was finished.

"All right then, Tran. You ready to blow this old tub?''

Pepper stepped down the stairs of the companionway to the lower deck. She'd only been gone a moment when the first shot sounded.

Pepper had lived aboard the *Miss Begotten* all her life, only home she'd known. Where her father made love to her the first time, where she brought home the first guy after the old man died, some hairy Italian who said he was a writer, and she rolled around with him for a couple of days before she asked him if he was going to write a story about her. Not unless you start doing something interesting, he said to her.

That's when Pepper told him he wasn't half as good as the sixty-year-old guy she'd slept with for ten years. And he wasn't. Premature ejaculator. Teensy dick. Nothing like her dad. The guy acted like she was joking. But Pepper let him know she wasn't. No, sir, that sixty-year-old man could keep going all night long, never let up. And he had the equipment a woman needed for her complete satisfaction. What exactly are you trying to say? the writer asked her. And quick as that, she said back to him, You're a writer, you ever come across the word *repugnant*? The guy didn't think that was funny and he got his clothes together and said a few impolite things to her and left.

But even with all the happy memories Pepper Tremaine had of the boat, there were just as many that went the other direction. In fact, some of the very same moments she could look at either way. Turn it a little this way and she could see the horror of her life with her dad. Turn it a few degrees the other direction and it was the rosiest childhood a kid could've had. Much as she loved that old ship, she guessed she hated it too. So when it came down to it, it wasn't that hard to sink the sucker.

It took her a few minutes of searching before she found her .357 Smith on a countertop in Greta's cabin. Not where she'd left it. She checked the cylinder. Two cartridges spent. She took the pistol to her cabin, got her ammo out, reloaded, then went forward to the engine hatch. She rolled the carpet aside, dragged open the heavy door.

Only the first squeeze was difficult, seeing the hull splinter and the gush of seawater flood around the big diesels. But after that, the rest came easy. She reloaded and opened up six more fist-size holes in the old wood hull, and stood there watching the water rise, coming slowly up to the deck.

She stared down at the seawater till it covered her

tennis shoes, soaked them through, which seemed to wake her from her dreaming, and she turned and hustled back up the steps to the upper deck where Greta Masterson, the pretty cripple, was screaming.

C H A P T E R

32

Seven orange life jackets and five white cushions were drifting, thirty, forty yards to the east, already bobbing in a fast current heading away from the boat. As Tran hurled the last of the white flotation cushions overboard Greta screamed at him again. Told him to stop immediately, drop his weapon. She was a federal agent. Tran didn't seem to hear her, mumbling to himself in the strange cadences of his own tongue. These lazy Americans, these ineffectual, boneless Westerners. Too many movies, too much booze, too many prayers to their indolent god. A reasonable mistake for an outsider to make, easy to miss the gristle below the blubber.

While Tran hurled the life jackets overboard, Thorn managed to pull the Colt from the bottom of his seat. He tucked the pistol into the crevice between his right hip and the aluminum plate of his chair. There wasn't a clean shot to be had. Greta and the fighting chair were squarely in his way. And then with Thorn trying to angle his chair to the right for a clear path to Tran, Pepper appeared, moving fast, coming right over to Thorn and jamming her hot barrel into his cheek.

"So where's these invisible people?"

"They're here now. They're among us."

"Yeah, why aren't they saving your ass then?"

"They're peaceful types. Conscientious objectors."

"Make love not war, huh? Those people?"

"That's right. But don't underestimate them."

She clicked the hammer back, digging the steel against a molar.

"You think I'm goofy? You think I'm some kind of cracker you can scare with ghost stories?"

"They're here," Thorn said. "Watching you. Like your conscience. They'll follow you to the end of the fucking earth, record everything you do. Present you with the list when you die."

Pepper stepped back and gave him a long look. She raked the hair from her face, rubbed the sleeve of her sweatshirt against her nose.

"Too bad we're not going to have a chance to get to know each other better," she said. "You're just weird enough, we might've been friends."

"Come on," Tran called to her. "The boat's going down. We must make haste, leave now."

Bean was sitting up, gripping his head—a melon split down the middle, about to fall into halves.

Tran pushed open the transom door and climbed down to the dive platform. As it settled deeper into the sea, the big yacht wasn't lurching as much as before. An ominous tranquillity.

Pepper walked over to Bean, pointed the pistol at his head.

"You could've had me," she said. "You could be going off right now to spend the rest of your life in my arms. But no, you had to punch me. You had to break my fucking jaw."

Bean stared up into the dark cylinder, his eyes cleansed of emotion, as resigned as he must have been that night on the hillside in Vietnam. Ready to go. Let it be finished. Take another ride on the great roulette wheel of rebirth, better luck next time.

"I committed some bad shit for you," she said. "I was willing to do about anything so you could get over your pain, 'cause I thought when it went away, you'd look up and see me standing there, see what I'd done, and you'd be grateful.

"But now I know how wrong I was. You don't have a thankful bone in your fucking body. You're one of those assholes who think it's all owed to you and you shouldn't have to do a damn thing to get what you want. Money, good looks, education. You think everyone is there to make you happy and take out your trash. And when you're in pain the whole goddamn world should stop and bow down.

"Well, that's the way a little kid thinks. That's the way I thought when I was five or six. But I got over it pretty quick. And most everybody else gets over it too, but you never did. You think 'cause your daddy didn't love you like you wanted him to, and 'cause you got a terrible agony where your legs used to be, that makes you more important than anybody else, it gives you some kind of fucking privilege to do whatever the hell you want. But no, it's just pain, Bean. Not a license to fuck up other people's lives. It's just this bad thing that's happening to you. That's all.

"And you could've had all the love any man could've stood. All you had to do was to've glanced up once and seen the way I was looking at you and you could have had every single bit of me. I tried to make myself over, learn the things I'd need to know to love you better.

But you never looked up. You couldn't even do it now. Not even to save your life. You don't see me standing here, still right to the bitter fucking end giving you a chance to say the words. All you see is whatever ugly fucking shitstorm is going on inside your own rotten head.

"A handsome guy like you, beautiful hair, beautiful eyes, hell, I was an idiot to fall for a guy like you. You probably can't even have sex. You're always feeling so fucking sorry for yourself, for how you didn't get loved enough or the right way, you got no idea how to go about loving somebody else. And that's sad, Bean. That's real goddamn sad is what that is. Even Pepper Tremaine is better than that. Poor dumb redneck cracker like me.

"So you're on your own now, buckaroo. Let's see how far you can get all by yourself for once. Nobody doing your work for you, nobody to boss around. Let's see how it is now, by god."

Pepper turned away from him and looked again at Thorn.

"You all have yourself a nice swim," Pepper said. "Maybe your invisible friends can keep you afloat."

She followed Tran down to the dive platform, where he'd hauled the Zodiac alongside. Stumbling to his feet, Bean called out to her and limped toward the transom.

The Zodiac's outboard roared to life and the raft began to glide away, surprisingly swift as it slithered atop the choppy sea.

Thorn grabbed for the Colt, but it bumped the chair's leather armrest and he fumbled for it and it clattered to the deck and slid into Bean's path.

Bean stared down at it, glanced at Thorn, then

dropped to his knees and scrabbled for the pistol. With a quick crank, Thorn surged forward and ran the hard wheels of his chair across Bean's wrist. The pistol squirted away and Thorn tumbled forward out of his seat and fell onto Bean's back and pinned him there.

But his advantage was brief.

Bean twisted out from under him. Sinew and muscle, hard as a snake. With a wrestler's squirming quickness, he was suddenly on top, his butt anchored to Thorn's belly. Thorn outweighed him by thirty pounds, but without the use of his legs, there was no way he could toss Bean off. No physical way, at least.

Thorn grinned up at him.

"Boy, oh boy. Pepper nailed your ass, didn't she, Bean? Sliced right down to the fucking bone."

Bean reached down and gripped Thorn's ears, lifted his head up and bounced it off the deck. Sparks danced at the edges of his sight and blood fluttered in his chest. Bean went out of focus for a moment, and Thorn spoke to his blurry image.

"One thing she left out though, something she had no way of knowing."

Thorn gripped Bean's wrists but could not peel his hands away. Thorn's ears were on the verge of tearing free at the roots.

"Those pictures on your wall. I look at them and I can see what was just outside the frame. Other people, Gaeton, Sugarman, Darcy, all our friends. Your mother, mine, our fathers. They were all there, Bean. It was always swarming with people. And there were lots of pictures of them too. But it was just those snapshots you saved. You picked them out of the pile and stuck them on your wall because they told the story you want to believe. The one that makes you such a tragic goddamn figure.

"I'm the one you picked to blame it on. Convenient Thorn, the kid who got more love than you. The one responsible for all the emptiness you feel inside. But you're dead wrong, Bean. You were the only son your father ever wanted. Yeah, maybe he loved your mother more than he loved you, but so what? You were number two. You were still in the center of every shot he took. You were the reason those photographs got taken.

"And here you've been looking for something that was missing all these years, feeling the pain of its absence, but the joke is, Bean, it was never gone. It was always there. The man who took those snapshots loved you, God help him, he loved you the best he knew how. And he still does. You and you alone. Even now, even knowing the shit you've been up to."

Bean let go of his ears.

"He sent me to fucking 'Nam. He sent his own son off to get killed."

"He did what he had to do. That's all. He had no choice."

"Bullshit. There's always a choice. He could've pulled strings like he did with you. You got out. He made sure of that."

"I never registered for the draft, Bean. My name was never on the list. Your father didn't get me out. He just ignored me."

Bean bowed his head as if he felt the sudden weight of the truth.

"He sent me, Thorn. He sent his own son."

"Maybe it was because he thought you were strong, Bean. You ever consider that? Because he thought you could be heroic and brave. Because he believed in you. Loved you."

"Well, he was wrong. I wasn't brave. I wasn't heroic. I got fucked up."

"And that's why you paralyzed me, Bean. To square it all up. Sitting there on your mountaintop, deciding who lives, who dies. That's why you did it, isn't it?"

Bean reached to the side for the pistol and picked it up.

Thorn held his eyes, things coming slowly back into focus. He lowered his hands, poised to knock the pistol free, wrestle it from him, whatever it took. But Bean set the pistol on Thorn's chest and he struggled to his feet.

"Somebody please shoot them before they get away," Greta said. "Or give the damn pistol to me."

The *Miss Begotten* was listing hard to port as Thorn climbed back into his chair. He rolled over to Greta. The Zodiac was already fifty yards away, sliding easily atop the waves.

"Second in my class," she said, holding out her hand. "Watch me."

Thorn lay the pistol in her lap. She raised it, steadied her aim for several moments, then squeezed off two rounds. Pepper and Tran swung around in unison and stared back at the yacht, but kept on going.

"Maybe you're a little rusty."

"Look again," she said.

He peered out at the inflatable and saw the two of them scrambling now, trying to wedge a towel into the hole Greta had blown in the side of the craft. But it looked futile, taking on water rapidly. All of them sinking into the same unfriendly sea.

"We should try to find something that floats," Thorn said. "Get ready for our morning swim."

For the next few minutes he and Bean scoured the upper deck. From the bulkhead wall, Thorn wrenched loose an old white life buoy with *Miss Begotten* printed on it, but the thing crumbled in his hand like a disk of sawdust.

They dug through the locker, all the storage drawers, but discovered nothing that would help. And the water was already rising up the stairway, waves sloshing over the sides every second.

"Can you swim, Greta?"

"I've had some practice lately. But I was wearing a life vest at the time."

"Well, come on, we need to get clear of this thing," Thorn said. "Before it sucks us down."

Monica saw the rubber raft about a mile away, rising up on a hill of water, then spilling down the other side. She took a heading on her compass and held the line as well as she could, but she didn't see the raft again or anything else for that matter. But then, of course, a freighter could easily be steaming past her, ten feet away, and if the waves were timed right, she'd miss it. Waves twice as high out here as back in the harbor. Scaring the ever-loving shit out of her, but she kept on going. What choice was there?

Down in the trough for half a minute, she gathered her courage, then held her breath, pushed the throttle forward, cut the wheel, and rode up the steep edge of a swell for a hasty and terrifying view from the crest, then almost instantly began the quick skid down the slope of the wave until she and her small boat were tucked again into another trough, twelve-foot walls of water on either side.

She almost ran them over. With a sudden glimpse of the orange life jackets, she jerked the throttle back. Two of them, a man with black hair, his face sagging toward the water, and a woman holding on to the back of his life jacket, towing him along.

Monica used the aluminum boat hook to drag them close. The woman was blubbering, spitting water. The man seemed dazed, his lips fluttered on each breath. Monica got them around to the stern, and unsnapped the dive ladder.

"Take him first," the woman said.

And Monica bent over the transom and grabbed the man's bright green shirt by the yoke and hauled him upward while the woman pushed from below. The man sputtered and moaned and floundered over the transom onto the bouncing deck.

In a sopping cream sweatshirt, the woman clambered up the ladder. On the top rung she lurched forward, thrown by the heave of another wave. Monica clutched her under the armpits, steadied her, then tugged her over the side.

The woman sat down on the deck beside the man. He was awake now, shivering, and muttering incoherently. Monica held the boat hook loosely in her right hand.

"Is he okay?"

"He's Vietnamese," the woman said. "That's just how he talks."

That was when Monica saw the pistol in her hand. And with sudden light-headed certainty, it came back to her. The two of them, a tall man and this tall woman, lit up by her headlights, both with pistols, bullets spraying her car as she hurtled past. Rover dead on the floor.

Breathing hard, the woman peered up at Monica and must've seen what was dawning in her eyes. It was all about eyes. Seeing clearly, reading the moment, reacting to the hard, inevitable facts.

Riding on a surge of utter certainty, Monica swung the boat hook at the woman's wrist. It wasn't anger, not fear, not even the desire for revenge. But a cold, fierce upwelling of instinct, as if some bestial warrior had wakened in her blood.

The gun skittered across the deck, banged into the console, and rebounded. And the big woman lunged for it, but Monica stepped toward her and chopped the aluminum staff across her wrist a second time. The woman wailed and rolled away. And though the boat pitched and reeled in the rising swells, Monica was steady on her feet. She stooped down and seized the gun and pointed it at her shivering passengers, and watched as each of them stared dismally into its small, dark eye.

Because Thorn's legs had not had time to atrophy, he was far more buoyant than Greta or Bean. When they first went overboard, Greta thrashed around for several moments, her head high out of the water, but her withered legs weighted her, and her chin began to slip below the sloppy sea. Thorn got to her in time, put an arm across her breast and towed her forward in some half-remembered Red Cross stroke.

A few yards away Bean ducked his head below the water and came up sputtering. He flailed his arms as he gulped air. Thorn swam over to him, Greta's body riding against his left hip.

"It's no good," Bean said. He coughed out a spray of seawater. "I can't get them off. Something's twisted, a buckle. Fucking legs are pulling me down, Thorn. Gotta do something."

"Okay," he said. "Hold on."

A wave surged under them and carried them high, and off to the east Thorn thought he glimpsed a small white fishing boat—a couple of people aboard. The sea dropped away, and in every direction there was nothing but the peaks and plateaus of gray water.

"Can you manage for a minute, Greta?"

"Do it," she said. "I'll be fine."

He let her go and sank beneath the water. Bean had opened his belt, pulled down his pants, exposing the buckles and snaps and Velcro fasteners that harnessed his artificial legs to his stumps. Thorn felt around, tried to read the array of clasps. He loosened what he could, tugged and ripped and got one leg free and it fell away. He was running out of air quickly, and as he was about to break off, he found on the other leg the twisted length of webbing that was jammed inside its metal buckle. He pried and jimmied the fastener, but only seemed to tighten the kink.

He floated to the surface, gasped, swiveled around to find Greta riding away on a rogue current, her face dipping below the waterline. He thrashed to her side, hauled her to the surface, and got her back in the swimmer's carry. She choked and spit up a mouthful of water.

"I'm okay," she managed. "I'm fine."

A few feet away Bean pumped his arms as if he were trying to launch himself into flight, but for every inch he brought himself above the surface, he dropped two inches below. Bobbing like that, he wouldn't be able to last ten minutes.

"You can't do it, Thorn," Greta said. "Just save yourself. Do what you can."

From his right, Bean lunged for him, took a panicked grip on Thorn's arm, levered himself up to get a clear swallow of air. Releasing Greta, Thorn gulped a breath just as he was forced below.

When he broke back to the surface, Greta and Bean were treading water furiously, heads tipped back, taking deep breaths, then holding them in like dopers with their precious smoke.

"Stay calm," Thorn said. "We can't panic."

"It won't work," Bean gasped. "You can't save us both."

"We'll take turns."

"What?"

Thorn paddled around to Greta and got her across the chest again and let her ride against the buoyancy of his hips.

"It's the only way," he said. "I keep one of you afloat till the other gets tired, then we'll swap."

Bean shook his head.

"Forget it," he said. "Everything's fucked. Goddamn drug doesn't work. Nothing works. It's all fucked."

"Don't give up, Bean. Hold on. Someone's coming for us."

"Who's coming?"

"Monica and your dad. Maybe others too."

"My dad knows?"

Thorn nodded.

"Everything."

"Fuck it," Bean said. "I'm wired wrong, man. You

were right. I been like this forever. I look at you, I look at my dad, and I don't get it.''

''Hold on, Bean. Save your breath.''

He pushed his head above the waves, arms working feverishly.

''Guys in 'Nam, you, my dad. Even Tran. Guys willing to risk their lives. Shit, I never understood that. I got something missing. A hollow place.''

''It's okay, man. We're going to get through this. Stay focused. We keep swimming long enough, they'll find us. They're looking now.''

Water splashing his face, Bean shook his head slowly.

''Fuck me. I should've done it right the first time.''

He swiveled and with a clumsy breaststroke he paddled down the backside of a steep roller. It crested over him, and Thorn, riding at the top with Greta on his hip, saw his old friend's head sink below the surface and disappear. Thorn struggled after him but Bean didn't show.

With a quick word of warning, he let go of Greta and dug beneath the surface and swam down into the dark and soundless water. Eight feet, ten, blowing out a bubble of air, then another. It was too dark to see, the turbulent current buffeted him about like a rudderless boat. He was about to give up; ride back to the surface, when he bumped Bean's arm.

Thorn seized a handful of cloth and tried to drag him back to the light, but Bean wrenched away, blew out a stream of bubbles that tickled past Thorn's face. And he sank.

Thorn made a final lunge for him but got only a handful of water, and with his lungs roaring, he stroked back to the surface.

Bean had given up and the deadweight of his artificial leg was dragging him down into the lightless reaches of the sea, a world the two of them had once explored as kids, holding their breaths longer than was possible, feasting on the outrageous colors, every twitch of fin and braid of coral. Swimming side by side, boys with absolutely no wish to become men. Who even now after all these years still wrestled with the deadly allure of those dreams—to return to a time when absolutely everything was imaginable and nothing hurt for long.

Thorn swam with Greta on his hip, a listless stroke, doing just enough to stay afloat, letting the sea decide their direction. Greta did what she could to help, swishing her arms through the water, treading, keeping her head light against Thorn's shoulder.

They didn't speak. There was nothing to say, no air to say it with.

It was an hour, a week, ten years of pitching seas, Thorn's arm as heavy and useless as water-logged towels, before they heard the burbling exhausts of a sizable boat.

Thorn had just enough strength left to raise an arm from the water and wave it overhead while he held Greta with the other. But the boat passed by without seeing them. And again there was only the slap and turmoil of the sea. Beyond fatigue, they drifted on in silence, another half hour and another.

And there was no future and no past. No memories or hopes of bright days to come that kept him going. There was only a gray world of water and sky and a woman's living weight against his own. There was breath and there was cold and a spreading numbness in his chest. But he dug his free arm through the water, stroked forward, dug and stroked without thought, without aim or direction, streaming north in a current that rode its ancient pathway, a deep river that swept along the continental shelf, drawn ahead by the earth's endless rotation. And all he felt was the strange comfort of being caught in the machinery of much greater forces. Swimming forward, saving himself and this stranger on his hip, not because he was worth saving. Not because of any drumroll of heroism in his veins, but because he was an air-breathing creature and was required by natural law to keep his head above the waterline. To dig deep through the water, to breathe, to stroke, to go forward into the gray immensity, one stroke, then another and another.

When the lifebuoy splashed a few feet away, Thorn felt no sense of joy or relief. He wasn't even sure it was real. As if perhaps unknowingly he had slipped across into the afterlife. But he guided them to the white circle, and hooked his arm through it and he and Greta managed to keep their heads out of the water as the rope grew taut and they were drawn to the boat's wide dive platform.

Doc Wilson kneeled on the dive platform and Brad Madison and a kid with long blond hair stood beside him holding the rope.

Riding the rough seas a few yards away was a small open fisherman, Monica behind the wheel, handling the boat just fine from what Thorn could see. Beside her Pepper Tremaine's wrists were lashed with rope to the rail of the console. Trussed to the opposite side was Tran in his bright green shirt.

Brad Madison and the kid dragged Greta out of the water, wrapped her in a big blue towel and muscled her up on board. And through the murky cloud of his draining consciousness he stared across the swells at

Monica, pretty and determined, with a grim smile for Thorn.

Bean Wilson and Brad helped haul Thorn up to the dive platform, where he lay for a moment, barely enough energy to breathe.

The doctor stared out at the gray water, his hair tossed in the wind.

"He didn't make it," the doctor said. "My son didn't make it."

"No, he didn't."

Thorn felt his blood going pale. His body rising weightless into a twilight of dull pink.

"I couldn't keep the three of us afloat," Thorn said. "We'd all drown. Bean realized that and he went off on his own so Greta and I could make it."

"You saw him go under?"

"Yes."

Dr. Wilson held tight to the stern rail and looked down at Thorn.

"He did that? My son did that? Sacrificed himself?"

"Yes, he did. He was very strong, very brave."

CHAPTER

33

Seventy percent recovery, they said. And even that was optimistic. Maybe he'd need a walker for life, braces on his legs. There were a couple of specialists who were convinced he'd be lucky if he ever wiggled a toe again.

For two weeks Thorn suffered through spinal headaches. Each time he tried to stand or sit a scalding spike drove through his frontal lobe. Dr. Wilson injected 10 cc's of Thorn's own blood into his epidural space and that seemed to help for a few hours at a time. But the headache returned whenever Thorn so much as considered lifting his head. His ears roared, the ceiling of his bedroom rippled like a highway mirage. The entire stilthouse swayed and dipped as though he were still riding twelve-foot seas.

A little at a time Monica filled him in on the news. Pepper and Tran in jail awaiting trial for first-degree homicide. Tran trying to pull some diplomatic immunity stunt, but so far it hadn't worked. Greta already back at work with the DEA. Brad Madison reprimanded and demoted. He and Greta dating cautiously. As for Dr. Wilson, he had decided to take a cruise through Alaska as soon as Thorn was well. And then last week, some small and twisted flotsam washed ashore near Vero Beach, three hours north, and after some dental checks, a name was put to the debris. Bean Wilson, Jr.

Early in the second week of convalescence, Greta Masterson rolled into his bedroom one afternoon with her daughter, Suzy. Greta held his hand and thanked him, then told Suzy that this was the man who'd saved her. A very courageous man. Suzy was pretty and serious and had long wavy blond hair and looked much like Greta must have looked.

"*Stubborn* is the correct word, Suzy," Thorn said through the roar of his headache. "Not courageous."

"Same difference," the little girl said, and patted Thorn on the hand.

Greta sat by his bed for an hour and she asked Monica about their life in Key Largo, about the fishing, about her job at the paper. Chatting like old friends. Monica showed Suzy her drawings and Suzy picked out her favorite—the one of Rover lying in the grass.

It was decided that when Thorn was feeling better they'd come back. They'd stay for supper. Greta would bring something. She made a mean vegetarian lasagna. They'd drink wine. They'd go out on the boat to watch the sunset.

"Well, okay, maybe not the boat," Greta said. "I guess I've had enough of boats for a while."

"Oh, yes," Monica said. "I'm with you there. Dry land is fine."

Thorn listened to them talk. Two women getting along very well. Some laughter, some jokes at Thorn's expense. Suzy playing quietly with Thorn's fly-tying tools. Thorn lay still and watched them.

Just before Greta left, she gave Thorn a kiss on his cheek and the cool print of her lips lingered for hours.

By late in April, Thorn's headaches subsided and shortly afterward he wiggled a toe. A few days later he swiveled his right foot, then his left. Every day, Monica bent his legs for hours, pumped them to his chest. Rough as a linebacker, relentlessly working the blood back into them.

She gave him no rest. Worn and gaunt, she cooked his meals and stayed at his bedside all day and night. Whenever he chanced to open his eyes, she was there, massaging, bending, working his legs.

"You're lazy," she said, one rainy afternoon, with distant thunder rocking the timbers of the house.

"Lazy compared to what?"

"The last guy I brought back from the dead was up and around in a week."

"Maybe I'm just dawdling because I like the leg rubs. You're learning to give a damn nice massage, you know."

"Why don't you try it? Today, right now. Get up, one foot in front of the other. You can lean on me."

"Christ," he said. "You're vicious."

He sat on the side of the bed, planted his feet on the rough wood floor. He smiled at her. She smiled back.

She bent down and helped him loop his right arm across her shoulders and hefted him up. His knees buckled and he sagged, but Monica dipped and swayed and propped him back up as effortlessly as an old familiar dance partner.

"I don't know about this," he said. "Maybe it's too soon. We should ask the doctor first."

"Hey, if I can support you, you can do your share."

"Jesus, you just don't quit."

"Damn right. I had a good teacher."

He took a step and then another.

"That's enough," he said. "I'm too heavy for you."

"Come on. You need to look outside, see the water, the sky. You need to be upright."

He made it into the living room. Out to the porch. Tottering and feeble but moving ahead. His legs prickled and burned as if they were waking from a twenty-year slumber, his bare feet numb against the floor.

Together they stood on the porch in the steady drizzle. When he turned to her, Monica's forest green T-shirt was pasted to her body, her hair shining. Down in the butterfly garden she'd planted a small stone angel and there were flowers blooming around it, lantana, yellow and red.

Blackwater Sound glistened like a silver tray picked clean of its treats. A single gull washed itself against the raw sky.

"You did it. You made it outside."

"We both did it," Thorn said.

"Mainly you."

Thunder rumbled out of the west. Dolphins rose and fell beyond the horizon—their pain silent and unknowable.

"Have I thanked you lately for everything you've done? Have I told you how much I love you?"

Monica didn't reply. She stepped out from under the weight of his arm and smiled at him as he gripped the rail, balancing again on the unsteady surface of the earth.

JAMES W HALL